LESSONS IN DESIRE

"How can it be that love and mating are two sides of the same coin, yet not the same?" Jilliana asked.

Ruyen ran his hand along her thigh, lightly caressing her until she trembled with delight. "That is desire. You want me, I want you. A man can feel desire and yet it does not always touch his heart."

"I see. You desire me—you love Katharine."

He pulled back, feeling slightly disturbed. Again, he tried to remember what color Katharine's eyes were, but he could not. He stared into bewildered blue eyes and pulled Jilliana back to him.

"I only know that I desire you more than I have ever desired a woman," he said, trying to be as honest as he could. "Let that be enough for now."

He kissed her, and she clung to him. She could not put a name to what she felt for him, but she knew it went deeper than mere desire. She worried about his safety, she grieved for the unrest among his people, and she feared what might happen. Could passion be this strong—if so, then love must be more painful than anyone could endure.

Books by Constance O'Banyon

Forever My Love
Song of the Nightingale
Highland Love Song
Desert Song
La Flamme
Once Upon a Time

Published by HarperPaperbacks

Once Upon a Time

⊲CONSTANCE O'BANYON⊳

HarperPaperbacks
A Division of HarperCollinsPublishers

HarperPaperbacks   *A Division of* HarperCollins*Publishers*
10 East 53rd Street, New York, N.Y. 10022

Cover photograph by A. Smith/Westlight
Stepback illustration by Pino Daeni

First printing: March 1996

Printed in the United States of America

HarperPaperbacks, HarperMonogram, and colophon are trademarks of HarperCollins*Publishers*

❖ 10 9 8 7 6 5 4 3 2 1

*Old friendships age well, outlasting
the passing of time.*

Patsy Blythe Robinson, I cannot remember a
time when I did not know you. Growing up together
we laughed, cried, and sang duets in church—you
made growing up fun.

And,
Jannette Baird Green, the sensible one—the miles and
spaces of time have only made you more dear to me.

And,
Velesta Black, with your infectious smile and
generous nature. You have been a constant friend,
and I thank you for always being there for me.

And,
Nelda Walker Reinhardt, I cannot think of
my teenage years without imagining you there
beside me.

Author's Note

Once upon a time there was a kingdom ruled only by women. It was a center of learning and culture unequaled anywhere in the world. So rich and prosperous was Talshamar that it was coveted by all rulers, but especially by the envious kings of England and France, its nearest neighbors.

Zealous scholars of later centuries virtually erased all traces of the existence of Talshamar from their historical accounts because they did not believe such a land could have existed. Still, the spirit of the tiny but valiant country has been held close to the hearts of women everywhere. The legend will not die, because stories of the daring and bravery of Jilliana, Talshamar's last queen, and the cunning of her ally, Queen Eleanor of Aquitaine, have been passed from mother to daughter for centuries.

In the year of Jilliana's birth, her kingdom had been free from discord for more than two centuries, but on her first birthday that idyllic peace was broken as King Henry II of England prepared to invade Talshamar and take its treasures as his own.

Did Talshamar really exist? I hereby pass on my account to those of you who believe in love, magic, and fairy tales.

Prologue

Kingdom of Talshamar, 1167

War had been raging with England for over a year, and the valiant, peace-loving Talshamarians could no longer hold back the powerful, well-seasoned forces of Henry II.

On their march to the capital city, the English troops had methodically destroyed all farms and villages that stood between them and their target, leaving those peasants who had managed to survive the brutal invasion without shelter or food for the coming winter.

Soon the outer walls of the queen's castle, the last stronghold of the kingdom, would be breached and Talshamar would fall.

Two riders took advantage of the moonless night and the lull in the assault to make their way clandestinely toward the royal castle.

"Who goes there?" cried a man-at-arms from atop the watchtower, his trained eye picking up the movement of shadows below.

"'Tis I, Sir Humphrey of Longworth, with urgent business for the queen. Lower the drawbridge, and hurry, man! The enemy is pursuing us like the hounds of hell."

Sir Humphrey and his companion were having difficulty reining in their war-horses, for the great beasts sensed the apprehension of their riders, and were prancing nervously, prepared for action.

"State the watchword," came the stoical demand from the sentry. "Anyone could claim to be Sir Humphrey. No doubt even old Henry of England knows that he is Queen Phelisiana's most trusted supporter."

"Damn you, man—" Sir Humphrey cried out in frustration, as he tried and failed to remember the password.

The guard remained impassive, and the gate remained closed.

Sir Humphrey ground his teeth in rage. He had narrowly escaped death that night, he had so many worries and responsibilities plaguing him that he had trouble concentrating, and this fool of a guard made him flounder around for a damn password. He forced himself to clear the exhaustion from his mind, ever aware of the sounds of pursuit in the distance. "Ah, I have it," he finally announced. "The Royal Scepter! Now let us in, damn you, or when Henry's men arrive, I'll toss you over the walls to their waiting arms myself."

"Aye, you be Sir Humphrey right enough," the guard said, more to himself than for the benefit of the men who waited. He shouted an order below and told Sir Humphrey and his companion to pass within.

The lowering of the drawbridge momentarily drowned out the sounds of battle that were drawing ever nearer. The riders entered the courtyard, their horses clattering over the wooden bridge that led into a second courtyard, where a man-at-arms bearing a torch awaited them.

"Follow me, lords. Her Majesty awaits you in the Great Hall," the guard said urgently.

Quickly the two knights dismounted. Their hurried footsteps took them through a maze of brightly lit corridors and finally into a chamber where Queen Phelisiana was hurriedly giving orders to her trusted adviser and palatine, Lord Kelvin.

The young queen's golden hair was uncovered and framed her beautiful face. She was bent over a map, her mouth set in a grim line.

Sir Humphrey's heart contracted when she looked up and her eyes met his. It was apparent that she was resigned to her impending fate, and he felt helpless to stave off Henry's cruel retribution.

"At last you are here," the queen said with relief. "I had so feared you would be unable to break through the enemy lines."

Sir Humphrey knelt before her. "Only death would keep me from my appointed task, Your Majesty."

Queen Phelisiana smiled faintly in acknowledgment of his devotion. "Rise, Sir Humphrey, and present your companion to me, for there is a need for haste."

The second man wore no insignia to betray his identity, but Queen Phelisiana knew he was a trusted knight of Queen Eleanor of England.

He stepped forward and bowed. "Sir James of Middleton, Your Majesty, and I bring greetings from my noble lady."

"Sir Humphrey has told you what is to be done?" the queen asked.

"He has, Your Majesty, and I am at your service. Queen Eleanor has charged me to render to you such aid as you deem necessary."

The palatine stepped forward, his expression stern. "Your Majesty is aware that I have grave misgivings about this venture. I am not convinced that we should rely on Queen Eleanor, who, after all, is Henry's wife. I question her purpose in aiding us against her own husband. What if by making Princess Jilliana her ward, we are placing our princess within Henry's reach?"

Sir James stepped forward. "I can understand your concern, but it is unwarranted. My queen has bid me assure you that Princess Jilliana will come to no harm while under her protection. I am to remind Your Majesty that Queen Eleanor has not forgotten when you stood her friend. She pledges that your daughter will not become a pawn of either her husband or Louis of France."

Queen Phelisiana smiled at Sir James, but her words were meant to assure her palatine. "Lord Kelvin, I would trust Eleanor with my life—more still, I trust her with the life of my only child."

The palatine still looked doubtful, but he made no further protest. "If I cannot sway you in this scheme, then I implore you to leave with the princess, Your Majesty. If you remain in Talshamar, you shall surely die or become Henry's prisoner, which might be an even worse fate."

The queen waved her hand dismissively. "I will not desert my people in this, their gravest hour. But be assured that by sending Jilliana to safety, I will deny Henry the final victory."

A nursemaid had been standing in the shadows, and now Queen Phelisiana motioned her forward. Lovingly, the queen took her two-year-old daughter from the nurse's arms, and dismissed the woman. The child slept peacefully and did not stir when her mother embraced her tightly.

The queen then reluctantly turned her attention to the two knights who would soon be entrusted with the safety of her daughter. "You will each pledge to me on your lives that the princess will come to no harm."

Sir Humphrey dropped to one knee, his face shining with earnestness. "Until the Princess Jilliana is returned to Talshamar, I pledge to keep her safe at the cost of my own life, Your Majesty."

She smiled gratefully at her liege man and then turned to Queen Eleanor's knight. "And you, Sir James?"

Sir James nodded grimly. "I pledge on my honor, and that of Queen Eleanor, that no harm shall befall the princess under my protection. I will accompany Sir Humphrey to make certain that Princess Jilliana safely reaches her destination, or forfeit my life in the attempt."

Sorrowfully, the queen touched her sleeping daughter's hand and placed a soft kiss on the rosebud lips. She knew that she was looking upon her child's face for the last time. Then with a sense of urgency, she handed the princess to Sir Humphrey.

Her eyes cleared and she straightened her back as the mother became once again the queen. "You must make haste. Leave by the secret gate at the perimeter of the castle grounds and take the mountain pass to safety."

Sir Humphrey's arms tightened about the princess. "Fear not, Your Majesty, her highness will be as safe with me as she would be sleeping in her own bed."

Queen Phelisiana's voice was unsteady. "You will ever stay near her, watching and guarding her in my stead, serving her as faithfully as you have served me?"

"This night I pledge my fealty to Princess Jilliana, Your Majesty."

"Then I am content." She handed a sealed parchment to Sir James. "Deliver this safely into the hands of your queen, and no one else. Tell Eleanor—" Her voice faltered. "Tell Queen Eleanor that I am forever in her debt."

"I will do as you command," Sir James vowed, admiring the brave young queen.

Queen Phelisiana then placed a golden object in Sir Humphrey's hand.

"This is the Great Seal of Talshamar," he said in puzzlement.

She nodded. "I place it in your keeping, Sir Humphrey,

and you shall give it to Jilliana on the day she claims her birthright."

Sir Humphrey bowed his head, trying to hide the sorrow that ripped at his heart. If the queen was relinquishing the Great Seal, she expected to die. He wanted to stay by her side and protect her from the enemy, but the road he must travel in her service lay elsewhere.

He placed the Great Seal into his doublet. "I will take it for safekeeping, Your Majesty," he said gruffly, "and one day return it to *you*."

Their eyes met, and there was much left unsaid between them.

"Go now, time is against you," Queen Phelisiana said urgently, then turned her back so that she would not be tempted to take her daughter in her arms once more and thus delay their departure.

The two knights bowed and backed to the door. Once they were in the corridor they hurried down dark stairs, going into the bowels of the castle, through a catacomb that led toward the edge of the royal grounds.

Sir Humphrey clasped to his breast his most precious charge, the sleeping Princess Jilliana, heir to the throne of Talshamar.

Once outside, they found fresh mounts waiting for them. Soon they left the castle behind and took the long winding road that led them through mountain passes and then finally down into a secluded valley.

On they rode into the night, both men conscious that the life of the little princess depended on them.

The sounds of battle could now be heard in the courtyard. A loud crash echoed through the marble halls as the enemy battered down the last barrier into the castle and swarmed inside. The Talshamarian Royal Guard fought bravely to deny the English entrance to the Great

Hall, but they soon fell before the larger, battle-hardened force.

In a white robe, with a golden crown set atop her head, Queen Phelisiana was composed as she watched five enemy knights approach her with swords drawn.

One of the knights, apparently the leader, smiled with satisfaction as he bowed to her. "Your Majesty, may I present myself to you? I am Lord Exeter."

Her voice was cold. "I have heard of you, butcher. I suppose you have come to take me prisoner."

He shrugged. "Regretfully, Madame, that is my directive."

"I shan't be going to England with you," she said quietly.

Lord Kelvin stepped to his queen's side, unsheathing his sword and facing the enemy. Cardinal Failsham, who had been praying in the chapel, rushed into the chamber to stand on her other side.

"Do not harm Her Majesty," the cardinal said, "or your soul will be damned for all eternity."

Lord Exeter appeared unperturbed by the threat. "This is not Rome's concern," he said, roughly shoving the cardinal aside and moving toward Queen Phelisiana.

Cardinal Failsham straightened his disheveled robe and bravely stepped in front of the queen, determined to protect her. "Are you prepared to stand before God and explain what you do here this night?"

"Out of my way, priest," Lord Exeter ordered, raising his sword in a threatening manner. "I have more fear of standing before King Henry if I do not carry out *his* orders than of standing before God if I do not carry out yours."

"Be at peace, good Failsham," the queen said, motioning for him to step away from her. "You must not interfere in this. Go instead to the task I set for you."

The cardinal reluctantly nodded and turned to do her bidding. The queen had drawn up documents that made him overlord of Talshamar until Princess Jilliana was old enough to ascend the throne. His footsteps were heavy as he left the chamber, knowing he must put the good of Talshamar before the life of its queen. He had given his pledge to her, and difficult though it might be, he would fulfill it.

"Dispatch this man to bring your daughter to us, Queen Phelisiana," Lord Exeter said, indicating Lord Kelvin. "She will also accompany us to London, as will any attendants either of you require."

Phelisiana's laughter was chilling. "Tell Henry that his bones will bleach white before he gets his hands on Princess Jilliana. As we speak, she is far from his treacherous grasp. Report to him that I have taken precautions so he will never find her. Indeed," she said triumphantly, "I have planned her future so well that Henry Plantagenet will not only pray that she comes to no harm, he will even want to protect her himself."

Lord Exeter looked at her suspiciously. "You speak in riddles. Say what you mean."

"Can you read, Lord Exeter?" the queen asked tauntingly. "I know reading is not a requirement for knighthood in England, while even the lowest servants in Talshamar are taught that skill at an early age." She smiled. "But even Henry has admitted that we are an enlightened people."

Lord Exeter glared at her. "I can read," he said with a snarl.

"Then look at this," she said triumphantly, thrusting a parchment at him, "and you'll understand how well I have robbed your king of his final victory."

He read the parchment and scowled at Queen Phelisiana. "What does this mean?"

"It means that if anything happens to my daughter, the king of France will be the legal overlord of Talshamar. I have named him my daughter's heir."

The knight moved to the wall sconce and held the parchment to the flame until it ignited. "So much for

France," he jeered, watching the document burn and then dropping it on the floor and crushing the charred remains beneath his boot.

Queen Phelisiana smiled. "What you destroyed is of no value, though I am certain that Henry would have liked to read it. The original document is safe with the Holy Father, Pope Alexander, and has been sanctioned by his hand. Did your liege lord think one of the richest fiefs in Christendom would so easily fall into his grasp? It will not be so—he will never have any part of Talshamar."

Lord Exeter motioned three of his men forward. "Take her prisoner. She will chirp less loudly once King Henry is done with her."

"I think not," she said calmly, halting the three knights in their tracks. "I already told you that I will not set foot on English soil."

"Then tell me where to find Princess Jilliana and we may allow you to remain in Talshamar," Lord Exeter said condescendingly.

"Never!" she answered, raising her head, her eyes stabbing into his.

"But you will tell us eventually," the warrior said with a cruel twist to his lips. "We have ways of extracting information from reluctant prisoners, be they royalty or commoner. You will soon beg to tell me everything you know."

As the three knights stepped forward, the queen raised her eyes to her palatine and quickly whispered.

"Do not allow them to take me." She took the point of his sword and placed it at her heart. When he resisted, she stayed his arm. "Good Lord Kelvin, I beseech you to end my life. If I kill myself, it will be a mortal sin. Allow me the mercy of dying by a loving hand."

There was no time for him to consider because when the knights realized what the queen intended, they rushed forward to stop him. With profound sadness, the chancellor nodded and pushed hard against the handle of his sword.

Queen Phelisiana gasped in pain, and almost immediately the front of her white gown stained a bright scarlet. She smiled softly at Lord Kelvin and crumpled to the floor to lie dead at his feet.

"Damn your eyes!" Lord Exeter cried, swinging his sword in a wide arc and slashing the palatine's throat with a single blow.

Lord Kelvin sank slowly to the floor to die in a pool of his own blood beside the queen he had served so well.

"His Majesty wanted Queen Phelisiana alive. He will surely punish us for her death," one of the knights muttered, his eyes darting from the dead queen to Lord Exeter.

"King Henry will quickly forgive us if we find Princess Jilliana," Lord Exeter answered. "Search the castle. Question everyone. Find someone who will value their life enough to tell me what I want to know."

Sir Humphrey and Sir James rode into the night and long into the next day, changing horses often along the way.

Soon the little princess would be under the protection of Queen Eleanor herself, to be hidden from the destructive hand of King Henry, and that of his adversary, Louis of France.

1

The church bells of Our Lady of Sorrow pealed loudly, reverberating across the lush green valley and into the peaceful Welsh village.

A frantic young girl hurried down the narrow lane, pulling her wimple low over her head to protect herself against the softly falling rain.

Even so, her white gown was hopelessly soiled and she paused in a futile attempt to brush away the mud. With a resigned sigh, she continued down the lane toward the convent.

There was apprehension reflected in the girl's blue eyes and she felt contrition within her heart. Once again she had missed morning prayers and Mother Prioress would surely scold her. It was the second time this month that she had been remiss in her duty.

Straining on her tiptoes to reach the latch, she finally succeeded in pushing open the heavy wooden gate and slipped inside, looking right and left to see if anyone was about. If she could sneak in the back door and make her way to her cell, perhaps she would not be missed.

But she held little hope that her tardiness would be undetected since Mother Prioress never failed to notice what went on around her.

By now the rain had stopped and a weak sun had broken through the low clouds, casting the garden in an eerie yellow light. As she entered the herb garden, the girl brightened when she saw that the gardener, Humphrey, was watching her progress with a bright smile.

She felt closer to Humphrey than to anyone at the convent. He always had time to stop whatever he was doing and talk to her. And when she was troubled, she sought him out, knowing he would listen patiently and then give her the benefit of his knowledge.

As he watched her approach, Sir Humphrey was dazzled. He was reminded of his youth, another time, another place, and another woman.

The love he had felt for Queen Phelisiana had transcended the physical to become complete dedication. The girl known only as Jilly to those at the convent was now the unknowing recipient of his selfless devotion.

It had been fourteen years since that stormy night when he and Sir James had taken Princess Jilliana to Our Lady of Sorrow convent with its high protective walls. It had not been difficult for him to convince Mother Prioress that he would be an excellent gardener for the abbey, so he had been able to keep his promise to Queen Phelisiana that he would watch over the princess.

Jilly's resemblance to the dead queen was uncanny. She had the same exquisite heart-shaped face. Each feature was perfectly formed, as if carved by a master sculptor. From her full mouth to her arched brows, she was breathtaking. Long lashes swept across sapphire blue eyes. Her raven-colored hair was the only characteristic she had inherited from her father.

"You'd best hurry, Mistress Jilly," Sir Humphrey said,

pulling his thoughts back to the present. "Mother Magdalene was just inquiring after you."

Jilly turned sorrowful eyes on Humphrey. He was a great bear of a man, with a wide chest and powerful arms. His hair was red and his face covered with freckles. He had soft gray eyes that always seemed to be dancing with mirth, especially when he spoke to her.

Sometimes she thought he was misplaced as a gardener, because his speech was much too cultured and he was obviously an educated man. She often fantasized that he was a great noble hiding from some cruel fate, who had found his sanctuary at the convent.

"I will surely be punished this time." She held out a crumpled bouquet. "I was gathering wild flowers on the cliff and forgot the time. They're for Sister Cecilia. She has been very ill, and I thought they might cheer her."

"You need have no fear of Mother Magdalene," Humphrey said encouragingly. "Even when she rebukes you, she has only your interest at heart."

Jilliana sighed. "'Tis not that I am afraid of her. It's more that I want so to please her and gain her respect. The pity is that I have always been a disappointment to her. I know that she feels I am frivolous and negligent in my duties to God's work. I never intend to be wicked. I just cannot seem to help myself."

Sir Humphrey smiled and shook his head at Jilly's innocence. She had no notion what evil was, and for that he was grateful. "You wicked, Mistress Jilly? I think not. I have oft times observed your kindness to others and seen you labor long at your appointed tasks without complaint. Do not chastise yourself so severely."

Jilly's lower lip trembled. "But there must be something wrong with me." Her eyes were clear as she looked into his. "I asked Mother Prioress again only yesterday if I might take the veil, and once again she informed me that

I am not meant for the Church. Humphrey, do you think I am too undisciplined to become a nun?"

"Not at all, Mistress Jilly. But Mother Prioress has great insight, and she speaks true. You are not meant for the Church."

"What will I do if I cannot take the veil?"

"There are those who will see to your future when the time is right," Sir Humphrey said kindly. "You must have faith and believe that."

"Faith is the only thing I do have." Jilly looked at the massive carved doors that led to the chapel. She could hear the clear tones of voices raised in song. There was no need for her to hurry now—it was too late.

"Humphrey, why do you suppose I am treated differently from the other students?"

He reached down and grasped a weed, pulling it free of the herb bed.

"In what way?"

"The other girls do not study all the subjects that I do. And Mother Magdalene does not reprimand them as severely as she does me when they fail to use courtly etiquette or proper grammar. Why do you think that is?"

"Perhaps you should ask her. As for now, consider how fortunate you are that Father Finn comes twice weekly to instruct you. Have you not told me how you love to read? I'd advise you to accept the privilege without question."

Jilly wrinkled her nose. "Perhaps you are right, Humphrey, but it makes me angry when the other girls taunt me. They think my studies are a penance for my transgressions, when indeed they are a blessing to me."

Sir Humphrey turned back to his work and they remained a few moments in companionable silence. Finally, he spoke: "Mistress Jilly, why do you suppose you have been given such a fine education?"

She thought for a moment before answering. "I have lain awake many nights wondering that myself. I believe that Mother Prioress is preparing me to work in some fine household so I can provide for myself." Her expression was wistful. "I cannot remain here forever. You may not realize this, but I am quite old for an unmarried maiden."

Sir Humphrey's lips twitched into an almost smile. "So you think you have unraveled the mystery, do you? You believe that you are being prepared for the life of a servant?"

"What else am I to believe?" She looked pensive and then troubled. "I am oft puzzled by many things, Humphrey. For instance, who are my mother and father, and why don't I live with them, or at least know their names? I once asked Mother Prioress who I was, but all she would tell me is that we are all children of God and that should be enough for me."

He ached to tell her the truth, but he knew the time was not now. "Put your worries aside, Mistress Jilly. In time you will come to know God's plan for you."

She gave a deep sigh of disappointment. He did not understand either. "I must be going now. I would not want Mother Prioress to see the mud stains on my gown."

Sir Humphrey braced his back against the trunk of a tree. "Yes, go along and see to your gown. And, Mistress Jilly, all will be well with you. This I promise."

She smiled at him gratefully. "I do not know what I would have done all these years if you had not been my friend, Humphrey."

He gave her a courtly bow. "I always stand ready to serve you."

She giggled at his gallantry. "It is I who will be served up as an example to the others after today." She clutched the now wilted flowers tighter in her hand. "I fear I shall never learn obedience."

Sir Humphrey watched her hurry away. So, she had not yet been told that tomorrow he would be taking her away from the convent. No doubt she would be frightened to leave the only home she'd ever known, but at least he could remain at her side until she reached her destination.

Jilly stood before Mother Prioress, her hands folded demurely, her head lowered in contrition.

"I had hoped you would outgrow that rebellious spirit that churns within you, Jilly," she sighed, "but it seems that my hopes are in vain. I have strived to curb your strong will and teach you patience and piety so you can lead a life of subservience, but in this I have also failed."

"I am sorry," Jilly said, wincing as she raised her eyes and saw the unforgiving expression on Mother Magdalene's stern face.

The prioress was small in stature and always spoke in a soft voice, but she could be formidable all the same. It was difficult to tell her exact age, but Jilly thought she must be very old, for her face was wrinkled and pale beneath her stark white wimple.

"Mother Magdalene, I know that I am a disappointment to you," Jilly said in a rush, "but I will try to do better in the future—truly I shall. You will find no more cause to chastise me."

The prioress held her hand out to silence the torrent of words.

"Tomorrow, Jilly, you will pass from my keeping." Suddenly her voice was soft, her eyes gentle. "And I pray that God will watch over you and teach you obedience as I was never able to do."

Jilly gasped. With tears in her eyes, she fell to her knees and grasped Mother Magdalene's skirt. "I entreat you, allow me to remain at Our Lady of Sorrow. I promise I shall strive every day to be obedient. I shall pray all morning and do good deeds all day. I shan't ever be late for vespers and I shall strive to be humble in all things."

Mother Prioress's expression hardened. "Stand up, girl," she ordered. "Do not grovel at my feet."

Jilly stood, her pride coming to her aid. "Can you tell me why you are sending me away?"

Mother Magdalene moved behind her desk to sit stiffly in her straight-backed chair, arching her slender hands as if in prayer.

"It is not I who am sending you away, child. I thought you understood that." She picked up a parchment and silently read it before shoving it into the folds of her gown. "I have orders that you are to be taken to Salisbury, in England. You will pack your belongings and be ready to leave at dawn on the morrow. Humphrey will accompany you on your journey."

Jilly was frightened and could feel her heart beating in her throat. "Why must I leave Wales? I am not English."

"Jilly," the prioress said patiently, "I know not who guided you to me fourteen years ago, but whoever they are, they wield great power. For some reason, I have even been required to make yearly reports to the pope in Rome concerning your health, your spiritual condition, and the progress in your studies."

Jilly's mouth rounded in surprise. "His Holiness is interested in me?"

"Perhaps I should not have told you that, so please forget I said it."

Jilly's mind was filled with questions, and she looked at the prioress pleadingly.

"I know not what or who you are, Jilly, and I cannot tell you more than I already have. Whoever your benefactor may be, I hope that you will comport yourself with dignity and act in a manner that will reflect well on my teachings."

Jilly again dropped to her knees as fear of the unknown overwhelmed her. "Will you bless me, Mother Magdalene?"

The prioress stood and gently laid her hand on the bowed head. "I give you my blessing, child, but only God can set your feet upon the right path and make you aware of your weaknesses. Pray that with his guidance you will become more humble in your actions."

When Jilly stood, she looked into Mother Magdalene's eyes, hoping to see some sign of affection or some indication that the prioress would be sad to see her leave—she saw none.

Mother Prioress led Jilly to the door. "Make yourself ready. Humphrey will take you to your destination. Be at the front gate before sunrise in the morning so you do not keep him waiting. Good-bye, my daughter."

There seemed nothing else to say. Jilly moved down the hall, her footsteps slow. Who was this mysterious benefactor that Mother Prioress had mentioned? Strange no one had ever told her before that someone was interested in her existence. She felt sudden excitement. Perhaps she would learn of her past when she reached England. Then she began trembling. What if she did not like what she discovered?

Jilly went directly to her cell, where she found a leather satchel lying on the bed. Sadly she packed her meager belongings. Then she dropped to her knees beside her small cot, raising her face in prayer. Tomorrow her life would be forever changed. And she was terrified.

The next morning when Jilly joined Humphrey at the front gate, the sky was gray and overcast, and it suited her mood. Sir Humphrey, however, was cheerful as he helped her mount a horse.

Jilly glanced back down the path toward the convent, hoping Mother Magdalene would come to say good-bye, or at least one of the sisters would wish her well. Of course, she reasoned when no one came, everyone would be at their morning prayers now and could not be disturbed.

She lowered her head so Humphrey could not see the hurt she felt inside. "I am ready," she said at last, turning her mount away from the convent and following Humphrey toward the distant hills.

They had been traveling for two weeks when at last they reached a small hamlet on the banks of the Avon River. Jilly raised her eyes to the towering castle just beyond the village.

"Is that to be our destination?" she asked.

"It is, Mistress Jilly."

"The castle seems so uninviting and somehow sinister," she said, determined not to like anything about England.

"You will find only a welcome there," he assured her.

"Will I meet the person who has been my patron?"

"As to that," Sir Humphrey replied, "you must wait and see."

He nudged his mount forward, and she followed. They passed almost unnoticed through the village on their way to Salisbury Castle, then rode across the wooden bridge that spanned the moat, where they halted before a guard.

"Who wishes to pass beyond?" the sentinel asked.

"Only a young maid sent to serve the castle," Sir Humphrey replied.

"I was told to expect a young lass, but no one said anything about a man. Who might you be?"

"I am merely her escort. I shall not be staying at the castle."

The guard looked at Jilly's plain attire and nodded. "She may pass within, but you may not."

Jilly opened her mouth to protest when Sir Humphrey smiled at her. "Go inside and you'll find a friend."

"But . . . I do not want you to leave," she said, tears filling her eyes.

Sir Humphrey looked at her, his heart wrenching because they must part. "I cannot remain, Mistress Jilly, but we will meet again. This I promise."

The guard motioned Sir Humphrey away, and at the same time the inner gate was opened to admit Jilly. She watched Humphrey until the gate closed behind her, blocking her view of him. She felt deserted and alone.

The guard, a thickset man with an unsmiling face, told her to dismount and then directed her to the rear of the castle and admonished her to use the servants' entrance.

How forlorn she felt as she tightly gripped the handle of her satchel and unhappily made her way down a worn path. When she reached the kitchen, she was greeted by a woman who seemed to have been expecting her.

"Be your name Jilly?"

"Yes, mistress."

"I am Mrs. Fillburne, the housekeeper. Please follow me."

"Am I to work in the kitchen?" Jilly asked, looking about at the beehive of activity, where copper pots bubbled on the open hearth and the smell of baking bread filled the air.

There was a startled look on Mrs. Fillburne's face. "I think not."

Jilly followed the woman through so many rooms that she soon lost count. She had never seen anything as magnificent as the castle, with its high-domed ceilings and rich furnishings. At last she was led to a small sitting room.

"Please wait here. My mistress will soon attend you," the housekeeper instructed her before departing.

The sun had set, and flickering rings of light from several candles reflected on the stone walls. Jilly waited in anticipation.

She looked about, comparing the furnishings of the room to the stark trappings of the convent. Age-old tapestries covered the stone walls, and richly colored rugs were scattered on the stone floor. On closer inspection, Jilly decided there was something feminine about the room. She had never considered that her benefactor might not be a man.

At that moment, the door opened and she turned to see a woman of such regal bearing that Jilly knew she was someone of import. Her blue silk gown swept out about her and her white headdress was adorned by a crown of gold.

The lady walked around Jilly, silently assessing her. Then she smiled.

"Yes, you will do very well."

Jilly curtsied. "Am I to be your servant, my lady?"

The woman smiled. "Not a servant, my dear. Rather you will be my companion and my pupil."

Jilly raised her eyes to meet the woman's. "I would be pleased to serve you in any way I can. I have been well taught."

"Know you who I am?"

"Nay, lady. I was not told your identity."

The woman emitted soft laughter. "I am called Eleanor."

Jilly's mouth opened in surprise as she looked at the golden crown atop the lady's head with new understanding.

"You are . . . Queen Eleanor of England!"

The beautifully shaped lips thinned into a smile. "So I am. Welcome to your new home. This is my prison, but for a time, it shall be your sanctuary."

2

1183

Armed knights rode two abreast through the winter-white drifts that blanketed the high road, their horses' hooves muted by the packed snow.

Behind them trudged a long column of foot soldiers with battle gear strapped across their backs. All eyes were alert to any movement that might announce that the enemy was at hand.

Prince Ruyen, of the Isle of Falcon Bruine, rode at their head, his black armor a stark contrast to the white of the snow. His ebony helm was adorned with the symbol of the royal family, a golden falcon, its wings spread wide in flight.

They had made the long voyage across the sea and were now on English soil, where they were to rendezvous with Richard, Duke of Aquitaine, rebellious son of King Henry.

The English king had turned his conqueror's eyes in the direction of Falcon Bruine, and Prince Ruyen was determined to stop his aggression before he reached the island.

Each warrior carried with him the grim realization that he might die in battle in this foreign land. But, to a man, they obediently followed their liege lord, Prince Ruyen, wherever he led.

The prince looked neither right nor left, but focused his eyes straight ahead. The raw sadness that filled his heart was hidden behind the helm: a messenger had reached him only that morning with word that his father had been fatally wounded and died while engaging the English in battle.

Though his father's death made Ruyen the king of the Isle of Falcon Bruine, he would remain uncrowned until he returned to his homeland. By tradition, he could not assume the throne until he stood in the High Chapel at Mountbaston Castle, where every previous king of Falcon Bruine had been crowned.

Through the visor of his helm, icy winds stung Ruyen's face as he approached the English village where he was to join forces with Richard. Snow covered the rooftops of the thatch cottages, casting the village in a ghostly white light.

Ruyen dismounted, his eyes trained on the roadway, watching for any sign of life. If Richard were in the village, why did he not show himself? Something was amiss, and Ruyen melted back into the shadows to remount his war-horse.

Suddenly the bells of the village church began tolling and the air reverberated with an ominous clamor.

"Make ready for battle!" Ruyen shouted as he wheeled his spirited mount about. His giant war-horse, with its immense haunches and muscled legs, easily carried his full-armored weight into the fray.

"Beware the archers behind the windows," he commanded, "and watch lest Henry's troops close in behind us."

Galloping forward with shield and lance raised for protection, he led his troops toward the woods beyond the village where they could take cover. He hoped that Richard's forces would be waiting for him there.

When they reached the woods, he signaled for his knights to spread out and form a horizontal line so they would not be an easy target.

"Be alert," he cautioned. "I know not if we will encounter friend or foe." Before he could say more, Henry's troops came at them from every direction.

The two armies met with a loud clash of armor and fierce combat ensued. Sword and lance fell from dying hands as the battle raged. The army of Falcon Bruine was hopelessly outnumbered, and still the brave men fought unceasingly.

Prince Ruyen broke his lance on an advancing knight and took his sword in hand. With bulging muscles, he wielded his weapon, felling his enemy. Then with a mighty swing of his sword, he dispatched one foe and then another. Bodies fell before his fierce onslaught. He slashed and hacked, crumpling shields and armor and driving his blade home.

Suddenly Ruyen's helm was knocked from his head by the blow of an enemy mace. He turned to meet the culprit, cutting him down with a forceful thrust. In spite of the bitter cold, blood and sweat stung Ruyen's eyes as he rode forward to meet his next opponent.

The evening light was beginning to fail and it became apparent to Ruyen that his decimated troops were surrounded on all sides. He realized the futility of their situation—without Richard's larger force, the battle was lost—still he and his men continued to fight.

Suddenly, the sword was wrenched from Ruyen's hand and a helmed knight thrust a blade to his throat.

"Yield or die, Prince Ruyen!"

"To whom do I speak?" Ruyen demanded.

Without lowering his blade, the knight raised his visor. "Sir Dudley, commander of King Henry's northern troops. Which will it be—yield or die?"

Ruyen raised his head proudly. "Sir Dudley, I choose death."

"Nay, you shall not die this day, Your Highness. Rather you will be taken to London and displayed as King Henry's conquest. It is there that you will face judgment for your actions against my sovereign king."

A heaviness settled over Ruyen as he looked around and saw the bodies of his dead knights littering the ground where they had fallen. Many of his foot soldiers had been captured, while others had scattered into the woods, and he prayed that they at least would escape.

He turned back to Henry's commander. "I will accompany you willingly to London if you will spare my troops, who were only following my orders."

The Englishman looked at him in a calculating manner. "I have your pledge on this?"

"You do."

Sir Dudley called to his men. "Cease fighting. We shed no more blood today. We have the Golden Falcon, allow the others to go free."

There were objections from the ranks of Prince Ruyen's knights, so he spoke to them. "'Tis done, go home. Tell my mother and sister what has occurred."

Sir Dudley shoved his sword into his scabbard. "They shall not find your sister on the island. She has already been taken prisoner and is on her way to London, where you will soon join her."

Ruyen's face turned ashen. "And what of my mother, Queen Melesant?"

"Of that I have no word."

Ruyen's eyes burned with hatred. "If Henry has dared harm my sister, he will rue the day."

Laughter broke out in the English ranks. "And what will he do?" someone called out. "Break the chains that we'll bind him with? King Henry must be fair trembling with fright."

Sir Dudley scowled at the man who dared defame such a noble warrior and ordered him to the back of the line. "Prince Ruyen is to be treated with the respect due his rank. Anyone who forgets that will bear the brunt of my anger."

Ruyen was reconciled to his fate, but he had to make certain that his soldiers would be released. "Have I *your* word, Sir Dudley, that my men will be allowed to return home to their families?"

"If each man swears to take up arms against King Henry no more."

"I give my pledge for them. They will not war against England."

Sir Dudley nodded in satisfaction. "Then they are free to leave."

Ruyen saw defiance on the faces of his knights, and they grumbled in protest, not wanting to abandon him. "Go home to your families," he said. "They need you now. There is nothing more for you to do here."

"We prefer to share your prison, Your Highness," one of his knights spoke up, voicing the thoughts of the others.

Ruyen looked upon the face of each knight who had fought so bravely at his side during their ill-fated campaign. Some of them had been his boyhood companions, and some had faithfully served his father before him. To a man they would sacrifice their own lives to save his, and all he could do was send them home in defeat.

"I order you to return to Falcon Bruine," Ruyen told them.

"But what shall we tell the people?" one of his men asked.

"Tell them to keep faith." Pride shone in Ruyen's eyes as he turned to his captor and held his arms out, waiting to be shackled. Though his actions were humble, there was no submission in his haughty manner.

"I am at your service, Sir Dudley," he said.

The commander motioned a soldier forward, and heavy chains were clamped on Prince Ruyen's wrists and tightened until they bit into his skin.

"I would forgo the chains, Your Highness," Sir Dudley said, "but I have my orders."

An English knight grabbed the reins of Ruyen's horse. As they started off, he was surrounded by an escort of twelve of Henry's elite guard. He turned back to look once more at the remnants of his army, but they had been swallowed up by the encroaching darkness.

Although the weather worsened and it was bitterly cold, they traveled all night without stopping, as if his captors feared pursuit.

Ruyen was oblivious to the cold and discomfort. He was a man in torment. His father was dead, his sister a prisoner, and God alone knew what had happened to his mother. He raised his head in silent agony, feeling the soft snowflakes fall on his face.

When the sun rose, they changed horses at a small inn, then resumed their grueling pace. Ruyen refused the food and drink he was offered at their infrequent stops. It was long after nightfall on the second day when they reached London. It was eerie, silent as they rode through the unlit streets toward the Tower.

It had stopped snowing earlier, but the clouds still covered the moon. With torches to light their way, Ruyen was escorted up stone steps. The shackles were removed from his wrists and he was thrust into a chamber and the door slammed and locked behind him.

"Oh, Ruyen," Princess Cassandra cried, rushing to her brother. "Is all lost?"

He enfolded his sister in his arms. "It would seem so." He then held her at arm's length so he could look at her closely. "Have they treated you well?"

"They have allowed me no woman to attend me, but I have been given palatable food, and as you can see," she said as she looked about the small quarters, "the rooms are not uncomfortable."

"You look pale." Ruyen was concerned with the sadness he saw in her dark eyes, and she appeared younger than her fourteen years. "What of our mother?" he asked abruptly.

Cassandra shook her head, reluctant to tell him that she suspected their mother had betrayed them.

"Is she dead?"

"No," Cassandra said in a choked voice. "When last I saw her she was very well indeed. She met Henry's emissaries at the gate, welcoming them into the castle like old friends. Then mother told me that I was to be taken away as a hostage and kept safe in one of Henry's castles until you and father yielded. But instead, I was brought to London and locked in the Tower."

Ruyen seemed incapable of speech.

There was uncertainty in Cassandra's heart, and she needed her brother's reassurance. "Our mother would never have allowed the English to take me had she known they intended to make me a prisoner rather than a hostage—would she, Ruyen?" she asked doubtfully.

Brother and sister stared into each other's eyes. Cassandra was learning what Ruyen had realized long ago: their mother loved no one better than herself, and she would do anything, sacrifice anyone, even her own children, to gain the power she craved.

The young princess gripped her brother's hand. "Must we prepare for death?"

He decided to be truthful with her. "Henry has long desired Falcon Bruine. Only you and I stand in his way. You understand what I mean, do you not, Cassandra?"

She nodded sadly, then proudly raised her chin. "I shall not shame our father's name if I must face the executioner's blade."

Ruyen held her, and she drew comfort from him as she had since childhood.

"The cause was lost from conception," he admitted. "We could not have won. Richard never came, and we rode right into a trap."

"I know, Ruyen. I heard the guards talking. I also heard them say that father . . . is dead."

He nodded grimly, wishing he could shield her from further hurt. "I was told that he died bravely, Cassandra, cut down as he rode at the head of his troops. It is what he would have wanted."

"I . . . loved him, Ruyen."

"Aye, as did I."

She looked dejected, as if there was too much sadness to carry on her slight shoulders.

"We do have one chance," he told her, trying to give her some bit of hope. "When Richard hears of our plight, he will attempt a rescue."

Cassandra was not fooled. "What can he do against his father? The walls of the Tower are thick. There is no escape for us."

"Richard would never desert a friend," Ruyen insisted. "If he did not join us in battle, there was a sound reason. He will try to help us, Cassandra, that you must believe."

Her eyes held a hint of hope. "I suppose."

"How fares Falcon Bruine? Did we lose many people? Were the villages damaged?"

"Mother's orders were that our people were not to raise a sword against the English, so there was no battle. She must have made a pact with Henry long before his soldiers arrived. Tell me she did this to save the people from being harmed."

"That is a question I would ask her, Cassandra. There are too many incidents that smell of treachery, and I would give her a chance to explain."

She raised sorrowful eyes to him. "I am glad that our father did not live to see Falcon Bruine fall to Henry Plantagenet."

"As am I," Ruyen agreed in a resigned voice, looking disinterestedly about the small quarters. There were several chairs, a scarred table, clean rushes on the floor and a warm fire burning in the hearth. Through an arched doorway he could see two small bedchambers.

Cassandra noticed her brother's exhaustion. Taking his hand, she led him closer to the fire. "Since you have no squire, allow me to aid you with your armor."

Wearily, he agreed.

"Have you eaten?"

"I want nothing," he said. "English food would stick in my throat."

After his heavy armor and chainmail had been removed, Ruyen took his sister's cold hand in his. "If it were in my power, I would spare you this." His free hand fell on her shoulder. "I am prepared to meet death, Cassandra, but I shall bargain with Henry for your life."

"Never! If you are to die, I shall stand beside you. I care little for a life without you and father. Do not ask any favors of Henry Plantagenet."

Ruyen lowered himself into a chair and leaned his head back, feeling bone weary. His thoughts turned to Lady Katharine Highclere, his beloved and his betrothed.

"Did you hear anything about Katharine? Is she safe?" he asked his sister.

"Mother told me that she and her father fled the island soon after you departed for battle."

He looked at her for a moment, sensing her disapproval. "Katharine's father must have forced her to leave. She would not have gone of her own will."

Cassandra did not share Ruyen's faith in Lady Katharine. Her brother was blind to his betrothed's many shortcomings. Why did he not see that she would always do what was in her own interest?

"You should take comfort in the fact that she is safe," was Cassandra's noncommittal reply.

"It is fortunate that we had not yet married, or she would be sharing this prison with us. My regret is that I shall never again look upon her face."

His sister's words cut into his thoughts. "Do not think about that now. You must rest."

He stood, moving to the smaller bedchamber. "Aye, I do need sleep."

"Ruyen," she said, her voice stopping him at the doorway, "will the winter last long?"

"Why do you ask?"

"I overheard a guard saying that political prisoners of import are rarely executed until spring. It seems Henry likes to turn the execution into a celebration."

"Father was fond of saying that as long as there is the flicker of life, there is hope."

"But then father is dead," she reminded him. Tears glistened in her eyes. "What a sad end for a proud and noble family."

He came back to her and pulled her into his arms. "If only Richard were king of England."

"Yes, if only," Cassandra said, brushing away her tears. "We must not think that. No one can defeat Henry, he has the power of the devil on his side."

Ruyen lay upon the narrow cot, too weary to think. His sister was right about one thing: they were the last of the Rondache family.

Now the crown of Falcon Bruine had fallen into King Henry's power-hungry hands.

3

The wind rattled the shutters while chilling drafts stirred the tapestries on the wall.

Queen Eleanor sat gazing beyond the moat of the impregnable walls of the castle. An ache that would not heal throbbed within her heart.

Once she had held sway over the most dazzling court in all Europe. She had been surrounded by brilliant scholars, poets, artists, and courtiers. Now, her husband had imprisoned her in this dreary, cheerless castle. It had become her exile from life, her tomb.

Ominous clouds swept across the skies and rain began to fall in great torrents, casting the world in darkness. Her eyes appeared incredibly sad as she glanced down at the parchment clutched in her hand. With a resigned intake of breath, she closed the window, shutting out the fury of wind and rain.

At length she rose and turned to her maid, Ameria. "'Tis time to summon Jilly. Bring her to me at once."

The servant nodded, then disappeared into one of the many corridors that led off the Great Hall. Her footsteps were noiseless as she ascended the wide stone steps that curved upward into the dark recesses, her candle flickering into the hidden shadows, casting them into muted light.

Jilly was halfway between waking and sleeping when her bed curtains were pulled aside and someone called her name. She sat up, blinking her eyes, to stare in bewilderment at the queen's maid.

"Mistress Jilly, Her Majesty awaits you in the Great Hall. She's asked that you come at once."

Without hesitating, Jilly pulled on her crimson velvet dressing robe, wondering why the queen would send for her at this late hour. Sliding her feet into soft velvet slippers, she nodded.

"I am ready."

They left the bedchamber and descended the stairs into grotesque shadows cast by the single candle carried by the maid.

But when they entered the Great Hall, Jilly was astonished to find dozens of candles ablaze. King Henry only allowed Eleanor a pittance, forcing her to conserve even the candles that lit her dreary existence.

Eleanor was seated on a cushioned chair and motioned Jilly forward, indicating that she should sit on the stool at her feet. There was affection in the queen's eyes as they rested on the lovely young woman who had been her pupil for more than three years.

"Your Majesty, you are not ill, are you?" Jilly asked in concern.

"Nay, my dear, I am fit enough."

Jilly felt a rush of relief, for she adored her benefactress. She waited patiently for Eleanor to tell her why she had summoned her so urgently.

The queen looked at her speculatively. At nineteen, Jilly was no longer the lovely young girl who had come to her, she was a beautiful woman. The ebony hair that tumbled about her face was a perfect frame for her pale skin. Her blue eyes were so deep in color that they immediately drew one's attention. Yes, she was lovely, and Eleanor hoped that would make the task she would set for her easier.

"How much do you remember about your early life?"

Jilly's brow furrowed in thoughtfulness. "My first memories are of the convent, and of the prioress, Mother Magdalene. She was the only woman who was constant in my life." She smiled in remembrance. "I believe Mother Prioress did not know what to do with me."

"She did as she was instructed, following my plan for you exactly. What else do you recall?" Eleanor prodded.

"I would have been lonely had it not been for Humphrey, the gardener. He is the man who brought me to you. He was a dear man, and I miss him every day because he was my one true friend. As I think about it, I cannot recall a time when Humphrey was not nearby."

"I had not meant for you to be so lonely, Jilly. But you will soon understand why it was necessary for you to be kept in seclusion."

She looked thoughtful. "How long was I at Our Lady of Sorrow, Your Majesty? I am not quite certain of what age I arrived there."

"You were taken there when you were but two years old, Jilly, and I had you brought to me when you were sixteen. On your next birthday, you will be twenty." Eleanor took her hand. "Have you no memories other than the convent?"

"Nay, Your Majesty, nothing." Jilly look reflective. "When I was young, I would pretend that I was the daughter of some great lord and that he would one day come to rescue me." Her eyes met the queen's. "How could I have imagined that you, Your Majesty, would be the one to take me away from the convent and give me a home?"

"Have you been happy here these last three years you have spent with me, child?"

"Oh, yes, Your Majesty. I have never known such kindness and contentment. I never want to leave you."

"This prison is not for you, Jilly. You are young and there is much you have yet to do with your life."

Jilly caught her breath, looking at the queen with growing distress. "You will not send me away, will you?"

"You are of an age when most women are already married, with babes clinging to their skirts."

Jilly swallowed hard, wondering what Eleanor was trying to tell her. "Have I displeased you in some way?"

"Nay, the opposite is true. You have been dutiful in your lessons and have not complained when you were forced to study long hours," the queen said, with a softness in her eyes. "Listen well and heed my words, so you will understand why I have insisted that you be as well educated as any man."

Jilly could only stare at Eleanor.

"We live in a society, constructed and administered by men," Eleanor continued. "I was once the heiress to a great duchy, Aquitaine. Our lives are not as different as you might believe, Jilly. My grandfather made Louis of France my guardian upon his death. Louis made certain that I married his son, also named Louis." Eleanor raised her brow in mockery. "The French are fond of the name Louis, and it is sometimes difficult to keep the numbers straight in my mind."

"Your Majesty, how are we alike?"

"You will see the comparison in good time. But I was speaking of myself. Being a woman, and not having the knowledge to govern, I was at the mercy of three kings. First Louis, my father-in-law, then Louis, my husband, and later, my second husband, Henry." Eleanor leaned against the back of her chair and studied her hands that were sparkling with jeweled rings.

"I was once beautiful, and the most powerful men in the world knelt at my feet."

Jilly looked at the queen's face, which was magnificently framed by a wimple and topped with a golden crown. She knew that the once glorious golden hair was heavily laced with white, and the queen's waist was thick from bearing many children. Still there was something beautiful and ethereal about Eleanor.

"Your Majesty, you are the loveliest of all women," she said in earnestness.

The queen's smile was soft. "Bless you, child, I think you are sincere. But I am growing old and I know it."

"If only . . . if only the king would let you out of this prison. I am very sad for you."

"Ah, yes, well, that's another story. Henry knows that if he releases me, I would again plot against him. It is the way it must be between us. As it is, he sometimes allows me to attend Christmas and Easter Courts with him and my children. I can't say that I enjoy it, other than the change in scenery—I don't like my sons very well; they have become thorns in my side. Richard, of course, being the exception."

"I have oft heard you speak of Richard with great affection. I would like to meet him someday."

"He will one day be king, although Henry would have it otherwise." Eleanor smiled. "My husband was furious when I made Richard duke of Aquitaine, although it was his right as our eldest living son. He wants the Aquitaine for his beloved John, as well as the throne of England." She looked annoyed. "How such a weakling as John could have issued from Henry and myself is beyond understanding."

"Why did you marry King Henry, Your Majesty?" Jilly asked.

"Oh, but Henry was magnificent when I first saw him." Eleanor's eyes took on a dreamlike expression. "Not handsome—more than that—powerfully built with a stock of red hair and an air about him that made other men seem like mere shadows. At that time, I was married to Louis, and was queen of France. I loved Henry at once. There are moments when I love him still." She sighed. "And this is where it has led. I am floundering in stagnant water, kept from the mainstream of living, forced to view life from the windows of my prison. And as for Henry, I have merely become an irritant to him. Where once I led armies against him, I am now no more to him than a boil on a horse's rump."

Eleanor smiled as if she knew a secret that no one else was privy to. "But this boil will join you to a golden falcon, *the* Golden Falcon, who will help you strike at Henry's pride." She closed her eyes for a moment, then opened them and looked hard at Jilly. "That's what Henry values most, you know, his pride. Kill his pride and you kill Henry. You will be my lovely instrument to inflict misery on my husband."

Jilly looked puzzled. What was Eleanor trying to tell her?

"There was a time when I was powerful," Eleanor continued. "Everyone listened to the sound of my voice. Now my words carry no farther than Salisbury. When I was first imprisoned, I was consumed with rage and later sorrow and then devastation. I am ever guarded by the watchful Fitz-Stephen, a noble loyal only to Henry."

"Fitz-Stephen is a most unpleasant man. 'Tis clever the way you smuggle messages in and out of the castle without his knowledge."

"True, true."

"Your Majesty, it is not fair that you must endure such a constricted life."

"Have no pity for me, child," Eleanor said. "I, who have traveled to Jerusalem and Antioch, been queen of two courts, both French and English, adored by knights and lords too numerous to count."

"It must have been glorious."

"Ah, well, now my days are spent listening to my ladies chatter, sing sad songs and spout bad poetry. Slowly I have begun to emerge from my prison, at least in my mind. I have found a purpose—a reason for being—a way to defeat Henry without ever leaving Salisbury."

"How will you do that, Your Majesty?"

"You may indeed ask. You see, Jilly, you shall be my weapon." Eleanor laughed softly and laced her slender fingers together. "Oh, how Henry will rage when he discovers that I have had you hidden away all these years, and when the time is right I'll make certain that he knows this was my doing. Even now, I can hear him roar and threaten. But in the end, he will be helpless to do anything about it. I have planned this carefully, waiting for the right moment—that moment is now! I bless the day your mother made you my ward."

"I am your ward, Your Majesty?"

"Of course. Did you think you were some little nobody that I took into my household out of pity?" Suddenly the queen's eyes were hard and cold. "Oh, no, my girl. There are those who would give much to find you. But I have hidden you well and waited . . . waited."

"Please tell me who I am," Jilly said, unable to believe that she might at last discover her identity.

"In good time, child, in good time."

It was clear that Eleanor was reflecting on her life tonight, and although Jilly was anxious to know about her own past, she must wait until Eleanor chose to enlighten her.

"I once entertained the thought that you would marry my Richard, but then I realized that might eventually please Henry, so I decided against it." A smile transformed the harsh lines about her lips. "The husband I have chosen for you will send Henry into a frenzy."

"But who am I, that you would consider me as a proper wife for Prince Richard?" Jilly cried, shaken by Eleanor's confession.

Eleanor waved her hand dismissively. "Your blood is as pure as any royal, more so than most. You are from a revered and noble family."

Jilly's mind could hardly comprehend all the queen was telling her. She was of royal blood!

"I vowed, Jilly, that what happened to me would never happen to you. I have made certain that you were taught by only the best scholars. It was no accident that I placed you under the tutelage of the prioress at Our Lady of Sorrow. She is a woman of great insight and wisdom. I only wish my sons were as learned as you."

"I have much to thank you for," Jilly said gratefully.

Eleanor looked pleased. "I am certain that your mother would be proud of the woman you have become. You will be able to best any man, Jilly."

"This is the first time you have mentioned my family to me." Jilly raised troubled eyes to the queen. "Is it because my mother and father were not married that I am unable to use my surname?"

"I can assure you that is not the case." Amusement danced in Eleanor's eyes. "Your father was a handsome devil, and I liked him quite well, even though he was impervious to my many charms. He loved only your mother. Unfortunately, he died before your birth."

Jilly was saddened to hear that the father she had just discovered was dead. She hungered for more knowledge about her parents. "Please, Your Majesty, what more can you tell me about him and my mother?"

"Your mother was an exceptional woman of great integrity, who placed loyalty and devotion to duty above her own life. I owe her more than I can ever repay. She stood my friend when it was dangerous to do so, and when many others turned away. She put herself between my husband and me, and even stayed Henry's hand when he would have struck me down. For her loyalty to me, your mother suffered Henry's wrath, and that is what ultimately caused her death."

Jilly gasped. "She is dead too!"

The queen took her hand. "I am sorry to tell you this

way. You see, your mother's death was caused by my husband's hand. Henry did not actually strike the fatal blow, but he is responsible for her death all the same."

Jilly winced in pain. "I always hoped . . . prayed that they were alive somewhere." Her eyes shimmered with unshed tears. "I have no family."

"Nay, my dear, you have not. But you have something that will sustain you even more."

Jilly looked anxiously at the queen. "What would that be, Your Majesty?"

Eleanor stood and walked to the open hearth, holding out her hands to warm them. She was always cold these days. At last, she turned back to Jilly. "There are only three people other than myself who know your true identity, Jilly—the two men who took you away to safety the night your mother died and the Holy Father in Rome."

"Who am I, that I must hide my name, and yet the pope knows my identity?"

"Before more is said, I must tell you that Jilly is not your real name. From this moment, you shall be known only by your true name, which is Jilliana."

"I . . ." The disclosure that she had been using a name that was not her own was such a shock that she could think of nothing to reply.

"Say the name," Eleanor insisted.

"I am . . . Jilliana."

"Forget that you were ever called Jilly," Eleanor said decisively. "Now, Jilliana, will you do everything that I ask of you?"

"Without question, Your Majesty."

"First, tell me what you know about the kingdom of Talshamar."

Jilliana was confused by this digression. "I think I must know everything there is to know. I studied about no country as much as Talshamar—but you know this."

"Tell me what you know of the royal family that rules Talshamar."

Jilliana thought she must have misunderstood. "There is no royal family. The consort died even before the queen gave birth to their d—daughter." Her heart was pounding and she stared at Eleanor.

"Go on, Jilliana, tell me what else you know about the family."

There was a growing awareness in Jilliana's mind, and it was as if all the things that had been a mystery to her were now becoming clear. "I know that the members of the royal family are all dead with the possible exception of— Princess Jilliana!" Now her words came out in a rush. "She has not been heard of since the night the castle was invaded by the English. Many people assume that the princess died that night, while others argue that she was hidden by friends of her mother."

Jilliana, looking pale and shaken, gazed into Eleanor's eyes. "I am Princess Jilliana!"

Now Eleanor's eyes were swimming with tears as she took Jilliana's trembling hand in hers. "Yes, my child, you are the true and only heir of Talshamar, and my dear friend Queen Phelisiana's beloved daughter."

Jilliana shook her head to clear it. "Of all the things that I ever imagined about myself, I could never have envisioned this."

Eleanor looked smug. "No, nor has anyone else. For seventeen years Henry has cast his power-hungry eyes in the direction of Talshamar, as did Louis and now Philip of France, and only your mother's ingenious plan has kept the kingdom out of their reach."

Jilliana withdrew her hand from Eleanor's and stood. "It is all too much for me to comprehend. I know from my studies that Talshamar is administered and governed by Rome. If the heir— If I do not come forward before my twenty-first birthday, the country will pass to the governance of France."

"Yes, and poor Henry has always known that to rule Talshamar and keep it from the French, he must find you and have you under his power. Even now, after all these years, he has not given up his search for you."

"I despise him for what he did to my mother." Her eyes were swimming with angry tears. "And for what he did to Talshamar."

"You must not forget that my husband is your enemy," Eleanor told her. "Heed me well, Jilliana, your subjects have been told that you live and will one day return and they only wait for that day."

Jilliana was suddenly frightened of the responsibilities that faced her. "My subjects?"

Eleanor lightly touched the aged parchment in her lap. "This is your mother's letter giving you into my care. With this, and the Great Seal of Talshamar, you will claim your rightful place."

Jilliana blinked her eyes. Now she understood why she had so diligently been taught the history of the Talshamarians, their politics and their customs. She had come to admire the bravery of the dead queen, never suspecting that she was her own mother.

"Now, I must ask you, child, have you heard of the Isle of Falcon Bruine?"

"Is it not far to the north of Talshamar?"

Eleanor's eyes gleamed. "Aye, it is. The ruling family there is Rondache. The king and his son, Prince Ruyen, supported my Richard against Henry in a recent conflict— a conflict that cost the king's life and caused the prince and his sister to be locked in the Tower."

"Do . . . you think they will die?"

"Henry will soon pass sentence on them. He will surely condemn them to death unless someone intervenes. However, it is within your power to save them both."

"How can I help them, Your Majesty? I do not even know them."

"Will you continue to follow my instructions and do all that I ask of you, no matter how difficult it might seem, Jilliana?"

"I shall."

Eleanor gave a triumphant laugh. "Then listen well and remember all I tell you. I will see you in your rightful place and repay an old debt to your mother. Make no mistakes, and do exactly as I instruct you, or Henry will find a way to destroy you."

The young woman's eyes burned with the light of vengeance. "I will make no mistake. I know not the face of my mother, but her voice calls out to me from the grave, and God willing, I shall answer my mother's cry."

Eleanor's eyes gleamed with elation. "Then all has not been in vain. I knew you would not fail me. In heeding your mother's voice, you will also serve others who stand in need of your help."

"But what is to keep Henry from imprisoning me and taking Talshamar?"

"Clever girl. Rome and France will prevent it."

"Surely my mother must have trusted the French king if she made him her heir, Your Majesty?"

"Only slightly more than she trusted Henry, which was not at all. But she was wise to pit the two adversaries against one another. The French king would see you dead without issue so he might claim Talshamar, while Henry must make certain that you live to deliver an heir. The pope has been your strongest champion. Know you this: neither Henry nor Philip will want to offend Pope Lucius by causing you harm. For to do so would surely cause their excommunication."

"Am I not in danger since I have no heir?"

"You will be safe in England. Especially if you succeed in snatching the Golden Falcon from the talons of death. First, however, you must be crowned queen of Talshamar. And this must be done swiftly, and in secret."

Jilliana felt overwhelming gratitude. "I begin to understand why my mother commended me to your care. How can I ever thank you, Your Majesty?"

A smile eased the tired lines about Eleanor's mouth. "My thanks will be when you are crowned queen and stand before Henry. Your cause will be a double blow to him. If my plan is successful, he will lose Talshamar, as well as the Isle of Falcon Bruine. I have waited long for this moment."

"How can I save Prince Ruyen and his sister?" Jilliana asked worriedly.

"I will instruct you on precisely what to do and say—but heed me well. Trust no one, especially not Henry."

"When do I leave?"

Eleanor looked at Jilliana as if she'd come out of a dense fog somewhere in the dark recesses of her mind. "Soon—very soon."

Eleanor then laughed. "At last I have you, Henry. How sweet will be the victory!"

4

What should have taken months to achieve, Queen Eleanor accomplished in three weeks. Jilliana was fitted with gowns of the finest tissue silk from Sicily and wool from Flemish weavers that was coveted by the English nobility.

Nimble fingers sewed elegant creations, working long days and well into the night. Rich, costly fur was sewn beneath a layer of crimson velvet to create a warm hooded cloak. Jilliana's headdress was made of the finest Belgian linen, which would be draped about her neck and shoulder to be fastened by a fillet of wrought gold.

Eleanor presented Jilliana with jewels that were so magnificent she could only suppose they came from the queen's own treasure trove.

She was puzzled by Eleanor's insistence that most of her gowns be white in color. When she questioned this, she was merely told that all would be clear in good time.

Eleanor now took Jilliana's teaching onto herself, instructing her for hours about the coronation ceremony that would take place before she reached London. They also rehearsed what to do and say when Jilliana stood before Henry. Jilliana listened carefully to each word—she must not fail!

At last the day came when Eleanor decided her charge was ready, except for the last and most important guidance, which she would see to herself.

Jilliana had been summoned and Eleanor waited for her appearance. Oh, if only she had wings so she could fly over the walls of her prison, Eleanor thought. How she would love to watch Henry's face when he learned Jilliana's identity. No matter. She knew Henry well enough to imagine his reaction—and she did have her spies at court.

When Jilliana entered, Eleanor faced her, her eyes hard like glowing coals. "You will recall that I mentioned the Rondache family to you, and told you that Henry would most likely pass a death sentence on them?"

"I do, Your Majesty. 'Tis sad."

"There will be a public announcement of their execution two weeks hence. I have carefully estimated the time it will take you to reach London. I want you to enter the city the very day that Henry passes sentence on the Golden Falcon and his sister. You must insist on being taken directly to Henry, and this is what you will say to him."

Although there were only the two of them in the room, the queen leaned close to Jilliana and whispered in her ear. The words she spoke brought a blush to the young woman's cheeks.

"But how can I profess such a lie, Your Majesty?" Jilliana asked in a shocked voice. "To do so would be publicly to disgrace myself and dishonor my mother's name."

Eleanor's eyes became cunning. "Oh, there will be gossip for a time, but no permanent damage. You have my word that when my son Richard comes to the throne all will be rectified, and the truth can then be revealed. You must say exactly what I have told you, or the Rondache family will perish. And lastly, I must warn you about Prince Ruyen's mother, Queen Melesant. My informant did not know if she has come to London, but if you should encounter her be wary. She is devious. Do not trust her. Remember she has aspirations to wear the crown of Falcon Bruine."

Jilliana frowned. "Why was she not taken prisoner with her son and daughter?"

"You may well ask," Eleanor replied dryly. "Melesant has always supported Henry, I suspect even against her own husband and son. She was once Henry's lover, in fact; until she lured him to her bed, he had been faithful to me. I hope she has grown fat and pockmarked."

Jilliana could not hide her shock at Eleanor's revelation, but she made no reply.

"Your mother would want you to follow my guidance in this and you have already promised that you would do so," Eleanor reminded her.

Jilliana nodded reluctantly in agreement. Surely Eleanor knew what was best. "I will do as you say, although it goes against my teaching to confess to a falsehood."

"Sometimes expediency must be implemented to serve justice. When you are queen, you will learn this, my dear." Eleanor smiled, showing white, even teeth and attempting to bring levity to their conversation. "I have heard it said that the Golden Falcon is practiced in bewitching and seducing the ladies. Beware also of him, and do not fall prey to his charms, lest you lose your heart."

"What shall I do in the event that Prince Ruyen denies my claim before everyone?"

"Then he would be a fool and deserve to die. But I have taken every precaution to ensure that does not happen. One who is loyal to me has managed to smuggle a message to Prince Ruyen. I only hope he understands the importance of what was relayed to him."

"I will do what I can." Jilliana's eyes were troubled as she gazed at Eleanor. "If King Henry believes my lie, then will I be forced to marry Prince Ruyen?"

Eleanor covered the girl's hand with her own. "Jilliana, you must understand that you were born to the purple, and that means you can marry only those of your rank. Think of this: Henry may very well want you for our son John. I do not believe you would like being John's wife."

Jilliana remembered seeing Prince John a year ago when he had visited his mother. Although she had not been presented to him at the time, she had observed him with the queen. His words had been oily, his eyes lusterless, small, and cunning, while his lips had been thick and pouting. She shuddered—no, she would not marry John! Even the unknown prince of Falcon Bruine was preferable to him. She lowered her head, resigned to her fate.

"I am most grateful to you for the lovely gowns and jewels. I will see that the jewels are returned to you as soon as I am able."

"I cannot take credit for providing the wardrobe or the jewels, my dear. They are donations from the people of your own country."

"But how?"

"You spoke to me of your friend, Humphrey, from the convent. In actuality, he is *Sir* Humphrey, one of your knights who pledged to stay near you. Loyal heart that he has, he bore his duties without complaint, and never broke the pledge he gave your mother. Even after you came to me, he remained in the nearby village, ever vigilant."

Jilliana found it painful to breathe when she thought what Humphrey—or, Sir Humphrey—had endured for her sake. "He spent years in menial servitude at the convent just so he could watch over me?"

"That is so. He also went secretly among your nobles to acquire what you needed to enter London in splendor. As you see, your subjects were extremely generous with their queen. You must know that you are well loved."

Jilliana glanced at the ruby ring on her hand. "I cannot

imagine why anyone would be so generous with someone they did not know."

"It is the loyalty people feel for their rightful ruler. I can assure you that you are important to all of Talshamar." Eleanor rose and moved to the door. "You must sleep now. Tomorrow you begin your long journey."

"Your Majesty, thank you for all your kindnesses. I shall miss you sorely."

Eleanor looked sad for a moment. "You have been a joy to me, child. I shall miss you and hope the day will come when we will meet again."

"I am frightened of what lies ahead."

Eleanor suddenly wondered if the girl was capable of the task that had been set for her. She was such a gentle spirit, perhaps Henry would destroy her.

"There is no need to be frightened, Jilliana. You have only to remember that your family name is older than that of the Plantagenets. Your family was ruling Talshamar when Henry's was yet heathen. Comport yourself with dignity at all times and you will not fail. Remember that you are a queen!"

Jilliana stood straight and tall, her eyes sparking fire. "I shall not forget."

Eleanor clamped the girl's arm, her tone suddenly hard and cold. "I must warn you not to underestimate Henry. He's sly and cunning and will try to thwart you at every turn. Do not allow him to humble you. Henry does not respect those he can manipulate."

"I shall never submit to his domination," Jilliana promised, raising her chin and straightening her spine. "When I stand before him, I shall remember that I am my mother's daughter—this I swear!"

Eleanor was pleased by the passion Jilliana displayed. This once meek girl had become consumed with the burning fires of revenge. Perhaps she would be a worthy opponent for Henry after all.

"Each step you have taken until now, Jilliana, has led you to the moment when you face my husband. You have been honed, schooled, and instructed since you first came under my care." Eleanor's face softened and she turned away. "Go now to your bed, child. You leave before sunrise tomorrow."

"I wish—I wish you were coming with me."

"Foolish girl, you know I cannot leave my prison. But you will be my ears and eyes and you will give voice to my words. In that I shall be with you."

Wishing she could say more, but knowing she had been dismissed, Jilliana left and slowly climbed the stairs to her chamber. She had realized tonight that while the queen was fond of her, the force that guided her life was her constant battle with her husband.

Eleanor loved no one as much as she hated Henry.

It was still dark when Jilliana was awakened by Eleanor's maid pulling her bed curtains aside.

" 'Tis time to rise. My queen has sent me to help you dress so you can be on your way."

Jilliana quickly got out of bed. Too excited to eat, she allowed the silent servants to aid her in dressing. The gown that Eleanor had chosen for her to wear today was a white silk, trimmed with golden embroidery. Her dark hair was braided and covered with a white wimple and veil. Sparkling jewels were slid onto her fingers, and bracelets adorned her wrists. Her trunks had been packed the night before and were now being carried below by several strong-backed men.

Jilliana watched the door, hoping Eleanor would come to say good-bye, but when it was time for her to leave, the queen still had not appeared.

She slipped a hooded cape about her to cover her finery, so that Henry's guards would not become suspicious.

When she reached the door, the men posted there paid little heed to her departure. They had been instructed to detain anyone who would enter the castle without permission; they had no orders to keep the queen's ladies from leaving.

As her trunks were being loaded onto a cart, Sir Humphrey appeared, leading a magnificent white horse. She clasped his hands in hers, her eyes shining with happy tears. "How I have missed you."

He nodded, his gaze lingering on her face, noting that she was a grown woman now. "Aye, and I missed you also, Your Highness."

Then he reached forward, his hands circling Jilliana's waist as he placed her onto her palfrey, then mounted a white horse himself.

"Shall we go, Your Highness?" he whispered, not wanting to be overheard by the two men who stood guard at the gate.

She smiled at him with great affection. "Yes, my dear friend, I am ready."

Jilliana turned to gaze up at Eleanor's window, her heart heavy. Apparently she was not to be allowed to say a final good-bye to the queen.

With her head high, atop a gold-trimmed saddle, and looking every bit a queen, she rode across the drawbridge. Down the winding road they went past the village and into the unfamiliar.

Eleanor stood at her window, watching Jilliana depart. Her heart was heavy, for she would miss the girl's cheerful presence.

"Go with God, my dear," she whispered, turning away. She suddenly felt cold and moved to stand before the fireplace, but the fire lent no warmth to the emptiness in her heart.

5

Neither Princess Jilliana nor Sir Humphrey spoke until they were well past the village. At last Sir Humphrey halted his mount so they could talk.

She reached out and laid her gloved hand on his. "I now know all about your loyalty. How can I ever thank you for the sacrifices you made, Sir Humphrey?"

He was speechless for a moment, knowing she was unaware how much she meant to him and the other people of Talshamar.

"Your well being is my reward, Your Highness. I can see you have thrived since last we met."

She suddenly felt like crying because they were no longer just Humphrey and Jilly. Their close relationship had been replaced by one of sovereign and subject—she almost wished herself back at the convent where he had been her friend. None of this could she say to him.

"Should we not ride on?" she said at last.

"Your Highness, first I must inform you that by nightfall we will join other Talshamarians, who will accompany you to London. Shall I explain what is to transpire tonight?"

Jilliana merely nodded, waiting for him to continue. In truth, events were moving swiftly. A few weeks ago she had thought herself one of Queen Eleanor's companions, now she found that she herself was also a queen. Although she was not yet comfortable in her new role, she schooled her face not to reflect her uncertainty.

"Tell me what I must do," she said at last.

"Your loyal subjects have been gathering for days in a secret place we will reach by nightfall. Since timing is so important, as soon as we arrive at that place, you are to be crowned. Queen Eleanor thought it best if you entered London as queen of Talshamar."

"How will this be done?"

"Cardinal Failsham has arrived from Talshamar to act as Pope Lucius's emissary."

"I know the cardinal. Do you recall he often visited the convent?"

"Yes, he came to see you so he could be assured you were doing well. By your mother's request, he has been acting as royal bailiff of Talshamar until such time as you return."

"I am certain that his has not been an easy task," Jilliana observed.

"We must hurry now," Sir Humphrey urged. "If you will allow it, I am told that His Eminence has everything you will require for the coronation. Will you agree to be crowned in this fashion?"

She was silent for a moment as she pondered his words. "The plan has merit—I see no other way it can be accomplished with such speed."

Jilliana could see happiness in Sir Humphrey's eyes just before he looked away.

"You cannot know what this day means to your subjects, Your Highness. Long have we waited for you to take your place as our sovereign."

She took notice of his silver armor and smiled. "You look very different from when last I saw you. How could I ever have mistaken you for a humble gardener?"

"Please forgive the deception, Your Highness. It was the only way I could fulfill my vow to your mother and remain near you."

Her eyes showed her concern. "Stay near me now, Sir Humphrey, for I fear I shall make many mistakes. I go into a future that I know little about. I must pledge my honor to men I do not know. I admit only to you that I am frightened because I may fail in my mission."

There was soft reverence in the old knight's eyes. "You will not fail, Your Highness. You are your mother's daughter, and she would have been proud."

He glanced to the east, where the sky had turned a rosy hue with the rising sun. "We should resume our journey, Your Highness. I would see the crown of Talshamar safely on your head before dawn tomorrow."

She heard the urgency in his voice and although many questions filled her mind, she did not give them voice. Instead she nodded.

"Then let us ride on, Sir Humphrey."

They rode silently all day, sometimes slowing to rest the horses, and sometimes going at a full gallop. Only once did they stop to eat, and at that time Sir Humphrey was watchful and tense, looking for any trouble that might arise.

It was almost dark when he led her off the road and down a narrow twisting trail. On they rode, until at last Sir Humphrey halted.

She tried to see his face, but he was no more than a dark outline. "Why do we stop here?" she inquired.

He dismounted and directed her gaze to a distant light. "That will be where your loyal subjects have gathered to welcome you. They have waited long for this moment, as have I."

She stared at the distant lights, now able to discern that

they were campfires. She could see many figures gathered about the dancing flames.

"Are they not risking danger of discovery by King Henry? Is it wise for so many to gather in one place?"

"It is the only way we could think of, Your Highness. Queen Eleanor herself was instrumental in the planning of your crowning. And have no fear, for we are now on the land of a lord who is loyal to the queen. Shall we proceed?"

She nudged her mount forward and Sir Humphrey fell in behind her as they continued down the narrow path. At last they reached the circle of light and Princess Jilliana was immediately surrounded by knights and solemn-faced barons who dropped to their knees and lowered their heads in homage.

Sir Humphrey helped Jilliana from her horse and she walked among her subjects, urging them to rise. She was not prepared for the love and adoration they poured out to her. She was further startled when she saw tears in the eyes of some of the men, or was it merely a trick played by the flickering light of the campfires?

Jilliana could not speak for the lump that was forming in her throat. These were her people and she immediately felt a bond with them.

Cardinal Failsham approached her, his expression solemn, as befitted the occasion.

"Welcome, Your Highness," he said, bowing to her.

"It is good to see you again, Your Eminence," Jilliana told him.

"I am honored that you remember me. I will be further honored if you will allow me to place the crown of Talshamar upon your head as I once placed it upon the heads of your grandmother and mother."

"Then I would have none other crown me."

"My regret is that you cannot be anointed before the high altar. Nevertheless, I have in my possession the Ring, Crown, Scepter, and Sword of Talshamar."

Suddenly Jilliana felt the blood of generations of queens flowing through her veins. She raised her head, a grave expression on her face.

"We shall not allow the place to deter us, Your Eminence. I am told by Sir Humphrey that we must make haste."

The Cardinal bowed his head. "That is so, Your Highness." He moved to a stand covered with golden cloth where several items had been placed. All those present gathered about as the cardinal turned to their princess royal.

In a clear voice, he uttered the words that had been spoken to crown generations of Talshamarian queens. He spoke first to those gathered near. "Princess Jilliana is your undoubted queen, wherefore all you who are come this day to do homage and service to her say yea."

"We do so come," came the answer from a strong chorus of voices.

"Are you, Princess Jilliana, willing to do the same to your subjects?"

Queen Eleanor had instructed Jilliana in her part of the ceremony, so she now answered in a clear voice. "I am so willing," she replied.

The knights spoke in unison.

"God save Queen Jilliana!"

The cardinal then stepped forward and anointed her with oil, first on the hand, and then on the forehead.

"God crown you with a Crown of Glory and Righteousness, that by the ministry of this our benediction, having a right faith and manifold fruit of good works, you may obtain the crown of an everlasting kingdom by the gift of Him whose kingdom endureth forever."

Jilliana bowed her head while he handed her the Great Seal of Talshamar. This she clasped in her hand and then held to her breast. Then she spoke, her eyes focused on the crown the cardinal supported upon a red velvet cushion.

"I uphold the most valuable thing that this world affords. Here is wisdom. This is the royal law. This seal is the oracle of God."

"God save the queen!" the knights said.

Jilliana could not help notice that the cardinal's hand trembled as he took the crown and placed it on her head. There was a long moment of silence, and she remembered that the last head this crown adorned had been her mother's.

The cardinal then stepped back and many voices spoke in unison.

"Your liege man of life and limb and of earthly worship; and faith and truth I will bear unto you, to live and die, against all manner of foe for your sake."

Jilliana found that the crown sat lightly on her head. She looked at the knights who had just pledged her their lives. She knew them not, and yet they were her subjects and she could feel their warmth reach out to her.

She felt the sting of tears when she saw tears in the eyes of these men who had just paid her homage, their voices blending: "God save Queen Jilliana. Long live Queen Jilliana. May the queen live forever!"

At last Sir Humphrey dropped to his knees and kissed the hand of his queen.

"Your Majesty, I swear my life and my earthly goods to your service."

Barons and knights approached her, each in turn, dropping to their knees and repeating the same pledge. She bestowed upon each a smile and a nod.

When the last man had made his pledge, Sir Humphrey held up his hand.

"Her Majesty is weary and shall seek her bed. On the morrow, we shall begin the long journey to London, and then, God willing, to Talshamar. Let not any man present allow harm to befall the queen."

Sir Humphrey escorted Jilliana to a tent that had been erected for her comfort.

"Good night, Your Majesty. I regret that you will have only one servant to attend you on the journey. Her name is Netta Dermot, and she will serve you until you find someone of your own choosing."

"Thank you, Sir Humphrey. How well I treasure your devotion."

"I had always hoped to live long enough to see you crowned. Tonight that dream came true." Suddenly he looked regretful. "Would that your coronation had been held in the Richmond Cathedral for all your subjects to witness. But, no matter the place, you are still queen of all Talshamar, and your subjects revere you."

She stared down at the Great Seal of Talshamar that she still clasped in her hand, knowing it was of great significance, but not yet understanding its power. "I pray that I will be worthy of them."

Sir Humphrey bowed and backed away a few paces. "You are the queen—you are most worthy." His eyes swept her face. "Have I not seen this for myself?" His voice cracked with emotion and he quickly turned away in embarrassment.

On entering the tent, Jilliana saw a woman she judged to be in her thirtieth year. She had flaxen hair and her eager brown eyes were filled with reverence.

"You would be Netta."

The woman dropped to her knees.

"I am, Your Majesty, and it is my honor to serve you."

"Thank you, Netta."

"Your Majesty, so long have we waited for you." She lowered her head, feeling she had said too much.

"Then help me disrobe, Netta, for I am very weary."

Obediently and deftly, the woman complied. Her crown and the Great Seal were placed in a velvet-lined chest, and soon Jilliana was wearing her nightgown, her long hair brushed and gleaming. She climbed onto a cot cushioned with a soft downy mattress and her eyes drifted shut.

Soon she was asleep, unaware that a quiet celebration was taking place among her loyal followers. They drank wine from Talshamar to honor their queen. Two knights did not join in the celebration, but instead stood before the queen's tent, ever vigilant and alert to any danger.

And so it was that the newly crowned sovereign of Talshamar spent her first night as queen, lost in dreamless sleep, not knowing that she had just fulfilled her nobles' dearest wish: to once more be under the rule of their own sovereign.

The sun had not yet broken through the night sky when Jilliana awoke. After a quick meal of fruit, cheese, and a delicious cream-filled bread that was served on a golden plate, Jilliana allowed Netta to dress her.

The woman appeared nervous when she reached for the crown. She held it, not knowing how to place it on her queen's head.

This brought a smile to Jilliana's lips. "'Tis only a symbol, Netta, you need not fear it."

"It is what it represents that awes me, Your Majesty. The honor of serving you is too great. That I was chosen out of all the women in Talshamar to wait upon Your Majesty has brought great respect to my family."

Jilliana was having trouble adjusting to her role of sovereign. She had lived a quiet, humble life, and to be suddenly so adored was somehow disconcerting. She took the crown from Netta and placed it on her own head.

"Come," she told the woman, striding to the tent opening, "I do not want to keep the others waiting."

When Jilliana stepped outside, a glorious sight met her eyes. Barons and knights, one hundred strong, were all wearing white, but for their golden chainmail. They were mounted on white steeds, their only ornamentation their family crests and helmets studded with brilliant gems.

Sir Humphrey, also dressed in white, came forward and helped her mount her horse.

"I trust you passed a pleasant night, Your Majesty?"

"Indeed, Sir Humphrey, I slept in comfort. 'Tis a glorious morning, is it not?"

"That it is, Your Majesty."

She smiled at him. She was finding it less and less difficult to adjust to the life she had been born to. But there was a mischievous gleam in her eyes. "Sir Humphrey, it must be difficult for you to think of me as your sovereign. You have too often seen me with dirt on my face."

He looked at her seriously. "I always saw the crown of Talshamar on your head. You have ever been my queen."

Soon the long column left the secluded glen and wound its way along the twisted trail until they reached the high road. What a splendid sight they made with scarlet banners flouncing in the wind and golden chainmail gleaming in the sun.

Everyone they met along the way gawked at the lovely young queen, with her stark white entourage. Eleanor had been wise in her choice of white, for how magnificent they appeared to the English peasants.

Word spread quickly to the villages and hamlets along the route, and as the cavalcade advanced, throngs of people gathered to greet them with waves and cheers of delight.

None knew the identity of the beautiful young queen, but all the same, they raised their voices to glorify her.

6

Henry was closeted with his minister and his bishops as they puzzled over the strange news that was filtering in from the outlying villages on the high road to London.

Henry was pensive as he spoke. "Say you that the cavalcade is dressed all in white, from tip of head to their steeds, and that they are led by a beautiful young noblewoman?"

"Yes, Sire. By my faith it is so. It is reported that they are even now within sight of London. Shall I have them detained at the gate?"

"Are they armed?"

"Indeed they are, but they have posed no threat to anyone along the way. In fact, it has been reported that they throw gold coins to the people as they pass."

Henry looked disgruntled. He always distrusted such generous gestures. "When they reach London, allow only the woman and two of her followers to enter the city. Disarm the others and place them under guard."

"Yes, Sire," the minister said, hurrying out of the king's bedchamber to follow his orders.

The mystery intrigued Henry, but he had no time to ponder his strange visitors. He moved slowly from his bedchamber to the throne room. This day he must render judgment on Prince Ruyen, a distasteful but necessary business.

Harshly whispered words rippled between the nobles who had gathered to hear King Henry's final judgment against the upstart Prince Ruyen and his sister, Princess Cassandra. Conjecture was widespread and wagers were placed involving the outcome of the king's ruling. Most believed the prince and princess would be condemned to death.

When at last King Henry entered, he ignored the waiting courtiers, focusing his attention on the light spilling through the high stained-glass windows, his mind already racing ahead to his decision. Whatever he decided today would be unpopular with many of his own subjects. But he would not tolerate audacious hotheads who supported his treacherous sons. Prince Ruyen would be an example to deter others who might be tempted to follow his troublesome offspring. Besides, the Isle of Falcon Bruine already as good as belonged to England.

Henry Plantagenet, the greatest lion of them all, was not an old man, yet his cropped short hair was heavily grayed, and his gray eyes had lost much of their luster. His complexion was ashen and he was now prone to obesity.

Though betrayed time and again by those closest to him, his shoulders were still straight, his head erect. He was a powerful man and those whom he counted among his enemies trembled at the thought of displeasing him, for his might was commanding and his reach long.

He had lost almost everything that really mattered, but not England—never England. He thought of Eleanor, imprisoned for plotting against him, and of his two remaining sons, Richard and John, who warred between themselves as well as against him. The vast lands he had conquered would likely be lost after his death, for which of his sons had the power to keep them?

"Bring in the prisoners," Henry told his lord chamberlain.

Prince Ruyen, although in chains, walked unhesitatingly beside his sister, his arms about her, supporting her, for she was ailing and weak from her imprisonment. He raised his head proudly, his eyes riveted on the man who held their fate in his hands.

King Henry's brow furrowed as he glanced at the haughty young prince, who many referred to as the Golden Falcon. He was a caged bird now. There was insolence in those dark eyes, but Henry knew how to deal with his sort. Prince Ruyen had been a formidable opponent— pity to destroy such a warrior. Grudgingly, Henry admired him, wondering if the young prince knew it was his own mother's betrayal that had caused his capture.

Princess Cassandra was a different matter, however. She was clearly ill and out of compassion he ordered a stool for her, but she shook her head, choosing to stand beside her brother. Henry had been told that she was but fourteen, and she held the hint of future beauty. There was a time when the sight of her would have stirred his blood, but no more. He was getting too old for the pleasures of the flesh.

Again, Henry looked at the prince, whose eyes still smoldered with the fire of rebellion. Oh, how well he knew what Prince Ruyen was feeling. Had he not once felt those same fires smoldering within himself?

"This is a sad moment for me," King Henry said in a voice that carried to the back of the large chamber. He shifted his weight, trying to find a comfortable position for his bulk.

A page, seeing the king's discomfort, rushed forward with a cushion, only to receive a scowl for his troubles. Henry did not like to show weakness before his subjects.

Henry continued to speak. "Your guilt has been pronounced by the high court, and it falls to me to render sentence for your crimes. As you know, rebellion must be punished or it will grow and fester into a cankerous sore. Although it would please me to be merciful, justice must be served."

Overcome by a dark and bitter hatred, Prince Ruyen spoke. "And you have ever been known for your mercy, have you not, Henry? Your wife is in prison and your own sons despise you. Tell my sister more about your mercy, maybe she will believe you, but I do not."

"By the eyes of God!" Henry roared, "your insolence will be the death of you. If you care not for your own life, care you not for your sister? If I had any notion of leniency, it is all but gone."

Ruyen was in a grip of rage and striving to keep his self-control. His voice was composed, hardly above a whisper, causing those in the back of the chamber to strain to hear. "I ask one boon of you, Henry."

Henry grinned, leaning forward and perching his chin on his folded hand. "You would ask a favor of me? Whatever can it be?"

"I ask only that you allow my sister to go free. She is innocent of any wrongdoing and should not suffer because of me."

Henry knew that if he provoked the young hothead he would surely condemn himself with his own arrogance. It was precarious condemning a royal family. He had been careful to gain the sympathy of the people, thus quelling any dissension in the ranks of his own nobles.

"You should have considered your sister sooner! You have no rights here since you have been tried and convicted of crimes against England."

Prince Ruyen clamped his lips in a severe line, but said nothing.

Suddenly, there was a stirring at the door and the two men-at-arms barred someone from entering the chamber. All attention turned in that direction.

"Determine the trouble at once," Henry said harshly to his lord chamberlain.

As the man rushed forward and then quickly returned, he bowed before the king.

"Well, speak," Henry demanded sourly. "Who has dared interrupt these proceedings?"

The lord chamberlain was accustomed to Henry's dark moods, so therefore was undaunted and leaned closer, whispering so only the king could hear.

"What?" Henry looked astounded. "What you say is preposterous! Have I not searched for . . ." His voice trailed off. "This cannot be."

"She claims to be Queen Jilliana of Talshamar and insists that she be allowed to attend this hearing because it concerns her."

Henry stroked his chin with a satisfied smile on his face. "So, after all these years in hiding, the young queen comes to me. If indeed she's telling the truth." He turned to the chamberlain. "But she is mistaken when she says this sentencing concerns her. Inform her that I shall grant an audience in my private chambers at the conclusion of these proceedings."

To Henry's amazement, a young woman appeared, dressed in white with a golden crown set atop her head. She glared at the guards who blocked her path. "Stand aside and allow me to pass," Jilliana ordered, pushing away the sword of one of the men. She advanced boldly into the chamber, flanked on either side by Sir Humphrey and Cardinal Failsham.

Silence fell over the chamber as they moved toward King Henry. Jilliana could hear whispers rippling through the crowd.

"Who can this beauty be?"

"Whence does she come?"

But her eyes were on the man who sat upon the throne. She stopped in front of Henry and stared into his puzzled eyes.

"Sire, I am Queen Jilliana of Talshamar," she said in a voice that carried to the far corners of the room. "If you condemn Prince Ruyen and Princess Cassandra to death, then you must also condemn me, for I carry within my body Prince Ruyen's seed."

King Henry was stunned, but no more so than Prince Ruyen. Henry's eyes went to the girl's stomach, but it was impossible to tell her condition since she wore a flowing surcoat.

Ruyen stared at the woman as if she had lost her mind. How dare she make such an outrageous claim. His sister looked at him in astonishment.

Suddenly, Ruyen remembered the baffling message he had received a fortnight ago. The servant who usually brought their meals had been replaced by another. As he served the food, the man had hurriedly whispered, while casting furtive glances over his shoulder at the guard. He had urged Ruyen to be alert for the chance that would come for him to save himself.

Ruyen had assumed that the man was sent by Richard. But as days passed and nothing happened, he forgot about the incident. And now this woman appeared—surely this was the opportunity the man had meant.

"You claim that you are Queen Jilliana of Talshamar," Henry said skeptically, "but how can we know that you speak the truth? It has long been our belief that Jilliana died in childhood."

Although Jilliana's heart was thundering against her breast and her hands trembled, she faced the king with clear eyes.

"I am indeed who I claim to be." She nodded at Sir Humphrey and he handed her an object wrapped in a velvet cloth. "Know you the Great Seal of Talshamar, Henry Plantagenet?"

"I do," Henry answered, his eyes narrowing.

She held the seal out for his inspection, but drew it back when he would have touched it.

"Then know that the seal is in my possession and that it signifies I am the true queen."

He nodded. "It looks to be the seal." He turned to Cardinal Failsham, knowing he would not put forward the claim of an impostor.

"Is this woman the true queen of Talshamar?"

"She is, Your Majesty. I have followed her progress throughout the years and know her to be the true heir to the Talshamarian throne."

King Henry nodded. "I accept your word, along with the evidence of the Great Seal." His eyes were piercing as he looked at Jilliana. "You have kept yourself hidden from us, when we wanted only to help you, Queen Jilliana."

Jilliana met his even gaze. "I have not been hiding, Henry. For these past few years I have been residing in one of your own castles. You are familiar with the castle of Salisbury?"

Henry's fist came down hard on the arm of his throne. "Eleanor! By the true God, she did this to me!"

Jilliana strived to hide her smile, wishing Eleanor could witness Henry's rage. "Did you not know that I was the ward of your lady wife?"

It was apparent that Henry was having a difficult time bringing his anger under control, but he would not allow everyone to see that Eleanor had bested him.

Slowly his red face whitened and he managed a smile. "Had you come to us sooner, we would have offered you our son John as husband."

Jilliana lowered her voice, so only those standing near could hear. "Why should I put my trust in the man who caused the death of my mother, and why would I want to marry your son, whom I dislike intensely?"

Henry's breath hissed through his teeth and his face stained red with anger.

"You dare say this to me?"

She moved to stand beside Prince Ruyen and clasped his resisting hand, praying he would not reject her gesture. She felt his hand tighten on hers in a painful grip.

Ruyen knew of Talshamar, and like everyone else, he had heard of the missing queen. If this was she, why had she come to stand beside him when it would surely mean her death? He did not understand or trust this woman, but he would not expose her just yet.

Jilliana raised her voice so everyone could hear. "I am ready to die beside the man I love and the father of my unborn child. Think you that the people of my country, and indeed the civilized world, will applaud our deaths?" She paused, ready to play Henry as Eleanor had instructed her. "Perhaps France being the exception. Philip could very well rejoice at my death."

King Henry roared to his courtiers: "Everyone out. *Now!*" Then he waited impatiently while the guards cleared the room.

"Now, what say you, young prince?" Henry demanded of Ruyen. "Does Queen Jilliana carry your seed?"

She drew Ruyen's startled gaze. He paused, looking deeply into eyes the color of a summer sky.

"I had not known about the baby," he said truthfully, deciding to trust this woman, who seemed to have no trouble manipulating Henry.

"But you have lain with her?" Henry pressed accusingly. "Surely you admit that."

"Being a gentleman," Ruyen said dryly, his eyes lowered to the woman, "I could hardly admit to that. I may lose my life, but I will never defame a lady's reputation."

Jilliana did not have to feign embarrassment because her cheeks flushed scarlet. She could not look at the prince, but hurriedly spoke before her courage failed her.

"I . . . love him, does that not answer your questions?"

Henry scowled as he felt Talshamar and Falcon Bruine both slip from his grasp.

"It seems instead of being queen of England, you prefer to cast your lot with a rebellious prince who would rather die than yield."

"I am not your chattel to do with as you desire. And until I reach Talshamar, I am under the protection of Rome." She raised her chin, remembering that Queen Eleanor had cautioned her not to show weakness. "I would rather die with the man I love, than live in a world without him."

Suddenly King Henry startled them all when boisterous laughter shook his ample frame.

"Gad, you're too much woman for John. If I were twenty years younger, I might consider taking you as my own wife."

Jilliana bit back her angry retort and said in a soft voice. "Twenty years ago, you already had a fine wife, Your Majesty. You still do."

Henry's face became impassive as if he were remembering. "So I did and do. Eleanor is still the best of them all." He nodded at Ruyen. "If I release you and Princess Cassandra, will you give your solemn oath that you will no longer raise your sword against England?"

Ruyen looked at his sister, who was at the moment bent over coughing and trying to catch her breath. If it only concerned him, he would gladly meet death, but how could he allow his innocent sister to suffer for what he had done. Still, the words were not easily uttered.

With a defiant look, he answered. "I do so swear, as long as England does not take up arms against me."

Henry glared, knowing that the young hothead would not yield further. He spoke to his lord chamberlain. "Let the word go forth to all counties and shires that the king of England is generous. This day I free a known enemy so he may return to his country and no longer take up war against us."

Jilliana was weak with relief. She had not failed Queen Eleanor. Now that the Rondache family had been saved from the executioner, she would be free to go home to Talshamar. Her dream did not last long, however, for King Henry chilled her with his next words.

"There is one thing that I insist upon before I release you, Prince Ruyen." Henry smiled blandly. He was aware that Jilliana had not spoken true about her relationship with the hotheaded prince. The two of them did not seem like lovers—they were more like strangers. He would wager that they had never laid eyes on one another until today. Eleanor had contrived the whole spectacle. God's blood, but that woman was like no other!

He leaned back, pondering his next move in their game of wits. He would make them play by his rules. This way the jest would be on Eleanor and not on him.

"I will see the two of you married at once. There need be no posting of bans," he said, stroking his beard. "Yes, you will wed without delay, for there must never be any question of the legitimacy of royal offspring—must there?"

"I— But . . . but," Jilliana stammered.

King Henry held up his hand. "Nay, do not thank me. It will be my greatest delight to make all the arrangements. I will have you each go to separate quarters so you might make ready for the nuptials. The wedding will take place this very day."

Jilliana glanced up at Prince Ruyen and saw his stormy features. Angrily, his eyes bore into hers, making her draw back in fear.

"I agree," Ruyen said at last, realizing she must be attempting to pass off someone else's bastard as his, "that there should be no question about the parentage of a royal heir, but I do not think it will be necessary for us to marry."

Jilliana felt relief until Henry spoke.

"I will have you each escorted to your own quarters and allow you time to agree to my plan." He smiled. "I am at my best when playing Cupid."

7

When the others were led away, and Cardinal Failsham attempted to accompany them, Henry called out to him.

"You will remain, Your Eminence." He stared with open hostility at the pope's emissary, waiting for them to be alone before starting his tirade. When the guard closed the door, Henry roared at the cardinal.

"Pope Lucius has known all along the whereabouts of Queen Jilliana," he said accusingly. "Even knowing that I was searching for her, he kept her from me. Why is this, Cardinal? After all the favors I have done for him and the Church, surely he owes me some consideration."

"If you will excuse me for saying so, Your Majesty, His Holiness owes his allegiance to a higher power than you. He was bound to keep Queen Phelisiana's confidence and to see that her daughter would someday mount the throne of Talshamar as is her divine right."

"Can there be no mistake? Is this girl truly the queen?" Henry asked.

"There can be no mistake. I christened her as a babe, and I placed the crown of Talshamar upon her head."

Henry gnashed his teeth in frustration. "Is it true that she has lain with Prince Ruyen?"

"Of this I have no knowledge. It has been some years since I have seen Queen Jilliana, until the night I presided over her coronation."

Henry's anger was boundless. "Where did this coronation take place?"

"I am not familiar with England, so I cannot say the exact location."

"Preposterous! You dance around the truth, Cardinal. How can I believe what you say?"

"By my profession, I am bound by the truth."

"Who besides yourself can confirm that this young woman is the true queen of Talshamar?"

"There were one hundred Talshamarians who witnessed the crowning. They were all nobles who would swear that she was their true queen. They would have no false queen sit on the throne of Talshamar, and neither would the Holy Father."

Henry knew when he was defeated. "So be it. But I know I have been duped. Neither of them will leave here until I see them wed. You will perform the ceremony, yourself, so you can report back to His Holiness, Pope Lucius, that I have helped produce a legitimate heir for Talshamar."

Cardinal Failsham also knew when he had been defeated. "The Holy Father's instructions to me were that I was to see Queen Jilliana crowned. He said nothing about her marriage."

"In this I decide."

"It will be my honor to officiate at the wedding," the cardinal said stiffly.

Henry's eyes became cunning. "Will Pope Lucius approve of the marriage, do you think?"

The cardinal looked away. "Only His Holiness can answer that."

Henry grinned and then laughed out loud. "I care little if it pleases His Holiness, but I am delighted about what this means to Philip. He'll no longer be the legal heir of Talshamar, and that will stick in his gullet."

"That is so, Your Majesty."

Henry's mood became sober. "I am not quite the fool Eleanor and her puppets believe me to be. You will go directly to Prince Ruyen and inform him that should he refuse the hand of Queen Jilliana, his life and that of his sister shall be forfeit. Then go to Queen Jilliana and tell her the same." Henry waved his hand in dismissal. "Go now, my guards will escort you."

"As you wish, Your Majesty," Cardinal Failsham said, bowing and backing toward the door.

Prince Ruyen and Princess Cassandra had been escorted to a small room, the door locked behind them. Ruyen helped his sister into a straight-backed chair and covered her with a lap robe he found in the window seat.

"Ruyen, who was that woman who claimed to know you? What trick does Henry play on us to condemn us to death and then snatch us back at the last moment?"

"I know no more than you, Cassandra. Is this the helping hand of Richard, or the destructive hand of Henry?" Ruyen angrily paced the floor, fury etched on his face. "I curse the day I ever set foot on English soil."

He propped his booted foot on a window seat and stared into the courtyard below, his mind alert to any opportunity of escape. There were heavy bars on the windows, and he deduced that they were somewhere above the kitchen because servants were unloading cheese from a cart. There would be no escape that way.

Ruyen turned back to his sister. "If there is a child, it is not mine. Perhaps the brat is some by-blow of Henry's and he thinks to obtain by stealth and trickery what he could not by conquest. Does he really believe that I will consent to marry a woman who is most likely one of his whores?"

"But what would Henry have to gain by such a marriage, Ruyen?"

"Falcon Bruine and Talshamar. If I marry her, accepting her as the queen of Talshamar, then the rest of the world will believe that is who she is. This would give Henry—who controls her—Talshamar and eventually, through the child, the Isle of Falcon Bruine."

Cassandra suddenly looked faint, and he noticed that her breathing was labored.

"You must not be concerned about anything, Cassandra. I want only for you to rest and regain your health."

"She was quite beautiful, was she not?"

"I hardly noticed."

"What will you do?"

"I know not. But I will forfeit my life before I marry Henry's impostor."

A hacking cough racked his sister's frail body, and when she could catch her breath, she spoke. "I am still willing to die with you. We will not allow Henry Plantagenet to control our destiny."

For a long moment, Ruyen stared at his young sister. She had been born ten years after him, and he had given her little thought until they had been imprisoned together. He had discovered that she was brave and steadfast, and he was ashamed when he saw love and trust shining in her eyes. He dropped down beside her and took her limp hand in his.

"Perhaps I spoke too hastily. I will decide nothing until I discern Henry's intentions." Ruyen knew that he would do anything Henry demanded to save his sister's life. He watched her eyes close and stayed by her side until she fell asleep.

Shortly, a key rattling in the door caught Ruyen's attention. He watched as Cardinal Failsham motioned the two guards to remain in the corridor while he closed the door.

Ruyen rose and joined the cardinal, who stood by the window. He noticed that the man seemed agitated.

"Your Highness, we have grave concerns."

Ruyen looked at him ironically. "At what point in the day did you make that assessment, Your Eminence? And what would make you concerned for me and my sister?"

Cardinal Failsham lowered himself onto the padded window seat. "Your troubles became mine when they became linked with Queen Jilliana's."

Ruyen looked skeptical. "I have never had reason to distrust a man of the Church until now. Why should you try to pass that woman off as a queen?"

Cardinal Failsham's eyes became piercing. "I can assure you that she is the true daughter of the martyred Queen Phelisiana. What you heard today in the chamber is true. Queen Eleanor has kept her hidden until now so she would be safe from the schemes of England and France."

"Why did she choose this day to come forth and why did she speak up for me?"

"We have long wondered how we would bring the queen out of hiding. There are those who wanted to see both you and her safe, thus your lives became intertwined. I fear they will become even more so."

Ruyen was still angry. "Ah, the marriage. And what does Queen Jilliana gain from this union?"

"What do you know of her?"

"Less than nothing."

"Allow me quickly to tell you what I can. She was taken from Talshamar the night her mother died. She is yet in danger, but you can save her."

"Why should I?"

"Because she humiliated herself today in order to save you and the Princess Cassandra. You would now be dead if she had not spun her tale so convincingly."

Suddenly Ruyen looked very weary. "There is no need to say more, Your Eminence. What can I do to help Queen Jilliana?"

"You can marry her," the cardinal said flatly.

"I am betrothed to another, whom I love. I have no wish to marry anyone but her."

Cardinal Failsham's eyes dulled. "For this reason alone, would you turn away from Queen Jilliana and leave her at the mercy of England and France?"

"What is the Church's interest in this?"

"The pope would see Talshamar under its rightful rule because of the promise he made to his predecessor, Pope Alexander. It seems our previous Holy Father was the cousin of Queen Phelisiana, a most devout Christian ruler."

"Surely there is someone more willing than I to become Queen Jilliana's husband."

"Think, Your Highness. Talshamar is one of the richest kingdoms in Christendom. It has fertile farmland and large vineyards, as well as being a seat of learning and the arts. It is a prize that has been coveted by many. It has been offered to you, while denied to others."

"A prize I neither asked for, nor covet."

The cardinal looked concerned, as if he were trying to think of an argument to sway the prince. Suddenly he knew how to reach him—he would appeal to his sense of obligation.

"I believe that love is not often the reasoning for royal marriages."

"Love played no part in my mother and father's marriage," Ruyen admitted. "I had hoped to be the exception."

"I would never have expected you to place love for a woman above the good of your country, Your Highness." The cardinal knew that he had hit a nerve, and he waited patiently as Ruyen paced back and forth in front of him.

"When would this marriage occur?" Ruyen finally demanded.

"Today, I should think."

"And what would be expected of me?"

The cardinal looked uneasy for a moment. "Queen Jilliana will not be free from danger until she produces an heir."

"Are you saying that once she has a child, I will be free of her?"

Cardinal Failsham lowered his eyes. "The Church does not sanction divorce . . . but an annulment can be obtained in special circumstances. I have taken the precaution of discovering that you and Her Majesty have a distant connection through your grandmothers. This could be enough to acquire an annulment."

"Am I to believe that if I impregnate the queen I would be granted my freedom to marry where I choose. Is that what you are saying?"

The cardinal looked noncommittal. "I am sure I could convince His Holiness to agree to an annulment . . . if you comply with our needs. Queen Jilliana gave you your life, and you will give her a child. I would say that is a fair interchange, is it not?"

"Why should I trust her to let me go when the time comes?"

"I believe she has as little liking for this union as have you. And what choice have either of you? King Henry would love nothing better than to seize Falcon Bruine and Talshamar for his own. The longer you remain within his grasp, the more likely it is that that could occur."

Ruyen was silent for a long tense moment. He thought of his beautiful Katharine and wondered what she would do when she heard he was married. He must find a way to let her know that this union was a farce from which he would free himself as soon as possible.

"You are right when you say I have little choice. And I am obligated to Queen Jilliana for saving our lives. I will agree to the marriage on the terms we have discussed."

The cardinal stood, smiling. "I will make the arrangements at once."

"What does the queen say?"

"I have not yet spoken with her. But she will do her duty, have no fear."

Ruyen turned away, listening to the fading footsteps of the cardinal. When he heard the door open and close, he turned to find himself alone with his sleeping sister. He was not certain he could trust the cardinal and he knew of no reason to trust Queen Jilliana. After all, she had so easily lied to Henry about carrying his child. What other lies might she tell?

In another part of the castle, Jilliana waited with Sir Humphrey. Her door was not locked, and there were no bars on her windows, but she felt like a prisoner all the same.

8

Although Jilliana's coronation had been secret, that was not to be true of her wedding, which was held at Westminster with as much pomp as could be arranged in one day.

Henry sent heralds forth throughout the land, announcing the nuptials. With great satisfaction and no little cunning, he sent a messenger to France to inform King Philip that not only had Queen Jilliana been located, but that she was to be married and would soon produce an heir. He signed Philip's letter with a flourish and laughed aloud when he affixed his seal. How he wished he could see the French king's face when he learned that Talshamar had slipped from his grasp. Henry would not allow himself to think that it was also out of his reach.

Jilliana wondered how her life could change so rapidly. Two months ago she had been a carefree maiden, thinking only of her lessons and attending Queen Eleanor. Had it only been this morning that she had entered London to confront King Henry and help free Prince Ruyen and his sister?

Nothing seemed real to her as she stood beside Ruyen Rondache in the elaborate cathedral and repeated the vows that would bind them together as husband and wife.

She turned her head slightly so she could see his face, for indeed she could not remember what he looked like. That was not surprising considering her whole attention had been centered on Henry Plantagenet that morning.

Prince Ruyen was dressed all in dark green, from doublet to boots. For a moment her eyes rested on his dark hair and the way the light shining through the stained glass window made it glisten like polished ebony. She drew in her breath as she looked into his dark, cold eyes and found them filled with contempt and loathing.

Ruyen's voice was harsh when he answered Cardinal Failsham. The words seemed drawn from his lips against his will and he spoke in a low tone.

"I do take Queen Jilliana as my lawful wife."

"And do you Queen Jilliana take Prince Ruyen as your husband and liege lord?"

She looked undecided for a moment before giving her answer, then spoke in a clear voice. "For the sake of my kingdom, I will set no one above me, save God. I agree to take Prince Ruyen as my husband, but I do not accept him as my liege lord."

There was a long moment of silence while everyone, including Ruyen, stared in shocked surprise at the young queen. There was a soft murmur of surprise when the cardinal continued the ceremony, asking the two of them to join hands. He seemed slightly amused at Jilliana's refusal to accept Prince Ruyen as her lord and master.

Jilliana turned her eyes to the cardinal as he spoke the final affirmation pronouncing them husband and wife. As they knelt beside each other, with hands joined, Jilliana thought the solemn mass would never end. At the same time, she prayed it would go on forever because she was frightened of what would happen when they left the sanctuary of the cathedral and she would have to be alone with this stranger she had just married.

Jilliana was not aware of the silence around her or that the mass had ended until she was aided to her feet by her new husband. In a daze, she accepted good wishes from the cardinal, and turned to look into the solemn faces of her nobles, who were in attendance. It was apparent that they did not understand the reason for the marriage.

She felt Prince Ruyen's hand on her elbow, guiding her out of the chapel, and they were flanked on each side by Henry's guards, a reminder that Ruyen was still a prisoner.

Once outside, Jilliana drew in a cleansing breath as she searched the crowd that had gathered to observe the wedding party. In the distance, she saw Sir Humphrey holding the reins of her horse. Jerking her arm free of the prince's grip, she moved quickly toward the security Sir Humphrey represented.

When the knight would have helped her mount, she felt strong hands about her waist and she was lifted onto her saddle by her new husband. Coldly, she turned to look at him.

"What do you expect from a wife, Your *Highness*?" she asked, deliberately emphasizing his lesser title.

"I expect nothing from you, Your *Majesty*," he sneered. "I would sooner see you go your way and allow me to go mine. After we are quit of England, that is exactly what will happen."

"Then we are in agreement. I did not marry you because of some unrequited love, Prince Ruyen. I did not shame myself before the English court because I pined to be your wife."

"Why then did you do it?"

Jilliana's lips trembled and she felt like crying. "Is it not enough to know that you are alive?"

Ruyen could swear that he saw tears in her eyes, but it might be a trick of the light. He had not noticed before how young she was or how beautiful. She was dressed in white from head to toe and all he could see was her face. He found himself wondering about the color of her hair. Her blue eyes were fine, and her lashes dark and long.

Suddenly he felt disloyal to his beloved Katharine. He would never love another as he loved her, especially not this brazen young woman who seemed to be in control of his life.

"We should leave," Ruyen said, noticing that Henry's guards were closing in around them to escort them back to the castle. "We seem to have attracted a crowd of curiosity seekers."

Jilliana nodded gratefully. When he mounted his horse and rode to her side, she decided to make an attempt to be pleasant; after all, they were both united by a common enemy.

"'Tis a pity your sister was too ill to attend the wedding."

"Yes," he said noncommittally.

"I hope you do not mind, but when I learned that your sister had no woman to see to her needs, I sent my maid to your quarters. I also sent word to Henry's physician to attend her."

"You took it upon yourself to do this." His tone was biting.

"I had to do it. You have no power to bargain with Henry, and I do. Should I have allowed your sister to suffer because of your pride?"

"Nay," he said stiffly, feeling his indebtedness to this young woman mounting. He did not like to be obligated to anyone, especially not someone who had already extracted a high payment from him for her aid.

"You acted compassionately on my sister's behalf," he admitted grudgingly. "I am again in your debt. If you have no objections, I would like to go at once and see how my sister fares."

"Then let us make haste. I am sure she will want to see you as well."

Ruyen felt the sun on his face and glanced up at the blue sky. Had he merely traded one kind of prison for another? Nudging his horse in the flanks he moved away with Jilliana at his side.

It occurred to Ruyen that only strangers had been in attendance at his wedding. Many had been Henry's representatives and the others were subjects of Queen Jilliana.

His eyes were drawn to the woman who rode beside him. Her face was in profile and her beauty touched a chord within his heart. He was not fool enough to believe she had sacrificed herself for him out of some noble gesture. Without a doubt, she had her own reasons for wanting the marriage. Cardinal Failsham had indicated she needed an heir. He ground his teeth together—he would hear the reasons from her own lips.

As they rode through the gates of Henry's castle, Jilliana halted and looked at Sir Humphrey and the others, who had been stopped on the other side of the gate. "Will you not come with me, Sir Humphrey?"

He saw the troubled look in her eyes. She was feeling frightened and uncertain and he wanted to take her away to safety, but he no longer had the right. None of the emotions he was feeling showed on his gaunt face as he tried to offer her some small comfort.

"Your Majesty, I have lodgings at the Bear and Bull Inn. If you have need of me, you have only to send word and I will come at once."

Jilliana nodded reluctantly. "I would ask that you attend me on the morrow. There is much we must decide."

He bowed his head. "Until tomorrow, Your Majesty." Sir Humphrey then turned his attention to the prince.

Lowering his voice, he spoke hurriedly so the queen would not hear. "I will expect you to be kind to her. If you are not, I shall surely cut your heart out."

Ruyen's eyes bore into the man. "It would take more than you to accomplish such a feat. But rest assured that I have no desire or reason to harm your queen." So saying, Ruyen moved through the gate to join Jilliana.

After dismounting, they entered the castle, and a guard escorted them to Ruyen's quarters. There was an awkward silence between them as they moved down the narrow corridors.

Netta had been listening for their arrival and whisked the door open. There was a worried frown on her face.

"I am glad you are here. I fear Princess Cassandra is desperately ill. She has complained of pains in her stomach and she is very weak and feverish."

"Has King Henry's physician seen her?" Jilliana inquired.

"He was with her for a time. He said she has a weakness of the lungs. He tied a poultice about her neck, although I doubt that will help her condition."

"As do I," Jilliana said with rancor. "The man is clearly incompetent."

Jilliana then turned to Ruyen. "May I see her? I might be able to help since I had training in healing herbs."

Feeling helpless, Ruyen nodded and the two of them entered the dimly lit bedchamber. When Ruyen saw his sister tossing upon her bed in febrile restlessness, he went to her and gently took her hand in his. Her condition had worsened since the morning, and it caused him great concern.

"Cassandra, it is I, Ruyen," he said softly. "Tell me where you hurt."

The girl merely groaned, flinging his hand away and turning her face into the pillow.

"Did the physician recommend any other treatment?" Jilliana asked her maid.

"Nay, Your Majesty, other than trusting in God."

Jilliana watched and listened to the girl's breathing long enough to discern that despite the physician's diagnosis, her lungs were clear. "I believe she has flux of the stomach. I know what is to be done. I will need cool water and towels, Netta."

When the maid moved to the other room, Jilliana spoke kindly to Ruyen. "I have seen this illness many times at the convent. With the proper medication, your sister will be cured."

Jilliana removed the smelly poultice from the girl's neck and flung it across the room. She then unfastened her own white overskirt and placed it across a chair.

By now Netta had returned with a water basin and linen towels and placed them on a side table. Jilliana dampened the cloths and laid them on Princess Cassandra, who was writhing in obvious pain.

"Netta," Jilliana said, "Go at once to the Bear and Bull Inn and seek Sir Humphrey." As she walked the servant to the door, she explained what she needed. "Inform him that I want these ingredients at once."

When the maid departed, Jilliana went back to her patient. "If you will step aside, Prince Ruyen, I will do what I can to help your sister. But I can do nothing with you in my way."

He stood his ground. "I have seen many grown men die of this sickness and she is but a child. You cannot help her. No one can."

"Who has stripped you of your faith? Your sister is not going to die," Jilliana said, rolling up her sleeves and wetting a towel. "If you want to be of help, leave her to my care."

Obediently he moved back. Jilliana might appear young, but she was confident and every inch a queen. "Once more it would seem I owe you my gratitude."

She placed another towel on the girl's forehead, all the while glaring at him. "I neither want, nor ask for, your gratitude. My concern at the moment is to alleviate your sister's suffering. I would do the same for anyone—even you in likened circumstances."

He heard the anger in her voice and wondered at the reason for it. He had married her, had he not? What else did she want from him?

By the time Jilliana had finished bathing the girl, she heard Sir Humphrey's gruff voice in the outer chamber.

Hurrying out to him, she took the herbs and potions he had brought and ground them up and added them to a flask of water.

"I see you are using Mother Magdalene's remedy for flux," he observed as he watched her.

"Yes, it always worked for her, let us hope it does the same for me."

Jilliana reentered the bedchamber, raised Princess Cassandra's head and encouraged her to drink. After much coaxing, the girl finally swallowed the bitter medicine.

Ruyen's sister was so young—so pale. Would she survive? Jilliana was not as confident as she pretended to be.

"I have done all I can," she said, turning to Netta. "I will want you to remain with the princess. Bathe her often with cool water and encourage her to drink liquids. In the morning, you will administer another dose of medicine. I'll see that you have a bed so you can rest as well."

Ruyen sat in a chair in the outer room, his eyes worriedly locked on the door to his sister's bedchamber. He had forgotten that Sir Humphrey was in the room until the man spoke.

"Her Majesty will do all she can to help your sister."

"But will it be enough?"

"Only God can say."

"God has paid little heed to me or my sister of late," Ruyen said bitingly.

"Sometimes He speaks and we are so immersed in our own needs that we do not hear His voice."

Ruyen's eyes were stabbing as he looked at the queen's man. "Are you then His voice?"

"Not I. But today you married a young woman who is pure of heart and deed, and I believe God speaks through her. If you will allow it, she can help restore your faith."

"I have had all the help from her I want. Who asked her to interfere in my life?"

Sir Humphrey smiled. "Perhaps God did."

There was a loud rapping on the outer door and Netta came from the bedchamber to open it. One of King Henry's knights stood there, his eyes sweeping past the maid to the room beyond. He had hoped to get a glimpse of the beautiful young queen everyone was talking about.

"You want something?" Netta asked coldly.

"I have a message for your queen."

"Then tell it to me."

He looked disappointed, but complied. "His Majesty, King Henry, is holding a banquet in honor of the wedding of Queen Jilliana and Prince Ruyen. Someone will come at seven o'clock to escort them to the Great Hall, where they shall be his honored guests."

"I will tell Her Majesty." So saying, she closed the door in the man's face—Netta had no liking for the English.

Ruyen had watched the whole encounter with a cynical twist to his lips. "The women from Talshamar, whether they be servant or queen, seem to hold men in contempt," he observed.

"Was it contempt that allowed my queen to save your life?" Humphrey asked. "Make no mistake about it—if she had not interfered today, you would be dead. I suggest you remember that and be thankful that she stood up to King Henry on your behalf."

"So you keep reminding me."

"As I perceive it, you do not deserve her."

Ruyen glared at the insolent Talshamarian knight. "I know that Richard is the instrument of my rescue. It is he who deserves my gratitude."

Sir Humphrey threw back his head and laughed. "Richard had nothing to do with your rescue."

"Who then?" Ruyen insisted.

"Mostly you owe your foolish head to my queen. I did not want to see her wed you today, nor did any of her subjects. I have heard nothing good of you, and she deserves a noble husband who will cherish her. I think that man is not you."

For some reason this man made Ruyen feel ashamed. He had not acted nobly and had only shown resentfulness toward Queen Jilliana. He looked into the clear eyes of her knight and found himself wishing he had this man's respect, although he could not have said why.

"Have no fear for your queen on my account."

"I made no empty threat when I told you that if you did harm her, you would not see another sunset."

Ruyen lowered his head. "You might be doing me a favor."

9

Ruyen was sitting beside his sister's bed, watching her slow but steady intake of breath. There was only a single candle flickering on a narrow table, its light falling on her face. She appeared to be resting easier and her color was not so pale. He swore that if he ever got her away from this cursed land neither one of them would set foot on English soil again.

There was a knock on the door and he bid whoever it was to enter. Netta stuck her head around the corner.

"The king's man has arrived to escort you to the banquet, Your Highness."

Ruyen would have preferred to remain with his sister, but he was in no position to refuse. "When in the den of the lion, walk the lion's path, hmm, Netta?"

She smiled. "I believe that is what my queen is doing."

"Is your lady ready?"

"She awaits you."

Ruyen gently touched Cassandra's cheek. "You will remain with my sister?"

"I shall not leave her bedside, Your Highness."

Ruyen was weary and this had seemed the longest day of his life. He did not relish spending the evening being entertained by Henry—but what choice had he?

He moved out of the chamber to find Jilliana with her back to him, gazing out the window. She was dressed all in crimson velvet, but for the golden headdress and golden crown set atop her head. She must have heard him, for she turned in his direction.

Ruyen was stunned by her beauty. Never had he seen such a perfect face, not even his Katharine could compare with her. He wondered how she could dress in scarlet and still appear so young and innocent.

"Shall we go?" he asked, offering her his arm.

Jilliana stared at him for a long moment. With his broad chest and wide shoulders, she found him extremely handsome. She had already seen his prominent dark eyes become piercing or flash like fire when he was angered. He was such a powerful presence that even as a prisoner he seemed in command of the situation. His gaze drew and held hers, and she wondered what he was thinking.

After a moment, she placed the tips of her fingers on his sleeve. "I like not the thought of dining at Henry Plantagenet's table. But, if we are to gain our freedom, we will have to allow him to play the bountiful host. By now he has probably convinced himself and others that the entire situation was his own idea."

Ruyen glanced down into clear blue eyes. "Do you know him so well?"

"I know him but little, but I know much of him. We shall attend his banquet so he can show his subjects how generous he is to his enemies."

"You will forgive me if I do not so readily accept that he is your enemy. I am still not convinced that you are not in league with that devil."

She lowered her silken lashes. "Your opinion of me

matters but little. I have helped you and I will soon ask help of you. Beyond that, we are nothing to each other."

"What can I give you that you do not already have?"

"I will tell you when the time is right. We must not keep our host waiting."

The banquet hall was crowded with nobles and their ladies. Long trestle tables were covered with white linen cloths, and magnificent tapestries hung on the wall. Everyone seemed to be talking at once, all speculating on the young queen and her husband, the Golden Falcon.

When Jilliana and Ruyen entered the room a hush fell over the hall. A servant bowed before them and led them to the high table, where the king waited.

"Welcome, welcome, my little lovebirds," Henry said, boisterously. "At last you are tied to one another. Come Queen Jilliana, sit to my right—you, Prince Ruyen, on my left. Eat, laugh, be joyful. This is your wedding feast."

The moment they were seated, meats and other delicacies were brought to the table. There was a continual progression of turnovers filled with chicken, cheese, and eggs. Courses of fowl, duck, geese, peacock, basted roasts of pork, mullet, sole, and lobster were offered to first the king's table and then the lower tables. Later, there followed plump figs, candied fruits, and tarts smothered with almonds and powdered cinnamon.

Ruyen insolently studied the people in the room, his eyes showing his dislike for them. Jilliana took a bite of succulent fowl, but found that she could not swallow. If only Eleanor were here to help her get through this evening. All she could think about was that Henry was responsible for her mother's death.

"Tell me, Jilliana—you do not mind if I call you Jilliana, do you—how do you like London?"

She raised her eyes to his. "Tell me, Henry—you do not mind if I call you Henry do you—how do you like Talshamar?"

For a moment, his mouth came together in a severe line. "I have not had the pleasure of visiting your country. It seemed that after your mother . . . died, His Holiness became the administrator, and I was ordered to stay away. I hope you will change that order, Jilliana, and we can be friends."

She lowered her eyes so he would not see the hatred reflected there. "I do not think that Talshamar would be good for your health, Henry. Imagine how devastated I would be if you visited my country and something untoward befell you."

Ruyen almost choked on his wine. She had the kind of courage he admired, he admitted to himself grudgingly.

Henry moved toward Jilliana menacingly, and Ruyen automatically reached for the sword that usually hung at his side.

Unperturbed, Jilliana smiled and raised her gaze to Henry. "The food is delicious," she said, taking a dainty bite from a fig, thus reminding Henry that their actions were being watched by the whole court.

"I am glad you show no fear of me—I would never harm you," Henry said.

"Nay, of that I am certain. It would not fit your plan for me to meet with an . . . untimely death."

He had a satisfied look on his face. "We shall keep you here so you will be safe until you give forth a son or daughter."

Now her eyes gleamed with a dangerous light. "I can assure you that if you keep me prisoner, I shall never have a child."

"But did you not tell me that you were already with child?"

She shrugged. "I spoke untrue."

Ruyen wondered if she knew what she was doing.

Henry nodded, not in the least perturbed. "I know. I knew it at the time, but it suited me to agree to this marriage. You will remain with us for a time, and we shall make you happy and see that you want for nothing. And of course, you shall have your husband to keep you company."

Jilliana came to her feet. "I will not remain in England, and you cannot force me to. I would remind you that I am under the protection of the Holy Father. How many times have you been excommunicated, Henry?"

He slammed his fist against the table, spilling a wine glass and jumping to his feet. "Your lips are moving, but I hear Eleanor's words."

"Then hear this, Henry Plantagenet, you cannot prevent me from returning to Talshamar."

They were standing, glaring at each other, while Ruyen remained seated. He saw no reason to interfere. Jilliana was handling Henry very well on her own and did not need his help. As for himself, he was starting to enjoy the banquet.

"Be reasonable, Jilliana," Henry said in exasperation. "You know the stipulations of your mother's bequest. I cannot allow you to return to Talshamar without an heir."

"And I will produce no heir while on English soil."

Suddenly Henry shook with laughter, surprising everyone—he loved a good fight. "Damn me if you are not magnificent! Half the world trembles when I speak, and you, a mere slip of a woman, dare dictate to me in my own realm."

"I will have my freedom," she insisted.

"So you shall. But it will not be in Talshamar. I will allow you to go to the Isle of Falcon Bruine with your husband. There you will remain until you give birth."

Jilliana's eyes flew to Ruyen. "But, I had not thought that . . ."

Ruyen came quickly to his feet and took her arm, pulling her against him. "That will be satisfactory," he said, seeing his one chance of escape from England. "I will take my wife, and we shall leave for Falcon Bruine."

Henry now turned his eyes to the prince. "In due time you shall, but I have taken precautions that will ensure you will cause us no more trouble. I have made your mother regent. Queen Melesant will make certain that you remain . . . shall we say, loyal to her English friends."

This was not what Jilliana had wanted. She could feel Ruyen stiffen beside her, and knew that he was angry also.

Ruyen felt rage boil up within him. His mother had always wanted to rule Falcon Bruine, and now Henry had placed it within her grasp. What he had feared was true— she had betrayed him to Henry Plantagenet! He would confront his mother when he reached home. Now, he just wanted to be free of England.

"I want to leave immediately—tomorrow," Ruyen said grimly.

"Not so soon as that," Henry said, playing to the audience that was watching and eagerly hanging on each word. "I am certain that your sister will not be able to travel for a while." He called to those at the lower table. "Ladies of the court, it is time for you to escort Queen Jilliana to her marriage bed. Her husband will remain with us until you have made her ready, then we shall join you."

There was ribald laughter as several ladies rushed forward, taking Jilliana's hand and pulling her toward the door. She wanted to protest, and she looked to Ruyen for help, but he only stared after her with a bewildered look on his face.

Jilliana had expected to be taken back to the chambers she had occupied earlier in the day, but she was led in a different direction. The women giggled and made lewd remarks about her wedding night. She was too stunned to react and too proud to object.

"Your Majesty," one of the women said enviously. "I have heard much about the prowess of the Golden Falcon. Would that I were the one to clip those wings."

"He's magnificent!" another said. "Those dark eyes pierce right through you. When he looked at me, I thought I would faint."

"Do not bother Her Majesty with your foolish chatter," an older woman scolded. "I am Lady Wentworth," she told Jilliana. "Pay no heed to these foolish magpies."

Jilliana did not answer, for they had reached their destination. The bedchamber was grandly furnished in white and golds—the royal colors of Talshamar. Jilliana wondered if it had been decorated for her benefit. It was just the sort of thing Henry would do to lull her into trusting him.

Jilliana saw that her trunk had been placed against a wall and her own night clothes had been spread on the bed. Before she could protest, she was undressed and her nightgown pulled over her head. Her hair was unbound and fell like a black curtain to her waist. Someone brushed it, while another hurriedly pulled the covers aside.

A feeling of anxiety was growing in the pit of Jilliana's stomach, for she knew what was to come. She had heard of the bedding ceremony. She was thankful that her white nightgown fit high on her neck and the ruffles fell to her wrists.

Lady Wentworth urged her to climbed into bed while the others smiled at her. "You are a beautiful bride. I have heard it said that all the queens of Talshamar are beautiful. Seeing you, I believe that."

Jilliana could not even respond to Lady Wentworth's kindness. Her throat seemed to have closed off and she could only lean against the pillows, clutching the covers to her chin.

"I know what you are feeling, Your Majesty, but there is nothing to worry about."

"I will gladly take her place—"

"Kitty!" Lady Wentworth scolded.

At that moment, the door was thrust open and several gentlemen entered with King Henry at the lead. His eyes were wide with admiration as they rested on Jilliana. He laughed jovially as he clapped Ruyen on the back.

"Ah, that I was younger and could have such a beauty waiting in bed for me." Henry turned to the others. "Let us leave the newlyweds, they do not need our instructions."

Everyone followed Henry out the door, and Jilliana could hear the laughter fading as they moved down the corridor.

She raised her eyes to Ruyen, who was studying her with intensity. So, her hair was black; he would never have guessed with her light coloring. He had seen many beautiful women, but none that could match her. She was so delicate, so lovely, that he felt a tightening in his loins.

He sat in a chair and leaned back, studying the pink tinge to her cheeks. "What do we do now?" he asked.

"I . . . told you that I would ask something of you when the time came."

"So you did. But perhaps you should tell me what it is, so there will be no mistake."

"I want—I need—an heir." He did not move, or bat a lash, so she thought he might not have heard her. She repeated her words, this time in a louder voice. "I need an heir."

Mesmerized, she watched his long sinewy fingers run down the arm of the chair.

"Before we discuss that, perhaps it is time that you explained some things to me. Who sent you here and why?"

She grabbed her long hair and flung it over her shoulder. "I do not know you, and thus far you have done nothing to inspire my trust. Why should I tell you anything?"

"How do I know that I can trust you?" Ruyen asked. "What if everything you have done thus far has been for show and you are Henry's ally."

"If you know anything about Talshamarian history, you know Henry was responsible for my mother's death. Why would I owe any allegiance to him?"

"Yes, I do know that. Who sent you to Henry on this particular day?"

"Someone who wishes you well."

"I know of only one such person in England, and that is Richard."

"It was not Richard, it was Queen Eleanor."

Ruyen's eyes narrowed and his jaw clenched tightly. "The royal whore! Why would she want to help me?"

10

Jilliana came to her knees, her dark hair swirling out about her, her eyes flashing turbulently.

"How dare you speak so of Eleanor! She has saved your life and that of your sister. I will hear nothing bad about her. Say that you are sorry."

Flickering candles cast rings of light upon her stark white gown and Ruyen thought that she looked like an avenging angel.

"Calm yourself, Madame, and tell me what Eleanor has done for you that you should be her champion?"

"She has done everything for me. She kept me safe from the time I was two years old until I came here to London. She sent me to help you and told me what to say that I might save your life. I am sorry now that I did."

He was thoughtful for a moment. "Then what you told Henry was to save me."

"Of course it was."

"Eleanor must really hate him. Perhaps I misjudged her, but why should she care if I live or die?"

"You attempted to help Richard, and for that she was grateful. Too many people misjudge Eleanor, but that is because they do not know her like I do. She is kind and generous. And if she hates Henry, who can blame her since he keeps her prisoner. You hate Henry, do you not?"

"Oh, yes. You despise him because he had your mother slain—I because . . ." His voice trailed off. "I have my reasons and they are my own."

Jilliana settled back against the pillows. "What do we do now?"

He removed his leather boots and then stood, unhooking his doublet. "I have had rather a long day. Do I join you in bed?"

"I . . ." She closed her eyes, feeling terribly shy. "Yes, if you please."

He laughed, noticing the blush on her cheeks, a phenomenon that he found most attractive. "I have seldom had a more enticing invitation. How can I refuse?"

"I suppose you know what is to be done?" she asked in all seriousness. "I would like a daughter, since Talshamar has been ruled by a queen for the last two hundred years."

Ruyen had just removed his short tunic, and he paused to stare at her. "A rather cold approach to lovemaking, is it not? I am not certain that I can perform on command."

She looked perplexed, and brushed a lock of hair from her forehead. "Then you will have to tell me what to do and I shall do it."

He sat down on the bed, taking her chin in his hand and looking deeply into her eyes. "My God, woman, how much do you know about lovemaking between a man and a woman?"

She looked remorseful. "I regret to say I know nothing. The only man at the convent was an occasional priest, and of course, Sir Humphrey."

"Convent!" he said in amazement.

"Yes, I lived there until I was sixteen, and then I went to live with Eleanor to complete my education."

His manner suddenly turned cold. "Did Eleanor tell you that you must have a baby by me?"

"Of course she did not! She only said that I must claim to be carrying your baby. It was I who realized my need for a child."

His hand dropped on her shoulder. "For what reason?"

"I am in danger until I produce an heir to secure the succession in Talshamar."

"I do not think you have thought this through. Has it occurred to you that if you have my baby, it will be my heir?"

"If I have a baby, it will be mine," she said indignantly. "You can get your own baby from someone else. Surely there must be some woman who is willing to give you an heir of your own. Did I not hear the women of Henry's court talking about how handsome you are and how they would like to be in my place tonight?"

His lips eased into a smile. "Now did they? Shall I seek one of them out tonight?"

Softly, Jilliana touched his hand. "I know what I ask of you is difficult, but you must understand how important it is to me."

"You heard Henry say that you will be going with me to Falcon Bruine?"

"For the moment, I will do as Henry wishes. But when I have my baby, he cannot keep me away from Talshamar."

"I did not know they made them as innocent as you."

"You make it sound like an insult."

"Nay, 'tis not that. But you are so young—too young in many ways. I would feel as if I was making love to a—" He stood up and moved away from her. He reached for his tunic and poked one arm into a sleeve and then another.

"Nay, Jilliana, I cannot do what you ask."

Her lips trembled, and she wondered what she had said to drive him away. Perhaps if she were to approach him differently? Jilliana slid off the bed and moved to stand before Ruyen. "Do you not think me pretty?"

They were standing near the window and it seemed as though the moonlight was trapped in her eyes. "I think you are beautiful."

"I know I could please you if only you will show me how."

His eyes dipped down to where the ribbon had come loose at the neck of her gown and the curve of her breasts were visible. He felt heat rising in his body. She could not know what she was doing to him, and maybe it was just as well.

"You would be well advised not to pursue this further. I have no desire to teach a virgin the art of lovemaking. Get back into bed."

She would not give up so easily. "Eleanor has always commended me on how quickly I learn. Who can I go to for instruction if not my husband?"

"I do not consider ours a true marriage."

"Do you— Are you in love with someone?"

"Yes."

She had not expected that admission to cause her pain, but it did. Her heart felt suddenly bruised. "I will take nothing from the woman you love. I only ask this one night of you. Is that too high a price for a man to pay for his life?"

He suddenly felt very weary. "Madame, there is no guarantee that one night together will result in the begetting of a child."

"Then you are no good to me. I shall travel to Rome at the first chance I get and petition for an annulment." She was quiet for a moment, then she shivered. "Of course, Henry cannot know that we have not been together tonight. Eleanor fears he might force me to marry John if I were free, and he said as much today."

"God's blood, not that milksop."

"It is no longer your concern. As soon as your sister is well, we shall take her to Falcon Bruine. Then I will release you from this marriage."

He felt that he had disappointed her. "It would be most generous of you to release me without gaining the one thing you desire."

She had not heard him. "I will have to hide again so Philip cannot find me, and of course Henry as well. I would not mind so much, but there are people in Talshamar who will think I am abandoning them to French rule." She raised her eyes to him. "What do you think I should do?"

He turned away, feeling his resolve slip. She had valiantly come to his rescue, saved him and Cassandra, and he had offered her nothing in return. He could sense her intelligence, although she was still very young and inexperienced. Seldom had he seen a woman with such a noble heart, certainly not his mother, perhaps not even Katharine. Talshamar would have a magnificent ruler in her; in this Eleanor had done well.

"What shall I call you?" he asked.

"I believe it would be appropriate for you to call me Jilliana . . . Ruyen."

"Jilliana, how can I make you understand that any child that would issue from you and me would also have a claim on my throne? Can you not see this?"

"I have learned that your father is dead. Does that not make you king?"

"You heard Henry say that he made my mother regent. Of course, she cannot remain in power without Henry's support."

"I find it difficult to comprehend why any mother would wrest power from her own son."

"Then you have not closely examined your Eleanor. She could tell you much about betrayal and deceit within her own family."

"If you continue with your cruel accusations, I shall no longer speak to you." She moved to the bed and sat down. "You may do as you please, and I will trouble you no more. You may find somewhere else to sleep."

He smiled. "I do not believe that Henry would allow me to leave this room tonight. Should we not pretend to play the loving pair? Our lives hang by a very thin thread."

"You hold your life much more precious than I do mine," she said haughtily. "Like my mother, I would rather die than live under the dictates of Henry Plantagenet."

"Life has little meaning to me," he told her, "as long as my people are not free. I was prepared to die this morning, and would have, had you not arrived with your preposterous tale."

Suddenly she felt pity for him. "These last months could not have been easy for you."

"You would have to know my mother to understand my concerns for my subjects. She loves only herself and is fond of beautiful and lavish trinkets. If my people are left to her mercy, she will impoverish them within a year."

"My mother died that I might live and one day rule Talshamar. That is the kind of love I understand."

"It is a kind of love I have never known. I would much rather my mother had died honorably than live dishonorably."

Jilliana agreed with him, but she did not say so. "What shall we do?"

"Go to bed. You must be weary."

"Would you like to lie beside me?"

"Yes, but I shall keep to my side of the bed."

"If that is your wish."

She moved under the covers and lay her head against the pillow. Was there something wrong with her that Ruyen did not want to give her a baby? It must be that he did not find her desirable. She closed her eyes and soon fell asleep, not even aware when Ruyen lay down beside her, turning his back to her.

If Jilliana but knew it, Ruyen was exceedingly aware of her nearness and found her very desirable. How easy it would be to reach out and touch her, take her in his arms and make love to her as she wished.

But he knew something that she had not yet realized— if she had a child by him, it would complicate both their lives.

It was a very long time before he fell asleep.

11

The golden light of dawn spilled into the room, filling the shadowy corners with light. Jilliana opened her eyes and carefully turned to her side, so she could study Ruyen.

In sleep he did not look nearly so fierce. Dark velvety lashes lay against his tan cheeks. His black hair fell across his forehead and curled about the side of his neck. His face was handsomely defined, his nose in perfect harmony with his full lips.

She had never been this close to a man, and she felt breathless. His hand was lying across his chest, and she noticed his long tapered fingers and the strength in those hands.

Jilliana had the strangest urge to press her lips to his, to reach out to touch his dark hair, but she dared not awaken him. She was disturbed by the strange emotions that had taken possession of her.

Quietly, she moved off the bed, lifted the lid of her trunk and removed a sapphire-blue gown. After struggling with her laces, she finally succeeded in dressing herself.

She ran a brush through her hair, covered it with a white wimple, then set her golden crown on her head to give her courage to face whatever happened today.

Softly she opened the door and stepped into the corridor. She glared at the guard that had been posted there.

"I am going to see about Princess Cassandra and I do not need an escort," she told him imperiously.

"I am here only to guard Prince Ruyen, Madame. I have no orders to restrict your movements."

She moved away from him and then turned back, undecided. "How will I find Princess Cassandra's chamber?"

"Madame, you have only to follow this hallway to the end and then turn right. Princess Cassandra's rooms will be the last door on the left."

She was surprised to see the girl sitting up and eating breakfast while Netta looked on with satisfaction.

"Your Majesty," the maid said smiling. "Princess Cassandra's fever broke last night, and when she awoke this morning, she demanded food."

Jilliana sat on a stool beside the girl. "We have not met formally, but I am Jilliana."

"I remember you. You made some strange disclosures about my brother to King Henry. I do not know why you would do such a thing when I know that my brother had never seen you before yesterday."

"What I told Henry was untrue, but I had to do it to save you and your brother from death."

Cassandra spoke softly. "I still do not understand."

"Think only of growing stronger and you will soon be on your way home. Will you like that?"

"Oh, yes." Cassandra looked at the beautiful woman with the golden crown of Talshamar upon her head. "You married my brother, did you not? I thought I heard someone say so."

"Yes. That, too, was necessary so the three of us can escape Henry. Do you mind so very much?"

The young girl lay back against the pillow. "I am glad you married Ruyen because I do not like Kath—" Cassandra looked down at her food as if she had said too much. When she looked into Jilliana's eyes, she was clearly distressed. "I believe Ruyen only married you to save me. Do *you* mind?"

"Nay, we both did what was necessary."

Cassandra looked at Jilliana in admiration. "Netta told me that it was your potion that healed me."

"Nonsense. It was your youthful resilience that made you throw off your illness."

Cassandra smiled weakly. "I like you and I hope you stay with Ruyen forever."

Ruyen awoke quickly and sat up, looking about him in confusion. It took him a moment to realize that he was no longer in the Tower. Remembering the events of the previous day, he turned to his side to find that Jilliana was not there.

He quickly dressed, then flung open the door to find one of Henry's guards posted there. Apparently his movements were still to be curtailed.

"I want to see my sister," he said, glaring at the man.

The guard lay his hand on the hilt of his sword. "I will escort you to her quarters."

Chafing at his imprisonment, Ruyen fell in step with the Englishman. When he stood before the door of his sister's quarters, he dismissed the man with a curt nod.

"I will not be needing your assistance any longer."

The guard avoided his eyes. "I will be standing just outside on His Majesty's orders."

Feeling angry, Ruyen opened the door and closed it firmly behind him. It did not sit well with him that he was still treated like a captive. But his concern for his sister drove every other thought from his mind.

As he advanced toward her bedchamber, he saw that the door was open, and he could hear voices coming from within. Stepping into the archway, he could only stare at the scene before him.

A very healthy-looking Cassandra was laughing at something Jilliana had said. Jilliana, with hands on hips, was speaking in an exasperated voice. It was not difficult to tell that she was mimicking King Henry.

"Nay, do not thank me. It will be my greatest delight to give the bride away."

Cassandra collapsed against her pillow in a fit of laughter. "You imitate the king so effectively. If he could only hear you, he'd most probably have an attack of apoplexy."

"He was rather condescending, do you not think?" Jilliana asked. "Poor Henry knew something was not right, but he could not discern what it was." Jilliana laughingly curtsied. "I am not yet finished with Henry Plantagenet."

Cassandra's eyes held a light of eagerness. "What will you do?"

"I have not yet decided."

"I am loath to interrupt this little tryst," Ruyen said, trying not to show his amusement. His eyes fastened on his bride, who was blushing prettily, embarrassed because he had caught her mimicking the king.

"Your sister is much improved," Jilliana said in a rush. "Is that not wonderful?"

"Indeed."

Cassandra threw her covers off and stood, turning around to show her brother how strong she felt. "I am all but well."

"So it would seem."

"Jilliana has a wonderful wit, and is so humorous, Ruyen. She has been entertaining me and making me laugh. Do you not find her amusing?"

"Oh, yes," he remarked drolly. "She has kept me amused since I have known her, which is all of two days."

He pointed to the bed. "Back you go. I will not have you overdo until you are completely well. The sooner you heal, the sooner we can leave."

Cassandra slipped beneath the covers, looking doubtful. "Do you really think Henry will allow us to return to Falcon Bruine?"

Jilliana plumped up the pillows. "He may not want to, but he will. He'll have no choice."

Ruyen handed his sister a tankard of apple juice that he found on a tray and indicated that she should drink. "I will believe it only when we put to sea."

Cassandra paused with the juice halfway to her lips. "Will you be going with us to Falcon Bruine, Jilliana?"

Jilliana met Ruyen's inquiring gaze. "I have little choice in the matter—I fear I must." She moved to the door. "Now if you will both excuse me, I have asked for and been granted an audience with Henry."

Ruyen caught her arm. "I should go with you. I do not trust him."

"He has asked that I come alone." She pulled her arm from Ruyen's grasp. "Besides, I believe you will find your movements are restricted."

He bit back an angry retort. She was right, of course, he could go nowhere without the guard following.

"Beware of Henry," Cassandra said in concern. "He is a devious man."

Ruyen started laughing. "It is Henry who should beware."

Brother and sister watched the brave young queen move regally out the door, never suspecting that inside she was trembling with uncertainty and fear.

Henry had arranged for his chamberlain and the Archbishop of York to stand behind the tapestry to witness his meeting with the young queen. Feeling confident that he now had the means to thwart Jilliana, he nodded to his guard to admit her.

As she walked toward him, he was touched by her delicate beauty. When she drew near, he could see that her blue gown seemed to reflect the blue of her eyes.

"It is good to see you looking so rested, Jilliana. Come sit beside me," Henry said, indicating the chair next to his.

"I prefer to stand, Henry. I will only require a moment of your time. I want to leave England."

"I hope when you do go you will remember how well you were treated, and that I am your friend."

"I'll remember everything I have ever heard about you."

"Ah, Eleanor again," he said. "How fares my lady wife?"

Jilliana was untouched by his pretense of solicitude. "You know that I did not come here to speak of Queen Eleanor. I want to know when I can leave."

"I might be generous if you suggest to Rome that I be made overlord of Talshamar until such time as you give birth to an heir. This would surely stay Philip's hand from harming you."

"But who would stay *your* hand?" Jilliana asked. "Do you think I have no knowledge of how my mother died?"

"That was unfortunate, I admit, and none of my doing. My men had orders to bring her to England. It was she who chose death. She impaled herself upon her own man's sword."

"Yes. Death over imprisonment. It is the same choice I would make, and I hope that if I am ever placed in such a position, I shall be as brave as my mother."

Henry's face whitened. "Are you saying that you would choose death over remaining in comfort here in England?"

"I am saying exactly that, Henry. Can I be less a queen than my mother?"

She watched his reaction carefully. First he was angry, then resigned, and then amused.

"I will allow you to leave as soon as I have proof that your husband has bedded you. You see, the servants that cleaned your bedchamber recounted that while you and Ruyen occupied the same bed, that is all you did."

Jilliana glanced down, pretending to study the hem of her gown. How could anyone know that she and Ruyen had not made love unless they had spies in the room? Nay, 'twas not possible, there would have been nowhere for them to hide.

She raised her head and glared at Henry, anger her best defense. "It is not for you to know what happens between my husband and myself."

"Those are my conditions," he said in a hard voice, determined not to be outmaneuvered again. "And I am sure you will admit it is a much better solution than impaling yourself on Sir Humphrey's sword."

Jilliana took a step backward, suddenly wanting to put distance between herself and the man she despised.

"We have nothing else to say to one another."

"I did not dismiss you."

"And I did not ask your permission to leave." She remembered what Eleanor had told her just before she left Salisbury. "And, Henry, you might remember that my ancestors were ruling while yours were still heathen."

Henry exploded with rage. He had often heard Eleanor use the same argument, mocking him with her ancient lineage. "You dare say this to me—you cannot even know the duties of a queen."

Jilliana raised her head haughtily. "I admit I have much to learn, but I will not learn it from you."

For a moment they stared at each other, neither willing to be the first to yield. Finally, Henry smiled.

"Gad, what a wife you will make. You are too much a woman to waste on that rebellious prince from Falcon Bruine."

"Nevertheless, I am his wife. You saw to that yourself."

So saying, she turned away and walked regally toward the door.

"Remember," he called after her, determined to have the last word. "I will expect proof that your husband has bedded you, Jilliana."

She forced herself to take slow steps when, in truth, she wanted to run.

After she had gone, the two men stepped from behind the tapestry.

"Will you allow her to leave London?" the archbishop asked.

Henry smiled slightly. "All is not as you might think. Queen Melesant is my confidante and ally. I must send a dispatch to her at once. She will know how to deal with her son and his new bride."

Once out of sight of the king's chamber, Jilliana leaned against the wall, hoping her trembling legs would support her. She was not certain if she had won or lost, she only knew that Henry had not been the complete victor. He wanted something from her, something more than Talshamar, and she did not know what it was.

She walked slowly down the corridor past the Great Hall and out into the fresh air of the courtyard. She moved down a well-worn path, needing to be alone so she could gather her courage.

Tonight she would have to beg a man to make love to her, and that thought was distasteful. She knew she was pretty, but there must be something the matter with her to make Ruyen reject her.

Perhaps it was thoughts of the woman he loved that made him resist her. Well, all she wanted from him was a child. Did he not see that he was the only one who could impregnate her?

It must be tonight.

12

Jilliana sat on a stool, wearing nothing but her shift, while Netta brushed her ebony hair until it sparkled in the candlelight. Until yesterday, Jilliana had only known old men, priests and scholars, no one who would awaken maidenly thoughts of love. Now her brow was furrowed with worry.

It should have been so simple to marry Prince Ruyen and save him from the executioner's block, then have his child to save herself from the machinations of Henry and Philip. If Ruyen would not teach her what to do, she would have to discover for herself how to proceed.

"Netta," she said to the maid, "I believe that you are married, are you not?"

"Yes, Your Majesty, my Tom and I were wed over ten years ago. He is steward of Sir Humphrey's estate, Longworth."

Jilliana was momentarily diverted. She had never thought of Sir Humphrey as having a home or a life away

from her. He had always served her so well and been so
attentive to her needs that it was difficult to realize that
he had a past which she knew nothing about.

"He must have given up a great deal for me," she
said, bemused by the loyalty of Sir Humphrey and
countless other people she did not even know who had
sacrificed so much to keep her safe all her life.

She realized that many Talshamarians had endured
great hardships on her behalf, and she was determined
that their suffering would not be in vain. But to be of use
to her people, her first duty was to produce an heir, and
she could not do it without Ruyen's cooperation.

Jilliana wished she could ask Netta about what happened between a husband and wife, but how could she
broach such a delicate matter with a servant?

"If you have been married ten years, you must have
many children, Netta."

The maid smiled faintly. "No, but I have not given up
hoping, Your Majesty. And if God never sees fit to bless
us with children, I'll never regret my life with Tom."

"It must have been difficult for you to leave your husband to serve me."

"My duty is to you for as long as you need me. My
only concern is that I not fail you."

"Would you like me to send for your husband so that
you may be together?"

Netta's face brightened, then she dropped her gaze.
"I would not ask it of you, Majesty. I know you have
many important matters that are troubling you, and I do
not want you to be concerned with my affairs."

"But you miss your husband?" Jilliana pressed, wanting to learn more about the first amicable marriage she
had encountered.

Netta's plain face was suddenly beautiful and her
eyes softened as she thought of her husband. "We've
known each other since we were children, and Tom is so

much a part of me, Your Majesty, that even when we are separated, I feel his presence."

Jilliana's expression was wistful, and she wondered what it would be like to have someone love her in that way. She was startled when she looked up and found that Ruyen had entered the room and was watching her closely, his face inscrutable.

She felt shy because she had to explain to him what had transpired between her and Henry.

"That will be all tonight, Netta. You should seek out your bed. I wish to be up and away from this place well before the noon hour on the morrow."

"An ambitious undertaking," Ruyen said in a sneering tone. "Have you told Henry your plans as of yet?"

Netta set the hairbrush aside and curtsied to her queen, preparing to depart.

"Netta," Jilliana said, "I will want you to sleep near Princess Cassandra again tonight. Even though she seems better, she may have need of you."

Netta bobbed a quick curtsy and hurried to the door. Something about the prince's mood made her apprehensive. It was clear that the queen and her new husband were not on good terms. But she was only a maid and the workings of royal minds were not for the likes of her.

When they were alone, Ruyen bowed with an exaggerated flourish. "Did you summon me?" he asked mockingly, his eyes raking her scantily clad body. The look he gave her made her very aware that he knew what she had in mind.

Jilliana raised her chin defiantly. "If you mean did I ask if you would wait upon me when you returned from your sister's chamber, then, yes, I did. I thought you might be interested in what Henry had to say about us."

Ruyen gave her a sharp glance. "Well, what did Henry say?"

"He said that neither of us could leave until"— her cheeks became flushed— "until . . ."

"Yes?" He said, more than a little irritated that she was allowed the freedom of the castle and he was not. "Until what?"

"Henry and I had a rather vehement discussion. He was at his most formidable."

"I dare say." He moved to the window and turned his back on her, staring out into the inky blackness. "I suppose you with your usual directness convinced Henry to allow us to leave?"

"Not . . . precisely."

"You should have tried charm. I understand it is a weapon women use very well."

"It did not work on you."

He still did not face her. "Did it not, Jilliana?"

"You have not agreed to give me a child. Is it because of the woman you love?"

"Katharine?" He mouthed the name softly. "Perhaps."

"Ruyen, Henry knows that we only . . . that we did not make love. How can that be?"

"Innocent," he hissed, fighting against the need to rush to her and take her in his arms, to crush those lips beneath his until she cried for mercy.

There was a long silence in the chamber. He had not known that she was beside him until he felt her hand on his arm. He turned to find puzzlement in her blue eyes.

"I had not considered that you might not be able to father a child. Is there something wrong with you?"

He opened his mouth to speak, but was unable to utter a sound. She could have said nothing that would have stunned him more.

"Well, is there something wrong with you?"

He grabbed her wrists, slamming her against his hard body. His eyes were like dark storm centers and his mouth twisted with rancor. "Why don't we just see, Jilliana."

He lowered his head, his mouth almost touching hers. "Remember, you have been begging for this."

Now she was losing her courage. She attempted to move away, but his arms tightened about her, holding her firmly against him. When she tried to turn her head, he captured her chin and held it firm.

Flinging her head back, she felt his warm breath on her neck. The trembling of her body was involuntary, and the feelings she was experiencing were unexpected and new to her.

When she felt his hot lips nestle in the curve of her breast, she closed her eyes, feeling a sudden weakness as his hands drifted into her hair and his mouth moved up her arched neck to settle softly on her lips.

At first she stiffened at the touch of his lips, then she sighed, pressing her mouth tighter against him, wanting to feel more of the glorious sensation he invoked. When Ruyen felt her respond, he deepened the kiss, and his hold on her became gentle, caressing, loverlike.

Jilliana was stirring his blood and he felt, once again, that he had broken faith with his Katharine. But the woman in his arms was so desirable and he ached to possess her completely.

He wanted to be the man who introduced her to deeper feelings, to control her body and even to meld with her mind. He wanted to know what she was feeling as his hand slipped beneath her shift, as he pushed it off her shoulders.

She gave a momentary cry of protest, suddenly afraid of the unknown. She had goaded him and tormented him into this action, why then was she so unsure that she wanted him to continue?

Modesty overruled her awakened passion and she crossed her arms over her breasts as her chemise fell at her feet.

His eyes ran over her silken body as his hand went to his tunic and he tore it away, tossing it aside. He wanted to rip the rest of his clothing off as his eyes devoured her sweetly curved body. Desire flamed through him with intensity when he traced a line through her ebony hair, which fell about her in a velvety curtain. Her waist was tiny, her hips rounded, just right to receive a man. Her legs were long and shapely, and her arched feet dainty.

Never had he seen a woman so perfect in every way and she was his to take, to hold, to do with as he deemed—she was his legal wife, and had she not asked for what he was about to do to her?

With a moment of doubt reflected in her eyes, she nodded and flung her head back when he came forward, lifting her in his arms.

Shyly her arms slid around his neck and she somehow reminded him of a frightened little girl.

"Are you sure this is what you want, Jilliana?" he asked.

"If this is what is required of me, I will strive to overcome my maidenly diffidence," she told him. "Do with me whatever is necessary."

Suddenly Ruyen shook with laughter. "Do not look on this as climbing the steps to meet the executioner's ax. It is not nearly so bad as all that."

He lay her down and she looked up at him with uncertainty when he sat on the side of the bed to remove his soft leather boots. When he stood to unlace his leather trousers, she nervously pulled the curtain of her long hair across her exposed breasts.

She gasped and sprang to a sitting position when he slid his naked body against her. She could not know that he was deliberately trying to shock her. There was passion in him, but anger as well—since he had known her, she had manipulated his life and he had been as helpless as a banner fluttering against a gale-force wind.

When he drew her into his arms he felt her tremble.

"If you wish to change your mind, I will understand."

Bewildered blue eyes were raised to him. "I will not change my mind. Our bargain is that you will give me a child, and I will give you freedom. Do you swear to this?"

"I have no wish to keep you. Whenever you want, you are free of me."

"Swear to me on your honor that you will execute no claim on any child I might bear from our . . . union."

"All I want from you is freedom."

"Swear this to me."

"I swear."

In a move that took him by surprise, she moved forward, touching her lips to his. A shock of pleasure flowed through his body as she pressed her naked body against his.

Promises were forgotten as he slid his arm about her and brought her on top of him, pressing and molding her against him, needing to feel all of her, craving the sweetness her satiny body promised.

"Jilliana, beautiful Jilliana, what are you doing to me?" he said softly in her ear. "I will have you now."

She felt his hot lips cover hers and she groaned with pleasure at the feel of his hard thighs and the swelling of his male member between her legs, while his hands roamed at will over her hips, pressing, tightening her body to his, invoking a rush of desire so strong that she could scarcely breath.

"I did not expect it to be like this. The feelings are . . . amazing," she said, turning her head and trying to drag air into her lungs. "Please do it now."

His desire for her intensified and he roughly turned her to her back, hovering over her, his gaze moving hungrily over her swollen breasts that moved enticingly every time she took a deep breath.

He softly touch her cheek and her eyes widened with bewilderment and aching passion. She allowed her eyes to move over the wide expanse of his chest and down to his tapered waist and flat stomach. She had not known a man's body could be so magnificent, or that a mere touch could send the blood running hotly through her veins.

"Do not forget, Jilliana—you asked for this. I would have had you walk away without touching you."

Ruyen tried to think of Katharine, but his body was betraying him. He wanted this naked beauty that lay beneath him—he wanted her in the worst way. As if it would excuse his own unleashed passion, a passion he had never felt for Katharine, he spoke in a harsh voice.

"I will plant my seed in you, then by the saints, I'll be rid of you."

13

Ruyen was touching her breasts, then her thighs, and when his hand slipped to the inside of her leg, she caught her breath, clamping her lips tightly together as he gently massaged her until she moaned.

White hot passion coiled through his body with such an intensity that he wanted to take her to him, to hold her thus until the wanting stopped. The sweetness of her almost drove him out of his mind with need.

He closed his eyes, trying to regain some measure of control over his racing heart. That he was wronging Katharine in his mind as well as with his body made him angry, and he took that anger out on the object of his desire, the woman who had taunted him until he had to have her.

Jilliana gasped when Ruyen thrust forward, driving his steely hardness into her. She twisted beneath him, her eyes wide, biting her lip to keep from crying out. She had not known there would be pain. But the pain did not last, and it was quickly replaced by a sensation so surprising that she turned her head from side to side, reveling in the newly awakened feelings he invoked as he plunged forward and then slowly withdrew, only to plunge forward again and again.

Her arms went about his shoulders and she planted kisses on his forehead, his eyes, and then when he raised his head, their lips met in a kiss so consuming that he groaned her name.

"Jilliana, what are you doing to me?"

She could not speak because his lips found hers once more and he ground his mouth against hers. He continued his tender assault on her body, and she found that if she met his forward thrusts it gave even more pleasure to them both.

Suddenly his thrusts became more forceful, and liquid, life-giving heat pulsed into her body. She held on to him tightly until he relaxed against her.

The only sound inside the room was their breathing that was slow to return to normal. Ruyen rolled over, taking her with him and keeping her at his side. In a move that surprised her, he laced his fingers through hers and raised her hand to his mouth, kissing it tenderly.

Jilliana reached up, touching his face and feeling the stubble of his beard. She looked into his eyes and saw softness there, the same softness she felt in her heart.

"I never knew making love could be so wonderful," she told him, allowing her hand to drift to his hair. "Is it always like this?"

He was quiet for a long moment. He pushed her hand away and moved to the side of the bed, where he sat upright. "What happened was no more than the coupling of two bodies. You want a baby, and I am merely attempting to oblige you."

She blinked at his coldness and tried to ignore the ache that throbbed in her heart.

She had felt so close to him only moments ago; had he not felt it also? Jilliana stared at his rigid back—no, he had merely done as she asked him. She wished he would look at her with the same softness he had when he was making love to her.

"Am I with child?"

Ruyen turned his eyes on her lovely face, that was partly in shadows. "If you are not, you soon will be. I'll mount you until your belly swells with my seed."

While he dressed, Jilliana slipped off the bed and retrieved her shift from the floor. Pulling it over her head, she tried to gather the courage to ask him a question that was pounding in her brain.

Ruyen was fastening his doublet when she moved to stand in front of him.

"Did you . . . have you done this with . . . Katharine?" she asked.

He swung around, pinning her with a glare. "Let us be clear on this one thing, Jilliana. Even though we are husband and wife, that does not give you the right to pry into my affairs. You will never speak to me about Katharine. I do not even want you to say her name."

Jilliana flung her head back as pride throbbed through her. "I know that you were betrothed to her, and I know that you love her. I neither ask for your heart, nor do I desire your goodwill. As you said, once I am with child, you are free to go to your . . . your . . . betrothed with my blessing."

He could only stare at the proud beauty that had so satisfied his body. Even now he wanted to reach out and clasp her to him. Damn her for being so desirable, and damn her for making him want her.

He nodded toward the rumpled bed. "Henry's spies can now report to him that I have bedded you."

Ruyen watched her belt her gown and place her wimple on her hair. She then took the crown of Talshamar and placed it atop her head and pulled on a blue brocade robe and clasped it with a golden broach. Ignoring him, she moved to the door, her back straight, her manner cold and distant.

"Where are you going?" he demanded.

She paused at the door, and turned to face him. "Just because we are married does not give you the right to inquire about my movements."

Ruyen clamped his jaw shut as his own words were used against him.

"However, since what I go to do concerns you, I will explain. I go first to see how your sister fares and then I shall seek out Sir Humphrey. I shall also ask for another audience with Henry. I must keep hammering away at him until he relents. You must be prepared to leave when that day comes."

"I say when I go and when I stay," he said, striking out at Jilliana in frustration. He had never before been in a situation where a woman was so in control of his life. It should be he who demanded to see Henry, and he who finally won their freedom. Of course, he was helpless because he was still Henry's prisoner, and while Henry wanted to keep Jilliana happy, he cared little about being in Ruyen's good graces.

Jilliana could not understand his attitude. "Very well, you remain here if you like, but as for me and my Talshamarians, we shall soon leave."

"You have more faith in Henry's word than have I."

"It is not my faith in him that will gain our freedom, it will be my ability to outfox the fox."

He stared at her in disbelief, knowing he had to make her understand what kind of man King Henry was. "You have won pittance from Henry thus far, and only because he allowed it. You are unworldly, and a man like Henry will eat you alive."

"I do not think so. He dare not antagonize me lest he offend the pope."

"Even if you did manage to win our freedom, have you thought how you will acquire the ships we need to take us to Falcon Bruine?"

"Have confidence in Sir Humphrey. He will arrange whatever transportation we need."

Jilliana watched Ruyen for a long moment, beginning to realize what he was feeling. It could not be easy for a strong, powerful man like him to be held as a prisoner. He was a man who had been stripped of his dignity by Henry, but no one could strip him of his pride.

"Have faith, Ruyen," she said gently. "We will prevail."

He looked into her eyes, wishing he had some of her faith.

"Ruyen," she said, "there is but one thing that troubles me, and that is whether my lords will be welcome on Falcon Bruine. Humphrey says that when we leave here we shall travel to the sea and most of my men will depart for Talshamar—but what of those who accompany us?"

"None of your men will be harmed in my country. They will be shown the greatest courtesy."

She looked at him with doubt. "Do you speak for your mother?"

"I speak for myself."

She nodded. "I trust you."

Without another word, she moved out the door and closed it behind her.

Ruyen stood there for a long time, trying to make sense of his turbulent thoughts. The world as he had known it had ceased to exist. His father was dead, his mother ruled Falcon Bruine. His thoughts turned to Katharine. She was as different from Jilliana as any two women could be. Jilliana's ebony hair felt like a curtain of silk as it slid through his fingers. Katharine's hair was golden in color. Jilliana's eyes were such a deep blue that they could look right into the heart of a man. He had seen those eyes flame with indignation, sparkle with humor, and soften with desire.

He paced the floor, frowning. What color were Katharine's eyes? Brown, he thought, or perhaps gray. How strange it was that he had never taken notice of Katharine's eyes.

Henry's messenger stood before Eleanor, waiting for her to read the king's dispatch. She moved closer to the candle and stared at the bold scrawl that she knew so well.

> *Madame,*
>   *It gives me great pleasure to announce to all Christendom that the daughter of your dear friend, Queen Phelisiana, has this day been joined in marriage to Prince Ruyen of Falcon Bruine. I hope you will be as pleased as I am at their union. Should you care to send your felicitations to the happy couple, you will find them ensconced in Falcon Bruine rather than Talshamar. I have placed Jilliana in the keeping of Queen Melesant, an admirable woman. As always, I hope your health is good and that you will not grieve overmuch at losing your student to a husband not of your choosing.*

Eleanor threw back her head and laughed lustily. It had taken many years, but at last she would be revenged on Queen Melesant for seducing Henry. She placed a parchment in front of her and dipped her quill.

Five weeks passed and Ruyen was still virtually a prisoner in Henry's castle.

Every night he would take a willing Jilliana into his arms and make love to her. As his passion for her grew, his restlessness increased. He could find no solace for the indignities he was suffering.

Even now Jilliana had gone to see Henry, as she did almost daily. He knew not what transpired at their meetings, for she did not confide in him.

Between Jilliana and Ruyen there was an uneasy peace. They shared a nightly passion, but now she rarely shared her thoughts with him. She had become quiet and subdued of late, and he wondered what was troubling her—though he never asked.

He lay back on the bed, thinking of Jilliana's silken hair, the softness of her skin. He was becoming too dependent on her. She was getting into his blood, so that all he could think of all day was the night to come when he would hold her in his arms.

He sat up—perhaps he had been too harsh with her. He should encourage her to talk about herself. When she returned today, he would try to make peace between them.

Ruyen watched the door, waiting for her return. An hour passed and then another, and still she did not come. Lying back on the bed, he thought only to close his eyes for a moment. Soon he nodded off and was lost in a dreamless sleep.

A short time later he was awakened by someone shaking him. Slowly he opened his eyes to find Sir Humphrey standing over him. "Her Majesty has sent me to help you prepare to depart."

Ruyen sat up, shaking the last remnants of sleep from his mind. Had he heard right? "Has Henry then given us permission to leave?"

The giant Talshamarian grinned. "Her Majesty has finally worn down his objections. This morning he relented."

Ruyen stood up to his full height, and still Humphrey towered over him by a head. "It seems to me that your queen always gets her way in everything."

"Pray God that it is always so."

Ruyen noticed for the first time that they were not alone. There was a young boy no more then twelve, carrying armor and a gilt-handled sword that he recognized as his own. It had been taken from him the day he lost the battle.

"How did you come by my armor?" he asked in amazement.

"My queen acquired all your belongings. Princess Cassandra told her that everything had been taken from you, so Queen Jilliana went to King Henry and demanded their return. This is my own squire, James, who has come to assist you as you dress."

Ruyen gently touched the sword that had been given him by his father—he had thought never to see it again. "Once more I am indebted to Jilliana."

There was pride in the older man's eyes. "You should have seen her today, standing before Henry without fear. She was magnificent!"

"Pity the poor fool who contrives to take her on, believing he can come out the winner," Ruyen said ruefully.

"Aye," Sir Humphrey agreed. "She is twice as good as any man, and three times as good as any woman."

Ruyen's eyes narrowed. "You have lived too long in a country ruled by women, Sir Humphrey, and have become too easily pleased."

Humphrey moved to the door. "I understand that your mother rules Falcon Bruine." He smiled, bowing slightly, not even waiting for a reply. "James will guide you to us when you are ready. Princess Cassandra is even now with Her Majesty. We await you at the outer gates."

Ruyen watched Humphrey depart and then nodded curtly to the lad, who rushed forward to dress him. His heart began to lighten—he was going home!

Ruyen was soon dressed in a clean white tunic and chainmail. He slipped into his soft leather boots and spurs and flung a black cloak fastened with a gold and jeweled pin bearing the falcon of Falcon Bruine about his shoulders. Ruyen took his helm and tucked it beneath his arm.

The squire fastened the chainmail and nodded. "Are you ready to leave, Your Highness?"

"Aye, lad, lead the way. I will suffer London no longer."

There was a sudden commotion at the door and it was flung open to admit Henry himself. He stared at Ruyen for a long moment and then smiled. "I felt it would be prudent to speak to you before you set out on your journey."

"I do not know why you thought you had to say goodbye in person," Ruyen said, slipping his hands into his leather gauntlets.

"I see your months of prison have not curbed your impatient tongue." Henry shrugged. "Nevertheless, I want to explain some things to you."

"I'm listening."

"You know that Queen Jilliana will be going to Falcon Bruine with you?"

"So she says. I have wondered how you convinced her to do that."

"It was simple. I told her that if she did not accompany you and Princess Cassandra, I would send you and your sister back to the Tower. Unlike you and me, she can be reached through her heart."

"Is this the only reason she goes with me?"

"It was the only weapon I could use to make her agree. She is a most unusual woman."

"You have no idea," Ruyen muttered.

"There is one other thing I wanted to make sure you understand. My troops will accompany you to the coast and see you on board ship."

Ruyen's jaw tightened. "Just keep them out of my way."

Henry laughed and walked to the door. "You will hardly notice them. Convey my respects to your mother."

He watched Henry leave. The man was certainly cunning—allowing them to leave, but still keeping them under his control. Ruyen walked to the door and pushed it open, but Henry was nowhere in sight and neither was the guard who was usually posted there. His heart grew lighter and his footsteps hurried—he was going home!

When he walked out of the castle, he found his sister already mounted and waiting for him.

"Look you there," she said happily indicating the horse he was to ride. "We shall all be riding white steeds, is it not wondrous?"

He pushed his booted foot into the stirrup and slipped into the saddle. "Do you feel well enough to attempt the journey home?"

"Oh, yes, Ruyen. I want only to leave this awful place forever."

A crowd of Londoners had gathered to watch the amazing spectacle. Jilliana moved among her people, many of whom she had not seen since entering the castle. She smiled at each in turn and spoke to them. As she would approach a knight or a baron, they would go to their knees and bow their heads, paying homage to her.

This is the scene Ruyen witnessed when he joined the Talshamarian escort.

"It is touching to see how they adore Jilliana, is it not?" Cassandra asked.

He could only nod.

Sir Humphrey placed Jilliana on her horse and she rode to Ruyen. "'Tis a most glorious day," she said, smiling.

"I never thought we would be leaving."

"I told you to have faith."

Their eyes locked and neither spoke for a tense moment. Cardinal Failsham came forward and gave his blessings and Jilliana turned to him.

"Your Eminence, will you not be coming with us?" she asked.

"Nay, Your Majesty. I go directly to Talshamar to prepare for your return. If God be willing, I shall be there to greet you when you arrive." His eyes went to Ruyen, "My blessings on you as well, Prince Ruyen."

"Until we meet, Your Eminence," Jilliana said, and then turned her attention to her husband. "If you will lead the way, we shall attempt to keep pace."

"God only knows I hope that I can keep pace with you," he said brusquely.

Jilliana looked past him to Cassandra and she spoke to the girl. "If you find the journey too tiring, you must inform me at once, and I will see that you have time to rest."

"I will not slow you down," Cassandra informed her, her cheeks flushed with excitement. "I feel completely recovered."

The people who had been gathered to observe the strange occurrence now moved back to allow the thundering horses to pass. Amid cheers and smiles, Queen Jilliana, Prince Ruyen, and Princess Cassandra rode past the Tower, each knowing that impregnable fortress could easily have been their permanent home.

Jilliana spoke to Ruyen. "I am glad to be quit of this place."

"On that we are in agreement."

He watched the way her transparent veil fluttered in the breeze and how regally she sat her white palfrey. If anything, she was even more beautiful than when first they had met—was it possible for a woman to become lovelier with the passing of each day? His lips firmed.

Why was she always on his mind? Had she woven a spell about him as she had the poor, unsuspecting Henry?

On they rode until they left London behind. Later in the afternoon storm clouds had gathered overhead and it soon began to rain, but the travelers did not slow their pace. Across the green English countryside they silently wound their way.

Jilliana looked upward, allowing the light rain to fall on her face. She felt satisfaction because she had accomplished all that Eleanor had asked of her.

She glanced over at her husband, who seemed cold and distant, a reluctant lover for certain. But he had kept his word, and she hoped she would soon have the baby she so desired.

14

Despite the hooded cape Jilliana wore, she was soaked through and very weary. It had rained unceasingly since they had left London.

She looked worriedly at Cassandra, fearing that the arduous pace they were traveling, as well as the rain, would cause her illness to return. She was relieved when the girl smiled at her.

Some time ago, Ruyen had dropped back to ride with Sir Humphrey. She supposed he preferred her knight's companionship to hers, but she did not care. It had been uncomfortable having to suffer his silent, brooding manner.

She glanced up at the sky, unable to gauge the time. They had stopped for an hour to eat, and twice since to rest the horses. She hoped they would soon stop and make camp.

Sir Humphrey, who always seemed to anticipate her needs, rode to her side. "Our camp is just ahead, Your Majesty. You will soon have a place of comfort and a well-prepared meal."

"How was this accomplished?"

"I have sent people ahead of us to make certain that your resting place each night will have every comfort."

She smiled at him. "It seems you have once more thought of everything."

He glanced up at the sky, noting that the rain was falling heavier now. "Let us hasten, Your Majesty, lest you suffer a severe soaking."

Sir Humphrey led the way off the high road, much as he had the night of Jilliana's coronation. Like a miracle, the rain stopped and the clouds parted to reveal a full moon.

When they reached the campsite, there were many fires burning and she could clearly see colorful tents, with each noble's banner waving in the breeze. The tents had been cleverly arranged in a wide circle, and she knew that the biggest and most grand, which was situated in the middle of the circle and bore the gold and white banner of Talshamar, would be her tent.

Sir Humphrey helped Jilliana dismount while Ruyen aided Cassandra. Then Ruyen disappeared while Sir Humphrey led Jilliana and Cassandra to the large tent.

Miraculously, Netta had arrived earlier to make everything ready. She now came forward and helped them remove their damp cloaks.

Cassandra was looking about the tent that had been prepared for Jilliana and Ruyen. Clean rushes had been strewn on the floor so they could keep their slippers dry. There were stools, tables and a cot large enough to accommodate two people. Everything had been done for their comfort.

"Does Your Majesty wish to rest, or will you dine now?" Netta asked.

"Let us dine. Then I want only to go to bed, and I do believe Cassandra should be served her supper in bed."

"Must I?" the girl asked in a disappointed voice.

"Yes, you must. You're just over your illness, and today was very taxing. We do not want you to have a recurrence of the fever."

"I suppose you are right. I would not want to become ill and slow our progress."

Jilliana could see the girl's disappointment. "As you grow stronger, you will be able to do more. I cannot forget how ill you were, and I want you to regain all your strength before we reach your home."

"Jilliana," she said in a voice that was no louder than a whisper, "it will not be a happy reunion when we reach the island. Eventually my brother will have to challenge my mother. Is that not sad?"

"I cannot help but think your mother will give up her title as regent in favor of her son. Having never known my mother, I do not really have experience of that kind of relationship, but I do know that my mother died that I might live."

"Aye, I am aware of the history of Talshamar. Queen Phelisiana's bravery is known and admired throughout Christendom." Cassandra ducked her head, her eyes filled with shame. "My mother is nothing like Queen Phelisiana. She would never give her life for either me or Ruyen. She worships power and . . . and although I have not said so to Ruyen, I believe that she betrayed him and our father."

While they were talking, Netta had been helping Jilliana into a burgundy gown, and because her hair was wet she wore it unbound and uncovered, wearing only a narrow jeweled crown.

Jilliana patted the young princess's hand comfortingly. "Surely you are mistaken about your mother."

"Nay, I am not, although I wish I were."

Jilliana wanted to distract the young girl, for if she spoke true, it was a great tragedy and could explain much of Ruyen's distrust. "How would you like it if I sent a minstrel to play and sing while you dine?"

Cassandra's eyes brightened and she touched Jilliana's sleeve. "I would like that above all."

"Allow Netta to help you into a dry gown, and then I shall send the minstrel to you. He is quite entertaining and Netta will remain with you."

Netta placed jeweled bracelets on her queen's wrist. "Princess Cassandra's tent is next to this one."

"Will you remain with her tonight should she need you?"

"Aye, Your Majesty. I shall go now to take her food. Sir Humphrey has asked that if you are agreeable, he would like you to join your nobles to sup."

"Yes, inform him that I will join him shortly."

Netta had reached the tent opening when Jilliana spoke to her. "Will Prince Ruyen be present?"

"I believe that Sir Humphrey has arranged for His Highness to dine with his sister."

Jilliana nodded. She understood that Sir Humphrey and her nobles wanted to talk to her in private.

When Jilliana entered the tent where her nobles had gathered, they all rose. She smiled and spoke to them, now able to put names with most of the faces.

Sir Humphrey led her to the head of the table, and when she was seated, her nobles remained standing until she indicated that they might also sit.

As vassals began serving food in an abundance that astounded Jilliana, she looked about her. Each noble was richly dressed. She had heard that Talshamar was a wealthy kingdom, and if they were any indication, it must indeed be prosperous.

Jilliana could see the expectancy on the faces of those gathered, and she realized it was time for her to speak to them as their queen.

"My lords of Talshamar, I know you must be wondering about me, and about the plans I have for Talshamar."

Everyone had stopped eating, their eyes on her.

"Having been away for so long, and having no memory of Talshamar, I am going to need the help of each of you. I welcome your guidance and advice. If you have questions, this would be a good time to state them."

A knight she knew as Sir Royce spoke. "Your Majesty, many of us do not understand why you are going to the Isle of Falcon Bruine, rather than to Talshamar."

"I understand your concern, and I will answer you thus, being as forthright as I can. I am certain that Sir Humphrey has explained to you that if I return to Talshamar without an heir, it would surely bring King Philip of France down on us. I will not have my people suffer a war if I can prevent it. So, I will go home only when I have given birth to a child."

"That is why you married Prince Ruyen?" Sir Royce asked.

"In part, it is, and I would say further, that any of you who wish to go home can do so now with my blessing. I see no need for you to be away from your families."

She looked down the long row of faces. "Do any of you wish to return to Talshamar?"

There was silence, so Sir Humphrey spoke. "If you wish to go home, you are free to do so, and with honor. Many of you will be leaving us when we take ship. I do not think Queen Melesant would allow so large a force to land on Falcon Bruine."

Still there was silence, until Sir Royce voiced his thoughts. "There are none here willing to leave you, Your Majesty. We all travel to the Isle of Falcon Bruine, to leave only when you are ready."

She felt a warmth surround her heart. If she could have embraced each of the nobles, she would have done so. "I am honored by your devotion, and I pray every day that I will be worthy of it."

The look of reverence on each rugged face proved that they thought her most worthy.

After eating a hearty meal and joining in conversation with her lords, Jilliana asked about their families, their children, and their estates. Slowly she was beginning to knit together in her mind a tapestry of her beloved Talshamar and its people.

When the last of the food had been cleared away, she sent a page to fetch Ruyen, and when he entered, she indicated that he should sit beside her. His face was inscrutable, his manner distant. No words passed between them as Jilliana turned once more to her lords.

"I would ask a boon of each of you. Will you not also extend your loyalty to my husband, Prince Ruyen?"

"Aye."

"Aye."

"Aye," came the steady reply as the pledge came from each man in turn.

This had come so unexpectedly that Ruyen was taken by surprise. He could think of no reply for such an honor.

"I thank you," Jilliana said, coming to his rescue. "I know His Highness also thanks you for your loyalty."

Now Jilliana rose. "My lords, I know you are weary and would seek your beds, but I would ask you to remain a bit to witness a ceremony that comes from my heart. I want to honor one who has been steadfast and has suffered greatly by being absent from his home and family on my behalf."

All the nobles rose, cheering while Sir Humphrey turned eyes on her, clearly touched by an honor that had come to him so unexpectedly.

"Rise, Sir Humphrey, and stand before me," she said, wishing her voice would not tremble, at this, her first official act.

He stood before her, his eyes questioning.

"If we were in Talshamar, we would have a proper ceremony. As it is, Sir Humphrey, I stand before your peers to bestow upon you, here and now, the title, earl of Baldridge, and furthermore, I hereby bestow upon you the title of palatine—which is only given to those of distinguished bravery—with the right to sit in my presence, and always to speak your mind. You will henceforth have all the privileges of the earldom of Baldridge, along with all the lands, castles, and moneys thereof. This I do in gratitude for all you have sacrificed for Talshamar, and for its queen."

Sir Humphrey remembered Jilliana questioning him on what titles had passed to the Crown because the family had died without issue. He had not known until now the reason for her interest.

She reached forward, taking his sword from its scabbard. "Kneel, Sir Humphrey."

He complied, lowering his head, fearing the others would see the tears gathering in his eyes. He could not remember a time when he had cried in his life, with the exception of the night Queen Phelisiana died, and now.

"I would have bestowed this honor on you in the splendor of Talshamar so that all might witness my gratitude for your devotion—but alas, that cannot be."

Touching his shoulder with his own sword, she smiled at him. "Arise, Lord Baldridge and face your peers."

He rose, fearing to look at her, lest she see his tears. "I will ask that you remain beside me to be my counsel, adviser, and keeper of the Great Seal of Talshamar."

He dropped back to his knees, taking the hem of her garment and raising it to his lips. "I have always been your liege man, and will serve you until death closes my eyes."

"Come," Jilliana said, smiling, "let us not speak of death tonight. Let us have wine to toast this happy circumstance. I wish all present to pay homage to his lordship."

There was merriment within the tent. A minstrel entertained them with his lute and sang to them Talshamarian songs.

For the first time Jilliana felt as if she belonged to this

people, and she was honored to be their queen. She watched with satisfaction as the other nobles hailed Humphrey, offering their heartfelt congratulations.

"How does it feel to be lady bountiful, to bestow honors on men who worship you already?" Ruyen asked, smiling dryly. "And as for your lords' loyalty, I neither sought nor welcome it."

She raised her face to him. "I would ask that you keep your dislike for me between the two of us. I do not believe my subjects would understand or approve."

He frowned at her. Dislike? He did not dislike her— why should she think such a thing?

She rose and everyone turned to her. "I will wish you all a good night. But you must not allow my absence to interfere with your entertainment."

Ruyen rose to walk beside her, following her into their tent. He watched as she set her crown aside and unhooked her overskirt.

"Jilliana."

She turned her head, watching him closely. "Yes."

"I do not dislike you."

"It seems to me that you do, Ruyen. I have known only your contempt since our first meeting. I know the reason for it, but I do not condone it."

He came to her, taking her hand. "How can you think I dislike you, when I admire you greatly?"

His hand was warm on hers and his fingers slid between hers. His voice was deep with feeling when he spoke. "At this moment I find myself reliving the night you gave yourself to me. You have so befuddled my mind that I can think of little else."

Dare she trust him? What about his Katharine? "Are you so easily befuddled, Ruyen?"

"It would seem so—if the woman has hair the color of a raven's wing, and lips full and ready for a man's mouth—yes, I am."

She felt him pull her against him, and she went easily into his arms.

She did not tell him that she, too, could not stop thinking of the intimacy they had shared.

15

Her skin looked like shimmering alabaster in the flickering torch light. Ruyen brought her against him, wondering what there was about her that brought the blood in his veins to the boiling point. It was more than the fact that her skin was like silk and smelled of some sweet exotic scent. His hands were roaming across her back in a circular motion.

"To think I knew nothing of you a few short weeks ago, and now you have complicated my life."

She pulled back and blinked her eyes at him, and painful words tumbled from her lips. "If that be so, it shall only be for a short time. When I am gone, you can resume your life as if we had never met."

He lifted her heavy curtain of hair and pressed his lips against the nape of her neck, causing a shiver of delight to dance across her body. Now that she had belonged to him, how would he put her from his mind when she left him? "How can I do that when I have become your prisoner, Jilliana?"

"You are not my prisoner, Ruyen. We merely made an agreement, and I intend to keep mine. I hope you will do the same. Is it not proof of my good intentions that I have agreed to go with you to Falcon Bruine?"

"It was not by your doing that you accompany me. Let us not forget that Henry ordered you to Falcon Bruine."

She moved away from him, concentrating on the wide cot that was heaped with soft sheepskins and covered with a silken coverlet.

"If I had not wanted to go with you, even Henry could not have made me."

He had to smile. She was probably right. She seemed to have little fear of anything, especially not Henry.

"Can you imagine," she said, turning to him, "Henry actually had a notion that I might marry John." Her eyes flashed as they did so often when she was indignant. "Nothing could ever induce me to become a part of that paltry family. Eleanor and perhaps Richard are the only two I would count as worthy."

"Humility does not seem to be in your nature, Madame. You rank yourself higher than the Plantagenets?"

"And you do not?"

Absently, she began to unfasten her shift and he came forward, deftly helping her accomplish the task. "Perhaps I should feel honored that you deigned to choose me."

"Eleanor chose you," she said absently. "I knew nothing about you until that first day I laid eyes on you."

"I surely knew nothing about you." His hand lingered at the back of her neck and he smiled. "Had I known about your temper, I might well have chosen death."

She turned quickly to face him, ready to do battle, when she saw the smile lingering on his lips. "My temper is not apparent to others. You seem to be the one who invokes anger in me."

"There speaks the female in you. To hear you ladies tell it, you are saints come down from Heaven to enrich the life of some poor fool of a man, when in truth you are Satan's daughters."

Jilliana somehow knew that he was speaking of his mother. How she must have hurt him. "Ruyen, I know that you have many problems facing you when you reach Falcon Bruine."

He raised her chin and held her gaze with his own. "I will not deny it."

"I don't wish you to misunderstand me, but I am offering you the sword arm of my Talshamarians if you should have need of them."

He smiled, but his eyes were sad. "No one can help me, Jilliana."

"Yes, they can. Do you know why I had my nobles pledge a loyalty oath to you tonight?" She did not give him time to answer. "I wanted you to have allies in the event that you needed them."

"My troubles are not theirs, Jilliana, or yours."

She moved to a camp stool and sat down. "I have been devising a plan that I believe may help you in your need."

He began removing his clothing. "How can you do more than you already have?"

"I—" She clamped her lips together, fearing he would misunderstand her reasons for helping him.

He waited for her to speak, wondering what was troubling her.

At last, she drew in a deep breath and looked at him. "Ruyen, I am prepared to have the Talshamarian crown placed on your head."

He stared at her in bewilderment. "Explain what you mean, Jilliana."

"I can make you a king!"

Doubt and distrust battled within him for dominance. "Why would you?"

"Many reasons. Firstly, your mother would never harm you if I made you king of Talshamar."

"And secondly?"

"I— You will be the father of my child. Your blood will run through my royal line through time."

"And?"

"How can I turn away from you when you need my help?"

He came to his feet as if the notion of depending on her charity once more was abhorrent to him. "Your sacrifice is declined. Have you forgotten that we already have a bargain? If I am your husband and your king, the pope might not honor his vow to release me from this marriage."

She felt as if someone had trampled on her heart. But her eyes were clear and there was no outward sign that he had hurt her. "I understand and I shall speak of it no more. I ask your pardon. It was foolhardy of me to consider such a scheme."

"I have not yet decided whether you were born with a generous heart, or you and Eleanor have concocted this notion to further embroil me in your schemes."

"I do not believe that Eleanor would approve of my making you king of Talshamar." She removed all her clothing except her shift and climbed onto the cot. "Let us pretend that I never made the offer. Consider it withdrawn."

He moved to stand over her, his eyes fastened on the way her dark hair fanned out about her lovely face.

"Do you want me to sleep with you tonight, Jilliana?"

She was quiet for a moment, then she finally whispered, "Yes."

She held her arms up to him, and he came to her, gathering her into his arms, holding her and wishing his body did not tremble so. He did not know what he would have done if she had said no. He had wanted to touch her all day. Riding beside her had been torture; he could not keep his mind off her. It was better after he had dropped back to ride with Humphrey because he had other distractions.

A growl issued from his lips as his mouth found hers and they came together in a heat of passion. His hands moved gently over her body and she pressed herself tightly against him. She did not question this enchantment that flamed between them, for it seemed that she existed for his touch, his lips, his body to take control of hers. It was right and natural, and she would savor it, until the day they parted.

Ruyen was suddenly angry that he should want her so desperately. He was no more than a stud stallion to her, someone to breed with, someone to give her the child she craved. If it had not been him, she would have found another to father her child.

He took her face between his hands, wishing he could crush the life from her, to end this torture she was putting him through. But when he looked into her blue eyes, they were soft and alluring, and, oh, how those eyes drew him to her.

He could no longer think of his anger. All he could think of was burying himself deep into her hot moistness and finding the paradise he had found there before.

He touched his face to hers, closing his eyes and allowing the fragrance of her to fill his being. His fingers ran lightly across her breasts, caressing, stroking, forcing a tortured moan from her lips.

In a frenzy of passion they quickly tore away the remainder of their clothing. They found themselves on the cot, and he dragged her beneath him while her hands clutched at him. He entered her with such force that it stole her breath. His jabbing forward thrusts rocked her body, and she had to clasp his shoulders to keep from being propelled from the cot.

"If you want to be treated like a brood mare, then damn you, that's how I'll treat you," he said hotly in her ear.

Jilliana was incapable of giving him an angry reply because at that moment Ruyen gentled his movements and he seemed to swell within her, the length of him extending deeper, deeper, until she wanted to cry out. She could not have said if it was pain she was feeling or ecstasy—she only knew that she ached, she hurt, she wanted him never to stop. Each forward thrust made her crave another and then yet another.

Now there was a new feeling that he had awakened in her inexperienced body. Something was happening to her—but what?

She trembled, she clutched at his arm, she cried out his name. His mouth smothered any further sound she might have made. At first the kiss was wildly passionate, intended to express his anger, but her lips curved to meet his and he plunged into her, deepening the kiss, and his possession of her body.

As their bodies trembled, shook and erupted, they clung to each other.

Jilliana had once heard one of the sisters at the convent telling another that there was much pain in childbirth. Was this what she had meant? she wondered. No, of course not, the sister would not have known what it felt like to have a man become such a part of you that you felt his every intake of breath, and could even feel the beating of his heart, and the softly whispered word as he spoke your name.

How did she feel about him? She could not have said, but she knew that when the time came for her to leave him it would be like tearing away part of her body.

He was pressing his lips against her breasts and she closed her eyes, loving the feel of him. She hoped she would not deliver a baby too soon. She wanted to remain with him longer—much longer.

"Do you think I am yet with child, Ruyen?"

He stiffened and pulled away. "If this night did not impregnate you, then you are barren, Madame," he said, rolling to a sitting position.

Where moments before she was feeling tender toward him, anger now burst forth. "Pray that it is accomplished, Ruyen. Think you that I like having to follow after you just so I might beget a child?"

He could not understand why he was so angry. He only knew that he resented her for using him only to produce a baby—it pricked his pride and made him feel less a man. He wanted to lash out at her, to wound her.

"I curse the day that you chose my bed."

Jilliana was confused. Had he not felt the wondrous joining of their souls with the joining of their flesh? Perhaps it had been nothing special to him, but she knew deep in her heart that she would never feel this way with anyone but Ruyen.

She turned her back to him, praying that she would not cry and let him see that weakness in her.

Ruyen dressed and moved to the tent opening. "I will seek another bed tonight."

Her voice was harsher than he had ever heard it. "After this night, I will not again require you in mine."

Huddling against the wall of the tent, she clamped her hands over her ears. She did not want to hear anything else he had to say.

When he left, her body shook with the deep sobs that she had kept under control. She cried herself to sleep.

A bright sun greeted Jilliana when she stepped into the fresh air. She pulled her white leather gloves on, while looking about her. The camp was astir as tents were being dismantled and horses saddled for the day's journey.

Humphrey led her horse forward. "I trust you rested well?" he said, looking at the circles beneath her eyes.

"Yes, I did," she answered, her eyes moving over the crowd of faces until she saw Ruyen. He was laughing with his sister and playfully placed her upon her horse. Jilliana wondered what it would feel like to have a brother who cared about her, or any family, for that matter.

"Let us depart," she told Humphrey.

He nodded his head and lifted her up to place her firmly in her saddle. He could tell something was amiss between the queen and the prince, but that was to be expected. Their marriage had not started out ideally, but perhaps the two of them would come to love each other. He hoped so. Humphrey liked Prince Ruyen. He had not expected to, but he had found that the prince was a man of honor and perhaps even worthy of Queen Jilliana.

They rode long hours, stopping only to eat and rest the horses. Ruyen did not come near Jilliana all day, nor did she want him to.

On their last stop, she chose a particularly handsome knight, Sir Edward Markem of Brisbane, and asked him to ride beside her. She would show Ruyen that she did not need him, and that other men admired her.

Sir Edward more than admired his beautiful young queen, he worshipped her. She had only spoken to him in passing, and to be singled out as her companion was beyond his fondest hope.

She laughed at his wit, and complimented him on his horsemanship. Not once did she look back at Ruyen.

When they stopped at the campsite that night, it was Sir Edward who lifted her from her mount and escorted her to her tent. That night she chose to have her meal in her tent and went to bed early—and alone.

She felt satisfaction in showing Ruyen that she had no more need of him. Let him go to his precious Katharine. Little she cared.

16

Three days had passed since Jilliana and Ruyen had quarreled. She saw Ruyen only from a distance, and that suited her just fine. She enjoyed Sir Edward's amiable companionship much more than Ruyen's indifference. Sir Edward was attentive and concerned about her comfort. She had not known that a man could be so courteous.

Each night she would wearily climb into bed, every muscle aching from the continuous riding. Tonight she was lonely and considered visiting Cassandra's tent, but thought better of it. Ruyen might be with his sister.

When she heard a familiar voice call out, she invited Humphrey to enter. She smiled brightly at him and bade him sit.

"You must have sensed that I needed a diversion, Humphrey. I tire easily of my own company."

He remained standing, his eyes fixed on the tip of his brown leather boot. She could tell that something was troubling him.

"Sit, my old friend, tell me what is the matter."

At last he dropped down on the stool, his eyes raised to hers. "It's about Sir Edward."

"He isn't ailing, is he?"

"Not in the way you mean, but ailing all the same."

"You speak in riddles, Humphrey. In what way does he suffer?"

"First, I should tell you something about the young knight. He was only belted last May. He is his father's only son."

"I know this. Sir Edward told me about his family. He has three older sisters."

"Aye, that he does. But did he tell you that he is betrothed to Lady Jane, a young woman from a good family that he has known all his life?"

"No, he did not tell me that. I hope she is worthy of him."

"I fear that when he returns to Talshamar, Lady Jane will find that he is less infatuated with her."

Jilliana frowned. "This is serious. What has happened to make him change his mind?"

Humphrey looked sorrowfully into her eyes. "You happened to him, Your Majesty. How can he go home to the young girl he is betrothed to when he has been blinded by your magnificence? All he can talk about is you. He can hardly sleep at night for planning what he will say to you next morn. He is suffering, Your Majesty. Cut him loose."

Jilliana shook her head and stood slowly. "How dare you say this to me! Think you that I would toy with Sir Edward's affections? I have said nothing to him that would make him think I hold him in any light but a trusted and valiant companion."

"Perhaps it is difficult for you to see yourself as do the Talshamarians. Your lords have lived and talked of the day when you would return. They loved you without ever seeing you, but it was the love a subject has for his sovereign. With Sir Edward it is different. You singled him out, allowed him to ride beside you. In his eyes, you bestowed your favor upon him."

She wanted to cry. Humphrey had never before criticized her, and it was an arrow to her heart. "Sir Edward knows that I have a husband."

"He also knows that your husband no longer seeks your bed, but rather prefers to sleep under the stars each night."

Shame burned her cheeks. "Am I then the jest of everyone because my husband does not want me?"

"Nay, Your Majesty. None here jest about the sovereign they adore. Like myself, they are sad that you were forced by chance to marry a man who does not suit you."

She placed her hand on his. "What shall I do?"

"Whatever it is, it had best be soon. Sir Edward has gone so far as to suggest he might challenge Prince Ruyen to a joust. That is why I have come to you, to stop this madness before it goes too far. Prince Ruyen is a seasoned warrior—he would probably kill Sir Edward."

"Oh, Humphrey, I thought I was lonely at Our Lady of Sorrow, but that was nothing compared to the loneliness I feel now. I cannot even bestow my friendship on those who serve me."

"I have heard your mother say the same many times. To be chosen to rule is an isolated road when you have no one to walk with you. Isolated, because you cannot reach out to your knights for comfort, lest they aspire to reach for the sun. You are all the glory of the sun to Sir Edward, Your Majesty. But in reaching so high, he would be burned to a cinder."

"I understand." Her eyes were swimming with tears. "I will cut Sir Edward loose as you suggested." She moved to the back of the tent and then turned to Humphrey. "Will you inform my husband that I want to see him?"

Humphrey bowed, and backed toward the opening. "I will do so at once, Your Majesty."

Jilliana paced back and forth while waiting for Ruyen. What if he refused her request? What would she do then? For that matter, what would she do if he came?

The tent flap was thrown aside and Ruyen ducked his head and entered. Chilling brown eyes stared into hers.

"You sent for me, Your Majesty?" he asked in a condescending voice, sweeping into an exaggerated bow. "I hastened to you as soon as his lordship informed me my presence was required."

She gave him her most disdainful look, her anger making it easier to say what she wanted to relate to him. She raised her chin just the merest bit, her eyes trained not on his eyes, but on his chin.

"I have something of a delicate nature to say to you."

He crossed his arms, towering over her. "Dare I hope you have missed me in your bed and are inviting me back? Or can it be that Sir Edward did not play your stud in my absence?"

She balled her fists and drew back, ready to strike him, but he caught her wrist, holding it in a firm grip.

"I would not attempt that if I were you, Jilliana. I have never yet struck a woman, but I could easily break that rule for you."

She jerked away from him, rubbing her wrist, certain that there would be a bruise there by the morrow.

"It was a mistake to think I could talk to you. You may leave now," she said imperiously.

He moved to stand beside her. "What ails you, Jilliana? Did you tire of your little game?"

"I never play games."

"Do you not? Mayhap Sir Edward could not see what you were about, but I did. Did you think to make me jealous by your childish attentions to a boy hardly old enough to shave?"

She was indignant because he had guessed exactly what she had been trying to do. "I, make you jealous? Why would I bother? I merely made a mistake in judgment and wish to rectify it."

His voice was soft and taunting. "So the flawless beauty has a flaw. She makes mistakes. Pity."

It took all her courage to look into his eyes and not turn away as she spoke. "Mock me if you must, and strike me if you will, but I am asking you to sleep in my tent until we reach Falcon Bruine."

He looked stunned, as if he had not expected this from her. "Have you missed me, then?"

"It isn't that. It seems I was heedless with Sir Edward. I did not know that he would—that he would . . . "

"Lose his heart to you," Ruyen finished for her. "Any fool could see that he worships you, but why should you care about his feelings when you were using him to torment me?"

Her eyes widened. "Did I torment you?"

She watched his mouth arch into a cruel smile.

"Jilliana, no man fancies another man walking in the field he has plowed."

She was livid. It had been a mistake to send for him. He was insufferable, and she detested him.

"You dare say this to me?"

His voice was hard. "Did he lay in your bed?"

"No man save yourself has lain in my bed. And you will not again."

He watched her face to discern whether she was speaking true. That first day she had ridden beside Sir Edward he had been consumed with jealousy, and had wanted to kill the young knight every time he looked at Jilliana with adoring eyes.

Each night he had lain on his pallet, envisioning Sir Edward caressing Jilliana's satiny skin. He had even placed his pallet so he could watch the entrance of her tent, staying awake most of the night to make sure the young knight did not enter.

She had done this to him, turned him into a fool, a dolt, who hungered for her smiles every bit as much as Sir Edward.

"You may go," she said after a long silence. "I do not want you in my tent after all."

He shook his head. "I'll go and gladly. But first tell me why you sent for me. And tell the truth because I shall know it if you do not."

She flung back her head. "It is nothing you would understand. I simply did not know I was hurting Sir Edward until Humphrey told me tonight. It seems I gave him hope that there could be something between us, and that was wrong of me. I do not want to hurt him any longer."

Ruyen had been watching her eyes as she spoke and saw the sincerity of her words. He had become cynical about women at an early age when he had learned that his mother bedded with many of his father's knights. He had known women who were titled, and those who were not, and they all played at love. They all liked to dangle a man until he squirmed. Even Katharine was well versed at this game. Was it possible that Jilliana was different?

"Then tell me why you singled him out to bestow your favor." He waited for her to spin some half-truth, or to invent some plausible reason.

She did not hesitate. "After the last night we spent together, I wanted to prove to you that I did not need you." She lowered her eyes, her long lashes sweeping her cheeks, and she looked very young and vulnerable.

Ruyen had never known a woman who spoke so truthfully, even if it put her at a disadvantage. Mayhap she had not yet learned to lie since she had spent most of her life in a convent. But she had surely learned something from Eleanor.

"I find the ground hard and uncomfortable. I will stay with you."

Jilliana was trying to keep her composure, but she felt it slipping. Being so near Ruyen made her want to reach out and touch him, to have him take her in his arms so she could lay her head on his broad shoulder and seek comfort there.

"You will not find the ground much softer here in my tent," she said, turning away.

His soft laughter made her turn back to him with an inquiring look.

"I have never won an argument with you since the day we met. You have put me in a spin, and I keep coming back for more."

"I do not believe you," she said haughtily. "No woman could best the mighty Prince Ruyen. No, you have no respect for any of us, except perhaps your sister and your lady love."

"Do you speak of Katharine?"

"Nay," she said tenaciously, "have you forgotten you forbade me to speak her name?"

He turned to her before leaving. "Any man who is foolish enough to forbid you anything, gets what he deserves." Laughing at her puzzled look, he swept her another bow. "With your royal permission, I beg to be allowed to fetch my bedding."

When he had gone, she stared at the flickering torchlight near the tent opening. He could be the most maddening man she had ever met.

She quickly undressed and got into bed. Turning her face to the tent wall, she waited. Moments passed and still he did not return. At last she heard him enter, but she pretended to be asleep.

Jilliana was aware of his every move. She could hear him making his bed, close to her. After he extinguished the light, she heard him removing his clothing, and she could envision his body, strong, muscled and so beautiful.

She sighed, wishing she had not been forced to ask him to share her tent. His presence disturbed her peace of mind.

After a long silence, she heard him laugh softly.

"Good night, Jilliana."

She did not answer. Long after she heard the steady breathing that told her he slept, she lay awake, listening to the noises coming from the camp. She could hear men laughing and talking, and finally even that ceased.

The long night stretched before her, and she had time to think about her new life that demanded so much from her. She had not realized that by favoring Sir Edward, she had hurt him.

She had grown up in a convent and then had lived a secluded life with Eleanor. Eleanor had prepared her for many things, but not the knowledge and insight into the mind of a man. Especially not a man like Ruyen. He was complex, brooding, and distrustful of others. More than that, he did not like her, and she did not know how to win his favor.

Turning to her stomach, she closed her eyes, waiting for the sun to rise. She was too troubled to sleep this night.

17

Sir Edward kept pace with Humphrey, his eyes on the man he despised most in the world, the queen's husband. He felt sick inside every time Prince Ruyen looked at the queen, touched her, or laughed at some witticism she made. It should be he, not the prince, who rode beside Queen Jilliana.

"I don't like what you are thinking, Edward. Put your feelings for the queen where they belong," Humphrey said abruptly. "She is not for the likes of you. She is royalty, you are not."

Edward's voice was harsh. "He is not good enough for her."

"Is any man? Certainly not you."

"He does not love her."

"Since when have you become an authority on love? Go home, Edward. Take your Lady Jane, and marry her."

"My heart is too full of love for the queen to think of any other woman."

"If the prince suspected what you are feeling, he would probably carve your heart out, and I would help him."

"He has no right!" the young knight said with fire in his eyes.

"He has every right. She is his wife."

"We all know why she married him. 'Tis a pity."

Humphrey glared at Sir Edward. "Cease your sniveling, or I'll run you through myself. Her Majesty was kind to you, nothing more. She is kind to everyone. She would never think of you other than as her liege man. God's blood, you are a fool if you can't see that Her Majesty loves her husband."

"Nay, she cannot love a man who is boorish, uncaring, and unmindful of her comfort. Were she mine—"

"She is not, nor will she ever be. You will not speak thus again, nor will you approach the queen unless she sends for you—and I think she will not."

Angrily, Sir Edward spurred his horse and galloped on ahead, out of reach of Humphrey's criticism.

Humphrey shook his head, wondering what would happen when Jilliana realized for herself that she loved Prince Ruyen. She had been too innocent and unworldly to be exposed to a man with Ruyen's appeal to women. On the other hand, Humphrey was not certain how the prince felt about Jilliana. He was a man who hid his feelings and was mistrustful of others. Humphrey was afraid that the two of them would never find happiness together.

Though Humphrey would stay ever near her to shield her against harm of the physical kind, he could do nothing to protect her from her own heart.

In the two weeks that followed, they set a steady pace. Soon they would reach the shore; sea birds now glided above them and Jilliana could taste the salty mist on her tongue.

It was late afternoon when they finally sighted the sea. The tents had been erected in a meadow of wildflowers with a forest of spiny woods in the distance.

Jilliana walked to the edge of a steep cliff, seeing several ships below flying the crimson flags of Talshamar.

Humphrey had taken charge and made certain that everything was in readiness. He was now directing the men to stow the cargo in the ships' holds.

Jilliana had decided that only one ship would make the voyage to Falcon Bruine, while the others would take her men home to Talshamar. If only she had not given Henry her word that she would go to Falcon Bruine, she could return to the land of her heart.

She heard footsteps and turned, finding Ruyen standing just behind her.

"I never thought to see my home again, Jilliana. I am impatient to return."

She watched men carrying supplies up long gangplanks. "Tell me about your island." She turned to look at him, watching as a slight breeze rippled through the strands of his dark hair and his brown eyes took on a faraway look.

"It is a fertile land that once yielded great harvests—that was in my grandfather's day. My father was more a warrior than a king. He spent most of his life in the Holy Land, fighting what he called a 'necessary war' against the Infidel."

"And your mother, did she also go to the Holy Land? I know Eleanor did."

"No, she remained behind, serving as regent."

"Like now?"

He did not answer for a long moment, and she could tell that he was troubled. When he did speak, it was not about his mother, but the land he loved.

"Being an island, Falcon Bruine has rarely been attacked by those from the outside. The waters are treacherous, and without an experienced pilot enemy ships know not where to anchor."

"Then Henry's troops must have had someone helping them who knew the waters."

The muscles in Ruyen's jaw tightened. He could not tell her that his own mother had probably given the English a map of the coast. "I have provided your captain a detailed map so he will have no trouble navigating the dangerous currents."

"Why did you leave?"

"Because my father found out that Henry was secretly negotiating behind his back to take over Falcon Bruine. We had no choice but to take up arms against England and try to place Richard on the throne."

"I have oft' thought that you did not truly believe in Richard's cause," Jilliana observed.

"Whether I believed or not had little to do with my reason for agreeing to join him. My father was an old man—I could not let him go to war alone—and I could not allow Henry to take over Falcon Bruine without a fight."

"Cassandra told me that you were not with your father when he died."

"It was Richard's plan that we split our forces. My father would come at Henry's troops from the right, I would come from the left, and Richard from behind. My father died, I was taken prisoner, and I have heard that Richard has now reconciled with his father."

She placed her hand on his shoulder. "Sometimes I can almost feel your pain. Have you been so betrayed that you can trust no one?"

Ruyen drew in a deep breath. "If one lives long enough, one will know betrayal many times. I have come to expect it as the rule."

She withdrew her hand. "Then I pity you."

His gaze dropped to hers. "Save your pity for those who want it. I do not."

She watched him turn and walk away, wondering what demons possessed his mind. He had no trust for anyone, no faith in anything—the exception being his young sister.

She turned back to the ships, thinking tomorrow would be a wonderful adventure, if only she were going to Talshamar. She would remain on Falcon Bruine no longer than necessary. As soon as she knew she was with child, she would ask Humphrey to take her home.

Night was falling when Jilliana returned to camp. She saw Sir Edward waiting for her in front of her tent, and she greeted him with a smile. He dropped to his knees and bowed his head. "Your Majesty, I have come to ask something of you."

She saw Ruyen talking to another knight nearby, but his eyes were on her, his expression inscrutable.

"Stand, Sir Edward, and tell me what it is that you want."

"Your Majesty, I beg you, give me the right to accompany you to the Isle of Falcon Bruine. Allow me to place my sword at your service."

Jilliana glared at Ruyen, who had crossed his arms and was now giving her and Sir Edward his full attention. Deliberately, she turned to look into Sir Edward's earnest blue eyes.

"I require you to travel to Talshamar and help with the preparations for my return. I will want you to see that the castle is made ready."

Disappointment was clearly written on his face. "I will do as you bid me, Your Majesty."

She moved to her tent and paused, looking back at the young knight. "And, Sir Edward, I will ask something else of you."

"Anything, Madame."

"I will want to meet your wife when I arrive in Talshamar. I believe I was told that you were betrothed to a Lady Jane."

He bowed to her. "I will always do as you ask. But may I speak honestly with Your Majesty?"

"You may."

"I love not Lady Jane, nor have I seen her since I was but ten and two. The marriage was arranged by our parents, and I have heard that she has no more liking for our joining than have I."

Jilliana thought for a moment. She believed the young knight spoke the truth, and she relented. "Very well, Sir Edward, you may accompany me to Falcon Bruine. My husband and I have need of those who are loyal to us. Do you understand my meaning?"

He could not meet her eyes. She was telling him that he had stepped over the bounds of chivalry. She was reminding him of his place—and it was not at her side.

"I want only to be your liege man."

Jilliana moved into her tent, not wanting to see Ruyen's smug reaction. She was somehow angry, and she could not have said why.

Princess Cassandra had witnessed Sir Edward's devotion to his queen. She thought him the most noble and handsome of knights. When he glanced at her, she smiled shyly, but he merely gave her a quick bow and hurried away.

Jilliana looked at Ruyen's pallet and kicked at it, wishing it was her husband himself she was kicking.

They had not shared a bed since the night they had quarreled about Sir Edward. Tomorrow they would sail for Ruyen's country, and she was more than a little apprehensive about what awaited her.

A brisk wind swelled the silken sails as Jilliana stood on board the ship that would take them to the Isle of Falcon Bruine. Her cloak was billowing in the misty breeze and she breathed in the salt air. She had never been on board a ship that she could remember, and she found it exciting. The crew all scurried about as if they had nothing in mind but her comfort and safety.

When she glanced to her right, she watched the three ships that were departing for Talshamar. It had been difficult to say good-bye to those she had come to know so well.

Humphrey stood beside her, sensing much of what she was feeling. "The world has never seen the likes of the celebration Talshamar will have to welcome their queen home."

"Are you certain they will welcome me?"

"Aye, more readily than you can imagine."

"Humphrey," she said without conceit, "it is not easy to know what is right."

"You speak of Sir Edward?"

"Aye."

"I was surprised that you are allowing him to accompany us to Falcon Bruine."

"I tried to send him home, and I suggested to him that he should marry his betrothed once he reached Talshamar, but he said they were not suited to one another. I thought that if I sent him away after showing him such marked attention, the others would ridicule him. Did I do wrong?"

Humphrey chuckled. "You did no wrong. I think the young nobleman has learned his lesson. And you are right, the others would have mocked him."

"This is all so new to me, and it is difficult to know what is to be done, Humphrey."

He placed his gloved hand over hers. "Since the crown was placed on your head, you have behaved as a queen should. I should think that the difficult part of ruling is in knowing when to be forgiving and when to stand fast." He smiled. "You have done both, and very well."

She drew in a trembling breath. "I am unsure of many things that I do, Humphrey. And, I am most assuredly frightened."

"But you do not show your fear, and that, too, is the mark of a queen."

"Humphrey, it seems as though my life has never belonged to me. Until now, I have been under the dictates of others. But when I reach Talshamar, that will change. I shall need you beside me at that time more than ever."

"I shall stand at your side as long as you need me," he assured her.

"What do you know of Ruyen's mother?"

"I know nothing good of her. She was the younger daughter of an unimportant lord from some obscure Castilian province—Visby I believe was the name of the holding. It is said that her husband never knew a peaceful day after marrying her. It is also said that she betrayed her husband and son to Henry, but this I do not know for certain."

"Eleanor warned me against her, and I can see why. I cannot imagine any woman allowing harm to come to her own children."

"That woman is ambitious and malevolent, and Eleanor was right, you must be wary of her. If she sees you as a threat, she will not hesitate to harm you. I have heard it whispered that she has knowledge of herbs and plants and is a master at the art of poisons."

"Eleanor chose me to save this family, and it looks as if I am not yet finished. They may be in as much danger in their homeland as they were in England." Jilliana stared pensively into the distance. "I like Cassandra, and I pity her because she seems so sad, but I do not know what can be done to help her. Ruyen is reluctant to accept anything from me, but it is not in my nature to stand back when someone is in need."

"I have noticed that about you, but sometimes you should think of your own needs. You should rest now, you look pale," he said gently. "There will be arduous days ahead."

Jilliana had been feeling light-headed, and the churning sea made her feel ill. "Yes, I shall go to lie down now."

Jilliana raised her gaze to Prince Ruyen, who stood in the bow of the ship. When their eyes met, he turned away.

She took a step toward the curtained area that had been erected to give privacy to her and Cassandra, then glanced over her shoulder at Humphrey.

"How long will it take us to reach Falcon Bruine?"

"With a fair wind, within the week."

Cassandra lay on her pallet, wondering how her mother would greet them when they arrived in Falcon Bruine. Would she be repentant, beg to be forgiven, or deny that she had helped the enemy? And how would her mother accept Jilliana? Henry would have made certain that she knew about Ruyen's marriage.

Cassandra had never met anyone like her sister-in-law, and the more she came to know Jilliana, the more she admired her. She was not quite certain how Ruyen felt about Jilliana though. Could he not see that his wife was worth three of Lady Katharine Highclere?

The young girl's mind moved to the Talshamarian knight, Sir Edward. Today she had watched him as he stood on board ship. He was like a golden god with golden hair and skin. She was sure that she would love him until the day she died, even if he hardly noticed her. If only he would look at her once the way he looked at Jilliana. But then, every man stared at Jilliana in awe. She was so beautiful that no woman could hope to be noticed when she was about.

Netta was plumping Jilliana's pallet to make certain there were no lumps, when the curtain moved aside and Jilliana entered, holding her hand over her mouth.

The maid rushed to her. "Your Majesty, you look pale. What is amiss?"

Jilliana unfastened her cloak and the maid took it from her. "I have been feeling sick since stepping on board, Netta. I did not want Humphrey to know because he worries so."

Jilliana dropped down to her pallet and closed her eyes. "Truth to tell, I feel extremely ill."

Netta touched Jilliana's forehead and was relieved that she had no fever. "It could be merely seasickness, Your Majesty, or it could be something quite different."

Jilliana sat up, running a trembling hand across her face. "What do you mean?"

Cassandra moved nearer, taking Jilliana's hand. "I have heard that one symptom a woman has when she is expecting a child is nausea."

Jilliana's hand tightened on Cassandra's and she looked at Netta for guidance.

"Ohhh," she suddenly cried, clamping her hand over her mouth. "I am going to be ill. Secure the curtains—I cannot allow the others to see me thus."

Netta had been kneeling beside her worriedly. "Can you wait until I return?" she asked, jumping to her feet and hurrying past the curtains.

Jilliana was sure this was what it felt like to die. Just when she thought she could hold back no longer, Netta was beside her, pressing a damp cloth against her forehead and placing a wooden pail beside her.

Jilliana retched until she was limp and then fell back on the pallet, groaning. Cassandra held her hand and talked to her encouragingly.

At last Jilliana smiled. "I believe the sickness has passed. I am sure it was nothing more than seasickness. There is no need to tell anyone that I was ill."

Cassandra and Netta exchanged doubtful looks.

"Jilliana," Cassandra said at last, "since I was raised on an island, I know much about seasickness. I have never known it to pass so quickly."

Jilliana sat up slowly. "I know so little about many things, Netta. Can it be that I am with child?"

"I cannot say for certain, Your Majesty. But if you are, the sickness will come again on the morrow."

18

The voyage stretched into nine days. Each morning, Jilliana was ill, a fact that was difficult to hide from anyone on board the small ship.

The men merely thought she had come down with bouts of seasickness, while Netta became convinced that the queen was with child. She prayed that it was so, for then they could return to Talshamar, where perhaps the queen would be happy.

It had not escaped Netta's notice that Prince Ruyen paid little attention to the queen. Even on board this ship with its limited space, he managed to avoid her.

The maid's loyal heart beat with anger. To her thinking, no prince of some small insignificant island was good enough for the queen of Talshamar. Her dear, sweet queen deserved someone to cherish her and love her. Not once had Prince Ruyen inquired about Queen Jilliana's health.

* * *

Humphrey was watching the rocky shoreline of the island rise out of the mist. He had never been to Falcon Bruine, and were it not for the circumstances of this voyage, he might have looked forward to exploring the island.

Ruyen stood beside him, his eyes dark and brooding, his jaw clamped together tightly. He thought of the morning he had sailed away with his troops to defend Falcon Bruine. He had not known that before he could return he would suffer the death of his father and the betrayal of his mother.

"I can see a tower in the distance, be that the castle?" Humphrey asked.

"Aye. That is my home."

The ship's captain lowered the billowing sails and the craft caught the tide, drifting toward the shore. Dropping the anchor in deep water, the captain ordered the small boats lowered over the sides.

Jilliana came forward, looking at the island with misgiving. There was a long pier jutting seaward, and in the distance she could see a road winding its way through a dense forest.

She felt Ruyen's hand on her shoulder and turned to him. "Falcon Bruine is lovely. You must be delighted to be home."

He did not answer her inquiry because he noticed the dark circles under her eyes. "I knew you were ill," he said with a frown, "and I was concerned, but I assumed you would not welcome my company."

She would have welcomed him, but she did not say so. "I believe men are of little use when a woman is ill. Cassandra and Netta proved to be admirable nurses."

He smiled faintly. "If you will allow it, I will assist you to the boat."

Jilliana nodded, looking down in trepidation at the small craft bobbing in the turbulent water.

Ruyen easily lifted her into his arms and descended the rope ladder. Once in the boat, he seated her on a cushion.

Before she could thank him, he had climbed up the ladder to aid his sister.

With rowers plying the oars, four boats caught the current and made their way toward land.

Queen Melesant descended the narrow stone steps, her splendid purple robe trailing behind her. Her headdress was a stark black, and the golden crown of Falcon Bruine sat atop her head. As regent she had no right to the crown, but little she cared; it was within her grasp and she would wear it.

She entered her private chamber to find her minister, Escobar Hernandez, waiting for her. Escobar had been her father's steward and had come to the Isle of Falcon Bruine with the wedding party thirty-five years ago. On Melesant's request, he had remained, gradually making himself indispensable to her through the years.

Escobar was not a tall man, but he was lean and carried himself straight. His skin was olive in color, and he had a great hooked nose and slightly irregular features—a plain man, who no one would ordinarily take notice of, and he often used that to his advantage.

A year after Melesant gave birth to Ruyen, she discovered that Escobar was a skillful lover who knew exactly how to set her body on fire. He had made himself useful to her in other ways, as well. She had made him her adviser after her husband's death, and where once he had crept into her chamber late at night, he was now free to come to her whenever she summoned him.

Melesant had made it clear to him, however, that when he was not in her bedchamber, he must treat her with the proper decorum her rank required.

"What news have you, Escobar? Is it true? Have the ships landed?" she asked, swirling her long robe aside and ascending the throne.

"Aye, Majesty, but there is only one ship."

Queen Melesant frowned. "I was told they left London with nigh a hundred Talshamarian knights. Can there be some trickery?"

"Nay, Majesty, my informant tells me that the queen of Talshamar travels with but twelve armed guards."

Melesant felt the tension that had been coiled within her slowly ease. She had been dreading her son's arrival. By now, he must know that she had aided King Henry, and she had expected him to return with a large fighting force.

"Does my son believe he can unseat me with a mere dozen soldiers?" she sneered. "How pitiful he will be against my Castilian knights."

Escobar bowed slightly. Everyone, even he, was hesitant to speak the truth, fearing it would throw the queen into a rage if she disagreed.

"It was wise of you to send for troops from Castile since most of the populace of Falcon Bruine remains loyal to your late husband. I have heard rumblings of dissent, for many of them believe that Prince Ruyen should be king."

Melesant's eyes narrowed, catlike, and her long fingernails dug into Escobar's arms.

"Ferret out the names of any who support my son against me, and I will have them thrown in the dungeon and beaten like curs."

Escobar watched as blood shaped from the gashes left by her clawlike fingernails. "It is not always easy to find traitors. While the people talk among themselves, they protect each other from outsiders. But we shall watch them more closely in the future. For now, they seem to fear our Castilians, and that alone should keep them from aiding the prince."

"Imbecile, you trust too easily. Set spies in the village and discover who incites trouble. Must I think of everything? Can you not take this situation in hand?"

Escobar knew that when the queen was in this mood it was best to humor her. He might be her lover at night, but in the daylight hours, she scorned and ridiculed him. He knew her moods better than anyone, and would endure what he must to be near her—she was like wine to his blood.

"Majesty," he said placatingly, "I will see to it at once."

"Do you think she is beautiful?"

"Pardon, Madame, of whom do you speak?"

"Ruyen's wife, of course. God, Escobar, you have only just returned from England ahead of them. You should be able to tell me something."

"I did not see her or talk to anyone who could give me a description of her."

"What you mean is, that you were merely a messenger. I should have sent someone else."

He bowed. "I did my best."

"I recall her mother," Melesant said thoughtfully. "All the men thought her beautiful, but I did not. She was too tall for a woman. Men do not like tall women."

Escobar knew when to flatter Melesant and when to keep his own counsel. This was one of those times when she needed reassurance that only he could give her. She had always been preoccupied with her appearance—it was her only feminine weakness, as he saw it.

"No one could compare with you, Majesty. You are most comely."

She looked pleased. "I was once reputed to be a beauty. I met my husband when my father took me to Paris. Papa was a diplomat and my husband was a guest of King Louis at some court function in honor of Falcon Bruine. I made certain that Broderick saw me to my best advantage. I wore my only decent gown and acted the coy maiden with him. Men always seem to fall for simpering innocence, and I played it well. He was so taken with me that he made me his queen, even though I had not a drop of royal blood in my veins." Suddenly her voice hardened. "But that is the past. Once I turned men's heads and they would do anything I asked of them, now it seems I must obtain their loyalty with force."

"You have always had my loyalty, Madame." His dark eyes held a hidden meaning. "You also have my heart and body."

Melesant recognized the passion that still raged between them.

"Yes, throughout the years you have been constant and loyal. But like everyone else, the day will come when you will betray me—they all do."

"Not I, Majesty." He reached out and clamped her arm and then allowed his hand to drift sensuously upward, then softly across her breasts. "I have been away from you for too long and my body burns for you."

Melesant closed her eyes—she had missed the feel of his hands on her body. She had often wondered why she was so infatuated by him. He was not appealing to look at—ugly really. She did not love him, and had never given her heart to any man. She had nothing to give because her body and heart were ruled by a strong ambitious mind. But she was possessive of Escobar and had warned him many times that if he ever touched another woman, he would breathe his last.

She did not object when he kicked the door closed with his foot, his hands still occupied with stroking her rounded breasts. She quaked when one hand plunged down the front of her gown, and she moaned, her breath coming out in gasps. He made her feel weak, and she wanted to strip her clothing off here and now and have him take her right here on the floor.

He pushed her gown aside and bent his head, sucking on one breast while fondling the other. She threw back her head, groaning and twisting until his wet, hot lips closed over her, draining her of all other thoughts.

He roughly lifted her gown, and undid the laces on his britches. They both knew that no one would dare enter a room when the two of them were together and the door was closed.

Backing her against a wall, he lifted her up past his waist, his eyes hard with passion. Slowly he eased her down, entering her and driving upward. He cushioned her head and plunged inside her while she groaned and clung to him.

Escobar felt a rush of triumph, knowing he could so easily control Melesant by using her passion against her. She had not realized, or perhaps did not care, that he had this power over her.

"Beautiful, beautiful," he muttered in her ear. Then his mouth clamped onto hers and he thrust his tongue in and out, keeping rhythm with his body movements.

She was mindless, she clung to him, whimpering, his movements now driving her into a frenzy.

When at last he had satisfied her needs, she lay limp against him and he guided her feet to the floor.

She stepped back, straightening her gown while he retrieved her crown and headdress and handed them to her.

Her manner was distant as she arranged her headdress and crown. "Escobar," she said, walking to the door, "when our visitors arrive, escort them to me in the throne room."

Unlike her, he could not so easily turn off his emotions. "Shall I come to you tonight?" he asked hopefully.

She gave him a disdainful smile which was meant to remind him that he was little more than her sycophant, and to demonstrate how easily she could put him from her thoughts.

Over the years he had become adept at hiding his feelings. "I shall greet your guests and bring them to you."

"Wait," she called, when he would have left. "Go at once to Lord Highclere's estate. Tell him I want him and Katharine to come at once."

"Do you think that's wise, since your son is bringing a new wife?"

Melesant's eyes narrowed and she purred, catlike. "Aye, I believe it is wise."

"Very well, Majesty," he said, turning away and leaving the room.

Melesant listened to his footsteps echoing down the corridor, and then the castle was silent. Her son loved Katharine Highclere, and she wanted to make this evening interesting, when the woman he loved met the woman Henry had forced him to marry.

With a malevolent smile, she hurried into her dressing room, where her maid was waiting. Melesant pushed the woman aside and flung open the lid of one of her trunks. Rummaging through her gowns, and tossing most of them aside, she finally found the creation she wanted.

Holding the heavily beaded black gown before her, she nodded in satisfaction. "Yes, Betty," she said to the maid, "this will do nicely."

The maid curtsied nervously. "Shall I help you dress now, Your Majesty?"

"Who else but you would perform that duty?" the queen asked in a harsh voice.

Betty had only recently been sent from the village to wait upon Queen Melesant. Everyone knew that the queen was not easily pleased and rarely kept a personal maid more than a few months.

"It is to be hoped," Melesant said, tossing the gown at the woman, "that you are better able to fill my needs than your predecessor was."

Betty's hands trembled. "I will strive to serve you, Your Majesty."

"Then, woman, bring me water, and help me bathe—I must look my best. Hurry—do it now!"

A short time later Melesant had bathed, and with the

servant's help, she was trying to wriggle into the gown that she had not worn since before Cassandra was born.

"Merciful heavens!" she cried, boxing the poor maid's ears. "Have you no notion how to dress your queen?"

Betty tried not to show her pain. She dared not tell the queen that the gown had been made for a much smaller waist. "I will attempt it again, Your Majesty."

"Lace the corset tighter," Melesant commanded. "I'll wear this dress and no other."

"Yes, Majesty."

The servant pulled and tugged on the laces of the queen's gown, but they would not meet in the back no matter how hard she tried.

"Never mind," the queen said, her anger plainly showing in the harshness of her voice. "I'll wear my cape and no one will know it does not fit."

"Yes, Your Majesty," the woman said, handing her the long purple cape.

"You may go now, but in future I will not require your aid in dressing. You can report to the kitchen and see what tasks they can find to suit your ability."

Betty lowered her head, grateful to be leaving the queen's personal service. In truth she detested the Castilian woman, as did most of the islanders. "Yes, Your Majesty," she said, hurrying to the door and feeling like a bird that had been set free from its cage.

Melesant studied her reflection in dissatisfaction. It mattered not that she would not be the most beautiful woman at the banquet that night. She was the most powerful—Henry had seen to that!

19

While carts were being loaded with their belongings, Jilliana walked to a slight incline for a better view of the island.

She was glad when Ruyen joined her because she had many questions to ask him. Eleanor had taught her about the importance of farming, mills, and vineyards, yet the fields she could see were neglected, as were vineyards, where grape vines were spindly stumps dying on rotted trellises. Against the horizon, she could see a village, and she wondered at its condition.

"What do you think of Falcon Bruine, Jilliana?" Ruyen asked.

"I am quite puzzled," she told him earnestly. "It is not yet noon, yet I see no farmers working the fields. Why is that, Ruyen?"

There was fury in every nerve of his body. Trust Jilliana to point out the obvious to him. "Of that you will have to ask my mother," he said bitterly.

"Are those salt marshes?" she asked, nodding toward a wooded area where swamp-like trees dipped their branches downward.

"Yes, the water is stagnant and will not support growth. Add to that the fact that the wind blows almost ceaselessly, and it rains most every day, thus many of the plants rot in the ground. Do you notice how the trees bind to the westward side of the island?"

"Yes, I see."

"That's from the wind off the ocean, sometimes so strong it is dangerous to be at sea. Many small craft are dashed against the rocks."

"I also see beauty here," she said. There were fields of wild flowers of a deep purple hue, and dense forests and mountainous terrain in the distance.

"I am glad that you see the beauty of my home, Jilliana. The pity is that Falcon Bruine has every harsh element known to nature, and few of the good ones. Those who live here are a hardy lot, and would choose nowhere else in the world to make their home."

Jilliana shivered when she looked beyond the village to see the great towered castle that appeared to be rising out of the dark clouds that hovered above it.

By now the horses had been brought ashore and saddled. Ruyen took Jilliana's hand. "I believe we should leave now. Already the wind is starting to blow."

He helped her down the steep incline and then grasped her around the waist and placed her on her horse. When he avoided her eyes, she could tell that there was much on his mind that was troubling him. She suspected it was his mother, but it was none of her affair. If what Netta had said was true, and she was with child, she would soon leave this harsh island that seemed as black and unapproachable as its prince.

Humphrey came up beside Jilliana and she could see the worried frown on his face.

"It would seem that Princess Cassandra is frightened about something," Humphrey told her. "Do you know what is troubling her?"

Jilliana glanced over her shoulder to see Ruyen's sister huddled near the boat. "I do not know, Humphrey, but there is much here I do not understand. Help Princess Cassandra mount her horse, and I shall keep her beside me."

Soon they rode away from the coast and up the winding road that would take them through the village and ultimately to the castle.

"Cassandra," Jilliana said, trying to sound cheerful, "your island is most wondrous, and like nowhere I have ever seen. Are you not pleased to be home?"

Cassandra looked at her with sad eyes. "I wish we had never come back. I . . . "

Her voice trailed off as if she'd said too much and Jilliana did not press her further.

When they reached the village, Jilliana saw that the roads were heavily rutted and empty of people. The village looked inhospitable with the doors and shutters closed. Rather than ride through as Jilliana expected, Ruyen halted in the center of town and the rest of the party waited behind him—for what she was not quite sure.

Slowly, people began to emerge from their houses, the eyes of the women mistrustful, the men with surly twists to their lips. What saddened Jilliana was that the few children she saw had shrunken bellies, and their eyes were large with hunger. She turned to look inquiringly at Ruyen, and she could see that he was clearly distressed by the pitiable conditions.

Suddenly a woman broke away from the crowd and ran toward Ruyen. Her actions startled his mount, causing it to rear on its hind legs. It took a moment for Ruyen to bring the animal back under his control.

He glanced down at the woman, and recognized her as Cassandra's old wet nurse. "What has happened in my absence, Lorna?" he asked angrily.

The woman looked quickly about her as if she were

frightened. "'Tis the Castilians, Your Highness. Everyone is afraid of them."

His brows met in a scowl. "What Castilians?"

Lorna spat in the dust. "The ones your mother replaced your loyal knights with. They outnumber us and take pleasure in terrorizing us, and there is nothing we can do but hide. Thanks be to God that you have returned!" She nodded at the Talshamarians. "You have not enough men to fight them."

Other villagers came forward, gathering about Ruyen.

"If you will lead us, Highness, we'll band together to drive the Castilians into the sea," a young man said, his eyes burning fiercely.

"Help us, noble prince," a woman cried out in despair.

Jilliana felt tears sting her eyes as she witnessed Ruyen's shame because he could offer his people no hope.

There was grumbling among the men, and Ruyen held up his hand for silence. "Have no fear. I will not desert you, nor am I blind to your plight, but you must allow me time to find out what has happened."

"Take the crown!" a woman cried. "It rightly belongs to you, Prince Ruyen. We would sooner see you king, than your mother regent."

Jilliana was finding herself the object of curious stares. One older woman with gnarled hands came up to her and touched her gown reverently.

"I n'er touched anything so soft—be this silk?"

"Yes, Madame, 'tis silk," Jilliana answered.

The old woman stared up at the lovely face and the crown atop Jilliana's head, and it seemed as if she was looking at the sun. "Who be you, pretty one?"

Cassandra spoke to the old woman. "Meg, this is Prince Ruyen's wife, Queen Jilliana of Talshamar."

Surprise and then shock registered on the old woman's face. "I heard 'bout the legend of that little girl that was to be queen, but we thought she was dead."

"Not at all," Cassandra told her. "This is indeed the queen of Talshamar."

Other women were gathering around Jilliana, pushing Meg back. Jilliana smiled at each of them and received timid smiles in return.

Old Meg elbowed her way forward again. "I'd be right pleased to see the look on Lady Katharine's face when she sees you. You're prettier than she be, that's for certain."

Jilliana raised her head and met Ruyen's eyes before he spurred his horse forward. Would she be forced to meet the woman he loved now that she had come to Falcon Bruine? She hoped not.

Humphrey whispered to Jilliana. "It might be prudent to toss coins to the villagers as we did in England. It appears they could use them."

"See that it is done, Humphrey." She removed a silken scarf from her neck and handed it to him. "And give this to the woman called Meg."

Jilliana nudged her horse in the flanks and followed Ruyen. She could hear the sounds of glee as the people gathered the coins that Humphrey tossed to them.

When they began the upward climb, Jilliana could see why the high grounds had been chosen for the site of the castle. It would be easier to defend against intruders, and every part of the island must be visible from the windows.

Jilliana had a feeling of foreboding as they reached the outer wall of the gray tower. Two men-at-arms passed them through a wooden gate and they were inside the main compound. The heavy gates closing behind them sounded to her like the knell of doom.

The compound was drab and cheerless, and there was a heavy feeling of evil in the air. Jilliana looked at the tears in Cassandra's eyes and reached for the girl's hand, squeezing it comfortingly.

"Do not worry, I will be with you."

Cassandra nodded, choking back the tears. "Did you

see our people? They are starving. How could this have happened in so short a time?"

Jilliana had been wondering that herself. "I am sure your brother will see that all is made right."

Ruyen joined them, his eyes riveted on the man who had suddenly appeared on the steps in front of them. Escobar, with a stiff smile on his face and his fingers laced together, bowed, but not too low.

"Welcome home, Prince Ruyen and Princess Cassandra. Your mother awaits within."

Jilliana shivered as she looked into the man's black eyes and saw that he had no soul.

"And you must be the beauteous Queen Jilliana. Welcome, welcome," he said with an oily tongue.

Ruyen gave the man a dark look. "Did protocol die with my father, Escobar? Neither my wife nor I require a welcome from you."

Jilliana and Humphrey exchanged glances, each wondering what kind of place they had come to.

The man only smiled, his manner over-polite. "What can you mean, Your Highness?"

By now Ruyen had seen that most of the guards within the gates were indeed Castilians. "What I mean, Escobar," he said through gritted teeth, "is that you will refrain from addressing my wife unless I decide to present her to you, which I doubt that I shall."

The man seemed undaunted as he stared back at Ruyen. "Then you have not heard. I am your mother's minister. It was she who sent me to greet you in her name and welcome you and your party home."

"Minister?" Ruyen said, his tone a growl, then lowered his voice and leaned toward Escobar. "Is that what they call sycophants and bed warmers under my mother's rule?"

Jilliana gasped at Ruyen's cruel words and moved closer to Humphrey.

Escobar's eyes grew cold, but he dared not show his dislike for the royal prince—not just yet anyway. He remembered all too well the day when Prince Ruyen was a lad of eight and had burst into his mother's room to find them in an extremely compromising position.

Since that day, Prince Ruyen had not spoken a civil word to him—but that did not bother the Castilian overmuch.

"Your mother asked that you go directly to her. You will find her in the throne room."

In a move that surprised Jilliana, Ruyen came to her, lifted her to the ground and then offered his arm. "Shall we see my mother?"

She nodded and placed her hand on his arm. "What about my knights?"

Ruyen spoke to a man-at-arms, who stood at the top of the steps. "See that the knights of Talshamar are made comfortable. Place them in the west wing." He moved forward, taking Jilliana and Cassandra with him. "My lord," he said to Humphrey, "you will want to accompany us and be quartered near your queen."

As they entered the castle, Jilliana had the strongest urge to run to her horse and gallop away. She wanted to get back on board the ship and leave this place before it was too late—if it was not already.

So her fear wouldn't show, she raised her chin, stiffened her back and placed one foot in front of the other.

The inside of the castle was as cheerless as the outside. The walls were gray and damp, devoid of warmth, and no tapestries hung on the wall to keep the wind from seeping through the cracks. The mistress here had done nothing for the comfort of those who dwelled within.

When Ruyen felt her hand tremble, he gave her a warm smile. "You have faced worse. Did I not see you take on Henry Plantagenet and win?"

"If I had prevailed, as you claim, Ruyen, I would not now be where I am," she reminded him.

He did not answer, but she felt him stiffen at her words.

Down the corridor, Jilliana saw that a door was standing open, allowing the light from the room to spill across their path. She prepared herself for her first meeting with Ruyen's mother.

Lady Katharine sat with her back straight, her hands tightly clutching the arm of the chair. She was burning with anger that Ruyen had married this woman and was bringing her here.

Melesant watched Katharine's rage with expectancy. She had approved of Lady Katharine as Ruyen's wife because her father, Lord Highclere, was a wealthy landowner, and Katharine was his only child.

She neither liked nor disliked Katharine, nor had she considered her feelings when she invited her for Ruyen's homecoming.

"What do you know of the woman Ruyen married, Your Majesty?" Katharine asked sourly.

Melesant shrugged. "I know nothing, except that she is the queen of Talshamar. Possibly she is old. Probably she is ugly. I suggest that we wait until they arrive to draw any conclusions. I can tell you that Ruyen did not marry her by choice."

"I have tried to understand why he would betray me, but I do not. My father is most disturbed by what has occurred."

Melesant had decided that she would try to placate Lord Highclere, until she learned more about this marriage Henry had arranged. "I can tell you, Katharine, my dear, that Ruyen has agreed to remain with this woman only as long as it takes her to produce a child. The pope's emissary as much as assured both Ruyen and King Henry that the marriage will be annulled once that is accomplished. The temporary nature of this relationship should be uppermost in your mind when you greet Ruyen."

Katharine's face whitened. "Even if that were true, Your Majesty, the child would be next in line for the throne of Falcon Bruine. What about my children if Ruyen should marry me?"

"King Henry wrote me a long account describing the matter. He insists that if there is a child, it will be the heir to Talshamar, rather than Falcon Bruine."

Katharine loved Ruyen, and it tore at her heart to think of him making love to another woman, even if she happened to be older, and even if she were as plain as Queen Melesant had suggested she might be.

"I am sure you have nothing to worry about, my dear," Melesant said, easily reading Katharine's thoughts. "Ruyen's feelings for you will no doubt be unchanged."

"Perhaps it will be too late for Ruyen to make amends," Katharine said sulkily. "My father was incensed about the marriage and has plans to send me to England." She looked teary-eyed. "It would be too humiliating for me to remain on Falcon Bruine with everyone knowing Ruyen passed me over for another woman."

Melesant was alarmed because she had not expected Lord Highclere to react to Ruyen's marriage with his pride instead of his head. "I will speak to your father, and convince him that no shame attaches to you. I can still see a future for you and my son, but not if you leave. Perhaps you do not realize that if Ruyen had not married this Talshamarian, he would now be dead."

The look Katharine gave Melesant as much as said she would rather see him dead than married to someone else.

There was the sound of voices at the door, and Melesant and Katharine turned in that direction.

Katharine rose, ready to face the woman who had taken Ruyen from her.

Melesant nodded toward the door that connected the throne room with a small chamber. "Wait in that room until I send for you. I will want to greet my children alone."

Katharine would rather have remained, but she did as she was told. No one disobeyed Queen Melesant.

Melesant waited with anticipation, the blood coursing through her veins. Ruyen was a worthy opponent, and she would savor his final defeat. He would want his father's throne—but it was hers, and she would not give it up for anyone, not even her own son.

20

Jilliana thought it would be best to allow Ruyen and Cassandra to greet their mother alone, so she remained in the corridor with Humphrey and Netta. When she noticed that Humphrey's hand rested on the hilt of his sword, she realized that he, too, was mistrustful of Queen Melesant.

Melesant watched her son and daughter advance into the room. She smiled, holding out her arms. "At last, the family is reunited."

Neither the brother nor sister went to her outstretched arms; instead they halted just inside the door.

"Not quite all, Mother. Our father is not here," Ruyen reminded her in a cold voice.

Melesant nodded and tried to look forlorn. "'Tis a pity. We shall all miss him."

"I am sure you grieve for him every day, Mother," Ruyen said without feeling.

Melesant decided to ignore Ruyen's sharp barbs, so she turned her attention to her daughter. Cassandra had always been so plain, with a thin, shapeless body and nothing remarkable about her. Now, however, she had filled out and her face was quite pretty. Melesant's first thought was that she might find a favorable marriage for the girl without having to disburse a large dowry.

"Cassandra, dearest child, come to me."

Reluctantly, the girl moved toward her mother, her steps measured, her eyes downcast. When she was near enough, she placed a quick kiss on the cool cheek that was offered her.

"Sweet daughter, how I have missed you."

Ruyen still stood near the door. "So much so that you allowed her to be taken by Henry's men and placed in the Tower, Mother? Cassandra and I were in prison and under the sentence of death. What we did not understand was why you remained free."

Melesant looked incensed. "How dare you insinuate that I would have allowed Henry to execute my own blood! If I had not bargained with him, I would surely have been locked in the Tower with you, and what purpose would that have served?"

"I did not see you standing beside us pleading for our lives the day we were to die. Were you in England that day, Mother?"

"Ruyen, you know I was not. But Escobar was there. He would have acted on my behalf."

Ruyen threw back his head and laughed. "Oh yes, Escobar, confidant of kings, wielder of power—" He was no longer laughing and his stomach churned with disgust. "Castilian lapdog. Escobar had no power to save anyone that day, Mother, nor did you. There was only one person who could save me, and she did so by becoming my wife."

Mother and son stared into each other's eyes, so much left unsaid. But the truth burned in Ruyen's eyes, and Melesant turned away from his accusing gaze.

Ruyen took Jilliana's reluctant hand and brought her into the room. "Mother, may I present to you my wife, the queen of Talshamar. Jilliana, this is my mother, the regent of Falcon Bruine."

Melesant realized that Ruyen had just elevated his wife above her by emphasizing that she was only a regent, while Jilliana was a ruling monarch.

But as always, Melesant was quick to hide her anger. "My dear," she said, going forward to greet Jilliana, "how will I ever be able to express my gratitude to you for the lives of my children?"

Jilliana leveled her chin. "There is no need, Queen Melesant. I do not expect gratitude for what I did."

Melesant allowed her eyes to move up and down her son's wife. Why had she thought Queen Jilliana would be an older woman? It was apparent that she was younger than Ruyen, younger even than Katharine. And what was worse, she was a beauty!

Her skin was creamy and flawless, her eyes an unusual shade of blue. She was haughty and regal, looking very much like a queen. Burning with envy, Melesant looked at the purple silk gown adorned with diamonds and pearls. The crown that sat atop Jilliana's white headdress was a golden circle set with diamonds and the biggest rubies Melesant had ever seen.

Melesant knew nothing of Talshamar. She had merely dismissed it as some obscure little kingdom, never imagining that it might possess great wealth. She must not be too hasty in condemning Ruyen's marriage.

Jilliana had been watching Queen Melesant. With her dark skin and fine features she might be considered pretty, but there was something about her that was disconcerting—an insincere note in her voice, a condescending manner that set Jilliana's teeth on edge. Her eyes were a deep brown like Ruyen's, but there the comparison ended. Ruyen's eyes were warm with feelings and often came alive with hidden passions, while his mother's were cold, mistrustful, and cunning.

"You are welcome at Falcon Bruine, Queen Jilliana." Melesant put her cold hand on her daughter-in-law's shoulder. "Or might I call you Jilliana?"

"Please do. And may I present to you my most honored palatine, Lord Baldridge."

Melesant turned to the red-headed giant who stood protectively beside Jilliana. As always, when she was near a man, her eyes sparkled and her smile was girlish. "I have never heard the term, palatine. What does it mean?"

Jilliana spoke. "Palatine has great significance in Talshamar. It means trusted adviser and true friend."

"Welcome, Lord Baldridge," Melesant purred. "We shall make certain that you are made comfortable. Shall I have a servant show you to your quarters?"

Humphrey shook his head. "Thank you, no. I remain with my queen until she dismisses me."

Melesant had not been prepared for the events that were unfolding before her. Perhaps it was not such a bad thing that Ruyen had married into the Talshamarian royal family.

At that moment, the connecting door off the throne room opened, and Ruyen watched in surprise as Katharine entered in a flurry of yellow silk. There was a pout on her lips, and her eyes stabbed into his accusingly.

When he did not approach her, she spoke in a hurt voice: "Ruyen, have you no welcome for me?"

Ruyen stood undecided between the two women, one his legal wife, and the other his chosen betrothed. At last, he moved to Katharine and took her offered hand.

"I had not expected you to be here," he said, noting the smug smile on his mother's face.

"And I," Katharine said snippily, "did not expect you to return with a wife."

She turned angry eyes on the woman who was the object of her hatred, but blinked in astonishment when she saw the lovely Talshamarian queen, who stood before her unflinchingly, as if to notice her would be beneath her dignity.

Jilliana had not been prepared for the hurt that took possession of her. However, she would not allow these people to see how she felt. "Queen Melesant, would you allow someone to show me to my quarters? I find I am very weary."

Cassandra rushed forward, taking Jilliana's hand and sending poisonous looks at Katharine. "I'll take you," she said, quickly leading Jilliana out of the room, but not before casting her brother an angry glare.

Ruyen realized that he still held Katharine's hand and he dropped it, not knowing what else to do. Why did he feel as if he had done something wrong?

"What an uppity bit of baggage," Katharine said. "How rude, not to wait to be introduced to me."

Melesant chuckled. "What a tangle. It cannot be pleasant for you, Ruyen, having to explain your betrothed to your wife. Perhaps you would like me to talk to Jilliana."

"Do you think that I am not aware of what you are trying to do? Must you always manipulate people without a care for their feelings?"

Katharine decided to play on his sympathy. "To be snubbed by the woman who has everything I wanted—you especially. It is difficult to bear."

Ruyen took pity on Katharine, whom his mother had used, to what end he could not guess. "I will have someone take you home. It cannot be pleasant for you here."

"Why did you do this, Ruyen?" Katharine demanded.

"We will talk another time." He turned to his mother. "You will both excuse me."

Katharine wanted to protest, but Melesant waved her to silence.

"I have invited Katharine and her father to sup with us. At that time, the two of you can talk. I shall be very discreet and place you beside each other at the table."

Ruyen could feel trouble in the air. No man should have three women who wanted to control his life.

"If you will both excuse me, I have matters that need my attention. You and I will speak later, Mother. There are many questions I still want answered."

As he left the room, Melesant's laughter followed him. "Think you he will not squirm tonight when he sits beside you under the watchful eye of his wife?"

"I wanted to scratch her eyes out. Who does she think she is to—"

"She, my dear," Melesant interrupted, "is a queen. You might want to remember that."

"I detest her."

"I do not think she holds you in high regard either. This evening should prove to be interesting."

"She was by far too haughty."

"As suits her station."

"She is not beautiful."

"No," Melesant said tauntingly, "she is more than beautiful. And from the looks of her jewels, wealthy as well. I must find out more about Talshamar and its queen."

"Ruyen has changed. He was . . . distant. I fear he loves that woman. How could he when he pledged his heart to me?"

Katharine's complaints were beginning to bore Melesant, but she decided not to alienate her just yet. She would play one woman against the other, and both of them against Ruyen, and her son would have no time to confront her.

"I am sure he still loves you, my dear, and who wouldn't?" A clever scheme was forming in her mind and she smiled as she spoke. "I would ask that you extend an invitation to that handsome cousin of yours. I will sit him next to Ruyen's wife. Perhaps he can entertain her."

"James will be pleased to attend. He has been curious about Ruyen's . . . wife."

"As I recall half the women on the island are enamored with him."

"He takes it as his due, Your Majesty."

"You have a handsome family, my dear. I will be glad to have you all grace my table tonight."

Katharine looked meditative. "I shall wear my most beautiful gown, the blue one. And I shall not cover my head. Ruyen always liked my hair. Yes, that is what I'll do."

Melesant watched the foolish woman bow and rush through the door. Did she really believe that Ruyen would notice her gown? All women were simpletons where men were concerned.

But not Melesant. She had decided long ago that no man would ever hold sway over her, and no man ever had—not her husband, and not any of the many lovers who had filled her bed but left her heart stone-cold.

She thought of Jilliana's palatine. He was so tall, muscled, a powerful man, but a bit too proud. It had been apparent that he disliked her. No matter. She would charm him and he would soon come to her at night when she sent for him.

At that moment, Jilliana was keeping a tight hold on her anger. It was obvious that Ruyen's mother had arranged for Katharine Highclere to be present today. She had seen how quickly Ruyen had rushed to the woman. Were they together now? Was he explaining to her how he had been forced to marry merely to save his life?

Netta was unpacking a trunk, and she watched the queen move absently about the chamber. It was a small room, devoid of warmth or comfort. The two wooden chairs had no cushions, and the bed was lumpy and smelled as if it had not been aired in a long time.

Netta dusted off one of the chairs before draping clothing across the back of it. "The servants here are malingering in their duties," she remarked huffily. "When I finish unpacking, I will remove the musty-smelling linens and tell the housekeeper that you will require clean ones."

"I feel as if I am in a cage with no escape, Netta. How is it that Queen Melesant takes no pride in her home, and provides no comfort for her guests? I believe she meant me to be uncomfortable. I have a feeling everything she does is done for a reason."

"I do not know of such things. Shall I lay out the green for tonight, Your Majesty?"

"No. I have no wish to dine with these people. I shall keep to my room. I want nothing better than to leave this horrid place as soon as possible."

"'Tis a cold, uninviting castle, Your Majesty. It makes me long even more for Talshamar."

"Fear not. The moment I know that I am with child, we will go home."

Netta nodded with satisfaction. "Shall I send word that you will be dining in your chamber?"

"Yes."

Before Netta reached the door, Jilliana called out, "Wait! I shall not cower in this room like a frightened rabbit. And I will not wear the green, but the white and gold of Talshamar, and all the trappings that go with it."

Netta smiled. "Aye, Your Majesty, you will dazzle them all."

21

Ruyen spent the rest of the day seeking out the knights who had accompanied him on the ill-fated campaign in England. This was not an easy task, since many of them had gone into hiding.

When at last some of them came before him, they were subdued and unwilling to talk, but after a while, he learned more about what his mother was doing to Falcon Bruine.

They spoke of a shortage of food, of unfair taxes being imposed on the people and about the Castilians who now guarded the castle. Reluctantly, one of the men admitted to Ruyen that his lands had been confiscated on Queen Melesant's orders. Ruyen also learned that many of the knights who had been loyal to his father had been executed as traitors.

Anger coiled within him because he had no army to send against his mother and her Castilians.

"Believe that I shall do all within my power to free this country of oppression," he told his loyal knights.

"Will you then take up our cause against your own mother?"

Ruyen's eyes blazed with an inner fire. There was no doubt in his mind where his loyalties lay. He would not allow anyone, not even his mother, to enslave his island.

"Be assured that I will go against anyone who brings harm to my people. But I am powerless to do anything at this time. Pass the word to all those who are loyal to be watchful, for when the moment is at hand, I shall surely call upon them to help defend Falcon Bruine."

There was guarded relief on the faces of his knights.

"I was sure when I heard that you had returned, Your Highness, that you would help us," one of them, Sir Donnely, cried.

"Keep the faith," Ruyen told them. "I will find a way to wrest this isle from all oppressors."

Angrily, he returned to the castle. However, when he sought his mother, he was told that she was away and was not expected until the evening.

Ruyen could not curb his impatience. He would confront his mother and demand that she step down and send her Castilians away. Falcon Bruine was in desperate need of leadership. His mother must be aware of the conditions in the village. He would do whatever was necessary to rectify the situation—or die in the attempt.

He went in search of Escobar and found him in the library bent over a desk. Slamming the door shut, he advanced on the man. "There is something I want you to do for me. Take whatever men are necessary and gather what sheep you can from the east farm. Amass fifty baskets of corn and nine carcasses of beef and take them directly to the village."

Escobar smiled smugly, knowing that the prince had no authority. "I dare not implement such an undertaking without Her Majesty's permission. You will have to speak to her, Your Highness."

Ruyen grabbed the little man by the doublet and yanked him so hard, he came sprawling across the desk.

"You will do as I say, and do it now, or you will find your throat slit from ear to ear. Your belly is full, but my villagers are hungry. I will not suffer them to wait until it pleases my mother. Do you understand me?"

"Yes . . . Highness," Escobar sputtered, "I will see to it at once. But you must tell your mother that this thing was done on your orders."

Ruyen flung Escobar back and he rolled across the desk and tumbled to the floor. Escobar was slow to rise and his eyes were wide with fright. "Your mother will not allow you to treat me with such disrespect. I am her chief adviser."

"You are a fool if you do not know that you are merely her toy," Ruyen said with contempt. "She uses you, nothing more. I wonder how my father tolerated you all those years. I better understand why he spent little time on the island."

Escobar had reached the doorway and was looking in the direction of the queen's study.

"Do not think you can go running to my mother, Escobar. Not until you have taken food to the village. I shall have men watching you to make certain that you do exactly what I have ordered." Ruyen walked toward him. "Do it now!"

"Yes, Highness—at once." The man pressed his body against the wall, sliding through the open doorway, trying to keep distance between himself and Ruyen.

Ruyen clamped his jaw shut, suppressing the urge to strike the craven little man. He had known for years that Escobar was his mother's lover—he was certain that his father had known it too.

He moved to the window and watched Escobar hurrying past the herb garden and down the path to the steward's cottage. The people of the village would have food before nightfall.

*   *   *

Ruyen was not to see his mother until the guests began gathering for the banquet. When he entered the room, he went directly to her, hardly able to mask his fury.

He nodded quickly to Katharine's father, acknowledging his presence, and then turned to his mother. "I want to talk to you."

The tension between mother and son made Lord Highclere uncomfortable, and realizing this, Melesant gave the man a charming smile while she patted Ruyen's arm.

"Forgive my son, my lord. You know that he has been away and we have much to discuss." She smiled at Ruyen. "But it will have to wait until our guests have gone—or perhaps tomorrow would be better."

"I think it will be sooner than that. There is much to settle between us, Mother."

Melesant felt sudden pride in her only son. He would make a worthy adversary, but she would win in the end. She had only to find the means to keep him under control—which she would do.

Escobar entered the room, and Melesant smiled while Ruyen scowled.

"Look, ye there, Mother," Ruyen said in a contemptuous voice, "your toad rushes to you. Mayhap he has something of interest to relate to you. I believe you will want to talk to me after you have spoken to him." Then Ruyen walked away in disgust.

Queen Melesant turned to Katharine's father. "Forgive my foolish son his rudeness, my lord. Like his father, Ruyen has no notion that it takes delicacy and diplomacy to rule."

Lord Highclere was a heavy man, in his late fifties. His first wife had died childless and he had married a much younger woman, who had given him his only offspring, Katharine. He spoiled and indulged his daughter and he was angered that the prince had married another while promised to his beautiful Katharine, but he did not say so to the queen.

"His Highness is fortunate that he has you to take that responsibility from his shoulders," Lord Highclere stated. "It was a wise move when King Henry made you regent."

Melesant glared at Escobar as he bowed before her, interrupting her conversation. "Majesty, might I speak to you on a matter of some import?"

Her eyes were chilling. "Anything you have to say will keep 'til the morrow."

"But, Majesty, it concerns your son. He—"

Her voice was hard. "Not now, Escobar!"

Ruyen was right, Melesant thought, Escobar was a toad. She ignored him and turned her attention back to Lord Highclere.

"As I was saying," she continued, "King Henry thinks he can control me, but he is mistaken. Know you why he made me regent?"

"Because you are wise in all things," Escobar clamored for all to hear.

Melesant sent the little man a poisonous look. "I was speaking to Lord Highclere." With cool assurance, she directed her speech to her guest. "Henry is accustomed to pitting his skills against his own sons, who are a rebellious lot. He thinks to keep Falcon Bruine in tumult and under his wide reach by causing trouble between my son and me. But he shall not succeed. Ruyen will not take the rule from my grasp, and neither shall I relinquish it to him."

Ruyen was making his way out the door when he almost bumped into Katharine. He steadied her with his hand and she smiled coyly up at him.

"Oh, Ruyen." She raised teary eyes to him. "I have missed you so terribly, and I am sorry for the way I acted this morning. It was all such a shock, and I will admit that I was angry with you for a time, but your mother has convinced me that you did not marry by choice."

His mind was still on the villagers and their plight. "I am sorry, Katharine, what were you saying?"

She placed her hand on his shoulder, her heart beating at the touch. "Knowing blue is your favorite color, I wore this gown just for you tonight."

"You look lovely, Katharine," he said absently.

"I also wore my hair down for you."

"Ah, yes, very pretty."

Jilliana and Humphrey descended the narrow, twisting steps behind the servant who led them to the room where everyone had gathered. Cassandra had been watching for them and she came forward, slipping her hand into Jilliana's.

"I fear this evening will have to be endured. Do you mind that Katharine was invited?"

Jilliana did mind, but she could not admit it even to herself. "She belongs here, I do not," she said at last, looking across the room at the beauty who seemed to have captured Ruyen's attention.

Jilliana had to admit that Katharine was beautiful. Her unbound hair fell to her waist and her blue gown was elaborately adorned with seed pearls. She was petite, had golden hair and a rosy complexion—just the kind of beauty that men preferred. At that moment, Jilliana despised her own dark hair and wished she was not so tall. Why did she feel so awkward and unattractive?

Every eye turned to Jilliana, who stood motionless in the archway. Humphrey, who knew her so well, guessed that she was ill at ease, although no one could tell it by looking at her. She was dazzling in white silk with gold trim. Her jeweled crown sparkled in the soft candlelight. She could not know that she presented a picture of grace and beauty that dazzled all those who looked upon her.

Cassandra squeezed Jilliana's hand. "Do not take to heart anything my mother or Katharine might say. They are people who are not happy unless they can make others feel lowly."

Jilliana realized that Cassandra was speaking from her own past hurts. The young girl must have been deeply wounded, and yet, she had a kind and loving nature. Why did her own mother not recognize Cassandra's wonderful character and treasure her?

Jilliana drew Ruyen's reluctant yet admiring gaze. He did not even feel Katharine's grip tighten possessively on his arm.

Katharine's voice was laced with malice when she spoke. "She would not be so pretty if the artificial paints were stripped from her face." Then she said in a loud voice that carried above the din. "I use neither rouge nor paint on my face. I need no beauty that can be put on in the morning and laid aside at night."

Ruyen frowned, stepping away from her. Katharine suddenly seemed not only silly, but vindictive as well, characteristics he had never been aware of before tonight. He still loved her, but she had changed—or was he the one who had changed? His eyes moved over Jilliana, who was talking to his sister. She was witty and intelligent, and could hold a man's interest not only by her beauty but with her knowledge as well. And he had been close enough to her to know that she wore no paint on her face, as Katharine had suggested.

Humphrey watched with silent fury. His queen was not being offered the homage she deserved. As of yet, no one save Cassandra had acknowledged her presence in the room.

Ruyen was on his way to his wife when he saw Katharine's cousin, Sir James, approach her. The young gentleman placed his hand on his heart and swept a deep bow.

Cassandra smiled at the young gallant. "Your Majesty, may I present Sir James Highclere, Katharine's cousin. Watch out for him, for he scoffs at life and views everything with humor. I look upon him as a friend, although he is something of a rogue."

Sir James's eyes burned with the brightness of precious stones. "Pay little heed to this child," he said with affection. "She is but a minx and would have you believe I have little principle, when the opposite is true."

Jilliana could not keep from laughing at the young man. He was nothing like his cousin.

"Indeed, Sir James," she said with a smile as she offered him her hand and allowed him to raise it to his lips. "I know of no better recommendation than to be a friend of Princess Cassandra's."

At that moment Queen Melesant brought Lord Highclere to Jilliana and presented him to her, thus giving Ruyen no opportunity to approach her.

"Shall we dine?" Melesant asked, nodding to a servant who had just appeared in the doorway.

Melesant offered her hand to Humphrey. "I have placed you on my right. Will you be my escort, Lord Baldridge?"

He bowed to her. "It would be my pleasure," he said, more to be courtly than from any satisfaction he felt at being singled out for her favor. He suspected that she would ply him with questions in an attempt to learn about Queen Jilliana and Talshamar.

The dining hall was well lit. Several squires served the meal, and Jilliana found it surprisingly delicious. One course followed another in rapid succession. The food was served on trenchers and wine in silver goblets.

Jilliana refused to look at Ruyen, who had been placed beside Katharine. She found it painful to see him so attentive to the woman who possessed his heart. Was he confessing his undying love to her and assuring her that the marriage was not of his choosing?

Jilliana was seated beside Sir James and she soon found herself being drawn into conversation with him and Cassandra.

"What do you think of our island, Your Majesty," Sir James asked.

"I . . . find it beautiful."

"Do not be fooled by its beauty. We have many obstacles that must be overcome before it can be a paradise."

Jilliana was interested in his ideas. "What obstacles, Sir James?"

"You would think that being an island, we would be blessed with rain, but that is not so. We have three great rivers, but they reach only the center of the island, leaving the farmers on the outer regions without water to grow their crops."

Jilliana took a sip of wine and then frowned in thoughtfulness. "I believe the answer to your problems would be aqueducts. The Castilians have mastered the technique quite well, and I am surprised Queen Melesant has not implemented this type of irrigation."

"I had not heard of this. As you might have been told, we are isolated from the rest of the world. Because of the dangerous crosswinds, few ships come to our shores—" He lowered his voice. "Besides, the Castilians that guard the castle are not a learned lot."

"As it was explained to me," Jilliana said, "the river headwaters are harnessed and diverted through a rock base. Since the outlet is much lower than the water source, gravity carries the water to its destination."

Sir James smiled widely. "Simple, yet I wonder that we have not thought of it. I must discuss your ideas with Prince Ruyen after dinner. Perhaps we can get more information and implement the aqueducts on our island."

Jilliana raised her eyes and found Ruyen glaring at her. Did he detest her so much that he would shame her for all to see?

She felt suddenly weary. The only people she liked on this island were Cassandra and Sir James. She wanted more than ever to leave, and perhaps she would soon.

Melesant was at her most charming with Humphrey.

She offered him special tidbits from her own plate and flirted with him outrageously.

"Tell me about your queen," she said slyly. "Is she popular in Talshamar?"

"I know of no one there who would not gladly die for her," Humphrey said. "We only await the day when she returns home to rule her people."

"I had worried when I heard about this marriage that Ruyen had been yoked to some poverty-stricken monarch who would be a drain on our treasury. If her jewels are any indication, Talshamar must be prosperous."

"My queen has no need of anything from Falcon Bruine," he said, choosing his words carefully.

"That is not quite true, Lord Baldridge, she wants an heir from my son." She placed her clawlike hand on his arm. "Is it true that the Talshamarians actually prefer a female ruler to a male?"

Again he chose his words carefully. He had a feeling that this woman never asked meaningless questions. He would not be drawn into her game, however, and would tell her as little as possible. "Our strongest rulers have been women. Queen Jilliana's mother was a great example of that."

"Ah, yes, but she died, did she not? Foolish for her not to cooperate with Henry."

"Foolish, Your Majesty? We in Talshamar think of her rather as a queen who placed the good of the people above all else."

"Yes, but she is still dead. What good can that do for Talshamar?"

"I wonder," Humphrey said, gauging his words carefully so that they would not appear to be an insult, "how many queens could be so revered after death as Queen Phelisiana."

Melesant became silent as she pondered his words. When one was dead, one would not care whether they were hated or adored.

"Is it true," she said at last, "that Talshamar is a wealthy realm?"

"Our children play happily and our people go to bed at night with a full belly," Humphrey told her.

"How can this be when Talshamar has been without a ruling sovereign since the death of Queen Phelisiana? I know not who was the steward in your young queen's absence."

"Before her death, Queen Phelisiana appointed a man of the Holy Church, whom she trusted above all others to oversee Talshamar until Queen Jilliana returned."

"Rome has been known to dip its hands indiscriminately into many treasure houses," Melesant said cynically.

"Queen Phelisiana chose her man well, and thanks be to God, under his stewardship, Talshamar has prospered."

Melesant's eyes glazed over with greed. She must find a way to control Jilliana. She glanced down the table at the diamond crown that sat atop the head of her son's wife, its brilliance sending prisms of light flashing across the walls.

Melesant's hand tightened on her wine glass. She would not be happy until that crown sat atop her own head.

22

After dinner, Jilliana watched Katharine hang on to Ruyen's arm, and she felt humiliated by his disregard of her feelings. She could not blame Lady Katharine for the poisonous looks she cast her way, but she did blame Ruyen.

She looked at Ruyen, his dark head bent to hear something Lady Katharine was saying to him. How had he explained their marriage to his lady love? Whatever he had said seemed to have appeased Katharine.

After conversing for a time with Sir James and Cassandra, Jilliana took leave of Ruyen's mother and left the room as quickly as she could.

Katharine watched her departure enviously. "Her gowns are quite nice, Ruyen. When a woman has a large nose, she must dress grandly to draw attention away from that defect. I believe her eyes are uncommonly dull, too, do you not think so?"

Ruyen looked down at Katharine, wondering what she was talking about. Jilliana's nose large? He had never thought so. He saw expectancy in Katharine's eyes and knew he was expected to make a comment.

"She dresses as a queen." He took her hand and raised it to his lips. "Now if you will excuse me, I have something that requires my attention."

Katharine's voice was hard. "You have not missed me at all. You are going to her?"

He had not seen Katharine jealous before, and he blamed himself for bringing out such an emotion in her. His voice was kind when he spoke to her. "No, Katharine, I am not. I am going into the village."

On his way out, Ruyen encountered his mother.

"Your little queen is quite lovely. I would like to know her better, yet it has not escaped my notice that she seems distrustful of me."

His words were cynical. "Why ever can that be, Mother? Perhaps she has felt my distrust for you and taken it as her own."

"Do not be bitter, Ruyen, it does no one any good. I know how you are feeling."

"You know nothing about me, Mother."

Melesant decided she must win her son's trust. She laid her hand on his. "Would you like me to dismiss the guests so we can have our talk now?"

He moved his hand away from hers. "Now is not a good time for me."

She stared after him as he moved out the door. He truly disliked her, and she wondered why she cared—but she did.

While Netta was helping her undress, Jilliana was becoming more annoyed by the moment. Ruyen had not spoken to her all evening, and the others must have noticed. Perhaps he had ignored her to placate Katharine, but whatever the reason, she felt the insult to the core of her heart.

"What kind of people are these, Netta, that they speak in riddles and hidden innuendos, never saying what they mean, and leaving one to puzzle on their purpose?"

"I have found the servants nervous and watchful of every word they speak. I have heard enough to know that they are fearful of being overheard by the spies who have been planted among them by that man called Escobar."

"We must be very careful, Netta. I trust no one here save Princess Cassandra. That child is like a rose growing on a thorn bush, an innocent living among vipers."

They both lapsed into silence while Netta brushed Jilliana's hair.

Jilliana could not keep her mind from straying to Ruyen. That he did not like his mother was easy to see, but was he so different from her?

At that moment, in another part of the castle, Humphrey followed a maidservant up a second flight of stairs, and down a long, dimly lit corridor. The servant had come to his chamber with a message that Queen Melesant desired his presence. He had somehow expected her to send for him, but he did not think it would be so soon.

The servant pushed open a door, bobbed a curtsy and hastily left. He entered the room with caution. Queen Melesant came forward with a glowing smile on her face. Her formal gown had been replaced by a dressing robe, and her dark hair hung loosely about her shoulders.

"I am glad you came, Lord Baldridge. I have many questions to ask of you, and we will not be interrupted here."

The chamber was unlike the rest of the castle. There was a rug on the floor and tapestries graced the walls. There was a huge bed with purple hangings and bed covering. "If this is your bedchamber, Madame, it would be best if I left. I would not like to cause gossip."

She sauntered up to him, her eyes like those of a feline, and she almost purred. "This is not my bedchamber. Only a few are allowed in this room. It is where I can be alone from prying eyes and no one ever comes here without invitation. If you are concerned about the servant who brought you to me, she is very discreet."

"It is late, Madame, and I am weary. Perhaps we can have this conversation on the morrow."

Melesant gave a throaty laugh. "I believe you are afraid of me, Humphrey. I have wondered all day what it would feel like to be crushed in those powerful arms of yours. You are a striking man."

She reached out and touched his cheek, and he took several steps backward.

"Why, my dear sir, you *are* frightened of me."

"Not frightened, Madame. I know you are just recently widowed, and as for myself, I have a wife."

"Your wife will never know, and if my husband were alive, I doubt he would care."

Humphrey stared into her eyes. "You are assuming, Madame, that I would want what you offer. I don't."

She could hardly believe that he was uninterested in her. No man had ever turned away from her when she wanted him—no man until now.

Perhaps he misunderstood her. She walked to him, allowing the sleeve of her dressing gown to fall off her shoulder and reveal her breasts. Her arms slid around his neck, and she pressed her cheek to his.

"It could be so good between us. I know it could."

He took her wrists and held them in a strong grip. "You will excuse me if I decline your offer, Madame. I have not to this day been faithless to my wife, and I will not start with you."

She hissed and jerked her hands free. Now that she was angry, she lapsed into a heavy Castilian accent. "Run away like a frightened little rabbit. I thought you were a man, but you're not! You'll be sorry for this."

"Good night, Madame." Humphrey left, closing the

door behind him, but he could hear the obscenities she hurled at him as he moved down the corridor. This woman was dangerous, and he must warn Jilliana.

Melesant lay beneath Escobar, her anger at being rejected by Humphrey driving her into a fervid frenzy. She rolled on top, straddled him and rode the wave of passion.

She smiled in satisfaction as Escobar groaned, pressing her tighter against him.

"Say no other woman can satisfy you as I," she demanded, running her tongue along the lobe of his ear.

"No one can!" he cried.

"You will never leave me," she said, biting his lip until she drew blood.

"Never."

When the act was completed, she felt strangely empty and unfulfilled. Escobar could no longer give her what she wanted. She would have to look elsewhere for a lover.

"I am weary tonight. Seek your rest in your own bed," she said, rolling to her side.

"Will you not want me again during the night?"

"I told you to go! Leave me in peace."

He moved off the bed and quietly dressed, all the while watching her rigid back.

"Are you angry about the food I distributed to the villagers?"

She turned over and sat up, her eyes piercing pinpoints. "You did what!"

"I tried to tell you earlier. I . . . thought . . . you knew—your son bade me take food and livestock to the villagers. He threatened to kill me if I went to you or if I did not do as he asked."

Melesant stared at him, but she was thinking of her son. There was so much anger eating away at Ruyen that it might become difficult for her to control him.

"Who are you more afraid of, my son or me?"

Escobar shivered. "This afternoon, I knew I faced death."

Melesant surprised him with her laughter. "So it begins. I had thought it would take longer."

He looked puzzled. "What begins?"

"My son's defiance. He is like me, afraid of nothing," she said with pride. "He will test my limits, but he will not win."

"You are not angry with me?"

She looked at him as if he were nothing. "I should be, but I'm not. You were merely the instrument my son used to strike the first blow at me."

"The villagers knew the food came from him. He is buying their loyalty."

She arched her brow at him. "And you helped him. You who have professed your lasting loyalty to me."

He backed toward the door. "I . . . had not thought of that. I will always stand beside you. Had I known—"

"This is not about you, Escobar. It is a battle that has been building between my son and myself for many years. You see, my son does not admire his mother, and he does not approve of you. He will bring me down if he is able." She gave Escobar a sly look. "And if I were you, I would avoid him whenever possible."

"I heard many rumblings among the people. It seems that food in their bellies makes them bold. They say Prince Ruyen is the rightful ruler. You must be careful, for they have no love for you."

Melesant arched her breasts toward him and pulled the covers aside incitingly. "And you will protect me from all my enemies, will you not, my brave champion? You will sacrifice your life for me?"

He came to her eagerly. "Yes, I shall. I would die in your stead, but I would rather live for you."

She ran her hand down her naked body, toying with him as a cat would toy with a mouse. "You still want me."

Escobar moved toward her eagerly. To him she had always been beautiful. He did not see the wrinkles or the sagging skin or even the gray in her dark hair. She was a queen, and when he was with her, he was touched by her magnificence.

Melesant threw back her head and laughed, pointing toward the door. "Well, I do not want you. After this night, you will never come to my bed again."

He shook his head, backing to the door. He had always feared the day she would tire of him, and that day had come at last.

"Leave!" she cried. "I cannot abide the sight of you. Go at once!"

He did not remember going through the door, nor did he recall going down the steps and out the side door to stand beneath the stars.

"No." He moaned, "No. I have waited too long for you to be free so we can always be together. No one can have you save me . . . no one."

23

Jilliana had been on Falcon Bruine for three days. In that time she had seen little of Ruyen. Most often he was away from the castle, and he rarely had his meals with the family.

Tonight he had dined with them, but Jilliana had excused herself directly afterward and gone to her chamber. She'd had no wish to be drawn into one of the family's sinister conversations. Also, she had not wanted to give Ruyen another opportunity to slight her before the others.

She tossed and turned on the lumpy bed, unable to sleep. Finally, with a heavy sigh, she slipped out of bed and moved across the room to stand at the window. Throwing wide the shutters, she allowed a cool breeze to fan her face.

A full moon hung in the sky like a huge ball, illuminating the countryside and allowing her to see all the way to the ocean. The island was lovely in the silvery moonlight, but in the light of day, there were flaws. And there was something evil here too; she could feel it in the very depths of her soul.

She was startled when she heard someone knock on her door. She thought it might be Netta returning, so she invited her in. However, the silhouette was a man's and she knew it would be Ruyen.

"You are not in bed," he said, stating the obvious.

"I could not sleep."

When he moved closer to Jilliana, her whole body seemed to be washed in moonbeams. He looked at the pert little nose that Katharine had criticized—it was perfect, like the rest of her.

"You left rather soon after dining, Jilliana."

"I was weary."

"Weary of the company?" His tone was biting. "Does the queen tire so easily of us island folk?"

She blinked at his stinging words. "I tire of pretense, rudeness, and unkindness."

He was standing closer to her now and she could feel his breath on her cheek.

"The other night I observed that you were entertained by James. You appeared to be engrossed in every word he spoke to you," Ruyen said accusingly.

She felt a sudden rush of elation—Ruyen was jealous! She felt no need to tell him that their major topic of conversation had been irrigation.

"It is true that I found Sir James to be pleasant company. He has many sides to him. He can be witty and amusing, but he has his serious side as well. Do you not think so?"

"James does not often cross my mind. I have never liked him overmuch."

"Pity, he speaks highly of you." Now she raised her eyes to his. "Why have you been avoiding me, Ruyen?"

He looked surprised. "Is that what you think I have been doing?"

"It appears so to me. I am sure everyone else thinks so as well."

"That was never my intention. I do not know if I can

make you understand what is happening on Falcon Bruine. There is much that requires my attention. Do you believe me, Jilliana?"

"Of course. You have always been forthright with me. I have known from the beginning that you love Lady Katharine. Although I found it somewhat humiliating to watch the two of you together, I was not unsympathetic to her plight."

"I was not speaking of myself or Lady Katharine, Jilliana. Much trouble has come to the island in my absence. I can say no more, but I do have a duty to the people who live here and I am attempting to—" He paused as if he had said too much. "But I will not bore you with such talk."

She turned her back to him. "Was there something in particular that you wanted to say to me?"

He wanted to slide his hands around her waist, pull her against his aching body, to bury his face in her sweet-smelling hair, so that her sweetness might drive away some of his devils.

"I know it hasn't been pleasant for you here. Would that I could have saved you from this."

She turned back to him. "Ruyen, Falcon Bruine is not what I expected. I have never seen such miserable conditions as I saw in the village."

He drew a long breath. "Do you think I tasted one morsel of food that first night or any time since? I have done what little I can to ease the hunger, but my people need more than food."

"Then they must be helped."

"Has it escaped your notice that I have no power here? Henry stripped me of everything. What I do must be done in secret. But I will not discuss this with you, for fear of placing you in danger."

She realized then why he had been so often absent. He was preparing to confront his mother. Why had she not guessed this before?

"Do not fear for me. Just do what you can for your subjects." She placed her hand on his arm. "Allow me to help you. Humphrey can leave tomorrow for Talshamar and return with enough food to see them through the winter."

Ruyen stared into her upturned face. "You would do this for me?"

"I would do this for anyone in need, Ruyen."

He lightly touched her face. "The world has not seen your like, Jilliana. I know of no ruler with your compassion. There are those who would destroy your sweetness and crush your spirit."

"Do you speak of yourself?"

He gently touched her lips. "Perhaps I am the greatest danger to you of them all."

She blinked her eyes. "Do not think because I was raised in a convent that I am weak, Ruyen. I have strength and I know how to use it."

He felt sorrow tug at his heart. "Beware, Jilliana. Your goodness may not be enough to battle the evil that is building about you. If it were in my power, I would send you away now."

"Will you allow me to help your people?"

"I thank you for your offer, but no." There was an edge to his voice. "What happens on Falcon Bruine is my responsibility. If they are to be helped it will come from me."

"Ruyen, it is not weakness to accept help from someone who gives it willingly. Should you change your mind—"

"I won't."

They were suddenly staring into each other's eyes, both remembering the times their bodies had blended. Her lips parted as he bent his head and pressed his mouth to hers.

The passion that they had tried to hide for so long ripped through both of them, fusing them together.

In a frenzy, they undressed and he lifted her in his arms and carried her to the bed.

They joined in a heat of passion, their lips hungrily touching. His hands were stroking, caressing as he became reacquainted with each soft curve.

"I have wanted this," he said, raising his head and looking softly into her eyes. "I tried to stay away from you, but I could not."

Her hand moved over his muscled shoulders. It was enough to know that he desired her. "I am glad you came," she admitted.

"When I am near you, I can only think of taking you to bed. I first took you by order of a king, but I now take you because I need you as surely as the air I breathe."

Their lovemaking was frantic, as if each feared it would be the last time they would be together. Jilliana yielded to his every need, and he took time to satisfy her as he had never done before.

Afterward, he held her tightly against him, drawing on her strength for the days ahead, the days when he must walk the path of life or death alone. If only he could get her safely away from here before the final confrontation with his mother.

"Ruyen?"

He kissed her fingers. "Yes."

"I am confused."

He shook with laughter. "I never thought to hear such a confession from your lips."

"Do not laugh at me."

He pretended seriousness. "Tell me what is troubling you, Jilliana."

"How can it be that love and mating are two sides of the same coin, yet not the same?"

He ran his hand along her thigh, lightly caressing her until she trembled with delight. "That is desire. You want me, I want you. A man can feel desire and yet it does not always touch his heart."

"I see. You desire me—you love Katharine."

He pulled back, feeling suddenly disturbed. Again, he tried to remember what color Katharine's eyes were, but he could not. He stared into bewildered blue eyes and pulled Jilliana back to him.

"I only know that I desire you more than I have ever desired a woman," he said, trying to be as honest as he could. "Let that be enough for now."

He kissed her, and she clung to him. She could not put a name to what she felt for him, but she knew it went deeper than mere desire. She worried about his safety, she grieved for the unrest among his people, and she feared what might happen. Could passion be this strong? If so, then love must be more painful than anyone could endure.

Jilliana was now certain that she was with child because she had missed her monthly bleeding. Soon she would tell Ruyen about the baby, but not now. Why did she hesitate? Because when she told him about the baby, she would sail for Talshamar.

She pressed her lips to his, knowing that she could not bear the thought of leaving him. Call it desire, or call it love, she needed him.

Suddenly she was reminded of her duty to her own subjects. She must not think only of herself. She must tell him now, even though it would set him free to go to Katharine.

She got out of bed and moved to the window, while his eyes followed her. She feared to look at him lest she change her mind.

"I have decided that I will be leaving in two days' time. I would leave sooner, but it will take that long for Humphrey to make the arrangements."

Ruyen came quickly to her, turning her face into the moonlight so he could read her expression.

"Why do you say this now?"

She tried to speak, but a lump had formed in her throat. His eyes were searching, probing, and she dropped hers before the intensity of his gaze.

"I am with child. There is no reason for me to remain longer."

She heard his sharp intake of breath. "So, you take my child and walk away."

She felt stinging tears form behind her eyes; she must not allow him to see her cry. "It is what we agreed I would do. I gave you my word, and I will keep it. Will you keep yours?"

He felt dazed, as if someone had struck him hard in the stomach. "Yes," he managed to grind out, "I will keep my word."

She touched his arm. "Ruyen, I have tried to tell you something before, but you have never listened to me. Even now, I am reluctant to do so."

He waited for her to continue.

"Does Lady Katharine understand that it was not your choice to wed me?"

The moment was so poignant, he had not expected her to speak of Katharine. She had just told him she was going to have his child. What in hell did that have to do with Katharine?

There was questioning in Jilliana's eyes. "Do you want me to explain to her what happened?"

"She has been told the truth."

"I believe I can make her understand that you never stopped loving her."

Anger riveted through him. "I do not need anyone to speak for me—certainly not you. Since the day I met you, I have not had control of my life. Woman, did God put you on earth to torment me?"

"Forgive me, Ruyen. I thought—"

He grabbed her, slamming her against his body, holding her so tightly she could scarcely breath.

"Forgive me," he breathed against her ear.

It was the first time he had asked her pardon. "For what, Ruyen?"

"For taking your body as you lay so softly in my arms willing to receive my seed. Forgive me for wanting you even now."

She touched his face, wishing she could express the words that begged to be spoken. She was so new in the world beyond the convent walls, and she had not yet learned the rules by which others lived.

"If I have caused you pain in any way," she said, "then I am truly sorry. If there is anything I can do to help you, you have only to ask."

He stared into blue eyes that seemed to have caught the reflecting moonlight. She was leaving. He would not be able to touch her, to watch the gentle way her hips swayed when she crossed a room. He would miss the sparkle in her eyes when she laughed, the kindness she had shown his sister and others in need. Poor Cassandra would be devastated when Jilliana left.

"Have you told my sister you will be leaving?"

"I have not said so, but she knows it will be soon. She and Netta know about the baby."

"You told them before you told me?"

She smiled. "They told me."

"There can be no mistake?"

"Netta is positive." She shook her head. "I will miss Cassandra. She has become like a sister to me."

He tilted her chin upward. "And what about me; will you miss me?"

Why did she feel the tightness around her heart? Why did she want to lie her head against his shoulder and have him hold her so tightly and never let her go?

"I— Yes, Ruyen, I shall miss you."

She turned back to the window, fearing she would cry.

Ruyen moved just behind her, his hands resting lightly on her waist.

"What if I ask you to stay?"

There was regret in her voice. "You know I cannot. You have your duties and I have mine. Our lives were ordained from the beginning and we cannot turn away from those who depend on us."

One of Ruyen's hands moved to Jilliana's abdomen, resting there gently. He was overcome with an emotion he had not expected to feel. Together, he and Jilliana had created a life. His child, whether it be male or female, would one day be the ruler of Talshamar. He would not see the child grow to adulthood, would not be a part of its life. Was he expected to forget that he was a father?

"What will you tell the child about me?"

She placed her hand on top of his and they shared a beautiful, heartbreaking moment before she spoke.

"I will tell her that her father is brave and noble, and that he is a man whose word can be trusted. I will tell her that her father is the Golden Falcon."

He had not known that she thought of him in that way. They had never spoken of their feelings, and it was difficult to do so now. Perhaps it was because they had both known from the beginning that they would have so little time together.

"You said her, Jilliana?"

"I feel it is a daughter."

His hand pressed tighter against her stomach. "I hope it is the daughter you crave."

"I would not mind if it were a son."

That thought was even more painful to him. A son that he would never know. "How will you answer the child when she asks why her father is not in her life?"

"I will make her understand that you gave her life, and then let her go." She turned to face him, her eyes filled with sadness. "Do you think I am so unfeeling that I do not know of your torture? When this all began, it seemed so simple. I would save your life and in return you would give me the child I need to save mine."

"We were just strangers at the plan's conception, Jilliana. That is no longer true."

"I would like to think ours is a friendship that will withstand the sands of time, Ruyen. I shall always remember you with great . . . affection."

"Will you?"

"Yes. Ruyen, please remember that this child is the only hope for Talshamar. Without an heir, do you think King Philip would allow me to live?"

"Will she be bastardized when the pope decrees that our marriage is annulled?"

"She will be the future queen of Talshamar, and none of my people will question her legitimacy."

"I know all the reasons for what we have done. But I did not consider the child as a real person."

Her eyes softened. "And now you do."

He pressed his cheek to hers. "And now I do." He brushed her tumbled hair away from her face and touched his lips to her forehead. "Would that I could have you once more before we part."

She took his hand and led him toward the bed. "On parting, I will give freely of my body."

His voice was gruff. "It will not harm the child?"

She smiled, lying back on the bed and holding her arms out to him. "This child will cling hard to life, and nothing, not Henry and not Philip, will shake it from my womb."

This time their lovemaking was impassioned and somehow pure. There was sadness in Jilliana's heart, for this would be the last time they would be together in this way. She wanted to remember this night for the rest of her life.

Gently, Ruyen held her to him, impressing the feel of her upon his mind. His lips moved over her face, then he sealed her mouth with a long kiss. She seemed to burrow into him and he took what she so willingly offered.

The moon was now directly over the window, and its golden light spilled on the bed, allowing him to see her face clearly.

He asked the question that had been haunting him all night. "Will you remarry?"

"I never shall. I want no other child save this one, and I will have no other husband."

He pulled back and looked at her. "Suppose something should happen to the baby? Have you considered what you would do in the event that should come to pass?"

She smiled. "Nothing will happen to this baby. You have my promise that she will grow up healthy and happy. The people of Talshamar will love and protect her, as will I."

Jilliana could see that Ruyen was still troubled, but he said nothing more. His eyes drifted shut and she pressed closer to him.

Long after Ruyen had fallen asleep, Jilliana lay awake, watching him. She carefully touched his dark hair, then pressed a kiss on his lips, which drew a sigh from him, but he did not awaken. She took his hand and held it in both of hers.

She tried not to think of Ruyen lying like this with Katharine.

The one thing she wanted most of all she could not have—she could not have Ruyen or his love. It was not meant that they should be together.

When the sun rose, she quietly dressed. Leaving the room, she went in search of Humphrey so she could tell him to arrange their journey home. It would be a bitter-sweet journey for her. Happy because she was going home at last; sad because she would never again see Ruyen.

Ruyen's life was here on the Isle of Falcon Bruine, and hers was in Talshamar, and the distance between the two could not be spanned.

24

It was still early, therefore few people were about as Jilliana moved down the path toward the stables, where she knew she would find Humphrey. He always rose early, and his first duty of the day was to visit the stalls where their horses were stabled.

Humphrey watched Jilliana's approach with a frown on his rugged face. "Is something the matter, Your Majesty?"

"Nay, good Humphrey. I have merely sought you out to tell you that we will be leaving as soon as you can make the arrangements."

He looked at her carefully, reading much in her expression. If she was ready to leave, it would mean she was with child. He smiled and took her hand, raising it to his lips.

"Then all shall be ready on the morrow." He dropped his voice so only she could hear. "I am ready to be quit of this island."

"As am I," she said wistfully. "The journey is to be mostly by sea, is it not?"

"Indeed, Your Majesty. It is hoped that you shan't suffer from seasickness as you did on the voyage from England."

"Have no concern on that, Humphrey. It was not the voyage that made me ill."

He nodded in understanding.

"Instruct the others that I will want to leave without delay. Is our ship still anchored off the island?"

"It is, Your Majesty. I will begin loading supplies immediately."

Humphrey watched her turn her gaze toward the castle. There was sadness in her eyes, and he guessed the reason for it—for had he not known her longer and better than anyone? She had been in his care for so long that he knew what she was thinking almost before she did.

"Your Majesty, are you certain that this is what you want?" he asked softly.

There was no pretense between them. "It is the way it must be. Ruyen and I must keep to our bargain."

She reached up and stroked the mane of a white stallion. "I am certain that Cardinal Failsham will be happy to see us. His health is not good, Humphrey."

"Aye, Your Majesty, that did not escape my notice. But you will soon take the burden of power from his capable but frail shoulders."

She turned to him. "I will see that the trunks are packed."

Humphrey watched her walk away with her head held high, but he knew that she was feeling pain. Had she discovered that she loved Prince Ruyen? Yes, she knew, although she might not yet have put a name to her feelings.

He would have given his life to keep her from harm. But he was helpless to protect her from a broken heart.

*   *   *

Ruyen stood before his mother, dressed in chainmail, his helm tucked beneath his arm.

Melesant was puzzled. "You look as though you are off to do battle. Against anyone I know?"

"I thought it only fair to warn you, Mother, that I will no longer tolerate your neglect of my people."

"*Your* people? Your association with the little queen must have muddled your thinking. I am regent here. Do you really believe that you can raise an army to come against me?"

"I can, and I shall."

There was a smirk on her face. "Foolish Ruyen, I have powerful friends."

He looked at the woman who had given birth to him, feeling no kinship with her. As a child, he had rarely seen her. He had heard her say often that she had an aversion to children. He could not remember a time when she had visited him in the nursery. When he was a young boy, he had wanted so desperately to please her so she would take some notice of him, but she never did. Now it no longer mattered.

"I will do what I can against you, Mother. I may face defeat, but you will not win either."

Melesant suddenly felt a sinking sensation. "I have no desire to war against you, Ruyen. Would it not be better if you left Falcon Bruine for a time?"

"And desert the people who need me most? I think not."

Her eyes were keen and probed deeply into his. "Will you leave your bride? Do you think I cannot see how your eyes follow Jilliana about? Poor Katharine. Think you she knows that you have fallen in love with your wife?"

"We were not speaking of my wife. I am asking you to yield to me, Mother, or face the consequences."

"My dear son, would you do harm to me?"

"I will do what I must. If you leave me no choice, I will crush you and your Castilians."

Melesant could see that he meant what he said. Henry

had made her regent, but she wanted more. She wanted to be queen.

"What is to keep me from throwing you in the dungeon, Ruyen? You know that you speak treason."

"You will not do that, not just yet. You like the smell of the hunt, and that will be your downfall."

"You have more of me in you than you would like to admit, Ruyen. That is why you know me so well."

"I know that you do not care about the populace of this island. Power is all you want, but you will not take it at the expense of the people."

"Perhaps we can reach a compromise. I admit I have been neglectful of the villagers. Suppose I allow you to help them. Do whatever it takes to pacify them."

"'Tis too late for that, Mother. The time when you could have helped them has passed. Do you not see their suffering? Do you care so much for yourself that you cannot hear the cries of those in torment?"

"God, but you are a son to be proud of, Ruyen. We could have obtained greatness together. Band with me now. We have Falcon Bruine and we can also take Talshamar."

He felt sick inside. "Your ambitions have made you mad. You cannot take Talshamar."

She laughed. "Can I not? With your help, it would be easy. Without it, it will be more difficult, but I shall succeed."

Suddenly his eyes were sad. She would never relent, and he could not allow her to win. "We have nothing further to discuss."

Melesant turned her eyes on her son, trying to see him as a young woman might. He was a handsome devil, perhaps too handsome. There was hardness in his eyes and a proud tilt to his chin.

"You are strong, Ruyen, and you owe that to me. Had I coddled you, you would not be nearly so fierce and unyielding."

His lip curled in contempt. "What fine gifts you bestow on your children, Madame."

"You should be grateful to me."

"Indeed."

Melesant started to reach out to him, but he pulled away from her touch. She smiled. "What of your wife?"

"I gave her my word that she could go when she was with child."

"Yes, yes, I know tha—" Her eyes widened. "Is she then with child?"

"It would seem so."

"I begin to understand. She is leaving?"

"Yes."

"So, you gave your word," she mimicked, "and you are allowing her to leave with my grandchild—the heir to the throne of Falcon Bruine."

"Remember this, Mother, Jilliana's baby is *not* the heir to Falcon Bruine. When the annulment is granted, I will relinquish all claims to the baby."

Melesant's face grew red with rage. "Annulment! You think to bastardize the child who will one day rule Talshamar! The pope will never agree to this."

"There you are wrong, Mother. There is an old law that allows annulment if there is close kinship between the married couple."

"You have no kinship with any Talshamarian."

"But I have, Mother. It seems Cardinal Failsham has discovered that our grandmothers were distantly related."

"'Tis too distant a kinship to matter."

"The pope has agreed that he will use this to give Jilliana her freedom."

Melesant's mind was spinning, everything was happening at once. She must do something quickly—but what? "You are certain that you will have the marriage put aside?"

"I am."

"Pity."

"I take leave of you now, Mother. When next we meet, it will likely be the downfall of one of us or the other."

"Does your bride know you are waging war against your own mother?"

"I saw no reason to tell her. She will be safely away before I come against you."

They both stared at each other and no warmth passed between them.

Ruyen's lips twisted in disgust. "I give you this one last chance to yield."

"Do you hate me so much?" She sounded almost regretful.

His voice was detached and devoid of feeling. "You are responsible for my father's death."

"I wondered how long it would take you to accuse me of that. Your father was a weak man and unfit to rule. You, of all people, should know this."

"He was my father. I have not yet spoken to you about your betrayal of me or how you allowed Henry's men to take Cassandra to England as a prisoner."

"You will not believe me, but I did not know that you and Cassandra were to be condemned to death. I tried to free you, but Henry is a stubborn man."

"You should be grateful to Jilliana then, Mother, for accomplishing what you could not."

She smiled and offered him her hand, which he barely touched, then dropped. "Pity it has come to this."

He turned and walked away, and she stared after him. She was almost sorry for what she must do next.

Escobar stepped from behind the brocade screen where he had been hiding. "Shall I have the guards stop him?" he asked.

"No. I want his movements watched so I can discover all those who would oppose me. Be discreet and find out where they are hiding and how strong they are."

Escobar bowed and hurried from the room, his dark eyes gleaming in triumph. The prince would soon be sorry he had treated him with such contempt.

Jilliana had been told that she would find Cassandra at the mews where the falcons were housed, so she walked in that direction.

Cassandra had not heard her approach, so Jilliana watched with fascination while Ruyen's sister trained a young falcon to return a lure. The bell attached to the bird's leg gave a tinkling sound when it glided on a strong wind current and disappeared from sight.

"That was quite fascinating," Jilliana said, shading her eyes and trying to locate the bird.

"Jilliana, have you noticed that our falcons are golden? Some have black on the tips of their wings, but most are solid gold. Nowhere in the world will you find falcons like the ones on our island," Cassandra said with pride.

"Is this where Ruyen draws his name?"

"Partly. But mostly because he won the name in battle. He is very brave, you know."

"Yes, I do know." Jilliana changed the subject. "I have read about this sport, but have never participated myself."

"I shall be happy to teach you," Cassandra said zealously. "I have just the right falcon for you. She is quite gentle. You may have her as your own."

Jilliana shook her head. "I will not be here long enough to train her, Cassandra."

The girl's eyes clouded with distress. "Are you going away soon?"

"Yes . . . tomorrow. I wanted to tell you myself before you heard it from someone else."

Cassandra dropped her head. "I have known that you would one day leave. I just did not think it would be so soon. I suppose Sir Edward will be leaving with you."

Jilliana had not realized until now that Cassandra had feelings for her young knight. She thought it best to pretend ignorance. "Talshamar is his home. He has family there."

"Aye, and the woman he is to marry."

"I believe so."

The falcon's bell tinkled louder and Jilliana could not reply because the bird had returned. Cassandra held out her hand and the falcon landed, its sharp talons gripping her padded glove. To calm the bird, Cassandra covered its eyes with a hood and handed it to the falconer.

She turned back to Jilliana, looking forlorn and lost. "I shall miss you. You have become my friend." Her little face was a mask of misery and tears gathered in her eyes. If only . . . if only—"

Jilliana put comforting arms about Cassandra. "I shall miss you as well. Were it possible, I would take you with me to Talshamar." Her expression brightened and she held Cassandra away from her. "Would you like to go with me if your mother will permit it?"

"Oh, yes. I would love it above all things! Do you think it will be possible?"

Jilliana wondered if it had been wise to raise Cassandra's hopes before talking with her mother. On the occasions she had observed Queen Melesant with her daughter, she had not seen any signs of affection. As a flower needs water, Cassandra needed someone to care for her, and Jilliana could not bear to think of leaving her here on this cold, loveless island.

"I cannot say for certain that your mother will allow it. Wait in your room, and I will come to you after I have spoken to her."

Cassandra was too fearful to hope, lest her mother crush those hopes. "Pray that she allows me to go with you, Jilliana. I want to see Talshamar."

As Jilliana left, Ruyen was just coming down the path to warn his sister of his intentions. When he saw his wife, he quickly stepped behind a hedge. Jilliana must not see him dressed in his chainmail because it would raise questions he was not prepared to answer.

She passed so closely that he could have reached out and touched her, and he wanted to, but he dared not. There could be no good-byes between the two of them, for he would always carry her in his heart.

Through the years, Ruyen had developed a cynical attitude toward women. Loving Jilliana had restored his faith. She would leave without knowing that she took his heart with her.

How insignificant had been his feelings for Katharine compared to the fire that raged within him when he thought of Jilliana.

He was glad she would be safely away before war raged across the island. The best thing he had ever done for her was to let her go.

25

Jilliana hurried into the castle, rushing past the Great Hall. She went directly to the library and rapped on the door, fearing she might lose her courage.

An imperious voice answered. "Enter."

Jilliana pushed the door open and found the queen sitting near the window. Melesant motioned her forward.

"So, you are leaving us, are you?"

"Yes, in the morning."

A black cat leaped upon Melesant's lap and she stroked it until the fur crackled. "It is not hard to determine that you do not treasure our hospitality, Jilliana."

Jilliana did not bother to deny Melesant's assumption. "I am anxious to go home. I have been away from Talshamar since I was very young."

The older woman's eyes became hard and her hand tightened on the cat, making it spit and leap from her lap. "Then you should not mind remaining with us longer."

Jilliana made no reply.

"Would you deny me the joy of witnessing the birth of my first grandchild?" Melesant asked.

"Ruyen has told you about the baby?"

"Did you think he would not?" The question was harsh. "Since coming to our island, no one could deny that you have been polite, leaving no doubt that you have been well taught in diplomacy." The regent stood, her eyes half-closed, a smile revealing even, white teeth. "Yet, you have kept your distance from me as if I were beneath you."

Jilliana had suspected from the first that she and Ruyen's mother would one day have a confrontation. She only wished that it had not been today because she wanted to take Cassandra away with her.

"If I have seemed distant, it is because I do not belong here. You were told that I married your son to benefit us both. We have done that and now I must leave."

Melesant bent to retrieve the cat, only to have the animal hiss and slap at her. Her hand tightened about the cat's neck and she squeezed.

Jilliana stared in horror at the cruelty she was witnessing. When she reached forward to stop her, Melesant set the limp cat at her feet and gave it a pat.

"He will remember this," Melesant said, "and know that I am his mistress and must be obeyed."

The feline lay still for so long that Jilliana feared it might be dead. But at last it rolled to its feet and sauntered away.

"That," Melesant said, "is true diplomacy. Power is the only way to master those around you."

Jilliana had never been so angry. "*That* was brutality. You could have killed the poor animal."

Melesant chuckled. "I know just how far 1 can go. For the first time in my life, I know the feeling of strength and power, and I will use it where I must."

Jilliana felt sickened by what she had witnessed. She must get Cassandra away from this woman. For the young girl's sake, she swallowed the bile that rose in her throat and pushed her anger aside.

"I was wondering if you would allow Cassandra to go with me to Talshamar? You have my pledge that she will be treated with the respect due her rank. I will further her learning and furnish her with a wardrobe. And when the times comes for her to marry, I myself shall provide her with a substantial dowry."

Melesant swept across the room, going to the window, and tapping her toe in irritation. "You still do not understand what I have been trying to tell you. You cannot take my daughter with you because you will not be leaving this island!"

Jilliana shook her head. "You cannot stop me!"

"Can I not?"

Jilliana backed toward the door, then turned with the intention of running to find Humphrey. But she encountered one of Melesant's guards, who blocked her way.

"Move aside," she commanded. "Allow me to pass."

Melesant came up behind her and spun her around. "The only place you are going is to your chamber. You will be locked in until you see reason."

Jilliana knew she was looking upon the face of true evil, and she was frightened, but she must not show it.

"Where is Ruyen? Why is he allowing you to do this to me?"

"Did you think my son would let a prize such as you get away?" she purred. "You carry within your body the heir to Falcon Bruine, as well as Talshamar. We must see that the baby is safely delivered. The one who has possession of the child, controls both countries."

"You are mad!"

"Nay, my dear, only practical."

"You would not dare do this." Terror filled Jilliana's heart. "I demand to see Ruyen at once. We had a promise between us. I kept mine, I expect him to keep his."

"My son is otherwise occupied and has left this unpleasantness for me to dispense with."

"Then I demand to see Humphrey."

"I regret that your arrogant Lord Baldridge and your other knights took exception when they were informed that you would be remaining with us. There was a struggle, and those of your knights who are not dead, are chained in my dungeon."

Jilliana's face drained of color. "You would not dare harm my Talshamarians. I will not allow such an atrocity." She turned back to the guard. "Step aside," she ordered.

She saw indecision in the man's eyes, but knew that he would do as his own queen commanded.

Melesant nodded. "Take her below and allow her to see the Talshamarians. But do not allow them to converse. Then take her to her chamber and lock her door."

Jilliana glared at Melesant. "We have not finished, Madame. Think you that no one will come to rescue me? Henry, himself, will not be pleased when he hears what you have done. Whatever else he is, he is a man of his word, and he did promise me that I could return to Talshamar."

"Henry is not king here. Know this: *I* say who goes and who remains. You remain!"

Jilliana had nothing more to say to Queen Melesant. She was so frightened for her men. What if Humphrey had been injured? What if he were dead? No, she could not bear to think of that.

She walked beside the guard, who led her through a darkened hallway, where they found steps leading down into the dark recesses of the castle.

Down, down they went, until they reached the dank chamber where wine casks lined the walls. She was led into another chamber where torches burned and in the dim ring of light she saw men chained to the walls.

Hurrying past darkened shadows that reflected ominous patterns on the rock walls, she cried out Humphrey's name. There was no reply.

The guard stepped in front of her, barring her path. "You can go no further. You heard the queen's orders. She will not allow you to speak to them."

He reached out to take her arm but thought better of it. He dared not lay a hand on a royal person.

"You cannot stop me," she said, pushing past him and running forward. "Humphrey, answer me. Are you hurt?"

The guard merely watched her, confused about what to do. He decided that Queen Melesant would never know if he allowed the Talshamarian queen to speak to her men before escorting her to her chamber.

Jilliana was almost faint with relief when she heard Humphrey's voice.

"Your Majesty, have they harmed you?"

She approached him cautiously, for he was mostly in shadow. She was fearful that he had been wounded or tortured. With a quick assessment, she counted only five other knights.

"I am not harmed, Humphrey, but what of you?"

"Merely embarrassed, Your Majesty, for walking into a trap and being taken unaware."

She looked into Humphrey's troubled eyes. "Where are the others?"

"Alas, Your Majesty, I know not for certain. Everything happened so swiftly." He shook his head. "I feel shame that I was negligent in my duty toward you. We were set upon by the queen's soldiers and hardly had time to draw sword. I make no excuses; I should have known this would happen."

"Do not blame yourself. I did not suspect Melesant's intent until it was too late. We have been betrayed."

Humphrey's wrists and ankles were chained and she placed her hand on his, before looking at the others. Sorrowfully, she did not see Sir Edward among them and knew he had been slain.

"Is there any hope that the others were merely wounded and are being tended elsewhere, Humphrey?"

"I fear they perished. I, myself, saw three fall."

Jilliana's eyes were burning and she turned to the guard who now stood beside her. "I demand that you release my men at once. If you do not, I will see that you are punished."

"We cannot do that, Your Majesty. We should leave now, or I fear there will be reprisals."

Humphrey's chains rattled as he tried to reach the man. "You dare not lay a hand on my queen, or I vow I will slay you with my own hands."

"You have nothing to fear from me, noble Talshamarian. 'Twas not I who struck today. Nor would I ever harm your queen."

He bowed to Jilliana. "We will leave now."

Jilliana looked back at each of her knights. "Not until I see that they are not suffering from wounds that need tending."

She looked them all over carefully, touching each hand, which drew a regretful smile. Three of them had wounds but they had been bandaged. It was little enough, but she was grateful for it all the same.

"Will they be treated well?" she inquired of the queen's guard.

"I know not, but I must take you to your chamber now or the queen will send someone to see what is amiss."

"Fear not," she told her knights, "for I shall not rest until you are free. Have courage, for I'll not desert you."

Humphrey tried to reach her, but fell back against the wall. "Be cautious, Your Majesty. Queen Melesant is corrupt."

The guard motioned her forward. She nodded, wishing she could share the chains with her knights. She was frightened for them and angry with Ruyen and his mother.

When they reached her chamber, Jilliana paused in the doorway and spoke to the guard. "You are not one of the queen's Castilian guards, and I have seen that you have compassion. I feel that you do not approve of what has been done to my men."

He looked about to make certain that no one was listening. "I had no part in it, Majesty. You must know this, the men will not be kept in chains, but moved to a cell."

That was little comfort to Jilliana. "Know you what happened to my men that were murdered?"

"I know not, Majesty."

She removed the ruby ring from her finger and pressed it in his hand. "Take this as payment. I beseech you to have my slain knights decently buried."

He handed her back the ring. "I require nothing from you, Majesty. But I shall do what I can to see your men buried. You should know that I am merely a man-at-arms, and have no authority."

"What of my ship and the captain and crew?"

"They have already sailed."

Jilliana could hardly believe they would leave without her. "How can that be?"

The guard knew he was saying too much, but he felt pity for the beautiful queen. "Your captain was told that a long sea voyage at this time would be dangerous for you . . . and . . . the unborn child."

"He would not believe this, knowing we were preparing to leave."

Again she thought she saw sadness in the guard's eyes. "I witnessed the meeting between the captain and Escobar Hernandez. The minister reminded the captain that you were ill on your voyage to Falcon Bruine and he was most sympathetic and understanding. He was told that you required him to return to Talshamar and tell the people that you will be delayed."

Jilliana felt the hopelessness of her situation. But she was not resigned to her fate. She would find a way to escape. She had to.

"Where is my maid, Netta? Has she been harmed?"

"I do not know, Your Majesty. You will have to ask the queen."

"What is your name?"

"I am Rob Gilbert, Your Majesty. Were it in my power, I would take you away from here. As it is, I will do what I can."

She smiled at him and his heart gladdened, for she was as brave and beautiful as he had been told. He had heard how she had saved Prince Ruyen's life by endangering herself.

"I have one friend here, Rob Gilbert, and I shall not forget your kindness."

With a heavy heart, she entered her chamber. She had not considered that Ruyen would break his promise to her.

The door closed behind her and she heard the grinding of a sliding bolt as she was locked in.

It was the sound of betrayal, the sound of heartbreak.

When Cassandra climbed the stairs with the intention of seeking her sister-in-law, two guards stood before the door to Jilliana's chamber and denied her entrance by her mother's orders.

Cassandra was determined to discover why Jilliana had been imprisoned. With her heart beating wildly, she hurried down the stairs to the lower level, where Jilliana's men had been lodged. It was empty, but their equipment was still there, as if they would soon return—or as if they had left in a hurry.

She had a sinking feeling in the pit of her stomach. If only Ruyen were here, he would know what to do. But she did not know where to find him. He had told her only that he would be massing troops to send against their mother, and that she was to remain in the tower so she would be safe.

Cassandra was frantic. The castle had become a fortress as her mother's troops prepared for war. The captain-at-arms would know what was happening, and she decided to pretend she was in her mother's confidence, thus gaining his trust.

She stopped in the garden and hurriedly picked an armful of primroses so she would look like she had been out for an afternoon stroll. With slow steps, she rounded the keep and confronted the captain of the guards, a burley man with hard, mistrustful eyes.

"Sir Arindel," she said, pretending a calm she did not feel. "Were you not surprised by what happened today?"

"Nay, Your Highness, the queen instructed me on what was to be done as soon as she learned of Prince Ruyen's treachery."

Cassandra was trembling with dread, but tried not to show it. "Yes, I cannot understand why my brother would go against our mother's wishes. But what was done with Queen Jilliana's men?"

"Pity to say, Your Highness, some of them were slain, the others are in the dungeon." He looked shamefaced. "I do not keep with attacking unsuspecting men. It would have been a slaughter if I had allowed it to continue. As it was, five of them died fighting valiantly."

She could only think of Sir Edward. Oh, please God, she thought, do not let him be among the dead.

"I will just go to the dungeons and see the men who have survived."

"I fear Her Majesty would never allow that. Her orders are that no one is to see the prisoners."

"You could take me there. I am very curious."

"I dare not, Highness."

"Then tell me where the encounter took place. I would like to see it for myself."

"They were lured to the walled garden, where they were told Queen Jilliana would be waiting for them. It was there we set upon them. And unless their bodies have been moved, the dead are there yet. Now if you will excuse me, Your Highness, I must see to the fortifications."

When he turned away, Cassandra dropped her flowers and ran down the path to the walled garden, praying all the while that she would not find Sir Edward among the dead.

Shoving the gate wide, she entered the garden and at first she saw nothing that would indicate a conflict. Moving down the yew hedges, she stood on tiptoes, and the sight that met her eyes made her feel faint. Several bodies were lying on the grass, obviously dead. She cried out when she saw that one of them was indeed Sir Edward!

Frantically, she ran down the row of hedges until she found an opening and squeezed through. With a heart-breaking cry she fell on her knees beside Sir Edward, lifting his golden head onto her lap, her tears falling on his face.

"Oh, please do not be dead," she cried, clutching his limp hand. She raised that hand to her lips and kissed it, then looked at it, puzzled. The hand was still warm. He could not have been dead long.

Just then he groaned and opened his eyes. She heard footsteps coming down the path and quickly stood, withdrawing her jeweled dagger from her belt and waiting for the intruder.

Although the man was from Falcon Bruine, he was her mother's guard. She glared at him while crying so hard that her words were coming out in gasps. "Have you no shame for what you have done?"

The guard did not answer.

"This man still lives, and I will not allow you to touch him. If you try, I shall drive my dagger into your heart! If my brother were here he would slay you himself."

"Nay, Your Highness, have no fear of me. I'll not harm the man. My name is Rob Gilbert and I will help you. You know my father. He is the forester and his cottage is in the woods. I shall take this Talshamarian there."

"How can I trust you not to go to my mother?"

"I give you my pledge that I will not do that."

She nodded, having no choice in the matter. "Why are you here?"

"Because Queen Jilliana asked me to see that her men were properly buried."

"You have seen her? She is well?"

"Yes, Highness. But if we are to save her knight, we must hasten. I will bring a cart to carry the bodies out of the castle and convince the guards that I am taking them to the church graveyard. Pray that I can convince the guard and thus sneak this man past him."

Hope rose within Cassandra's heart. "Yes, do—please hurry."

She turned back to look at the ashen face of the man she loved. "I will come to your father's cottage tonight and treat his wounds."

Cassandra was frightened and she wished that her brother was there to help her. It would not be easy to go against her mother, but someone had to.

"Ruyen, where are you?" she cried. "I need you to tell me what to do."

26

Cassandra walked along, leading a packhorse, a dark-hooded cloak covering her hair and shading her face. She hunched her shoulders as she neared the gatekeeper. When he waved her through, thinking she was a villager, she hurried in the direction of the woods.

Night was almost upon her and she hoped she would not lose her way.

"Your Highness," someone called to her.

Cassandra was relieved to see Rob Gilbert just ahead.

"I have been watching for you, Highness, so I could lead you safely through the woods."

She was grateful for his assistance, for in truth she had dreaded the dark woods. "How fares Sir Edward?"

"My father has dressed his wounds, and while deep, they are not of a dangerous nature."

"Think you we can trust your father not to account to my mother?"

"Aye. My father served your father faithfully. His loyalty is now to Prince Ruyen, the rightful king."

Cassandra nodded in satisfaction. "Then take me to Sir Edward at once."

They moved down the twisted path and deep inside the woods. At last Cassandra could see a faint light in the distance. When they reached the cottage, Rob Gilbert opened the door and waited for her to enter.

She recognized his father, William, and nodded at him. "How is your patient?"

William pulled a curtain aside, and to Cassandra's relief, she saw that Sir Edward was sitting upright on a straw pallet, while a woman she thought to be Rob's mother spooned thin broth into his mouth.

He quickly came to his knees, his eyes burning with challenge. "I warn you," Sir Edward threatened, "I shall not be taken alive."

"You need not be concerned, Sir Edward, you are with friends. I have come to help you."

"I trust not anyone of the Rondache family," he said bitterly.

William Gilbert stepped forward, placing a restraining hand on Sir Edward's shoulder. "I'll not have you insulting Her Highness, when it was her that seen you was brought to us. She's saved your life."

"We have no time for distrust," Cassandra said, handing Sir Edward a pouch.

The knight looked at the princess as if seeing her for the first time. She had thrown off the hood of her cape, and her raven-black hair glistened in the soft light that came from the one lantern in the cottage. Her features were so soft, and so evenly placed that he was sure she must be an angel sent to earth to guide him.

"The pouch contains all the gold I could obtain to aid you on your flight, less the amount I gave a ship's captain to take you away from Falcon Bruine. Do you think you are strong enough to sit a horse?"

Sir Edward stood with the aid of Rob Gilbert, but he still felt weak. "I must get to my queen."

"You cannot help her. You are but one. She is being

kept prisoner by my mother. But Jilliana is in no danger until she has given birth to the baby since my mother is interested only in the child."

When Sir Edward took a step, he stumbled and would have fallen had not Rob steadied him.

"You must be well enough to travel. It is not safe for you to remain here," Cassandra said, going to him and touching his forehead, then nodding in satisfaction when she discovered he had no fever.

"It grieves me to leave my queen."

"You can better help her if you do as I tell you. You must go to Salisbury Castle and seek Queen Eleanor's aid."

"Queen Eleanor cannot even help herself, how can she help my queen?"

"Jilliana trusts her above all others—she has told me this. If she trusts the English queen, there must be a reason. Go to her."

Sir Edward was struck by the intelligence of this young girl. He noticed how fiery her eyes had become as she spoke to him. She was not a girl, but a brave young woman with a loyal heart.

"When does the ship leave?" he asked, heartened by her calm assurance.

"Soon. Rob will go with you and see you safely on board."

"Pardon, Your Highness," Rob said, smiling. "I have never left the island, but have always wanted to. I will accompany Sir Edward, if you will allow it."

Relief showed on her face. "Aye, he has need of you. You will have my gratitude for your devotion."

Sir Edward stood up straight, managing to keep his balance, and trying not to think about the pain. "I will not fail in my duty."

"You must not," Cassandra said. "Jilliana's life may depend on your success."

"Let us leave now," Sir Edward stated firmly.

Cassandra nodded. "Rob, you should skirt the village, and draw as little attention as possible. Have you clothing for Sir Edward?"

Rob studied the man for a moment. "Aye, we are of the same height; he can wear my clothing."

It was but a short time later that Cassandra watched Rob help Sir Edward onto the back of a horse. She rushed forward when he slumped over.

"You are too ill to travel." There was distress in her voice as she touched his shoulder. "If only Ruyen were here, he would know what to do."

"Why is he not here, can you tell me this?"

"Civil war is about to erupt between my mother's followers and those who are loyal to my brother. I fear your queen has been caught in the middle."

Sir Edward straightened, and placed his hand on her silken head.

"Do not distress yourself, and have no fear for me. I will rest once on board the ship, and be healed before I stand before Queen Eleanor."

"I do not know how you will gain entrance to her castle since it is guarded. But you must find a way."

He brought her close to him, his lips brushing against hers. "I shall see her, and I shall return, my angel. Will you be waiting for me?"

In wonder, Cassandra reached up and touched her lips, her heart thumping against her breasts. "I shall be waiting."

Jilliana languished in her chamber, seeing only the queen's servants. She had heard nothing of the fate of Humphrey and the others. At first she hoped that Ruyen would relent and come to release her, but as the hours passed, that hope diminished.

She had thought him noble and honorable, but he was

not. He was no better than his devious mother, and had intended all along to betray her.

Thus far she had refused to eat. She sent word to Melesant that not one morsel of food would pass her lips until her men were released from the dungeon and she was allowed to leave Falcon Bruine.

A battle of wills developed between Queen Jilliana and Queen Melesant. Jilliana was prepared to give her life and that of her unborn child to gain freedom for her men.

She heard someone at the door and turned her face weakly in that direction. Escobar Hernandez slid the bolt aside, entering without knocking, a smug smile on his thin lips.

Jilliana weakly eased herself to a sitting position and glared at the odious man. "I did not invite you into my chamber. Leave at once!"

He gave her a disparaging glance. "I am sure you would rather talk to me than Queen Melesant. She is not as understanding as I."

"I want my maid with me now!"

He poised his hand and gave her a malevolent smile. "Only the queen decides that."

"Return to your queen and tell her that I do not care to speak to underlings."

Escobar's eyes hardened. "You will talk to me or no one."

"Then it is no one."

He pulled up a stool and sat beside her. "You must see reason. The queen has asked that—"

Jilliana moved off the bed and walked to the window, as if dismissing him. She was so weak she feared she might faint, so she gripped the window ledge, leaning heavily against the wall.

"Her Majesty wants you to eat. She has authorized me to tell you that the kitchen will prepare you any delicacy you desire."

Jilliana still did not acknowledge his presence, presenting him with her back.

She could hear his exasperated sigh. "You will talk to me sooner or later."

She faced him now, her head tilted high. "Minister, tell your queen that I refuse to eat."

"She won't like it."

"I can imagine that. It would be difficult for her to explain to Henry how I starved to death on the Isle of Falcon Bruine. He will be most displeased when Talshamar passes to French rule. Remind Queen Melesant that the motto on my family's escutcheon is *Before dishonor, death.* Also remind her, underling, that my mother died by that creed, as will I."

Escobar was not adept at hiding his feelings. His neck and face stained a deep red. "You would not do this. Think of the child."

"I will speak no more to you, sycophant. Take my message to your taskmaster."

Escobar wrenched the door open, angrily locking it on the other side. He had hoped he would be the one to induce Queen Jilliana to eat, thus endearing himself to Melesant once more.

In his dealings with the Talshamarians, he was finding them to be far too arrogant for his liking. He had little doubt that this woman would starve herself just as she threatened.

With misgivings, Melesant watched Escobar approach. "You saw Jilliana?"

"Aye, but she is a stubborn wench. I like her not."

"I am certain that she feels the same sentiment for you, Escobar."

"She refuses to eat. She's ready to die, sacrificing the child she carries unless you release her men and allow them all to leave."

Melesant turned around, her robe flaring out about her, her face a mask of rage. "I will not have it, I tell you. *I will not!* She will obey me!"

"I think she won't."

"What do you know, little man?" Melesant cried, taking out her anger on him. "You, who were born a commoner, cannot possibly understand someone born to the purple."

He could have reminded her that she was not of royal blood either, but he dared not. He knew she envied and hated the young queen because she had been born to rule.

"I know of nothing you can do to make her eat."

Melesant paced back and forth. "I have to think. There has to be a way. I must have the baby, or all is lost."

"She's asked for her servant. Perhaps that woman could entice her to eat."

"You do not know these Talshamarians, if you believe that. It's more likely that the woman would die with her mistress just to foil me." She raised her fists toward the ceiling and shook them. "I detest all Talshamarians!"

Escobar took several quick steps backward. "We could slay her men. That might make her yield."

Melesant looked at him with surprise. "Excellent! You have come upon the very thing that may well defeat her."

He blinked, not understanding. But the queen was pleased with him and that was all that mattered.

"Escobar, think you she will oppose me if I threaten the lives of her men?" Her eyes gleamed with pleasure. "I would enjoy cutting the heart out of the man Humphrey myself."

Melesant threw open the door to Jilliana's chamber and entered with a flourish, anger showing in every jerky step she took.

Jilliana weakly stood, holding on to the bedpost for support. "I wondered how long it would be before you came, Melesant."

"Then you know why I am here."

Jilliana faced her, unafraid. "Allow my men to go free and I will willingly stay on Falcon Bruine."

"You will remain, willing or not." Melesant pushed Jilliana back on the bed and stood over her. "Heed my words, Queen of Talshamar. I have been informed that you are not eating. If you do not eat, your men will suffer for your willfulness."

Jilliana rolled to the other side of the bed and stood once more. "What do you mean?"

"Just this. For every meal you miss, one of your men will miss a finger . . . and I shall start with your watchdog, Humphrey."

Jilliana's face paled. "You would not dare do such a foul deed. It is inhuman!"

"Oh, I will do it right enough. I seldom make idle threats. I shall have your maid bring you anything you want to eat. If you refuse, try to imagine Lord Baldridge's screams as his fingers are lopped off. Think about this: if you miss three meals, he loses three fingers."

Jilliana felt the room spin and she eased herself back on the bed. "I will eat. Please do not harm my men."

Melesant laughed triumphantly. "I admire you more than ever, because you are not too proud to admit when you are beaten."

Jilliana wanted to lie down, but she did not want Ruyen's mother to see how weak she felt. "I find no shame in relenting to save those I care about."

Melesant turned away in satisfaction. No matter how Jilliana tried to hide it, she was in torment, and that brought her great satisfaction. She left abruptly, slamming and bolting the door behind her.

Jilliana dropped her head in her hands, trying to gather her shattered thoughts.

Now the tears that she had held back swam in her eyes. She sobbed until the last remnant of her strength was spent.

Her situation was desperate. There was no hope for her or her baby. She was the prisoner of a madwoman!

27

Ruyen arrived at his father's hunting lodge, hoping for the peace and tranquility he had often found there in the past. Today, however, that tranquility eluded him.

Chaos raged across the island, and his people were suffering. They needed his direction, but how could he help them when he was floundering himself? Someone had to stop his mother, and it must be him. But he could not do it without the support of the people. Would they follow him and take up arms against their queen? More importantly, could he destroy his own mother?

He took the path that led up a steep incline and stood atop the cliff that jutted out over the sea, offering a magnificent view of the island.

To his left, he could see the Talshamarian ship far out at sea, its crimson sails weaving in the harsh breeze. That ship took Jilliana away and he would never see her again.

Well, good riddance to her. She had been nothing but trouble to him since their first meeting. She did not need anyone. That woman would always be in command of her own fate, and if life did not conform to her expectations, she would merely find a way to bend the circumstances to her will.

An intense sea breeze cooled his face as his thoughts turned once more to Falcon Bruine and the troubles that faced him. He glanced back at the lodge, remembering happier days when he had hunted with his father. They had ridden over the green hills in pursuit of stag and boar. But because of his mother, those days were gone forever.

In defiance, he tossed a stone into the sea and watched it skip across the waves and drop into the churning tide. He took the path that led down to the sea and walked along the beach, his footsteps leaving imprints in the sand that soon disappeared in the ebbing tide.

A fine spray of water dampened his face and it seemed to clear his mind. He knew what Jilliana would do if anyone threatened the peace of Talshamar. She would gather her forces and dispatch the Judas, and that is what he must do. Ruyen smiled reminiscently. Jilliana was glorious, there was no doubt that no woman, living or dead, could equal her in tenacity.

He suddenly stood stock still. When had he begun to love Jilliana? Had it been that first day when she stood before Henry, defying him so courageously—or had it been the first night he had taken her body to his? He blinked his eyes as his mind cleared even more. How could he have allowed her to leave without telling her how he felt? She was his wife, and if he lived through this war, by God, there would be no annulment!

He climbed back up the cliff with determination. When he reached the hunting lodge, an awesome sight met his eyes. It seemed that the whole village had gathered there. He looked from one familiar face to another, and the men, women, and children bowed to him as he walked slowly among them.

"Why gather you here?" he asked of no one in particular.

An older knight stepped forward. It was Sir Piermont, whose son Byran had died fighting beside Ruyen in England. The man's care-worn face was pale with age, but his dark eyes were alive with the light of rebellion.

"I knew your son well," Ruyen said. "He was a valiant soldier, who brought pride to his family's name."

"That he did, Your Highness. And if he were here today, like the rest of us, he would offer you his sword arm, his loyalty, and his life," the old knight said.

Ruyen was overwhelmed by such devotion, for he had not expected it. As the moments passed, the number of people continued to swell. Knights, peasants, and villagers stood together united in a common cause—to fight beside the man they considered their rightful king.

Ruyen was quiet for a long moment as he chose his words carefully. "Know you all who stand within the sound of my voice that civil war is the ugliest of all wars, for we shall be fighting against many of our own countrymen, even our own families."

"We have thought of this," Sir Piermont told him, "but nothing could be worse than the conditions we are forced to endure at the hands of the Castilians. Yes, and those of Falcon Bruine who have turned against us to side with our enemies."

"There will be great casualties," Ruyen warned.

"There are casualties every day from starvation because of the high taxes imposed on us," a woman called out, and the multitude murmured their agreement with her.

"You are our rightful king," Sir Piermont stated with feeling. "We will have no other in your stead. What we want to hear from you is whether you will stand with us against your own mother."

In Ruyen's heart there burned the fire of long-dead kings. These were his people and they were offering him their fealty and their trust. He unsheathed his sword and pointed it to the heavens.

"I will fight with you though the enemy be my own mother. This I swear!"

A deafening shout went up among the people and there was jubilation on each face. The flame of patriotism swept through the crowd, making them all one voice.

Ruyen turned to Sir Piermont, knowing the old knight had fought many campaigns with his father and was a seasoned warrior. "You will be my commander. Have the women and children sent to the far side of the island where they will be safe. Gather weapons and have new ones forged. We must be prepared."

"Aye, that we must, Your Highness," the old knight agreed with a spark in his eyes.

"I am depending on your superior knowledge, Sir Piermont. Set up camps in the woods and post guards to alert you should danger come. Put men to work building ladders and amassing ropes, chains, and weapons. It will be nigh impossible to breach the walls of the castle, but we shall gather our forces and cut off the castle's source of food and water, forcing them to surrender."

"I will see to it at once, Your Highness," Sir Piermont said with certainty, mentally selecting the strongest men to carry out his orders.

"We need to build our defenses carefully," Ruyen continued, "even though my mother is not a strategist in warfare and Escobar is certainly no great brain. I calculate that the castle will fall before winter loosens its grip on the land."

"Aye," someone in the vast crowd yelled. "We'll starve the devils out."

Ruyen's eyes saddened as he thought of his sister. "That we will, but you must all realize that many of our own people work in the castle and they will suffer hunger, maybe death, before the siege is over."

Sir Piermont proudly raised his head, his faded blue eyes moving over the faces in the crowd. "I stand ready to serve the son as I served the sire."

The loud roar of assenting voices was heartwarming and chilling at the same time. Ruyen realized that the results of his actions here today would ripple across the island and none of his people would ever be the same. They would be victorious, of that he had no doubt, but at what cost?

"We must disperse now," Ruyen urged the people. "My mother has her spies and they will become suspicious if they learn of this gathering." He turned to the women who would be most affected by war. "Go to your homes and gather only what you will need to survive. Each of you will know hardship for a time."

The women were silent as they pondered his words. "Better to starve with a friend than dine with the enemy," one of them called loudly, drawing vigorous nods from the others.

Ruyen turned away to gather his shield and armor. He must warn Katharine to leave Falcon Bruine with all haste or be caught up in the war—he owed her that much.

It was dusk when Ruyen rode into the gates of Greenleigh Keep. A servant led him immediately to the garden, where he found Katharine. She wore a pale green tunic and a darker green surcoat, and her golden hair hung freely down her back. She was a very handsome woman, but Ruyen was not moved by her beauty as he had once been.

When she saw Ruyen, Katharine's mouth rounded in surprise and her face paled. "What are you doing here? It is not safe for me to be seen with you."

Ruyen tensed. "Why say you this, Katharine?"

"There is talk of war. It is said that you will fight against your own mother."

"That's why I came to see you," he said.

"Why must you do this, Ruyen? Can you not accept things as they are? Your mother cannot live forever, so if you only bide your time, you will be king without this silly little war."

Disappointment showed in his eyes. "I had hoped you would understand, Katharine."

She glared at him. "Did you think what this would mean for us?" she asked accusingly. "Have you no thought for our future?"

Ruyen's voice was cold. "There is no future for us, and I confess that I thought only of the people who are suffering under my mother's rule."

Katharine felt her heart contract. How had she lost Ruyen's love?

He looked at her as if seeing her clearly for the first time. "I only came to warn you that Falcon Bruine will no longer be safe. You and your father still have time to leave if you make haste."

Her lips trembled and a lone tear trailed down her cheek. "Why should you care what happens to me?"

He felt uncomfortable. "I have a high regard for you, Katharine, I always have had."

She lifted her eyes to him, deeply ashamed of the way she had behaved since learning of his marriage to that Talshamarian woman. She could never have him as her husband, but perhaps it was not too late to redeem herself in Ruyen's eyes.

Her smile was etched with melancholy. "Do you not know that a woman needs more than a man's regard? She needs to be madly loved, to be his only love. I realize now that you never loved me as much as I love you. I believe you have fallen in love with your Jilliana."

"I never meant to hurt you, Katharine. Can you forgive me?"

She visibly flinched, then smiled sadly. "Pity, Ruyen, I would have made you an admirable wife."

He shook his head. "Alas, I fear I would have made you an abominable husband. You deserve better."

She shook her head and then pressed her hand to his shoulder. "Ruyen, have you tried to settle the differences between you and your mother without bloodshed?"

"My mother listens only to the voice that comes out of Castile, but I intend to speak to her again."

"You should be careful, Ruyen. Father says that there are strange happenings at the castle."

"What kind of happenings?"

Suddenly her eyes took on a look of concern, reminding him of the old Katharine. "There is talk that Queen Jilliana never left the island. My father says that her men have either been captured or put to death, and that she is being held prisoner by your mother. Go at once to your wife, Ruyen. I fear she may have need of you."

He stared at her in disbelief. "My mother has gone too far this time. If she has harmed Jilliana—"

"You will be careful, Ruyen?"

He hardly heard her words. What a fool he had been for not seeing Jilliana safely aboard her ship. He had known the way his mother's mind worked, and he should never have trusted her.

Anxious to leave, he spoke hurriedly to Katharine. "Thank you for telling me about Jilliana. You should leave Falcon Bruine in all haste."

"I shall. My father has said that France is lovely this time of year."

"Good-bye then, Katharine. I wish you happiness."

She came to him and placed her hand on his sleeve. She realized that even if Queen Jilliana had not come into his life, she would never have held Ruyen's heart.

"Your mother is dangerous. Watch out for her and Escobar." She kissed his cheek in farewell, but he seemed to look right through her. She knew that his mind was with the woman he loved.

Ruyen hurried out of the garden and mounted his horse, riding like a man possessed. Rather than approach the castle from the front gate, he rode to the side where supplies were delivered to the kitchen.

"Admit me at once," he called up to the lone sentry who guarded the gate.

Immediately the gate was thrown open and Ruyen rode inside. As he dismounted, he observed that extra guards had been posted in the outer courtyard, so he entered the castle by the kitchen. As he hurried across the stone floor, he drew several startled looks from the cooks and their helpers. No one could ever remember a time when the prince had been in the kitchen. He spoke to no one as he climbed the back stairs that led to the private chambers.

Ruyen's steps were hurried as he rushed down the dark corridor. He stopped at the corner and then dropped back, pressing his body into the shadows. A Castilian guard stood before Jilliana's chamber, and the man seemed alert to all that went on around him.

"Your Highness," an oily voice Ruyen despised spoke from behind him. Turning, he looked down into the cunning eyes of Escobar Hernandez.

"I have been expecting you, Your Highness."

"Where is my mother, Castilian swine?"

Escobar's eyes narrowed just the merest bit at the prince's insult. "She is resting at the moment and does not wish to be disturbed."

Ruyen watched as Escobar's hand moved to the dagger he wore at his waist, and the man toyed nervously with the jeweled hilt.

"I would not do that if I were you, little man," Ruyen warned. "I could slice your throat from ear to ear before you could brandish that toy."

"You mistake me, Highness. I would not be so foolhardy as to draw blade against one of your strength and might. I have no wish to sacrifice my life when there are others who can prevent you from reaching your wife. You did come to free Queen Jilliana, did you not?"

Ruyen shoved Escobar aside, but the Castilian quickly planted himself in Ruyen's path. "If you could see around that corner, Your Highness, you'd notice the guard who stands before your wife's door. And, there are other soldiers within the sound of my voice. I have but to call out and they will come to me."

With lightning quickness, Ruyen whisked out his sword and placed the point at Escobar's throat. "It is fortunate for me that you came along. Otherwise, I would not have so worthy an accomplice."

Escobar's eyes darted to Ruyen's face and when he saw the raw hatred there, he knew that he looked into the face of death. "You cannot win in this, Your Highness," he said in a trembling voice. "Surrender to me, and your mother will be lenient with you."

"Fool, if I fail in my task, you will never live to see it," Ruyen hissed. He spun Escobar about so his back was to him and then jerked Escobar's dagger free of its sheath. "Dismiss the guard," he said, pressing the dagger against Escobar's spine. "Make one mistake, and you're a dead man. Now, inform the guard that Queen Jilliana is to be placed in my charge."

"He will not believe it," Escobar said spitefully. Then he yelped as he felt the sting of the dagger as it pierced his skin.

"Then you must be very persuasive," Ruyen spat, "or you will die at his feet!"

Escobar knew that the prince made no idle threat, and would not hesitate to end his life.

As they approached the guard, Escobar nodded at the man, trying to sound natural, but it was difficult to keep his voice from trembling as he felt blood drip down his back.

"You are relieved of duty," Escobar said hurriedly.

"Will you require no guard at this door?" the man asked, looking from Escobar to the prince suspiciously.

"Can you not take orders?" Ruyen stated firmly. "Do you question authority?"

"No, Your Highness, it's just that—"

"You stand relieved of duty."

The guard bowed. "As you wish."

Escobar watched his only hope disappear into the dark recesses of the hallway, and then even the man's footsteps faded into silence.

28

Jilliana sat near the window with her sewing in her lap, trying to catch the last dying rays of the sun. Netta had gone below to the garden, where she was allowed to pick roses each day to brighten up the dreary chamber. When the door opened, Jilliana thought it was her maid returning. She was astonished when Escobar landed at her feet, groaning in pain.

She stood quickly to face her husband, who seemed to loom over her. At last she could vent her anger on him. "What is the meaning of this, Ruyen?"

"There is no time to talk," he told her. "Have you a cloak?"

"At last I can tell you what I think of you— You blackguard—miscreant—knave!"

His lip curled in annoyance. "I have no time to swap insults with you." He jerked her cloak from a peg and thrust it at her. "Put this on and hurry."

She crossed her arms and tapped her foot. "Why should I?"

Ruyen let out an impatient breath. "Do as I say, and do it now, Jilliana."

Her voice was even and cold. "I will not."

He grabbed her arm and thrust her toward the door. She was about to blast him with an angry retort, when Escobar stood, a satisfied smile on his thin lips.

"Ah, the trials a man must endure at the hands of a reluctant woman."

Ruyen shoved Escobar against the wall. "I will hear no more from you, spineless ass."

To Jilliana's astonishment, Ruyen brought the handle of a dagger down hard against Escobar's temple and the man crumpled to the floor to lie still at his feet.

Without ceremony, Ruyen took Jilliana's arm and pulled her to the door. "If you want your freedom, you had better come with me and do exactly as I tell you."

That was all she needed to hear. She flung the cloak about her shoulders and nodded. "I agree to come with you only because I see no recourse."

He stepped into the corridor, looking left and right, then motioned for her to follow. When he took her wrist, she had to run to keep pace with his long strides. He led her down the back stairs and into the kitchen. Thus far, luck had been with them, for no one had challenged them.

Amidst looks of astonishment from the kitchen servants, Ruyen hurried Jilliana out the door and into the courtyard. Without ceremony, he swung her onto his horse, then climbed on behind her. Guiding the animal toward the side gate, he steadied the horse until they were safely outside the castle walls.

Drawing a deep breath of relief, he nudged his horse into a gallop. Soon the hue and cry would go out that Jilliana had escaped, and he wanted to be far away when that happened.

She held her body rigid so it would not come in contact with his. To her, Ruyen was still the enemy and she did not trust him. "Where are you taking me?" she demanded.

Grinding his jaw at her high tone, he spoke. "At the moment, where no one will find you."

Hot fury coursed through her. "If this is another scheme you concocted with your mother—"

"Jilliana," he said in exasperation, "later you can call me names and wish me to hell all you want. But for now, spare me the sound of your voice."

His arrogance went through her like a destructive wind. With indignation, she tightened her lips and became even more rigid, but she said nothing more to him.

On they rode, skirting the village and entering the thick undergrowth of vine-covered woods. Nettles tore at her sleeve and branches slapped against her face. Just when she thought she could stand it no longer, they rode into a clearing and then were racing along a stretch of sandy beach.

As the sun made its exit with blazing splashes of fiery color across the western sky, Ruyen jumped from his mount and stared in the direction of the merchant ship that had disappeared from the horizon.

"Damn!" he swore, turning his eyes to Jilliana. "I had not thought they would sail today."

With curious regard, Jilliana stared at him. "Do you mean you were going to set me free?"

His dark eyes sparked anger. "I cannot imagine you would think I would want to keep you. You have been nothing but trouble from the very first day."

Suddenly her heart was soaring with elation. He had not betrayed her! She slid off the horse and went to him, placing her small hand into his. "How could I ever have doubted you?"

He looked at her, his dark eyes burnished with flecks of gold in their fathomless depths. "You had every right to doubt. It seems no one is what they pretend to be and one cannot tell friend from foe until it is too late."

Gently, she brushed her hand against his face. "The

fear—the captivity—was all worth it to find that you had kept your word to me."

Sardonic amusement played on his lips. "Careful when you look at a man like that, Jilliana. You might give him reason to hope."

She glanced steadfastly at the swelling waves, then raised her eyes to fix him with a level stare. "Sometimes, Ruyen, hope is all we have."

With a sharp intake of breath, he grabbed her to him, pressing her close. "I do not know what tomorrow will bring, Jilliana, but for this moment, allow me to hold you as if you belonged to me."

She threw her head back, her eyes soft with the light of love. "I will never belong to anyone save you."

Ruyen laughed and brushed the sand from her cheek. "Then I have won the greatest treasure of all."

For a long moment they stared into each other's eyes, looking for, and finding, the love they sought. Gently his lips moved over hers as if he were testing her response. When her mouth softened beneath his, his kiss became possessive, bruising, impressing his ownership on her.

Suddenly Ruyen realized that they were standing in the open where anyone could see them. Lovingly, he lifted her in his arms, then shoved his foot into the stirrup and climbed on the horse, keeping her tightly against him. "You belong to me," he told her.

"Heart and soul," Jilliana replied. Suddenly she felt such a deep love for him that she could not look into his eyes, but buried her face against his broad chest.

Ruyen nudged his horse forward. She loved him, he could see that now. Tomorrow would bring separation and war, but tonight belonged to them.

By now the moon shimmered through the branches and Jilliana raised her face to him. "Where are you taking me?"

"To a secret place that I have never shared with anyone else."

She touched her lips to his cheek. "I don't care where we go as long as I can be with you."

His expression was serious. "You do know that I must send you to safety tomorrow?"

"I do not want to leave you."

"You must. There will be war, and I do not want you caught up in it."

She frowned, knowing what he must be feeling. "You will fight your mother."

He hoped she would understand. "I must."

"Yes, it is the only way."

He slid his arms about her, bringing her tightly against him. "I must find a ship to take you to Talshamar."

"I am not afraid. Let me stand beside you in what you must do."

Ruyen's heart swelled with pride in her. She was fearless and loyal, something he had never encountered in a woman. "You must think of the child," he reminded her. "No matter what, promise me you will do what is best for you and our baby."

She closed her eyes, laying her head against his shoulder. "I promise."

Jilliana lost all sense of time as his mouth moved up her neck, toyed with her ear and brushed her lips. His hands moved over her swollen breasts and she nestled against him. The love she had so newly confessed made her ache for total fulfillment.

He dipped his head and covered her lips with a searing kiss. Jilliana had not realized that they had stopped. Ruyen lifted her from the horse and carried her down a path.

The night was magical, and with a full moon hanging in the sky, it seemed almost like daytime. Thousands of stars twinkled against an ebony background while flirtatious fireflies were carried on the evening breeze. The melodic sound of some exotic night bird sweetened the air, and somewhere in the distance Jilliana could hear the sound of rushing water.

"Are we almost there?" she asked breathlessly as he paused to taste her tempting lips once more.

He lowered her until her feet almost touched the ground, but with strong hands pressed her to his body. "We have arrived," he said against her lips.

She turned and watched, entranced by a rushing stream that glistened like silver. "It's lovely—almost magical."

He turned her to face him. "You make it magical."

Their mouths met and fused. Slowly their bodies drifted downward onto the sweet summer grass, the wonderful aroma enhanced by wild clover.

"I love you, Jilliana," he said, holding her as gently as he would the most fragile flower.

"And I love you," she answered, her eyes glowing as if lit by hundreds of candles.

He gently traced the outline of her face with his thumb. "You do know that this may be the last night we can ever have together?"

Sadness filled her heart as she nodded her head. "Yes, I know."

His hand drifted into her hair and he pulled her forward. "I will make this a night you will never forget. I will always remember you as you are now, with the starlight in your eyes and moonbeams reflecting off your hair."

She took his face between her hands and a sob broke from her lips. "Every night of my life, when I am alone in my bed, I shall relive this moment with you."

"Jilliana, some people have a lifetime together and never know love. We are fortunate, we have only one night, but a lifetime of love."

There were softly murmured words, gentle caresses, lips that hungrily sought reassurance, but created only an aching need. Ruyen slowly and deliberately undressed her, savoring each moment, then she did the same for him.

At last they stood before each other in all their naked glory. He held his arms out to her and she seemed to float to him.

Suddenly touching was not enough. Hot passion flowed between them, fusing and molding them into one body, one mind, one love.

Hardly able to control his passion, Ruyen spread her legs and plunged into her, but remembering the baby that was nourished there, he gentled his movements.

"No one has ever loved as deeply as I, Ruyen," she breathed in his ear.

He could not speak for the pain her words caused him. He felt tears fill his eyes, and was unashamed because of the deep love they shared.

"My heart, my love," he murmured. "Time is our only enemy."

Her face was wet with tears, and he gently kissed them away. They rode the waves of passion. Intoxicating pressure was building inside Jilliana, and she cried out when her body experienced glorious pleasure.

Throughout the night they lay beside each other, sometimes talking softly and often their minds meeting in silence. Jilliana did not want to fall asleep because she did not want to miss one moment of this time with Ruyen. But just before dawn, she drifted off, while he held her cradled in his arms, his lips pressed against her sweet-smelling hair.

The sun was still below the horizon when Ruyen kissed her awake. She stretched and wound her arms about his neck.

"Why did you let me sleep?"

He smiled. "I like watching you. You are beautiful." He gathered her in his arms. "Can you swim?"

"Of course not."

He laughed as he waded into the water while she clung to his neck. "Then you will just have to trust me."

Lovingly, she pressed her cheek to his. "I trust you with my life."

As the sparkling water washed over them, they laughed, splashed, and played like two children just discovering life. Then the sun lit the sky with its golden light and Jilliana became silent, for their time was nearing its end.

Without a word, Ruyen took her hand and led her out of the water. Gently, he helped her dress and then dressed himself.

His eyes were soft as he looked at her. "It is time for us to leave."

"How can I bear it?" she asked.

"You must."

"What about my men, and what about Netta. I cannot leave without them."

"Jilliana, I will do what I can to help them. But you must leave today. You promised."

She lowered her head, praying she would not cry. "I will keep my word."

There, with the morning mist covering the land and the sun spiraling through the branches of the tall trees, they embraced.

"Oh, Ruyen, we wasted so much time fighting each other. If only . . . if only—"

Jilliana never finished what she was about to say. Loud voices called out and horses snorted and reared about them. They were surrounded by Queen Melesant's soldiers!

Ruyen pushed Jilliana behind him and lunged for his sword that lay just out of reach.

"Hold, Your Highness," Escobar said, his eyes darting up and down with excitement. "Do not make me give the order to end your life."

"Bastard!" Ruyen cried as he gripped the handle of his sword. Rolling to his feet, he stood before Jilliana. "Your fight is with me. Let her go, and I'll accompany you peace-fully."

Escobar laughed and his cold lusterless eyes moved over Jilliana in appreciation of her beauty. "I think not, Your Highness. Your mother has asked that I bring you both to her."

With a loud cry, Ruyen ran at Escobar, brandishing his sword.

"Stop him!" the Castilian cried. "Do not let him get to me!"

Jilliana cried out, reaching for Ruyen. She screamed as arrows tore through his body and he fell backward into the sea.

She ran to him, pulling and dragging him from the blood-colored water. "Ruyen," she cried, lacing her fingers through his. "What have they done to you!"

He had been struck by three arrows, and the front of his jerkin was covered with blood. His eyes were so sad as he looked at her. "My dearest love, do not cry . . . remember me . . . and tell our bab—"

His head fell sideways and he went limp. Pressing her lips to his, she stood slowly, facing the man who was responsible for Ruyen's death.

"You will die for this," she said past the sob that was building in her throat.

Escobar looked frightened, not of Queen Jilliana, but because Queen Melesant might very well take his life for killing her son.

With a booted foot, he turned Ruyen over, staring at him for a long time to make certain he was not breathing. "Bring him along later," he said to one of his men. "Give me time to explain to the queen."

Jilliana slumped forward into a shadowy world of blackness. She did not want to live in a world without Ruyen.

29

Queen Eleanor, surrounded by her ladies, listened to the young minstrel play the lute and sing about her days of glory. In irritation, she held up her hand for the singer to stop.

"I want no more morose songs about the past. I want happy songs. Ladies, dance, laugh, be merry."

So saying, she left the gallery, indicating that she wanted to be alone.

These days her prison was becoming too hard to bear. Perhaps it was because Jilliana was no longer with her. The girl had given her a purpose and allowed her to strike out at Henry from her walled prison.

Life no longer held challenge or meaning. The days were too empty, the nights too long.

When she reached her sanctuary, away from the others, she leaned her head against the window and looked out at the bleakness of the day.

"Your Majesty."

Eleanor looked up at her maid. "Have I a letter from Richard?"

"Nay, Your Majesty, but there is something quite odd, that I think you might want to know about."

"What can that be?"

"I was below in the kitchen arranging your tea tray when two men came to the door. They looked to be beggars, and cook, being soft-hearted, offered them bread and admonished them to be on their way. And what do you think?"

Eleanor looked indifferent. "You tell me."

"One of the men said he must get a message to Queen Eleanor."

"Why should I listen to a beggar?"

The maid's voice rose with excitement. "Your Majesty, he said he had come from your ward."

"I have no war—" There was the merest shimmer of hope in her eyes. "What else did this person say?"

"The one man said that he was from Talshamar, and I believed him."

"Where is he?" Excitement was growing within Eleanor. "Bring him to me at once."

"I was certain you would want to see them. They are just outside the door."

Eleanor was poised and regal when the two men entered. They stood several paces from her while she looked them over. They merely looked like beggars to her, and none too clean either.

"Which of you said he was from Talshamar?"

Sir Edward bowed. "'Tis I, Your Majesty. I am Sir Edward, one of the knights who accompanied Queen Jilliana to London and then on to Falcon Bruine."

"Why then are you not with Jilliana now? Why do you come seeking bread at my door?"

"Your Majesty, terrible trouble befell my queen. I know not if she is alive or dead."

Eleanor motioned the man closer so she could watch his eyes as he spoke. She could usually discern when someone was speaking the truth.

"Why say you this, Sir Edward, if that is your true name?"

"A small number of us accompanied the queen to Falcon Bruine." He dropped to one knee and lowered his head. "I feel such shame. It was my duty to keep the queen safe. I have not done so."

"What has happened to Jilliana?"

"Her Majesty has been locked in her chamber and is not allowed to leave. Queen Melesant plans to keep her there until she has the baby."

"What is this? Did you say that Queen Jilliana is with child?"

"Aye, Majesty. We were preparing for our homeward voyage when we were set upon by Queen Melesant's soldiers. Some of our men were slain and others taken to the dungeon."

She read truth in his earnest eyes. "Stand up, Sir Edward, and tell me what happened to Humphrey."

"I am told that he is one of those in the dungeon. I did not see him among my slain countrymen so I believe it to be true."

"You appear to be a resourceful young knight. How is it that you escaped when the others were killed or captured?"

"I was wounded and left for dead. Had it not been for Princess Cassandra and Rob Gilbert, here, I would surely have died."

Eleanor restlessly moved up and down the floor she had paced so many times in the past. She was wondering why Queen Melesant had so brazenly committed such an offense. With her quick mind, she finally understood and shook her head.

"The Castilian queen believes that she can control Talshamar if she takes Jilliana's baby. To control Talshamar, Jilliana would have to be dead, and that I shall never allow. A plague on Melesant—from the devil she came, from the devil she will return!"

"But what can we do, Your Majesty?"

"Do not look so dejected, sir knight," Eleanor said with confidence. "I have defeated more able opponents than that silly queen. She is no match for me."

"But, Madame, you are a prisoner."

Eleanor laughed softly. "You have given me purpose just when I thought I would die if I had to spend another day listening to my silly ladies chattering and gossiping. Ameria, escort these men to a room and prepare a bath. Sir Edward, you shall dine with me tonight and we will plan our stratagem."

Sir Edward had heard much about Eleanor and most of it bad. After today, he would be her most staunch defender if anyone tried to defame her name. Cassandra had been right to send him here, for Queen Eleanor had readily agreed to help him.

Cassandra flattened her body against the wall, listening to her mother rage at Escobar. "*You fool!* You killed my son, and for this you shall pay!"

"He tried to kill me, Majesty. What could I do?"

"Ruyen was a better man than you will ever be. Do you believe I would trade my son's life for yours? *Never!*"

Cassandra pressed her hand over her mouth to keep from crying out in pain. Ruyen dead, how could that be! She swallowed a sob and turned her attention back to her mother.

Melesant's fingers curled into tight fists as she spent her fury on Escobar. "You dared to take it upon yourself to harm my son!"

He had never seen her so enraged, and he moved quickly out of her reach. "I saw no other recourse. I had to stop him. He had betrayed you."

"You are a little man," Melesant said contemptuously, "and little men have little thoughts. Do you think I could not have controlled my own son? Have I not done so before?"

"Yes, Majesty." Escobar cringed as she vented her fury on him. "What would you have me do?"

"You have already set events in motion that cannot be stopped." She advanced on him and he drew back. Although she did not raise her voice, he flinched. "When next you decide that you can dictate policy on Falcon Bruine, that is the day I send you back to Castile minus your head!"

"Yes, Majesty."

"Get from my sight. I no longer want to look upon you."

"Yes, Majesty."

"Go!"

Escobar scurried out the door, passing Cassandra without seeing her. When she entered the room, Cassandra found her mother slumped in her chair, her eyes filled with tears.

Cassandra knew that for her own safety, she must play the innocent fool. "Why are you sad, Mother?"

Melesant stiffened her back. "I have sad tidings, daughter. Your brother has been . . . is dead."

Cassandra clutched her hands, trying not to cry. "But how could such a thing happen?"

"Does it matter? He's dead."

The pain was almost too great for Cassandra to bear. "I . . . want to see his body."

Melesant dabbed at her eyes. "His body was taken away so no one would make a martyr out of him. I'll soon bring this rebellion under control."

"I want to see my brother's body," Cassandra insisted.

"Silly girl, I told you no one will know where he is buried. I have had him laid to rest in secret."

Anger choked Cassandra. Her mother was an unfeeling monster, and she wanted to confront her and accuse her of causing Ruyen's death. It might have been by Escobar's command, but it was her mother's doing none the less.

Instead, Cassandra moved to the door, her head lowered, as if in prayer. Her mother saw her as no threat, therefore her movements were not restricted. She would go now to the village and question the people. Surely someone knew where Ruyen had been buried.

All was quiet in the huntsman's cabin deep in the woods. Outside the cabin, armed men waited, their faces careworn, their swords at hand should trouble come.

Sir Piermont stood over his wounded prince, his aged face furrowed with worry. Prince Ruyen's wounds were deep but he was still alive, and the old knight prayed he would recover. He turned to his squire. "No one but those of us who are gathered here must know that Prince Ruyen is alive. We must guard this secret with our lives."

The huntsman's wife, Mert, spooned foul-tasting medicine into Ruyen's mouth, and he shoved her hand away, groaning.

"It was luck that you found the prince when you did, or he would have died from his wounds. As it is, he may die still, but at least he has a chance," Mert said.

"It was not luck that led us to the prince in his need," Sir Piermont told her. "We followed three of Escobar's foreign soldiers into the woods, knowing they were up to no good. We overheard them say that the queen had ordered her son buried in an unmarked grave. Now those Castilians occupy the grave they dug for our prince."

Ruyen was fighting his way out of a dense fog and he called out to Jilliana. His mind was filled with torment because his reckless actions had only prolonged her suffering and she was once more his mother's prisoner.

"I must save her," he said weakly. He tried to rise, only to have persistent hands restrain him.

He recognized Sir Piermont's voice. "You must not move, Your Highness. Your wounds are severe. You must rest and grow stronger before you can help anyone."

The chill of the room made Ruyen shiver, and though he fought to remain conscious, he finally gave up his struggle and surrendered to the blackness that engulfed him.

"There," the old woman said in satisfaction. "He'll sleep through the night."

Melesant stormed into Jilliana's chamber to find her lying on the bed, her eyes swollen from crying and dull with pain. She was obviously grieving over Ruyen, and that nettled Melesant.

"Did you think you could escape me?" she raged. "You have not lived long enough to battle me and win."

Jilliana eased herself off the bed and stood defiantly before Ruyen's mother. "You must be in torment knowing you caused the death of your own son."

Melesant moved around the bed and stood at the window. "When one is placed in power, there are many things one must do that are distasteful." She shrugged. "I would much rather my son were alive, but he knew the risks if he defied me."

"Ruyen would rather have died with honor than live with dishonor."

Melesant whipped her head around and her eyes gleamed with hatred. "You think you knew him so well. If you had not muddled his brain with your soft ways and swaying hips, I could have won him to my side."

"Ruyen was most concerned for the people of this island. Even if I had not been here, he would have warred against you, and he would have won because he had the loyalty of the islanders."

"Little good it did him."

"I pity you, Melesant. You killed the best part of you when you killed your son."

"Do not pity me, Jilliana, rather pity yourself. I am free, you are not."

"Yes, but you paid a high price, did you not."

Melesant wanted to strike Jilliana. She had come here to humble her, to taunt her, but she found in Ruyen's wife a strength and courage she could only admire. "A high price indeed, but worth it since I will soon hold the scepters of both Falcon Bruine and Talshamar."

"You will never reign in Talshamar," Jilliana told her.

"You do not understand, do you? I will rule through the child you carry. When your baby is born, it will be taken from you. But fear not that the babe will be harmed. I shall take particular care of its health and make it my heir."

Jilliana could not hide her horror. "You cannot have my baby!"

Melesant laughed gleefully. She had found a way after all to bring Jilliana to her knees—the child. "Oh, but I can."

"You would do this to your own son's child?"

"Let me tell you, my girl, I have done many things, performed many tasks that would offend your delicate sensibilities. I bear no shame for anything and ask pardon of no one."

Now Jilliana was frightened, not for herself, but for her unborn child. "Have pity, Melesant. Do not take my baby from me."

Melesant swept to the door, then turned back to her prisoner. "I have every right to the child." She smiled maliciously. "Unless you have bedded someone besides my son and are now attempting to pass the brat off as Ruyen's."

"You are disgusting."

Only Melesant's eyes seemed alive in her stone face, and what she saw in those eyes made Jilliana shudder.

"Only consider," Melesant said smoothly, "without your child, Falcon Bruine has no heir except Cassandra, and I fear my daughter is addle-brained and could never rule this island."

"You are mad. There is nothing wrong with Cassandra."

"Perhaps not, but it matters little. I will give you something to ponder. Every day brings you closer to delivering your baby, and before you can even lay eyes upon it, that child will be mine." Now her voice was silken and she smiled slightly. "Is this not a bitter thing to endure, Jilliana?"

"I will find a way to defeat you," Jilliana said, raising her chin and denying the tears that gathered behind her eyes. "You may ponder that."

Melesant laughed and left the room.

Jilliana held on to the back of a chair so tightly that her knuckles whitened. In truth she was trembling like a leaf on an aspen tree. Never had she felt so alone.

"Ruyen, my beloved," she sobbed, "what am I to do to save our baby?"

30

Because of her son's popularity with the people of Falcon Bruine, Melesant had tried to keep Ruyen's death a secret, but of course that had not been possible. Every day for weeks the islanders gathered outside the castle, not saying anything—just staring up at the walls.

Angrily, Queen Melesant ordered them to be driven away. But the next day, they returned in larger numbers. It was unnerving, and Melesant was trying to think of a way to end their silent siege.

After a while, she began to ignore them. Without Ruyen's leadership, the people were no more than a disorganized mob, with no mind, no direction, and no hope.

Jilliana languished in her chamber, her anger smoldering, her heartbreak too painful to bear. She could still not believe that Ruyen was dead. It was all so senseless. She swore that if God in His mercy saw fit to release her from her prison, Queen Melesant would one day pay for what she had done.

And so the weeks turned into months, and autumn stretched into a long winter. One day followed another and everyone on Falcon Bruine seemed to be waiting for something to happen, but what that was they did not know.

As Melesant predicted, those who had supported Ruyen floundered without his leadership. Those who backed her watched the sea, fearing reprisals when the Talshamarians learned their queen had been captured.

Jilliana's spirits plummeted with each passing day. When she stood at her window so high above the ground, she felt like a caged bird, and she was reminded of Eleanor in her prison. It was hard to have hope when there was none.

"Your Majesty," Netta said with concern. "You look pale. You do not get enough sun and fresh air."

"There is no help for that, Netta."

"You need proper clothing since yours no longer fit. And your wardrobe is not suited for winter. But then you did not expect to pass the winter on this island."

"I will just have to make do with what I have. Queen Eleanor has been a prisoner far longer than I and she has endured it."

"Yes, but she had the use of a castle, and you have but this room."

Jilliana smiled faintly. "I do not mind this small space. It suits me. What I do miss is the long walks I took at the convent. I remember the mornings when the grass was still wet with dew. I miss the aroma of wood smoke and the way the earth smells just after a rain. Mostly, though, I miss Ruyen."

Netta's eyes were filled with tears. "My poor lady, it breaks my heart to see you pining away for your dead husband. If I could rid you of the pain, I would do so."

Jilliana picked up her sewing and took several small stitches before laying it aside once more. "Netta, I believe there is something we should talk about. You know that Queen Melesant is never going to let me leave here alive."

Netta's throat became choked with sobs. "I will not believe that. You are too good and kind to die. I will not believe that there is no hope."

"Dear Netta, do not weep for me. I do have one hope—you are that hope."

Netta dried her eyes and looked puzzled. "Me?"

"Yes. Netta, I know how you would like to return to Talshamar and be with your husband and family."

"I would never leave you."

"Netta, I have tried to think as Melesant thinks and I know that when I am dead, she will not allow you to live either."

"I have thought this also, Your Majesty. But it matters not. My place is at your side."

"But there is hope for you. I must convince Melesant that my baby will need someone from Talshamar as nurse."

Netta looked surprised. "You would want me to care for the royal child?"

"I would trust no other."

"But if you die, I will not want to live."

"You must, so you can one day tell my baby what has happened and instill pride in her. Will you do that for me?"

Netta's shoulders slumped. "Aye, Your Majesty. The pity is that the closer it gets to the birth of the child, . . . the closer it gets to—"

"I know, Netta. But we will not think of that. There is something else I want you to do for me."

"Anything."

Jilliana lowered her voice. "Is there anyone in the kitchen that you can trust?"

"I am not certain. I believe many do not approve of what has happened to you. The head cook is a jolly-faced woman who is always inquiring about you. You know she bakes those special cakes for you."

"Do you think she could be trusted enough to get a message to Cassandra?"

"I think so. I shall ask her, but it may take time to see her alone."

"I am worried about the princess. I know she has no part in this. She must be so saddened by what has happened, and I want her to know that I believe in her innocence."

Jilliana walked to the bed and lay down. "I am very weary now, Netta. I'll just rest for a bit."

She turned her face to the wall. Sleep was the only freedom allowed her. For while she slept, she dreamed of her beloved. He was alive and holding her tenderly in his arms as he had done their last night together.

At that moment, there was a loud pounding on the door. Jilliana sat up and watched as two guards entered unannounced.

"Why are you bothering Her Majesty?" Netta asked, standing between them and Jilliana.

"Queen Melesant told us to take your lady's jewel coffers and her trunks."

Netta knew the coffers contained many valuable jewels as well as the crown of Talshamar. "You cannot have them."

"It matters but little, Netta," Jilliana said, fearing her loyal maid would protest too much and one of the men might hurt her. "Let them take what they will."

After the guards had left, Jilliana and Netta sat in silence for a time.

"That is the last of it," Jilliana stated. "I have nothing else for Melesant to take but my baby and my life."

"She is evil."

Jilliana moved off the bed and walked to the window. "Aye, that she is," she said, watching a flock of birds in perfect formation arch across the blue skies. Winter still blew its frosty breath down on the island, and she knew that in spring her baby would be born.

She touched her stomach, loving the child that grew there, because while she had the child, she still retained that small part of Ruyen. She had faced defeat, but she would not be defeated. Ruyen had taught her that.

Spring was late. The wind was howling past the battlements and snow was flying in a frenzy of white. Inside the small bedchamber, Jilliana was in the thralls of labor and she gritted her teeth to keep from crying out in pain.

Since a guard was always posted outside the door, Jilliana clamped her hand over her mouth and groaned.

"Netta, I must not cry out," she gasped, as another pain ripped through her body. "I must bear this in silence, lest Melesant's man hears and reports to her."

She held Netta's hand tightly while she arched her body. "Oh, Netta, the pain is so bad."

The maid wiped a damp cloth across Jilliana's forehead. She was witnessing a kind of courage that she could only admire. How could the queen suffer so much pain in silence.

"If I could bear it for you, I would do so, Your Majesty."

The two of them had shared so much that Jilliana felt affection for this woman of humble birth. Now she must call on Netta's strength because hers was ebbing. The pains had begun just after the midnight hour and now it was almost noon.

Netta had made several trips downstairs. First, she had gone to fetch water, then linens and towels. She dared not leave Jilliana alone again, for the pains were more frequent and it was surely time for the baby to be born.

"It is taking so long, Your Majesty. Should I not get help for you?"

"No, no! If Melesant learns of the birth of my baby, she will take it from me. I want to keep it with me as long as I can— We must—"

Just then another pain pinned Jilliana to the bed and she moaned, turning her head from side to side. She wanted to scream because it felt as if a tight vice was squeezing her body. This one seemed to last longer than the others, and when it subsided, Jilliana was so weak she could scarcely raise her hand.

"Netta, will it be much longer?"

"I know so little about childbirth, Your Majesty," Netta replied sadly. "I pray the child comes soon."

Jilliana whimpered softly and twisted her body as a tight wave of pain engulfed her.

Netta felt fear grip her—the baby was being born! Gently she took the head in her hands and guided the tiny body as it finally emerged. After the cord was clipped, she wrapped the child in a warm blanket and held it lovingly in her arms.

"Your Majesty, it is a girl—a princess!"

Jilliana's tense body trembled and her head fell back against the pillow. She was so weary, all she wanted to do was sleep. "Is she all right? Should not a baby cry?"

Netta laughed. "She is perfect. The princess did not cry because she wants to remain with her mother. It is a miracle, is it not?"

"Yes, a miracle," Jilliana said weakly.

Netta handed the little princess to her mother. Jilliana smiled as she touched the small hand and then placed a kiss on the soft cheek.

"She is beautiful."

"Aye, like her mother."

Their eyes met, and both women knew that the child would soon be taken away. They could not keep her birth a secret for long.

"Put the child to your breast, Your Majesty. You have the means of feeding her, and it will help prevent her from crying."

As the rosebud mouth closed on Jilliana's breast, tears rolled down her cheeks. "How can I ever give her up?"

Netta had no answer, but her eyes were filled with pain. She had come to know the compassion and kindness of the queen, and that someone as evil as Melesant should torture her so made her angry.

"I will go below to fetch you something to eat. You will need nourishment to regain your strength."

"So I can be strong for the execution, Netta? How do you suppose they will do it?"

"I . . . cannot . . . think it will . . . happen." Netta rushed to the door and rapped three times, the signal to the guard that she wanted to leave the chamber.

Jilliana pulled the cover over the child, lest the guard see her. When she was alone with her new daughter, she gently swept her hand over the tiny head.

"My dearest daughter, I gave you life, but I cannot protect you for long." She closed her eyes and tears of anguish squeezed through the eyelids. "I hope that you will one day learn about your father, and how he gave his life for you and me."

Jilliana knew now the heartbreak her mother must have felt when she had sent her daughter to safety, knowing she would soon die. Like her mother, she would not be allowed to see her daughter grow to womanhood.

On entering the kitchen, Netta was so engrossed in her own thoughts that she paid little attention to those about her. It was her habit to prepare a tray for Jilliana and she did so now. The cook nodded to her.

"Netta, if you will go into the storeroom, there is extra cheese for your lady."

Netta was about to refuse when the cook nodded. "Go, now— Go. She will like the cheese."

Netta had intended to speak to the cook about Princess Cassandra as the queen had urged, but there had never been a moment when they had been alone.

When she entered the storeroom, she saw a slab of cheese on a round table and took up a knife to slice it when someone spoke up behind her. She was startled when she heard Princess Cassandra emerge from behind a large barrel.

"Quickly, Netta, how is your mistress? Does she fare well?"

The maid stared into the young girl's eyes, wondering if she dared trust her. The queen trusted her, and she might be their last hope.

"She is not well."

"Oh, I feared as much. I have been frantic for her safety."

Netta decided to confide in the princess. She lowered her voice lest they be overheard. "Her Majesty gave birth to a daughter, this very day. No one knows."

Cassandra's eyes filled with tears. "We must act quickly, then, for Jilliana is in grave danger now that the child has been born."

"What can we do?"

"Tell her not to lose heart. Sir Edward has survived and has just returned from Queen Eleanor with a plan to save her. She must be ready to act quickly when the opportunity comes. It must be soon."

There was hope mirrored in Netta's eyes. "I will tell Her Majesty what you have said."

"Go now, quickly! We do not want to arouse suspicion."

Netta grabbed up a large hunk of cheese and placed it on the tray. "Oh, bless you, Your Highness. You have given me hope. But have a care, for to help my queen is to bring danger to yourself."

"I shall."

As Netta climbed the stairs with a spring in her step, she did not know that black, malevolent eyes watched her from an open doorway.

Queen Melesant shook her head and drew back into the library, motioning for Escobar to follow her. "Your assumption is absurd. Jilliana would have been screaming and everyone would have heard her if she was giving birth."

"The guard reported to me that the servant has been acting suspiciously all day. He said that he had to let her out several times and she came downstairs on one pretense, then another. It is my belief that Queen Jilliana is having her baby, or perhaps she has already delivered."

Melesant walked hurriedly out the door, heading for the stairs. "I'll just see for myself."

Jilliana was propped against pillows, holding her sleeping daughter, when she heard the sound of the lock sliding and the door was thrust open.

She clutched the baby to her as Melesant stormed into the room, her eyes blazing, her face distorted with fury.

"So, foolish girl, you thought to keep the child a secret from me?"

Netta would have stepped between Jilliana and her mother-in-law, but Jilliana shook her head. "This is my baby, and you cannot have her."

"Ah, so it is a girl." Melesant walked closer, peering at her granddaughter, and her shadow fell across the infant's face like an evil omen. "Give her to me."

Jilliana's grip on her daughter tightened. "No, I will not!"

"I think you will." Melesant called over her shoulder. "Step inside, Escobar, I may have need of you."

Jilliana became a mother fighting for her young. She slid off the bed and hurried toward the open door, but before she could reach freedom, Escobar blocked her path. His smile sent shivers down her spine.

She turned back to her mother-in-law, her eyes pleading. "I beseech you, do not do this. Do not take my baby. I am willing to do anything you ask, but let me keep my baby."

"So, the mighty queen of Talshamar is humbled and

begs like any of the common people," Melesant said, enjoying Jilliana's torment.

Jilliana fell to her knees, still clutching the child. "Yes, I'll beg or do anything you ask of me, only do not take my daughter."

"Grab her!" Melesant shouted to Escobar. "Hold her fast."

He grasped Jilliana about the waist, while Melesant ripped the child from her arms. For the first time since she had been born, the infant began to cry.

Netta's loyal heart was burning with indignation. She rushed to Jilliana and gathered her into her arms. "Give the princess back to Her Majesty. You cannot do this to her."

"Out of my way, toad," Melesant said, sweeping to the door and out of the room.

Jilliana held her hand out entreatingly, but the door slammed behind Melesant, and the bolt ground into place. Jilliana sank to her knees and lowered her head until it touched the floor. She could hear the sound of her daughter crying. It became fainter, and then she could hear it no more.

"Oh, God, watch over my baby," she moaned. "What will happen to her?"

Netta sadly shook her head. "Allow me to help you into bed, Your Majesty."

Jilliana stood up, tears swimming in her eyes. "I do not care what happens to me. I died a little the day Ruyen died, and I died again today when they took our daughter."

Weakly, Jilliana fell back on the bed. "I have failed, Netta, in all that was expected of me. What will become of Talshamar?"

"Here, now, Your Majesty," Netta said gently, "I have something to tell you that will give you hope. Princess Cassandra has said that help is near."

Jilliana stared out the window at the bleak sky. "There is no hope for me."

31

Cassandra hurried toward the dining hall, where her mother was entertaining an emissary who had arrived from Castile the day before. She had run all the way from the woods, and she slipped into her chair, trying to catch her breath.

"You are late, Cassandra," Melesant accused.

The lie came easily to the princess's lips. "I was in the nursery with the baby. She likes to have me rock her and sing to her."

This seemed to pacify the queen. Cassandra had to be careful so her mother would not suspect her. Sir Edward had come this morning and she had been with him while they plotted Jilliana's escape.

Cassandra noticed that her mother was wearing one of Jilliana's gowns. Since Jilliana was smaller than the queen, the seamstress had been instructed to let the dress out. Cassandra ground her teeth, attempting not to show her anger, for her mother was also wearing Jilliana's jewels.

The girl's eyes moved to the Castilian emissary, Count Renaldo Ortiz, who had been placed on her mother's right. Cassandra observed her mother's exaggerated movements and her girlish laughter. She had seen this all before and she recognized the posture—it was always the same when her mother took a new lover. She would ply him with attention, then tease and taunt her poor victim with the audacity of a milkmaid.

Count Renaldo had a wife and seven children in Castile, but that did not seem to matter to either of them. Her mother could be very charming when it suited her, and it was easy to see that Count Renaldo was flattered by her attention.

"Your Majesty," he said, "allow me to offer you my condolences for the death of your son. It is a tragedy."

"Yes," Melesant answered with two bright spots glowing on her cheeks. "He was slain by that rabble who would see war come to our island."

"My illustrious Majesty bade me assure you that he will send troops to help you stop the rebellion, although we ourselves are having our own troubles with the Moors."

Melesant placed her hand on the count's. "I know who my friends are, and I will not be ungrateful."

Cassandra raised her wine glass to her lips and paused. "Count Renaldo, did my mother tell you that she has only last week become a grandmother?" she asked softly.

The man looked startled. "But, Your Majesty, surely you are much too young to be a grandmother."

The look Melesant cast her daughter was pure poison. "After you have finished your meal, you may be excused, Cassandra," she said in a hard voice.

"I would have a word with you first, Mother," the princess persisted.

There was a warning in Melesant's eyes. "Anything you have to say can be said later."

Cassandra was having a hard time hiding her dislike for her mother. She would never forgive her for Ruyen's death. "But, Mother," she said smiling, "the matter concerns the woman upstairs. You know she—"

"Cassandra!" Melesant interrupted, coming abruptly to her feet. "I command you to say nothing further on this matter."

Her daughter blinked her eyes, managing to look innocent. "This matter will not wait, Mother."

"You will excuse us, Count Renaldo. It seems my daughter has something of import to relate to me—" Her eyes burned into Cassandra's, "that cannot wait."

The Castilian rose and bowed, raking the queen with his dark eyes. "Of course. I shall await your return, Your Majesty."

Melesant led the way to the small chamber off the dining hall. She was livid when she closed the door and turned to her daughter.

"What, pray you, was the reason for your behavior just now?"

"I did not think it was wrong to mention the baby or Jilliana. Does not the count know of them both? Everyone else in Falcon Bruine does."

Melesant tapped her foot in irritation. "To be cursed with such a daughter," she said to no one in particular.

"I merely wanted to ask something of you. Perhaps it can wait."

"Now that we are here, tell me what it is," her mother said in an intolerant voice. "But be quick about it."

Cassandra gathered her courage. "The cook has sent word to me that Netta has asked for a priest to attend Jilliana. Will you allow it?"

"I have no time for this now. Why do you bother me with such foolishness?"

Cassandra shrugged, as if it made no difference to her. "Very well, but I am told Jilliana is very weak, refusing to eat again. I believe she wants to starve herself to death. Would it not be wise to allow a priest to see her? If she should die, he can later say it was from her own will."

A smile slowly spread over Melesant's face. "I see . . . yes, what a clever girl you are, after all. You can take care of the details, Cassandra. Get a priest from the village."

Now Cassandra's heart was thundering inside her. "Someone will have to alert the guard at Jilliana's door to admit him when he arrives."

"Yes, yes, I shall have Escobar tend to it." Melesant's mind was already on the handsome man who was waiting for her in the dining hall. Tonight she would invite him to her bed, and he would eagerly comply. "Find Escobar now and send him to me. I shall tell him what to do."

"Yes, Mother."

Cassandra turned away, forcing herself not to run. She had not been able to save her brother, but she would save Jilliana or die trying. She smiled at her own daring. Her mother was not even suspicious of her motives because her mind was occupied with her new lover. The first obstacle had been overcome, but the most difficult one lay ahead.

Jilliana was very ill. Her cheeks were pale, her eyes had dark circles beneath them. Netta knew it was because she had given up all hope and did not want to live. She did not even move or take notice when the door was opened and someone entered.

A priest and a nun stood just inside the door, waiting for the guard to close it, but the guard seemed interested in observing them.

Netta rushed forward, dropping to her knees and taking the priest's hand. "Thank God you have come, Father. My queen needs your spiritual guidance."

The priest withdrew his hand and turned to the guard. "Close the door, my son, so that this poor woman may have her privacy."

When the door slammed and locked, Sir Edward threw

off his hood and so did Cassandra, who wore the habit of a nun.

Sir Edward rushed to the queen. Dropping down on his knees, he looked into dull eyes that had once been so brilliant and was stunned. "Your Majesty, I have come to take you away."

It took Jilliana a moment to focus her eyes. When she saw Sir Edward, she clutched his sleeve. "My baby," she moaned, "they took my baby."

He looked at Netta and Cassandra. "We must hasten. Help her into the habit." He moved away and turned his back while they were dressing the queen. He had come just in time. She would not live long if he did not get her away from here.

Jilliana tried to push Cassandra's hands away. "No, I just want to lie down. I do not want to leave. Do you think me so craven that I would desert my imprisoned people or my child?"

Cassandra grabbed Jilliana's face between her hands and whispered harshly. "Someone has to stop my mother, Jilliana, and it can only be you. You cannot think of yourself. You must think of the people of Talshamar and Falcon Bruine. They need you."

Jilliana's vision seemed to clear and at last she nodded. "I will try. Help me stand."

In no time, she was dressed in a wimple and robe. She reached out her hand to Cassandra. "Thank you for what you have done. But will you be punished?"

"Do not think of that. My mother has a new lover who occupies her attention. Netta and I will keep up the pretense that you are still here for as long as we can, and give you all the time you need to escape. If we are fortunate, they will not discover the deception until you are away from the island."

Jilliana took Netta's hand. "I am loath to leave you. You have become my trusted companion."

Sir Edward took her arm and supported her weight. "We must hurry, Your Majesty. If you delay, all may be lost. You must walk past the guard without my help so he will not become suspicious. Are you able to do that?"

Jilliana drew in a steadying breath and took a tentative step. "I am."

Sir Edward glanced at Cassandra. "I have never known anyone quite like you. I wish we could have known each other better."

She smiled sadly, wondering if she would ever see him again. There was no time to tell him how she admired his courage. "I shall get into bed and pull the covers over my head, so the guard will believe I am Jilliana."

Sir Edward rapped on the door and waited for the guard to open it. "Lower your head," he instructed Jilliana, "and poise your hands as if you are praying."

She followed him out, hoping her legs would carry her.

Sir Edward paused before the guard. "Peace be with you, my son."

As they moved away, Jilliana expected the guard to discover the deception and come after them. When they reached the stairs, she breathed easier. But when she took several steps, her legs went weak and Sir Edward took her arm.

"Keep your head low," he whispered. Then he raised his voice so anyone who might be about could hear. "You should not be sad for Queen Jilliana, it is a far better place she goes to than this troubled world, Sister Mary."

Each obstacle was met and overcome, and at last they were outside the castle walls.

A bitter, cold wind stole Jilliana's breath, and she braced herself against its onslaught. With forced steps, she followed Sir Edward, startled when she saw the two donkeys they were to ride. He helped her onto the shaggy animal's back, and he mounted the other.

For a moment, Jilliana thought she might burst out laughing. He looked so ridiculous with his long legs dangling from the donkey's back and almost touching the ground.

"It would look suspicious if a humble man of the church rode a fine steed," he told her.

It had snowed earlier, but now the sky was clear. On the back of the gaunt little donkey, she rode with her head down, through the village, and no one seemed to pay them any heed.

Several times Jilliana felt weakness wash over her, but she kept a tight grip on the reins, praying she would not fall. On they plodded, past fishing boats that had been moored because of the rough sea.

At last they rounded a cove and several men came forward. Without ceremony, Sir Edward dismounted and took Jilliana in his arms. "You can cling to me now, Your Majesty, we are almost safely away."

She laid her face against his shoulder, wanting to cry, but she was just too weary. She tried not to think of the daughter she was leaving behind, not to mention Humphrey and her other knights imprisoned in the dungeon. She thought about faithful Netta. How would she forgive herself if anything happened to her? And brave little Cassandra had put her life in danger for her sake. Jilliana wondered what she had done to deserve such devotion.

She remembered Ruyen's last words, beseeching her not to forget him, as if she ever could. She would return to Falcon Bruine to get her daughter, and at that time, she would show Melesant no mercy.

Jilliana was wrapped in warm furs and placed in a boat while several men rowed to the ship that was riding the restless waves.

When she was on board, the sails dropped and pride surged through her when she saw the flag of Talshamar snapping in the wind.

She had escaped!

Sir Edward saw her swaying on her feet and again lifted her in his arms.

"We have provided warm quarters for you, Your Majesty." He smiled. "You sail for home."

She pressed her face against his, loving him not as a man, but as a loyal subject who had endured many hardships for her sake.

"Yes," she said weakly, "take me to Talshamar. There I shall find a way to free the others and take my daughter home where she belongs."

"We shall return with such a force that Falcon Bruine will tremble beneath the onslaught of our army," Sir Edward stated fervently.

He carried her below and gently laid her among the soft furs. "I regret you will have no lady to attend you. Should you need anything, I shall be within hearing and you have only to call."

Jilliana closed her eyes, too weary to even thank the young knight who had risked his life to rescue her.

Above deck, the crew was clambering about, tying off sails and bringing the ship into the wind. The storm was worsening. It was as though the heavens opened and sleet pounded the small craft. Violent gusts of wind made the sailors' lot miserable, for it was bitterly cold.

But within the heart of each man, there was gladness. Their queen was at last on her way home to Talshamar, where she belonged.

For the first week of the voyage, Jilliana was so ill and sick at heart that she lay upon her bed, wishing she had been left to die. But under the gentle care of the men on board, she began to throw off her gloom. She forced herself to eat so she would regain her strength.

Amazingly, by the second week, there was color in her cheeks, and she joined them on deck.

At this time, Sir Edward handed her a letter from

Cardinal Failsham explaining to her what would occur
when she finally reached Talshamar. He explained how
her subjects' fervor had risen to a crescendo upon learning
of her imminent arrival, and many were already celebrat-
ing in the streets. He admonished her to keep faith and be
diligent in her prayers.

Jilliana wondered how she could face her people when
her heart was breaking.

32

Melesant's black eyes were pinpoints and her hands were clawlike as she grabbed Netta and flung her against the wall. The maid crumpled to the floor and Cassandra dropped down, protecting her with her body.

"Do not touch her again, Mother!" she said threateningly. "I will not allow it. None of this is her doing."

Melesant was taken aback. Cassandra had never shown such spirit. She had not thought she was capable of it.

"You are no daughter of mine, if you side with my enemies," Melesant said with a snarl.

Cassandra helped Netta stand. "I have never been anything to you. I was my father's daughter and you killed him. I was my brother's sister and you killed him. You are the betrayer, Mother. You have even made a prisoner of your grandchild, though you have not seen her since the day of her birth."

Like a caged animal caught in a trap, Melesant raged at her daughter's duplicity. "Quickly, fetch the guards," she told Escobar, who had discovered the deception. "Jilliana may still be stopped."

"She is safe from your clutches, Mother. She left the island three days ago."

"Enough, Cassandra! I will have you placed in chains if you continue to defy me."

"Will you have the whole world placed in chains, Mother? All your enemies will come against you now, you know. I can almost feel pity for you."

"Ingrate!" Melesant cried. "I gave you birth and you have no feelings for me. I should have locked you away, but no, I trusted you. That is a mistake I will not repeat."

"You did not trust me so much as you thought me incapable of deceiving you."

Melesant did not deny Cassandra's accusation.

"I have remained in this chamber three days and nights to allow Jilliana time to escape. The simpering smile of your new lover engaged your attention, or you would have known that something was amiss."

For a moment Melesant was speechless. Her daughter had never defied her, and she had certainly not spoken to her with such contempt. "I am warning you, Cassandra, do not continue."

"What will you do, Mother, lock me in the dungeon?" Cassandra withdrew her jeweled dagger and tossed it on the floor. "You once gave me this, and now I give you leave to use it on me if you dare. You took my brother's life, now take mine!"

Melesant glared at her daughter. "I leave the knife so you can use it on yourself. Your flesh will rot on your bones before you leave this room."

She turned to the guards. "Take the Talshamarian woman below and throw her in the dungeon with her countrymen. As for my daughter, she will remain here alone, until she's had time to think about her actions."

"I am sorry, Netta," Cassandra said, as two men roughly led the maid away. "I'll pray for your safety."

Melesant was watching her daughter with a strange

expression on her face. "You would do better to pray for yourself. Ask me to free you, and I may consider it," she said.

Cassandra raised her head. "I would never ask anything of you. You killed any feelings I had for you when you killed my brother."

"How come you by this haughty manner?"

"It is nothing you would understand. It's called honor, Mother. It is putting another's welfare before your own. I learned it from Jilliana."

Melesant sneered. "You might as well enter a nunnery. I have no use for you, and from this day forward, I shall take no interest in your future."

"You never have, Mother."

Melesant left the room and ordered the door locked behind her. Her children had been a disappointment to her, and Jilliana had escaped. Well, she was not beaten. She had the baby, and as long as the child was under her care, she still wielded the power.

It was still dark when Jilliana began to dress herself. Fine gowns and trappings had once more been provided for her by her generous people. This was the day she had long awaited. Soon she would step onto the soil of her beloved Talshamar, and in honor of the occasion, she wore a shimmering white silk gown and golden surcoat.

When she appeared on deck, rough-faced sailors dropped to their knees, paying homage to their young queen. Many gazed at her adoringly.

Sir Edward bowed to her and offered her his arm. "Never has a queen been more worthy," he said with feeling.

Jilliana looked out upon the sea and thought of Eleanor, who had hatched the plan to smuggle her out of Falcon Bruine. So many people had helped her, and at great risk to themselves.

She must not fail them. She must not!

The minutes that passed seemed like hours. Jilliana breathlessly waited for the mist to part so she could catch her first glimpse of Talshamar.

In the last week, it was as if they had left winter behind and sailed into spring with warm, sun-kissed skies.

An invigorating breeze touched her cheek, and she closed her eyes, feeling excitement stir within her.

"There, Your Majesty," Sir Edward pointed out, "see where the sun has burned away the mist?"

She was speechless as she saw the green land shimmering like a fiery emerald. Gentle waves touched the shore and stately palm trees weaved in the soft tropical breeze.

Jilliana felt a lump forming in her throat, and she could not speak. When the ship drew closer to land, she could see a multitude of people waving and calling her name.

She closed her eyes and said a silent prayer that she would not disappoint those who depended on her.

"Are we not getting too close to land?" Jilliana asked, noticing the figures were growing larger; she could almost see their features.

"Your Majesty," Sir Edward said, "Talshamar is blessed with deep harbors, therefore our ships are able to dock at the piers you see there. It is only moments before we drop anchor and lower the gangplank."

"Then I shall go below and fetch my cape."

"Allow me to get it for you."

She shook her head. "I will need this time to compose myself."

Sir Edward watched her move gracefully across the deck, feeling pride in her. He spoke to the captain, who also watched the queen. "This is a glorious day for Talshamar."

Jilliana flung the crimson cape about her shoulders and fastened it at her neck with a diamond clasp. Her hand shook as she reached for the ceremonial crown of

Talshamar that Cardinal Failsham had requested she wear on her arrival.

It was a circlet of gold open-work, adorned with clusters of sapphires, diamonds, and emeralds. Atop the crown were four *fleur-de-lis* and a diamond orb set with huge stones. The arch of the crown was decorated with doves carrying olive branches in their beaks. It was magnificent!

Jilliana felt unworthy to wear the crown that was last worn by her mother, nevertheless she placed it on her head, feeling the weight of it go all the way to her heart.

"I have come home, Mother. I pray the daughter will be worthy of the mother."

She heard the anchor clanging and the sound of the gangplank groaning into place. Taking a deep breath, she moved out of the cabin.

When she reappeared on deck, a poignant silence fell over the waiting crowd. The sight that greeted her took her breath away. As far as the eye could see, there was a magnitude of people.

A calm settled over her and she no longer felt tense. These were her subjects. She had been born and trained to govern them, and she would strive every day of her life to rule them forthrightly and with compassion, as her mother had.

A beaming Cardinal Failsham moved up the gangplank to take her hand. Jilliana could not help but notice that he was limping. She was sad to see that he had aged since last they had met.

There was deep feeling in his voice when he spoke to her. "Welcome home, Your Majesty." He held out his arm. "We should not keep the people waiting. Many of them have been here for a week. Yesterday, when fishing boats sighted your sails, the crowd began to swell. The consequence you see before you."

"Shall we go?" she asked, placing her hand on his arm and descending the gangplank.

Jilliana could not know the sight she presented in her royal robe of crimson velvet. The crown glittered on her ebony head, and her face was so lovely that she brought gasps from the crowd.

Her older subjects, who remembered her mother, exclaimed that it was like Queen Phelisiana had returned to them.

Jilliana smiled as she was led to the waiting horses, while her subjects dropped to their knees to pay homage to her.

"God save the queen. Long live Queen Jilliana!" they chanted in unison.

She was mounted on a high-stepping palfrey with a gleaming white coat. She was soon joined by high-ranking lords and their ladies. Sir Edward rode to her left and Cardinal Failsham to her right. Amid great splendor, the solemn procession made its way toward the castle.

There was jubilance in the air, and people were laughing and crying at the same time. At last Talshamar had a queen!

All along the way, women threw flower petals in their path. Jilliana caught sight of an old man, his face wrinkled, his hands gnarled, with tears rolling down his cheeks.

At one point, a child broke away from her mother and ran toward Jilliana with a bouquet of crumpled flowers clasped in her hand. Jilliana halted her mount lest the child be trampled, while her mother and father ran forward, scolding her for bothering the queen.

"I'm sorry, Your Majesty," the mother apologized. "It's just that she has been so excited about your coming. She has talked of nothing else for days. I will see that she is properly punished."

Jilliana smiled into the troubled little face. "You will not punish this child. What is her name?"

"M . . . Mary Hawkins," her mother replied.

"Mary, how would you like to ride as far as that bridge with me?"

The child's eyes rounded with wonder. "Oh, please, Your Majesty."

"Place her upon my horse," Jilliana told the father. "And walk beside us so she won't be frightened."

The mother looked startled, but the father scooped up his daughter and placed her in front of the queen.

The child laughed up at Jilliana as they continued their journey. There was an uproar from the crowd, who loved the gesture.

"That is what your mother would have done," the cardinal said reminiscently. "She loved the people and they loved her."

As Jilliana held the small child, she thought of her own daughter and her heart ached. When they reached the bridge, she handed Mary back to her father. Removing a golden cord from her cape, she tied it about the child's head.

"Thank you for riding with me, Mary."

The child startled everyone when she reached forward and kissed Jilliana on the cheek. "I love you," she said.

Jilliana laughed and turned to the child's mother. "Mistress Hawkins, when Mary reaches her seventh year, bring her to me and I will see to her education. Do not forget."

"We will remember," said the father, bowing his head, and feeling deeply honored that the queen should take an interest in his daughter. Wisely, the mother looked deeper and saw the sadness in the queen's eyes and knew that she was grieving for her dead husband.

As they rode away from the sea, Jilliana noticed the rolling farmlands and woodlands where Sir Edward told her there was an abundance of game. They passed great orchards, gardens, and dense wooded areas, as well as neatly kept farmhouses, and green valleys where sheep and cattle grazed.

There were fields of golden grain along the roadway, and Jilliana watched women carrying crocks of milk, and happy children herding geese. It was a peaceful scene and one that made her heart swell with pride.

"Your Majesty," Cardinal Failsham told her, "Talshamar produces one of the world's finest wines for export. Another export is fine-grade marble from quarries in the mountains. The castle itself is built of our own pink granite. You will find no finer castle anywhere."

By now they had reached the castle, and Jilliana was inclined to agree with him. Nothing could have prepared her for the magnificent structure that spread out before her like a precious jewel. From her vantage point, Jilliana could see seven wide reflecting pools mirroring the great turrets, projecting towers and keeps.

"It is quite unlike the cheerless strongholds of England and France," the cardinal continued with pride. "You will appreciate the gracefully carved archways and windows that open to the north to reveal a breathtaking view of the ocean beyond. And if you take a deep breath, you will smell the fragrance of orange and lemon blossoms."

Jilliana was feeling too many emotions to speak. She looked at the colorful flowers spilling over the high walls of the castle. As they entered the inner courtyard, the servants who had been going about their assigned tasks stopped and bowed until Jilliana passed.

Sir Edward helped Jilliana dismount, and she walked up the wide steps to the castle.

She was home at last.

33

Jilliana had never imagined anything as lovely as her home. She walked across marble floors that were polished so brightly she could see her reflection. On the white stone walls hung priceless tapestries and thick velvet coverings.

She could better understand why Talshamar was so coveted by its neighbors. There was wealth here, and wealth meant power and strength.

When Cardinal Failsham escorted her into the huge antechamber, Jilliana found it filled with nobles and their ladies awaiting her arrival. Each was presented to her by Cardinal Failsham, and she greeted them graciously, making a mental note of each name and face.

After Jilliana thanked them for their loyalty to her while she was in exile, the cardinal dismissed them so the queen could retire to her chamber before the evening festivities.

But Jilliana was too excited to rest. This was her home and she wanted to see every cranny, so Cardinal Failsham became her willing guide.

Candles too numerous to count gleamed through the open portals. Coming from the chapel somewhere nearby, she could hear the melodic sounds of monks saying vespers.

In the gardens, she walked past musical fountains and tall sculptures that had been carved by masterful hands. She had lived here as an infant, yet nothing was familiar to her.

At last they reached her mother's study, and the cardinal stepped back so she could enter before him. Jilliana stood in the middle of the room, turning in a circle. She had never seen so many books—they lined the walls on three sides. Seeing a portrait, she moved toward it, her steps measured, her eyes on the face of her mother. Except for the golden hair, it was like looking at an image of herself.

Her mother was dressed as a huntress, draped in gossamer with bow and arrow poised. One bare foot rested upon the Golden Orb of Talshamar, and the other was atop a coiled snake. The words beneath the portrait read *Before dishonor, death.*

"No one has used this room since your mother. It was kept cleaned and aired, but it is just as she left it for you."

"I would like to be alone, if you don't mind."

He nodded. "I understand. I shall see you at the celebration banquet tonight then, Your Majesty."

After the cardinal had departed, Jilliana stood silently looking at the face of her mother, who appeared regal and unapproachable until you looked into her eyes, which were soft and almost innocent. When this portrait was painted, her mother could not have been much older than Jilliana herself. There was a dull ache inside her because she could not remember the woman who had given her life.

The scent of some unidentified flowers filtered in on the afternoon breeze as Jilliana moved to her mother's desk and sat down. She gingerly ran her hand over the smooth surface. Her mother had been the last person to sit at this desk. It was a moment so touching that it brought tears to Jilliana's eyes.

Carefully, she opened a drawer and found a ledger where her mother had kept account of her daily appointments, each meticulous entry done in her own hand.

With a sigh, Jilliana closed the book, knowing she would read it at a later time.

When she left the queen's study, Lady Darby, one of the women she had met earlier, was waiting for her.

"Your Majesty, I had the pleasure of being your grandmother's, and later your mother's, Lady of the Robes. I would be honored to serve you in that capacity until you appoint someone of your own choosing."

Jilliana smiled at her, knowing that because of the woman's advanced age it would be a difficult task for her. Still, she could see by the shine in Lady Darby's eyes that she was eager to help.

"Thank you. Later, I will want to hear about my mother and grandmother. I am sure you knew them very well."

The older woman chuckled. "I can even tell you about your own antics when you were a babe." Her eyes softened. "We all adored you."

Jilliana looked regretful. "I can remember nothing about that time, Lady Darby."

A huge four-poster bed with blue velvet hangings trimmed in gold dominated the queen's bedchamber. Soft rugs were scattered on polished floors. As Jilliana looked at the bed, she turned wistfully to Lady Darby.

"Have I time to rest before dressing for the banquet?"

The woman nodded decisively. "Of course you do. You are the queen." Her eyes twinkled. "Therefore, the banquet cannot begin without you."

She helped Jilliana undress and pulled the covers aside so Jilliana could climb into bed. Hardly had her head hit the downy pillows when she fell asleep.

*   *   *

The evening was warm and balmy. Musicians played in the gallery while the chamberlain greeted new arrivals and presented them to the queen. It was almost a relief to Jilliana when the dining room doors were thrown open and they left the Great Hall.

Seated at the high table, Jilliana was glad that Eleanor had meticulously trained her in her duties. Dressed in shimmering silver, she presided over the banquet with a watchful eye to everyone's comfort.

Dining was a formal affair in Talshamar. The Grand Master of the castle, bearing his staff of office, led an elaborate procession of servants bearing covered dishes.

The tables was laid with richly embroidered cloth, which reached the floor on all sides. Hands were washed from golden bowls with scented rosewater and dried on crisp linen.

Every dish was tasted before being presented to the queen, a ritual that made her smile. She could imagine no one on Talshamar who would wish her harm. Cupbearers carried napkins on the shoulder while serving the queen's table, but placed them on the arm when they moved to the lower tables.

Jilliana talked and laughed at witticisms and presented the face of merriment to delude those who did not know her. But Sir Edward was not fooled by her lighthearted performance. He recognized the pain in her eyes, and he knew that she was thinking of her daughter. Once their eyes met, and he gave her an encouraging nod.

After the last course had been served—there had been fourteen courses—Jilliana stood, allowing the others to do the same.

"I will ask you to excuse me since I have matters that need my attention. Continue enjoying the entertainment." She spoke hurriedly to Cardinal Failsham. "Accompany me. I have something of import to discuss with you."

He followed her out of the room, and when they reached her study, she turned to him, her eyes troubled.

"Your Eminence, I have much to learn, and I have many questions without answers. I need your wise counsel."

He held the armchair for her and she sat down, looking even more troubled.

"I stand ready to help you in any way I can, Your Majesty."

"You know about my daughter."

"I do. Sir Edward told me, and I told the other lords."

"I . . . How would the people feel about—" She looked at him with agony in her eyes. "How can I ask them to go to war with Falcon Bruine?"

He sat down himself, as if to stand was an effort, and she noticed again how frail he was. He was quiet for so long that she thought he would admonish her for speaking of war.

At last, he raised clear eyes to her. "You are the queen. If you ask them to go to war, they will follow you without question."

"But have I that right?"

"You alone have the right to declare war."

"I fear for my daughter. It was difficult to leave her with that woman, even though I had no choice at the time. Queen Melesant's mind is not stable, and I do not know what she might do. Besides, I have a responsibility to those I left behind and I shall not rest until they are free."

"Then you must war against her?"

"I have a plan, but if it does not work, I may have to ask men to fight for me. I hesitate to send men into battle when they might lose their lives."

He shook his head. "When you are the ruler of a country, you must make many decisions that will cost lives."

"Wars cost money."

"Talshamar is a wealthy country and continues to prosper. The treasury is filled to overflowing."

The cardinal was being so noncommittal when she so needed his advice. Why was he being so evasive?

"Can we win a war against Falcon Bruine?" Jilliana asked.

"We will have the advantage, Your Majesty, since we have many ships and they have few."

"But they have soldiers that have been trained in warfare, and Talshamar has not been to war since my mother fought King Henry—and lost."

"Your armies are capable. I would not hesitate to pit them against any force in the world."

"Again, I ask you if it would be wrong to declare war?"

"Let us put it to the people and allow them to have a voice. We will begin with your guests." With trembling hands, he gripped the side of the chair and stood. "Shall we ask them?"

She nodded and they walked together to the Great Hall, where they could hear the sounds of merriment.

The cardinal stopped her before they entered. "A word of advice, Your Majesty. Do not ask them. Tell them. I believe you may be amazed at their reaction. Have you forgotten that the little princess is your heir and their future queen?"

"It seems so much to ask of them when they do not even know me."

He chuckled. "They know you, and have followed your progress through the years. They were never told that you were residing at Our Lady of Sorrow, but they gathered outside the castle gates once a year, on your birthday, anxiously waiting to hear how you were faring. They would want to know everything I could tell them, from the time you first learned to ride, to the time you left the convent, then when you married Prince Ruyen."

And all that time she had thought she was alone. Jilliana's heart was softened even more for the people she had been born to rule. "I never knew anyone cared."

They entered the chamber, and as soon as everyone realized that Jilliana was among them, they fell silent. She walked to the middle of the room and began to speak.

"I have made a decision that will affect every Talshamarian man, woman, and child. As you all know, Queen Melesant holds my daughter captive. I will try to free her by diplomatic means, but if that fails, I will be forced to declare war on Falcon Bruine to secure her release."

The men rushed forward, cheering her decision, and the women nodded their heads emphatically.

"We will bring home the little princess," one of them was heard to say. There was a murmuring of agreement.

"We will never allow an outsider to take one of ours away from us. We fight to the death!"

Jilliana caught Cardinal Failsham's eye and he smiled.

"I will ask that my barons attend me tomorrow morning," Jilliana said, "so we can plan our strategy. If there are any who are not present tonight, see that they are informed about the council."

She was about to withdraw when she saw Sir Edward standing alone, seemingly downcast, and she realized that his rank would not allow him to be included. He had certainly proven himself fearless and daring, and although he was young, she trusted him, and he was just the man she wanted in command of her troops.

"Sir Edward," Jilliana said, "because of your devotion and bravery, I hereby grant you the title of baron. I will be placing you in command of my army and will also bestow upon you the rank of general. I call upon all present to acknowledge my baron, Lord Markem."

He looked disbelieving, but his eyes shone with pride and he was immediately surrounded by those who congratulated him. Jilliana withdrew. What was to come next would be difficult, but it was necessary.

She asked Cardinal Failsham to return with her to the study. Once she was there, she stood at the window, where her mother must have stood many times. Even though there was no moon and it was pitch black, she continued to stare into the night.

At last, she turned to Cardinal Failsham. "I have decided to enact a law that will have far-reaching consequences. It is the only way I can see to defeat Queen Melesant and free my daughter from her grasp."

"I cannot think what would bring that about short of war."

"I will draw up a decree that will prohibit a woman from ever ruling Talshamar after me."

The cardinal stared at her in astonishment. "Surely you understand the consequences of such an action? You would be without an heir, and at risk from Philip of France."

"I have considered that, but it is the only way to ensure my daughter's safety."

"When do I leave?"

She looked bewildered. "You?"

"Of course. We have no ambassador to Falcon Bruine, and I am the obvious one to carry the dispatch to Queen Melesant."

She looked at his sunken cheeks and his stooped shoulders and her heart ached for him. "You have done so much for Talshamar. I want to lighten your burdens, not add to them."

"I am growing old, and would like nothing better than to live out my life in peace. But I served your mother, and I'll serve you until I am no longer needed."

Jilliana went down on her knees before him and his trembling hand rested on her head.

"Pray for me, Your Eminence. I fear for what I must do."

He raised her face and looked into her eyes. "I will keep you in my prayers. But no matter what happens, remember that you were born to be queen, and if you have to go to war, then do it with a vengeance—do it to win!"

34

Queen Melesant, never having been devout in her faith, swept into the anteroom in a bitter mood. Her eyes were hard as she stared at the man, his red regalia identifying him as a cardinal of the Church.

"Your Eminence," she said, yawning behind her hand. "To what do I owe the honor of entertaining one of the pope's high officials?" The tone of her voice indicated that she was more annoyed than honored.

"As it happens, Madame, I come not as a representative of His Holiness, but as a messenger from the queen of Talshamar."

Melesant had been pretending to study the lace on her sleeve and her head snapped up at his announcement. "So, she sent you to plead with me. If Jilliana believes that I would release my granddaughter to you, she is mistaken."

"Her Majesty had hoped you would place the princess in my keeping." Now his eyes were boring into hers. "It would avert war—a war you shall surely lose."

Her laughter reverberated off the high ceilings. "Am I supposed to quake and fall down, begging for mercy? I will not be threatened, Cardinal."

"You should take the threat seriously. If I do not return to Talshamar with the princess, Queen Jilliana will send her armies to take her."

"Do not threaten me, priest. These castle walls have never been breached."

"They will be."

Her heart was beating with tempered fear, but she would not allow Jilliana's puppet to know that. "Send your armies. We shall cut them to pieces!"

"Your Majesty, I have here a parchment that you may find of interest."

He held it out to her and she batted it away, sending it sliding across the floor. He shrugged. "No matter, I shall tell you what it says."

"I care not."

He suddenly felt very weary. This woman would never listen to reason. "It merely states that after the present queen, no female will ever again become ruler of Talshamar."

Melesant's face turned white, and her lips tightened in rage. "She would not do this."

"I can assure you that it was not an easy decision for Queen Jilliana to make, but she did it none the less."

Melesant shook her head vigorously. "No. No, it is a farce. If I gave the child to her, she would reverse her decision."

"Queen Jilliana knew that you would question the document's authenticity, so before I came here, I went to the pope. His Holiness affixed his seal to the document, which makes it binding."

Melesant had never expected this. "Is Jilliana mad! She could lose everything, including her life. Philip will surely come against her when he hears of this."

"But that is not your worry, Madame. Your concern should be with Henry of England. He will surely destroy you when he learns what your actions have brought about."

The cardinal saw the fear in Melesant's eyes. She rubbed her temples as if her head ached, then she smiled. "Jilliana will have to go to Henry and tell him it was all a misunderstanding. If she does that, then I shall send the child to her."

"Queen Jilliana does not trust you. You have no recourse but to release the princess into my keeping."

She walked back and forth before him, clasping and unclasping her hands nervously. "I knew Jilliana was trouble the moment I saw her, with her regal airs, and her lofty attitude."

"May I see the princess?"

"Nay, I will not permit it."

"Is she well?"

"What— Oh, yes, yes. She is under the care of my daughter, Cassandra."

"I will tell Her Majesty that. She trusts Princess Cassandra."

"She should. She turned my daughter against me. It is only right that I take her daughter in retaliation."

"What message do I give Queen Jilliana?"

Melesant's face was distorted by anger. "Tell her that she will rot in hell before she ever sees her daughter."

"Then we have nothing further to discuss." Cardinal Failsham bowed his head just the merest bit. "I pity you, Madame, because the force that you have unleashed this day is more powerful than you can imagine. I do not believe your island kingdom will survive."

So saying, he turned and moved out the door. Once outside, he filled his lungs with fresh air.

He was soon mounted and ready to leave the foul island. With his party of twelve knights, he rode through the gates, toward the sea. His hopes had been dashed—he had failed. If only he had been allowed to take the princess home to her grieving mother.

"Your Eminence," Cassandra called out to him, her eyes on the castle. "May I speak to you?"

He halted his horse and looked down, at first not recognizing the girl. She was dressed like a peasant, and it took him a moment to realize who she was. "Princess Cassandra!"

She stepped back, so no one from the castle would observe her speaking with the Talshamarians and report to her mother. "Is Jilliana well?"

"Her health is good, yes. But she grieves for her daughter."

"Tell her that I am watching over my niece. The child is thriving."

"That will be some comfort to her." He looked into Cassandra's eyes. "I must warn you that there will soon be war between Talshamar and your island."

For a moment he saw pain in her eyes, then she smiled sadly. "It is the only way. Will Jilliana accompany her army?"

"I would think so."

"Inform her that my brother lives."

"What say you? Prince Ruyen is alive!"

There was both joy and sorrow in her expression. "I found out only today that he survived his wounds and has raised an army. Tell Jilliana that Ruyen will strike against our mother soon, Your Eminence."

"Will your brother raise sword against the Talshamarians when they land to take the princess?"

"I cannot speak for my brother." Cassandra's eyes clouded over. "Tell Jilliana it would be better if she did not come to Falcon Bruine to be caught up in our civil war."

"Are these your words or your brother's?"

"They are mine, but I think only of her safety."

"I will tell her, but I do not think it will make any difference. If you can manage to bring the little princess to me, then war between your country and mine could be avoided."

"I regret that is not possible. I am never left alone with my niece." She moved closer to the cardinal and raised her face to him. "The reason I sought you out is to tell you that my brother has managed to free the Talshamarians from the dungeon. When you get back to your ship, you will find them already on board. My mother has not yet discovered their escape, so I would urge you to return to your ship and get under way without delay."

"Thank you, Your Highness," Cardinal Failsham said kindly. "I will tell my queen that not all on Falcon Bruine are her enemies. If I know Queen Jilliana, she will instruct her troops not to harm the population, but you should know that in any conflict there are casualties and some-times the innocent suffer. Warn your people of the impending war and advise them to seek shelter and not hinder Queen Jilliana's passage, for she is determined to rescue her daughter."

Cassandra stepped away from him. "You must leave quickly, Your Eminence. Pray that all goes well for my country."

The battle between Ruyen's troops and his mother's was fierce, but short. The siege started at daybreak and lasted only until the noon hour, when Ruyen's troops stormed the walls and were joined by those loyal to him within the compound. There was little resistance as he fought his way to the main entrance of the castle, and no one tried to stop him when he moved toward the Great Hall.

Angry voices could be heard from the villagers who had converged on the castle. "Send the Castilian whore back to Castile! Let the true king rule!"

When he entered the throne room, Melesant was wait-ing for him.

"So, it's true. You are not dead," she said without feel-ing.

Ruyen motioned the soldiers who accompanied him to withdraw, then he coldly faced the women who had given him birth, feeling nothing but revulsion for her. She had wanted to rule so desperately that she had betrayed those closest to her, and in doing so had brought about her own downfall.

She looked him over, satisfied that he had not suffered from his wounds. "Have you no greeting for your mother?"

He wondered how her mind worked that she should expect him to pick up the threads of his life and act as though nothing had happened between them.

"You are beaten, Mother."

She sighed. "You are bitter against me. I can hear it in your voice."

"Bitter? I hope not. Remorseful for what must be done to you, most probably."

Melesant looked uneasy and avoided his eyes. "I have changed, Ruyen. I no longer want to rule Falcon Bruine. I propose that you be crowned king without delay."

"You have no say in the matter. Your troops have been slaughtered and there is no one to stand at your side."

She shrugged. "Little I care. I have decided to leave Falcon Bruine for good."

"That is precisely what I had in mind for you. But what made you come to that conclusion, other than the fact that your supporters are all dead?"

"If you must know, that silly wife of yours has declared war on us and demands my abdication." Melesant shook her head. "And if that is not bad enough, the king of Castile is sending troops with his own demands that I consolidate my power for the glory of Castile."

Ruyen tensed, knowing he faced another battle. "When do the Castilians arrive?"

"Their sails have already been sighted. And here I am, caught in the middle of two armies and Henry demanding that I come to England at once and explain why Jilliana has disinherited her daughter or he will attack, too."

"It looks like you have quite a dilemma, Mother."

"I blame Jilliana entirely. I sent dispatch after dispatch begging for a truce, but she sent them back unopened. Did you ever suspect she would be so unreasonable? And you cannot believe that she has disinherited her own daughter. If that be so, why does she come for her?"

He was not following his mother's ranting. "Where is the child?"

"She's quite safe. Cassandra is seeing to her care. Jilliana is a fool to wage a war over a mere child."

Ruyen was sickened by her. "You would never understand a woman like Jilliana. Did you not think she would grieve over the loss of her child? You brought this on yourself, Mother. Now I must mass troops to fight the Castilians who will soon land on our shores."

"Why would you do that? You will need them to help you against Jilliana."

"Do you think I would support the Castilians against my own wife?"

Melesant looked perplexed. "You can do what you will, Ruyen. My ship sails with the tide."

His lip curled in disgust. "So the mighty queen attempts to flee when she cannot face the results of her own actions."

"You can say what you will, Ruyen, but there was a time when you could have stopped me."

"Perhaps, and for that I bear the blame. Somehow, I cannot find it in me to be the one to strike you down, Mother. You may leave the island, but I shall be the one to choose your destination."

Melesant nodded, only too happy to have gotten off so easily. "I'll go anywhere as long as it's far away from here," she said.

"Where is Escobar?" Ruyen demanded.

"He is already aboard the ship."

"Just what I would expect of the cowardly little man."

He walked to the door and called the guard. "Go to the ship in the harbor and find Escobar. Bring him hither and lock him in the dungeon."

Melesant knew it would do no good to beg Ruyen to let Escobar accompany her. What did it matter, she was tired of him anyway. "What will you do to Escobar?"

"He will be executed as a Castilian spy," Ruyen said without remorse.

Melesant realized her son could be pitiless. She was indeed fortunate that he was allowing her to live. She walked to the door. "I'll just be leaving now."

"Not yet, Mother. I am placing a man I trust as captain of the ship, and the vessel will be searched to make certain you do not take anything with you that belongs to the treasury of Falcon Bruine . . . or Talshamar."

She suddenly smiled. "You know me so well, do you not? You will find the jewels and gold in my trunks. Leave me enough so I will not be destitute." She looked puzzled for a moment. "What destination have you chosen for me, Ruyen?"

He was quiet for a moment, knowing he was about to pronounce the sentence of death on his own mother. "You will be sailing for England. I feel I must warn you that the Tower can be quite uncomfortable. I know this from personal experience."

She gasped. "You would do this to your own mother?"

"Perhaps it will not be as bad as you think. Henry may be in a forgiving mood."

"You know that is not so. He will demand my death! I will not go to England."

Ruyen shrugged. "Remain if you like, but if I were you, I would choose Henry over Jilliana. She will be far more merciless should she find you here when she lands."

Melesant looked defeated. "You win, Ruyen." When she walked out the door, he knew he was looking at his mother for the last time. Even after all she had done, he felt a pang of regret. She would soon face Henry's wrath, and her fate would be death.

He placed his hands on the chair and lowered his head as waves of regret washed over him. It was not an easy task to send his own mother to her death.

It was much later when Ruyen entered the nursery and found Cassandra standing over a sleeping child. When she heard him, she swung around, her jeweled dagger clutched in her hand. When she saw it was her brother, she dropped the dagger and ran into his outstretched arms.

"Oh, Ruyen, it is over. Falcon Bruine is free."

He held her away from him, taking in her appearance. Her face had matured in the last year and she was lovely. "You might want to go to our mother's chamber and tell her good-bye. I am sending her to England."

They stared at each other for a long moment, knowing the consequences of his actions. "Do not blame yourself, Ruyen. It is the only thing you could do."

"You know that there is to be war with the Castilians?"

"I had heard their ships have been sighted. It cannot be avoided, Ruyen, but we shall win against them."

He moved around Cassandra and glanced down at the sleeping child. Her head was covered with golden curls and she looked so like an angel, soft and pink. He could not resist touching her tiny hand. He was overcome with a rush of emotions. There was a lump in his throat he could not swallow.

Cassandra touched his arm. "Ruyen, there is more that I must tell you. To save her daughter, Jilliana drafted a decree that prevents any female from becoming queen of Talshamar."

Ruyen closed his eyes. "So that is what mother meant. It must have taken great courage for Jilliana to disown her only heir. She gave up everything for the baby." He looked at his sister. "I thought all women were like our mother.

Jilliana has proven me wrong, time and time again, and so have you."

"You love Jilliana," Cassandra said.

"Even if I do, there can be no future for us. Too much stands between us."

"What will you do?"

"I prepare to fight the Castilians. They will be on our shores within a day." He lifted his sister's chin. "If I fall in battle, you must see that the child is safely reunited with Jilliana."

She nodded solemnly. "It will be done."

Jilliana felt her knees go weak and she lowered herself onto a chair. "But I saw him fall," she said in disbelief. "He died holding my hand."

Cardinal Failsham knelt before her. "His sister says he lives and I believe her. Does this make a difference in what you must do?"

She thought for a moment then shook her head. "No difference at all. The attack goes forward. Everything is in readiness; we sail for Falcon Bruine within the week." She motioned for him to sit beside her. "But you will not be going, my dear friend. I have need of you here."

"Are you only saying this because I am ill?"

Jilliana laid her hand on his. "Nay. I do this because if anything happens to me, my people will need your wise counsel."

She stood. "Now, if you will excuse me, I want to see Humphrey and the men who were imprisoned."

Jilliana hurried out of the library to the anteroom where Humphrey and the other knights waited for her. Her face brightened and she went first to Humphrey, clasping his hands.

"This is a happy day for me, dear friend. It gladdens my heart that you are safely home." She turned to the others, speaking to each in turn. "I have ordered the kitchen to prepare each of you your favorite meal, and I have sent for your families so you can be reunited."

Humphrey's eyes moved over her face fondly. "We are hardy enough to sail with you to Falcon Bruine," he told her.

"I will need you all with me, so rest and regain your strength. Later, I want to hear the details of your release." She looked about the room with a puzzled expression on her face.

"Where is Netta? Has she already gone to the village to see her husband?"

Humphrey's expression was one of sorrow. "She did not survive the ordeal, Your Majesty. Melesant was particularly harsh with her because she helped you escape. Her last words were of you."

Sadly, Jilliana turned away. Here was another sin to lay at Melesant's feet. Sweet, loyal Netta dead. How could that be?

"Have someone go to her family and tell them the sad news. Impress upon them that she died well."

Later, when she entered her bedchamber, Jilliana sat for a long moment pondering the sad task that lay ahead of her. It was not her wish to go to war. It had been forced upon her. Therefore, it must be won at all costs. But her heart was singing. Ruyen was alive. *He was alive!*

Then she thought of the battle that was to come and it brought an ache to her heart. She would be forced to march across Ruyen's island, slaying his people. If only there had been another way, but Melesant had left her no choice.

Jilliana would free her daughter, whatever the cost.

35

As the early morning mist cleared, Falcon Bruine fishermen were the first to spy the scarlet sails of the Talshamarian ships. A messenger was sent to the castle to inform King Ruyen, while the villagers took refuge within the protective walls of the castle.

Troops were massed at the gates, but Ruyen did not send anyone to intercept the Talshamarian fleet that was fifty ships strong.

Lord Markem had expected resistance at their most vulnerable spot, as they disembarked from the ships, but no one opposed them. Horses were brought ashore for the advance guard, then they were followed by the foot soldiers.

It was late afternoon when the last of the arms and equipment were unloaded and they began the march to the castle.

Jilliana rode between Lord Markem and Humphrey. As they neared the village, they had still encountered no resistance. But there were signs of battle all about them. Many of the cottages had been burned and in fact were still smoldering.

"What do you think has happened here, Lord Markem?" Jilliana asked, looking to her general.

"There has been fierce fighting, and I would say quite recently."

"But who?" Jilliana asked fearfully, because it looked like Ruyen's followers had been defeated.

"I would suspect civil war," he replied. "There must have been a great loss of life."

Cautiously, they left the village behind, still encountering no one. When they were in sight of the castle, Lord Markem ordered the tents erected and a command post established. Guards were placed a horse length apart, their eyes ever watchful for signs of trouble.

They made preparations to attack the castle in the morning with the rising of the sun.

It was almost evening when Jilliana emerged from her tent. To everyone's astonishment, she was dressed in silver chainmail, which was covered with a scarlet surcoat. The Great Sword of Talshamar hung from a silver belt at her side, and she carried a silver helm beneath her arm.

Humphrey looked at her with growing dread. "Just what are you about, Jilliana?"

"Queen Jilliana," she reminded him, with her chin set in a stubborn line. "I am going alone to the castle to ask for an audience with Queen Melesant. I must try one more time to get my daughter back before blood is spilled."

"Then I shall accompany you."

"No. You are needed here, Humphrey. I go alone."

"But, Your Majesty," Lord Markem added his protest to Humphrey's, "you must not put yourself in danger. Allow me to go in your stead."

She clamped her helm on her head and secured the strap. "I go myself, and I go alone. Bring me a horse," she ordered. "If I have not returned by morning, attack the castle."

Both men would like to have prevented her going, but knew it was useless to try.

Jilliana's prancing palfrey was led forward. The white horse wore a long silver panoply, which covered most of its face and fell short enough so as not to entangle the animal's legs.

"I still do not like it," Humphrey said, helping her shove her foot into the stirrups and mount astride.

She placed a hand on his shoulder. "If there is any chance to avoid war, I must take it. We are the stronger force and will breech that wall without difficulty before noon tomorrow. We have no quarrel with the people. It is their queen I want."

Humphrey nodded and stepped back. She was after all his sovereign and she must be obeyed.

With a low snort and the clamoring of the silver bridle, her horse moved slowly away from camp. All eyes watched with concern as Jilliana rode across the open ground between the Talshamarian camp and the castle.

Her horse pranced and tossed its head, and she pushed her booted foot more securely into the stirrups.

As she neared the outer wall, there were more signs of battle. The acrid smell of smoke burned her nostrils and black swirls dissipated into a blood-red sky. Jilliana was concerned that they had seen no signs of life since their arrival.

Tense moments passed as the Talshamarians watched their queen ride bravely toward the enemy's stronghold. In each man's heart was the desire to protect her—to die for her if the need arose.

When Jilliana reached the wall, she called out to the sentry. "I am Queen Jilliana of Talshamar. Lower the bridge. I will have word with your queen."

There was no answer, but the spiked gate lowered with a loud clinking sound.

Jilliana tried not to show her fear as she rode past armed men. It was so silent that the sound of her horse's hooves echoed through the courtyard. No one attempted to stop her progress. When she reached the castle, a man held the reins of her horse while she dismounted.

"I will speak to your queen," she told him.

He motioned for her to follow him.

Jilliana's spurs made a tinkling sound as she moved across the stone floor. She did not hesitate, lest she lose her courage. Perhaps she had been foolish and was allowing herself to fall into Melesant's hands once more.

When she approached the throne room, a man-at-arms threw the doors open to admit her. Still no one had spoken a word to her.

Cautiously, Jilliana entered the room, her hand resting on the hilt of her sword, though she knew not what she would do with it if there was trouble.

She stopped, and her eyes went to the end of the long room. Melesant was not present, but on the dais, dressed in a purple surcoat and wearing the crown of Falcon Bruine, sat Ruyen and oh, her heart sang at the sight of him. His dark eyes seemed to look past her helm, right into her heart.

Cassandra stood beside him and smiled softly at the baby she held in her arms.

Jilliana did not stop to consider her actions. As she ran toward her daughter, she threw off her helm and removed her gauntlets, dropping them as she went. When she reached Cassandra, she took the baby from her, tears of happiness filling her eyes.

Ruyen motioned for the guards to close the door, and he watched longingly as Jilliana rained kisses on their daughter's face. It was as if the child knew her mother, for she squealed with delight.

"Oh, Cassandra, she has grown so! I missed too much of her life."

"Not so much, Jilliana," Cassandra assured her. "She is but one year old tomorrow. And I can tell you everything you want to hear."

"I am taking her home with me." Her eyes dared Ruyen to oppose her.

Ruyen had been on the battlement, watching as Jilliana had ridden toward the castle. God had never created another woman such as her. Every deed she had ever done had called on courage that few men possessed. Yet she had seemed fearless as she entered the castle alone, still thinking that his mother was queen.

"Take your baby and return home, Jilliana," he told her. "No one will stop you."

She raised her eyes to his and saw love shining in the dark depths. Her heart was thundering in her breast. "Not just yet, Ruyen. There is something I would ask of you." She handed the child to Cassandra. "Take her to Humphrey so he may know that all is well."

"Is Edward with you?" Cassandra asked hopefully.

"Yes, and he will be most happy to see you."

Cassandra smiled brightly as she gathered her niece in her arms and hurried out of the room. She hoped that Jilliana and her brother would come to an understanding because they loved each other.

When they were alone, Jilliana turned her attention to her husband. It was hard to act queenly when all she wanted to do was run into his arms. She loved him so desperately that it was painful for her to look into his eyes after believing for so long that he was dead.

"You seem to have recovered from your wounds," she remarked, making polite conversation. Why was she so nervous?

He smiled. "I was fortunate."

"Where is Melesant?" she asked, her eyes going to the crown that sat atop his head.

"I believe you will understand why I could not pass a death sentence on my own mother. Therefore, I sent her to England."

Jilliana nodded in satisfaction. "I could easily have driven my sword through her heart, and was prepared to do just that. But I know that Henry will do what you could not."

Ruyen wished he dared reach out and touch her shimmering hair to see if it was as soft as he remembered. "What a bloodthirsty wench I married. Must I fear for my life lest you run me through?"

She casually moved to the second throne and sat down, throwing her leg over the arm—most unqueen-like. "There was a time when I would have done just that. With regret, but I would have done it all the same."

"But now?"

"You know that I could never do you harm."

He leaned his head back and turned to look at her. "What do we do now?"

"War between our countries has been averted."

Ruyen smiled. "So it seems."

"I thought it strange that we were allowed to land on your shores unopposed."

"Jilliana, that is because my armies were ordered not to spill one drop of Talshamarian blood."

"I can see that they spilled someone's blood. With whom did you do battle?"

He could hardly concentrate on what she was saying. He ached to touch her, but she seemed so distant. "First, I battled my mother's troops, who offered little resistance, and then a Castilian fleet that came ashore and offered considerable resistance. As you can see, I was victorious."

"I am glad, Ruyen."

Ruyen stood up and walked down the few steps that took him onto the stone floor. "I was not sure if I would have to battle a beautiful, blue-eyed hellion who came charging at my castle to take on my armies single-handedly."

He had his back to her, and Jilliana would have sworn that he was afraid to face her. She rose and moved to stand just behind him.

"I thought I would never see you again, Ruyen."

He turned slowly to face her. "So, Jilliana, do we war, or do we make peace?"

"I told you that I have something to ask of you. I have a dilemma that only you can help me with."

He shook his head. "I remember your last dilemma. It ended in my giving you the daughter you wanted. Being a father is new to me, but I find it difficult to let my daughter go. We have become quite good friends, she and I."

"That is part of what I want to talk to you about. You know that our daughter cannot become queen of Talshamar?"

"That was an ingenious plan." There was pride in his voice. "You outwitted my mother, and that is no easy task."

"Ruyen, will you hear what I have to say?"

"A small voice warns me against it, but go ahead, Jilliana."

"It is really quite simple. When Philip of France learns that Talshamar has no ruler after me, he may well decide to press his claim."

Ruyen narrowed his eyes. "What are you asking of me?"

"I need a son. Two would be even better."

Every muscle in his body tensed. "Are you asking me to be the father?"

"You are my husband. Who else would I ask?"

He started laughing and she stared at him. This was not the reaction she had expected.

"Jilliana, Jilliana, is there anyone like you?"

"Ruyen, I also want you to rule jointly with me in Talshamar. That would be my protection in the event that you can only give me daughters."

"What!"

"I will promise to be as little trouble to you as possible. If I ask it of my Talshamarians, they will readily accept you as their sovereign."

Ruyen's eyes moved over her face lovingly. He had feared that after today he would never see her again. He could hardly hide his joy at what she was proposing. He spoke with humor: "If bedding you is the only way to save you, I will consider it, Jilliana."

"You would not regret it, Ruyen." Then her eyes danced with laughter. "Of course, I may have been a bit rash in promising not to cause you trouble. For some reason, I have always been a trial to those about me."

He moved back to his throne and sat down. "Jilliana, call me a fool if you will, but I have decided to help you with your dilemma. It may be difficult for us to be together because I will never abandon Falcon Bruine."

"Of course you will not. You shall be king of both. I am not suggesting that we unite the countries, we shall merely unite the crowns." She startled him when she reached up and gently touched his face. "I am ready to swear fealty to you as I would not on the day we were wed." She dropped to her knees, her eyes raised to him reflecting sincerity. "I pledge my devotion to you in all things, King Ruyen."

He took her arm and lifted her up to him. "Is there more that you will pledge to me?"

"Aye, Ruyen, I pledge you my heart."

He drew in his breath. "You still love me?" he asked in wonder.

Her eyes were shining and he could see the truth in their depths. "I never stopped loving you, Ruyen. Not even when I thought you were dead. Now, I offer you the crown of Talshamar, asking only one thing of you."

He wanted to scoop her into his arms, to crush her to him. "And what would that be?"

"Sons, Ruyen. I want many sons."

"Do you want nothing for yourself?"

When she did not reply—the first time he had ever known her to be at a loss for words—he drew her into his arms.

"Sweet, sweet Jilliana, I love you as no man has ever loved a woman. You restored my trust and gave me back my faith." His eyes darkened and he pressed his cheek to hers. "I will do as you ask, but I will expect something from you as well."

She was crying and kissing his rough cheek. "Anything, Ruyen, anything."

"We will never again be parted. When I am in Falcon Bruine, you will be beside me. When you are in Talshamar, I will be at your side." His eyes softened. "As for you becoming subservient, I would have you stay the way you are." He laughed, feeling lighthearted. "I cannot imagine a time when you would not state your mind. It is what I love about you most."

"Oh, Ruyen, I never thought you would love me."

He kissed her lips and then gathered her even closer. "I never thought I would not."

Epilogue

1189

It was early spring, and a warm sun had melted the last of the snow and ice, thus swelling the rivers and streams of Falcon Bruine where Jilliana and Ruyen spent half the year, dividing their time between the two countries.

The previous year, at Yuletide, Talshamar and Falcon Bruine had united into one country, much to the delight of their subjects, for each benefited by the union. Already mapmakers had marked the change, and new banners waved proudly over both lands: the symbol of a golden falcon clasping the Talshamarian scepter in its talons.

Eleanor, Queen Mother of England, watched Jilliana's two sons playing in the sunny garden, while their older sister, Princess Phelisiana, kept a watchful eye on them.

"'Tis a lovely place to raise my godchildren, Jilliana. If I had it to do over again, I would have taught my offspring to love and respect each other as you have obviously done." Eleanor then smiled. "No, most probably I would have made the same mistakes."

Jilliana clasped her benefactress's hand. "I am happy for you, Eleanor. Richard is king and you are free of your prison. I always prayed for this day."

"I had only to outlive Henry." Eleanor dismissed the subject with a shrug. "You look happy."

"My family is happy, therefore so am I. You did hear that Cassandra and Lord Markem married and are expecting their first child, did you not?"

"Of course. But we were speaking of you, my dear."

Jilliana's face took on a glow. "Ruyen is what every woman wishes for in a husband."

Eleanor looked satisfied. "I chose well for you, did I not?"

Jilliana smiled. "Indeed you did."

"What are you two gossiping about?" Ruyen asked, coming up behind them. "Can a man join this little domestic scene?"

Eleanor brightened as she always did when there was a handsome man about. "Richard has told me that Talshamar and Falcon Bruine both flourish under your rule."

Ruyen pulled Jilliana close to him. "I have help."

Eleanor laughed. "I taught her well, did I not?"

"You did that, Eleanor." His eyes dropped lovingly to Jilliana. "Sometimes too well."

"I see I am not needed here," Eleanor said, rising slowly from the bench. "I'm off to England. Richard has need of me there." She brushed a kiss on Jilliana's cheek. "I wish you happiness always."

"God go with you, my dearest Eleanor."

"And you, child."

Jilliana and Ruyen watched Eleanor move toward her horse with a spring in her step. Several attendants scurried about to see to her comfort, and she took their devotion as her God-given right.

"I would not have enjoyed my happiness nearly so much if Eleanor had not been freed from her prison," Jilliana said contentedly.

Ruyen touched his lips to hers, while their daughter grabbed onto her father's leg. He picked up the little princess, who lay her head against his shoulder.

"The women in my family have me just where they want me."

Jilliana laughed. "So we do."

Humphrey and Lord Markem stood at the edge of the garden, observing the happy scene.

"Talshamarians will speak of Queen Jilliana long after we are all dead," Lord Markem observed. "They will write songs and recite poems about her greatness and bravery."

"Aye, that they will," Humphrey agreed. "But this is today, and we are blessed to be numbered among those who bask in her glory."

Let HarperMonogram Sweep You Away!

Once Upon a Time by Constance O'Banyon
Over seven million copies of her books in print. To save her idyllic kingdom from the English, Queen Jilliana must marry Prince Ruyen and produce an heir. Both are willing to do anything to defeat a common enemy, but they are powerless to fight the wanton desires that threaten to engulf them.

The Marrying Kind by Sharon Ihle
Romantic Times *Reviewer's Choice Award–Winning author.* Liberty Ann Justice has no time for the silver-tongued stranger she believes is trying to destroy her father's Wyoming newspaper. Donovan isn't about to let a little misunderstanding hinder her pursuit of happiness, however, or his pursuit of the tempestuous vixen who has him hungering for her sweet love.

Honor by Mary Spencer
Sent by King Henry V to save Amica of Lancaster from a cruel marriage, Sir Thomas of Reed discovers his rough ways are no match for Amica's innocent sensuality. A damsel in distress to his knight, Amica unleashes passions in Sir Thomas that leave him longing for her touch.

Wake Not the Dragon by Jo Ann Ferguson
As the queen's midwife, Gizela de Montpellier travels to Wales and meets Rhys ap Cynan—a Welsh chieftain determined to drive out the despised English. Captivated by the handsome warlord, Gizela must choose between her loyalty to the crown and her heart's desire.

And in case you missed last month's selections . . .

You Belong to My Heart by Nan Ryan
Over 3.5 million copies of her books in print. As the Civil War rages, Captain Clay Knight seizes Mary Ellen Preble's mansion for the Union Army. Having been his sweetheart, Mary Ellen must win back the man who wants her in his bed, but not in his heart.

After the Storm by Susan Sizemore

Golden Heart Award–Winning Author. When a time travel experiment goes awry, Libby Wolfe finds herself in medieval England and at the mercy of the dashing Bastien of Bale. A master of seduction, the handsome outlaw unleashes a passion in Libby that she finds hauntingly familiar.

Deep in the Heart by Sharon Sala

Romantic Times *Award–Winning Author.* Stalked by a threatening stranger, successful casting director Samantha Carlyle returns home to Texas—and her old friend John Thomas Knight—for safety. The tender lawman may be able to protect Sam's body, but his warm Southern ways put her heart at risk.

Honeysuckle DeVine by Susan Macias

To collect her inheritance, Laura Cannon needs to join Jesse Travers's cattle drive—and become his wife. The match is only temporary, but long days on the trail lead to nights filled with fiery passion.

Harper *Monogram*

Buy 4 or more and receive FREE postage & handling